THE BARRISTER'S BED

TINA GABRIELLE

ZEBRA BOOKS
KENSINGTON PUBLISHING CORP.
http://www.kensingtonbooks.com

ZEBRA BOOKS are published by

Kensington Publishing Corp.
119 West 40th Street
New York, NY 10018

All Kensington titles, imprints, and distributed lines are available at special quantity discounts for bulk purchases for sales promotion, premiums, fund-raising, educational, or institutional use.

Special book excerpts or customized printings can also be created to fit specific needs. For details, write or phone the office of the Kensington Special Sales Manager: Attn.: Special Sales Department. Kensington Publishing Corp., 119 West 40th Street, New York, NY 10018. Phone: 1-800-221-2647.

Zebra and the Z logo Reg. U.S. Pat. & TM Off.

ISBN-13: 978-1-4201-2275-6
ISBN-10: 1-4201-2275-4

First Printing: July 2012

10 9 8 7 6 5 4 3 2 1

Printed in the United States of America

For Gabrielle,
my angel love.
God has blessed me beyond measure.
I love you.

ACKNOWLEDGMENTS

Writing a book is a challenging task that I could not have accomplished without support. My sincere thanks to my wonderful agent, Stephany Evans, for her enthusiastic support of my Regency Barrister series. Thank you to my editor, Audrey LaFehr, at Kensington Books, who gave me the opportunity to hold the published books in my hands. Thank you also to my family and friends for their amazing support.

And as always, thank you to my readers. Without you, there would be no books!

Chapter 1

May 10, 1819
London, Old Bailey Courthouse
Honorable Barnard Bathwell, presiding

"You're a bastard by birth. How could you inherit anything?"

"Me father wanted me to 'ave it," Pumpkin O'Dool explained.

"So you just broke into your stepmother's home and took this?" Prosecutor Abrams strode forward, a gold pocket watch dangling from his fingers.

"Well, I knocked first, I did," Pumpkin claimed. "She peeked through the curtains and saw me and never opened the door."

"And yet you still took the watch. Your illegitimacy prevents you from inheriting property from your father," Abrams argued.

James Devlin jumped to his feet from behind the defense table. "Objection, my lord. Mr. O'Dool's illegitimacy is *not* in question. What is in question, however, is the missing will. If the prosecution had exerted as much effort in locating the will as it did in prosecuting a grieving son, we wouldn't be in court today."

Judge Bathwell, a squat fellow whose bewigged head

barely cleared the top of his perch, drew his lips in thoughtfully and looked to Abrams. "Has the prosecution any idea where the will is?"

Prosecutor Abrams shook his head. "No, my lord. The solicitor that drafted the will is deceased. The original was given to Mr. O'Dool's stepmother. It has not been found."

"No doubt stuffed under her mattress," James drawled.

"Objection!" the prosecutor shouted.

Six of the twelve members of the jury guffawed; two others eyed the prosecutor with a critical squint.

And that's when James Devlin knew he had them.

Juries disliked overaggressive prosecutors more than thieves. Pumpkin O'Dool was an impoverished bastard and without a written will saying otherwise, he was entitled to nothing.

No one understood this more than James.

But at least Pumpkin O'Dool wouldn't be sentenced to death today.

Sunlight poured in from the windows and heated the crowded courtroom. The spectators' gallery was packed with observers seated on wooden benches, and the air thrummed with excitement. Commoners in worn dresses and patched corduroy jackets sat beside wealthy merchants and nobility in fine gowns and tightly tied cravats. Women avidly fanned themselves as the temperature in the room rose with each passing minute, and perspiration formed on the men's foreheads, like water beads on good butter.

All were drawn to the Old Bailey. They had come to witness a man sentenced to hang, only to now champion his cause. Court, like the theater, contained the extremes of man's behavior.

James turned his attention to the twelve members of the jury. A mostly rough lot, he had initially thought. One of the jurors had a battlefield of wrinkles, none of which were laugh lines. Another juror had hands dyed the color of dark coffee and an unkempt beard. A tanner, no doubt. And yet another was barely twenty, with golden curls and the face of a cherub.

A trill of feminine laughter and a shout turned his head. Pumpkin's stepmother, a heavyset woman with dyed red hair and painted lips like a thread of scarlet, sneered at Pumpkin O'Dool from the front row. A balding man with a drinker's veined face sat beside her, his thigh brushing her skirts.

Hardly the grieving widow. She wasted no time in finding a lover, James thought.

The stepmother's features twisted into a maddening leer. Raising a finger, she pointed at Pumpkin and shouted out, "Thief! Cur!" She then turned to stare at James and eyed his black barrister's gown and wig with disdain.

James cocked an eyebrow, and his lips twitched in amusement.

The remainder of the trial consisted of Prosecutor Abrams arguing the deficiency of a will and James emphasizing the stepmother's motive for the will not to be found followed by three witnesses who testified as to Pumpkin's "upstanding" character.

In the middle of Prosecutor Abrams's closing, a shadow of annoyance crossed the judge's face. "That will be enough from both barristers. As it is time for luncheon and all relevant evidence presented, I ask for the gentlemen of the jury to consider their verdict."

It was the jury's fifth verdict of the morning with a half a dozen more trials to conclude before the end of the day. They gathered in the corner, their faces animated as they gestured wildly at one another. They whispered, yet every few words could be heard across the courtroom from "guilty" to "bastard" to "harsh sentence."

Three minutes later, the foreman, a middle-aged alchemist with eager brown eyes behind thick spectacles and a stained shirtfront, stood. "We the jury find Pumpkin O'Dool not guilty of housebreaking and theft."

Pumpkin O'Dool cried out with joy; his grin reached from ear to ear as he shook James's hand. Spectators shouted encouragement at the verdict and jeered at Pumpkin's stepmother.

The woman rose and departed the courtroom in a huff, her lover rushing to keep up with her.

A court clerk passed the pocket watch to James, who in turn handed it to his client. "The jury believed your story that your father wanted you to have this," James said. "Now stay out of trouble, Pumpkin. And don't get caught selling that watch or 'walking' into any other dwellings."

Pumpkin winked. "The watch is the least my old man could do fer me. Ye understand, don't ye?"

Yes, I do. Only I won't even get a bloody watch from my father, James mused.

Judge Bathwell's gavel rapped as a prisoner in shackles was led forward by two guards. James nodded at Abrams, whose vexation at losing was quite evident by the prosecutor's unfriendly, thin-lipped stare. Abrams turned away, pressed to prepare for the next case. Not a second was wasted at the Old Bailey.

James gathered his papers and made to leave the courtroom, aware of every eye in the spectators' gallery following him. It was rare for a criminal defendant to be represented by a barrister, let alone to win against the Crown's prosecution.

James reached the double doors when a voice stopped him.

"A word, Mr. Devlin."

He turned and looked down into the eyes of an old woman who sat in the last row. Dressed in a gray gown with a large onyx brooch that resembled an enormous spider pinned to her shoulder, she sat stiffly on the wooden bench, her hands folded in her lap.

It can't be, he thought.

Yet the unmistakable scent of her perfume—a cloying floral fragrance—wafted to him.

The Dowager Duchess of Blackwood.

"What are you doing here?" he asked.

"Is that any way to greet your grandmother?"

He chuckled a dry and cynical sound. "It's been years since I've seen you, so yes."

Her expression was one of pained tolerance. "You always were rudely straightforward."

"Why are you here?" he asked.

"I've come with grave news. Your father is dead."

James stiffened. He shouldn't care, and yet he felt a sharp jab in his gut as the knowledge twisted inside him.

Bitterness spilled over into his voice. "You needn't have delivered the news personally, Your Grace. A note would have sufficed."

She glanced around the courtroom, her lips tight and grim, before returning to look at him. "We need to speak privately. Is there a quiet place in this circus?"

James regarded her with a speculative gaze. There was a client consultation room, but damned if he would cloister himself in the small room with her until he knew what she was after.

"Is that necessary?" he asked.

"My carriage then?"

The consultation room suddenly held more appeal. He could walk away when he chose. "Follow me." He inclined his head, and she stood to her full height of five feet.

She was a formidable woman, with noble bloodlines and the bearing of a queen. With her shrewd eyes, her steel-gray hair pulled back in a tight bun, and the ramrod posture of a British brigadier, James had witnessed both debutantes and titled lords cowering at her aura of respectability and propriety.

They walked side by side out of the courtroom, James's tall frame towering beside hers. The hallway of the Old Bailey was bustling with activity, barristers dressed in black gowns ushering witnesses to and from courtrooms. Clerks carrying stacks of briefs and litigation documents scurried to their assigned judge's chambers.

Halfway down the hall James stopped before a door with a brass nameplate labeled CLIENT CONSULTATION. He opened the door and held it as the dowager duchess marched inside.

The room was lined with bookshelves containing well-used law books. A battered desk sat in a corner and wooden chairs occupied the rest of the space. Unlike the crowded, over-heated courtroom ripe with the odor of unwashed bodies, the air in the small consultation room was stale and dusty. She glanced at her surroundings with haughty distaste before choosing a chair. James seated himself opposite her.

"Is there not a cushioned chair in this place?" she asked.

He ignored her and took off his barrister's wig. He ran his fingers through his dark hair and exhaled before looking in her indigo-blue eyes, the exact shade of his own. "What is so imperative that you visit me in person and request to speak privately?"

"I told you, your father is dead."

"And I'm sorry for that, Your Grace. I assume my half brother, Gregory, is busy dealing with the responsibilities of inheriting the dukedom."

"Gregory is not the new duke."

"Whatever do you mean?"

"You are the new Duke of Blackwood."

For a heart-stopping moment he stared and wondered if he had heard her correctly. Then the truth dawned, and he laughed bitterly. "What joke do you play?"

"This is no joke."

"May I remind you, Your Grace, that I am a bastard by birth."

Her aristocratic nose rose an inch higher—a feat he would have previously believed impossible—at his choice of words. "So we had all believed. But circumstances have come to my attention. Your parents were legally wed before you were born."

Again he merely stared, at a loss for words. James prided himself on his composure. Very little shocked him whether in the courtroom, in his chambers at Lincoln's Inn, or in the bedroom. But this woman had managed to render him speechless twice in one minute.

What game did she play?

She sat forward in her chair and looked at him intently. "It's true. Your father confessed to me on his death bed. I've always known that your mother was a parlor maid and she had run off with your father when he was seventeen. I had accounted it to drunken stupidity on your father's part after coming home on holiday from Oxford. Only days ago did I learn he had legally wed the girl at Gretna Green. Your mother died four months later, birthing you. Your father returned home and dutifully did as I bid and married your stepmother. She birthed Gregory before she too died. So you see you are the legitimate son, the new Duke of Blackwood."

He knew his mother had been a maid, of course. His grandmother and half brother, Gregory, had cruelly and repeatedly reminded him of that fact in his youth.

"You need to take over your responsibilities at once," she said, her tone authoritative.

"After years of being shunned by the family as the bastard, you now tell me it has all been an inaccuracy, and I am to step up to my responsibilities?" he asked incredulously.

"It was an unfortunate mistake."

An unfortunate mistake? Could she truly be even colder than he had believed?

"Don't be so ungrateful, James," she said tersely. "I saw to your every financial need. Your clothes, your tutors, the best education at Eton."

James sat very still, his eyes narrow. "How did he die?"

"It is of no consequence now."

"How?"

She gave an impatient shrug. "He was leaving his solicitor's office after selling off one of his country properties when he collapsed. He died a week later when his heart gave out."

"Which one?"

"Pardon?"

"Which country estate?"

"Wyndmoor Manor."

"Why would he sell Wyndmoor?"

A hint of exasperation flickered across her face. "Why does it matter?"

It mattered to him. Wyndmoor Manor was the only safe haven he had known as a boy, the only place the old duke had ever treated him as a true son. But he refused to explain himself to the woman sitting before him.

James rose in one fluid motion, intent on leaving and putting as much distance between himself and his grandmother as possible. The collar of his barrister's gown felt as if it was cutting off his supply of air, and he needed time to digest the shocking news. His hand touched the doorknob.

"Well? As my grandson and the legitimate Duke of Blackwood, what do you plan to do first?" she demanded.

James swung around, his eyes cold. "Buy Wyndmoor Manor back."

May 25, 1819
Wyndmoor Manor, Hertfordshire

There was a man outside her window.

Bella Sinclair had heard his footfalls, and the sound had her jumping out of bed like a skittish doe. An instant's panic had squeezed her chest, and she'd thought Roger had come into her bedchamber.

But Roger was dead.

Thank the sweet Lord. Roger lay in a cold grave.

She flew across the room and pressed her back against the wall. It was a chilly May evening and the cold from the plaster wall seeped through her thin nightdress. Gooseflesh rose on her arms. Taking a breath, she dared a quick glimpse out the window.

There. Just behind the azaleas, skirting the rosebushes. A black-dressed figure moved stealthily.

She doubted any other woman would have heard his movements, but years of practice had heightened her senses. Her hearing was attuned to the unwelcome sounds of a man's stockinged footsteps, the creak of a floorboard at the threshold of her bedchamber.

Again she looked out the window, the curtains gripped in a clenched fist. With dismay, she realized she had lost sight of him. The full moon seemed bent on scudding from behind one dark cloud to another. The shadows below looked like stalking cats. She scanned the front terrace, the fountain, and the gardens beyond until she spotted him.

The figure made his way to the front door.

Wyndmoor Manor was empty save for Harriet, who was in her seventies. As she'd moved here only days prior, there had been no time for Bella to interview and hire additional servants.

Heart lurching madly, she grabbed the closest thing to a weapon she could find, a fireplace poker, and tiptoed out of her bedchamber. The hallway was dark as pitch, but she dared not light a candle. Early this morning she had explored the halls and rooms of the manor with the excitement of a child experiencing her first country fair. She knew the width and length of the hallway and the number of steps that led down the grand staircase. For the first time in seven years, a house felt like a home to Bella.

How dare any stranger invade here!

She felt for the unpacked trunks and crates that sat in the hall midway to the landing. She slipped down the stairs, her breath escaping her as her bare feet touched the cold marble vestibule. She darted behind the front door and clenched the poker tightly in both hands above her head.

An orange glow passed by the window of the door. The stranger had lit a lamp.

How odd.

The doorknob rattled.

Locked. She had been sure to lock it before retiring.

The intruder would be forced to break a window or force the lock. Blood rushed through her veins like an avalanche.

Then she heard the jangle of keys and the distinctive sound of a key sliding in the lock.

Impossible.

The dead bolt slid aside and the door opened. A dark cloaked figure stepped inside.

She swung the poker downward with all her might.

He moved so swiftly she barely had time to gasp before she was thrust against the wall and a hard body slammed against hers. The poker fell from her grasp and clattered across the marble floor. Her scream was cut off by a large palm pressed against her mouth.

"Don't," a masculine voice said curtly. "No screaming to bring your criminal acquaintances bearing down on me."

He held the lamp high with his other hand, and she realized with alarm that he had managed to disarm her and pin her against the wall with one hand.

Fear and anger knotted inside her, and her heart thumped against her rib cage. Every solid inch of him was pressed against her. He was a tall man, broad and lean. The lamp lit half of his features, and she looked into blue eyes so dark they were almost black. Wavy jet hair framed his chiseled features. He shifted his weight, and she felt the muscled hardness of his body. His expression was taut, his jaw tense.

"I'm going to let you speak, but no screaming. Understand?"

She nodded, and he leaned to the side and kicked the door

shut with a booted foot. Placing his lamp on top of a nearby crate, he released his palm from her mouth and rested it against her throat.

"Who are you?" she croaked.

"James Devlin, the Duke of Blackwood."

A duke? Good lord, what was a duke doing at Wyndmoor Manor?

And yet, he had said the title stiffly, awkwardly, as if unpracticed in pronouncing it. Her mind raced and she wondered if he was truly a duke. Perhaps he was a local member of the criminal class who had heard of the new mistress of Wyndmoor and had come to pillage and steal whatever he could get his hands on. It made more sense. What duke traveled alone without a crowd of servants and a fancy, crested carriage?

His eyes raked her form, and she was highly conscious that she wore her nightdress without a wrapper. "Now it's your turn. Who are you and what are you doing in my home?" he demanded.

"My name is Bella Sinclair. I am the owner of this manor."

If she thought she couldn't be more alarmed, she was wrong.

He arched a dark eyebrow, the expression making him appear even more sinister. "You're lying. As of yesterday morning, *I* am the owner of Wyndmoor Manor."

Chapter 2

Bella's first instinct had been correct. James Devlin was not a member of the nobility, but a criminal.

She swallowed hard, lifted her chin, and boldly met his hard stare. "I assure you, I'm not lying. Whoever you are—and I doubt that you are a duke—I demand you leave at once."

His hand dropped from her throat. He stood inches away, and she felt the heat emanate from his body through her cotton nightdress.

There was a lethal calmness in his eyes. "You demand?"

Her pulse beat erratically at the threatening undertone in his deep voice. She knew she was in a precarious position, but instinct told her if she backed down or showed the slightest fear, he would swallow her whole.

"I will summon the constable," she insisted.

"The constable? And pray tell me, Miss Sinclair, just how would you accomplish that?"

"It's *Mrs.* Sinclair."

"*Ah.* Where is your strapping husband?"

"Bella?" A voice sounded from the top of the landing. "I heard noises. Are you down there?"

No, not Harriet!

Anxiety spurted through Bella as an old woman dressed in

a blue robe carrying a heavy candelabrum slowly descended the stairs.

"Do not trouble yourself, Harriet," Bella called out. "It is only a lost gentleman, and he was just leaving. You may go back to bed."

Bella turned to the stranger, her gaze imploring. "She is just an old servant. Please, if you are who you say, you will not harm her," she whispered vehemently.

His brows drew downward in a frown. "I never intended to harm anyone."

Harriet reached the bottom of the stairs and started across the vestibule. "A lost gentleman in the middle of the night?" She came close, holding the candelabrum high with both hands. Candlelight fully illuminated the man's features.

The chiseled planes of his face were arresting and elegant at once. His dark curling hair was cut short, and his lips were firm and sensual above a strong chin. His eyes weren't as dark as she had initially thought, but an extraordinary indigo. He needed to shave, but it was the middle of the night and most men would be in need of a razor, and the dark bristles only added to his rugged appeal. He was dressed in formfitting trousers and a white shirt that molded to impossibly wide shoulders.

Bella realized he was intently regarding her as well. His sharp eyes seemed to strip her of her nightdress, and she was thankful her unbound hair covered her breasts.

He bowed to Harriet. "Pardon the late hour. My name is James Devlin, the Duke of Blackwood. I had no idea the house was temporarily occupied."

Harriet's mouth opened and closed like a fish, and she looked to Bella.

"Temporarily?" Bella said.

"The previous owner never mentioned renters."

"Renters?" Bella said.

"Do you have a tendency to repeat people?" James asked.

"Only when they make little sense," Bella snapped.

"You think I'm a burglar?"

"What else am I to think of a man breaking into my home in the middle of the night?" Bella retorted.

Harriet gasped; Bella held out her hand to silence her and confronted the man.

He drew his lips in a tight smile. "I didn't break in. I lit a lamp and used a key. Have you ever heard of a burglar using a key?"

"You could have stolen the key," she accused.

"I purchased Wyndmoor Manor yesterday morning. In my excitement to see the place, I rode here straightaway."

"You must be mistaken, sir." Bella refused to address him as "Your Grace" when he was as far from being a duke as she was from being a duchess. "*I* purchased Wyndmoor Manor three days ago."

"From whom?" James asked.

"Sir Redmond Reeves," Bella said.

"Interesting indeed since Reeves sold the property to me as well."

"Again I insist that there must be a mistake. Why would Sir Reeves sell Wyndmoor Manor twice? Surely you purchased another property in Hertfordshire. Legal documents are complicated. Perhaps you misinterpreted them."

His laughter had a sharp edge. "Now that is highly unlikely. I've been a barrister for over ten years. I can interpret a legal document while intoxicated."

"A barrister! You said you were a duke. And to think, you accused me of lying!"

James sighed. "What I said was true. I am a barrister. I recently inherited my father's title."

"Hmmm. You really do think me a fool. What sane man would trouble himself by purchasing a small property such as Wyndmoor Manor so soon after inheriting a dukedom? Don't you have more pressing matters to attend to in London?" Bella asked.

A bright mockery invaded his stare. "Indeed. But my reasons do not concern you."

Bella stiffened and placed her hands on her hips. "Prove what you say."

"I shall return tomorrow morning with the deed to Wynd-moor."

"Why did you not carry it with you?"

His voice carried a unique force. "As I said, I had no idea the house was occupied. Do not fret, *Mrs.* Sinclair. I left the deed at a local inn—known as the Twin Rams—as I was in need of a hot meal and a fresh horse. I will return tomorrow with the proper documents."

He opened the door and turned back to glance at Bella. "I suggest you locate and procure your deed as well because this is the first and last night I will spend elsewhere. Starting tomorrow, I will sleep in the master's chambers of Wyndmoor Manor."

"He may truly be the Duke of Blackwood," Harriet said.

Bella shook her head. "I cannot believe his story. It makes no sense."

Bella sat on the edge of her bed in her nightdress as Harriet rubbed her shoulders. After Bella's mother had died when she was just a babe, Harriet had arrived as Bella's nursemaid. She had soothed Bella in the same manner when she had cried over a broken toy or a stubbed toe. Bella closed her eyes and tried to relax as Harriet's fingers worked a knot between her shoulder blades. Only this time, Bella remained tense.

"Bella, luv, there was something about the man that makes me believe his story. I've known frauds before, including your late husband, but I don't believe James Devlin is one of them," Harriet said.

Bella's deceased spouse had been the most talented of frauds. Roger had easily convinced Bella's father to consent to their betrothal when she was seventeen, and Roger had concealed his evil nature from the rest of the world.

Only Harriet had remained loyal to Bella, for she knew Roger as the monster he had been.

"We must be prepared in case Blackwood shows up tomorrow with a deed to Wyndmoor Manor."

Bella looked at Harriet. "But how? I have the deed."

Harriet kissed Bella's cheek and went to the door. "You'd best go find it, Bella," she said, closing the door behind her.

A knot tightened inside Bella as she sat on the bed, her fearful and angry thoughts centering on James Devlin. After seven years of misery as Roger Sinclair's wife, her husband's death had finally freed her of the bondage of their marriage. Her relief had been short-lived, however, as she'd learned that her wealthy husband had not left her a shilling. Instead, he had bequeathed his entire fortune to the church. He had been hailed a hero in death, as in life.

Fraud. Charlatan.

But still Bella was free, and she would gladly accept poverty over forced servitude to her husband.

No one had suspected the cruelties Roger had inflicted on his pretty, young wife. He had quashed her budding ambitions as a writer—her one passion and desire in life—and he had often threatened to dismiss Harriet in order to control Bella. But his most dastardly deeds had been the incidents of physical abuse when he'd come to her bedchamber intoxicated.

Roger had not stopped there, however, and had successfully isolated her by spinning a web of lies and deceit about his young wife's mental state. After his death, the townsfolk of Plymouth had been wary and distrustful of Bella. Even the vicar and his wife had turned their backs. Alienated from everyone, Bella had fled.

Her substantial dowry, which had aided Roger in building his investments and wealth, was gone, along with her mother's jewels. Her mother had died when Bella was an infant, and her father had perished in a carriage accident after her marriage. Bella's future had seemed precarious. Then she had received word that a great aunt had died childless and had left Bella with a tidy sum of money.

With Harriet by her side, Bella had planned to travel to London and start a new life in the crowd and bustle of the city. Along the way, she had stumbled upon Wyndmoor Manor and had instantly fallen in love with its rolling hills, grassy lawns, working fountain, and elegant manor house. She had pictured herself writing her articles here, free to send them off to any London paper of her choosing.

The closest town of St. Albans was only a day's coach ride to the city, and she could receive newspapers and easily send and receive mail. Wyndmoor was small for a country property, only a hundred acres, but beautifully kept, and upon inquiry she had been thrilled to discover that the owner was willing to sell, and the rent from the tenants was more than sufficient to maintain the place.

A home at last. Financial independence at last. A life without fear at last.

Bella's thoughts returned to the present. She rose from the bed and hurried across the bedchamber to a small trunk, the only remaining item from her mother. It was inlaid with an ivory and mother-of-pearl lid that was curved on the top and flat on the underside, and the workmanship of the trunk's lid was exquisite. Bella stored a miniature portrait of her parents inside along with her books, notes, and unpublished articles and novels, and other important items. Placing the candle on the floor, she lifted the lid and searched until she withdrew a packet of legal documents tied with brown string.

Sitting on the floor, she clutched the papers to her chest and took a deep breath. She forced herself to calmly focus on her future until her courage and determination hardened like a rock inside her. She was no longer a young bride, easily intimidated and dominated. No man would ever take advantage of her or control her again.

Wyndmoor Manor was not just her home now, but her salvation.

And whether or not James Devlin was truly the Duke of Blackwood, if he believed he could easily take it all away, then he best be prepared for the fight of his life.

James stormed into his room at the Twin Rams Inn. The door slammed against the wall causing a cheap print to clatter to the floor.

His manservant jumped out of the chair in which he was sleeping. "What's amiss?" Coates shouted.

James cursed. "What the devil are you doing in my room?"

"Waiting up for you."

The candle Coates held burned low, and the room was dim. James stalked forward and promptly walked into an end table.

"Damn!" James cursed again and rubbed his bruised thigh.

Coates rushed to light a lamp.

"I need a drink." James hobbled to the chair Coates had previously occupied and sat.

Coates hurried to pour a whiskey and handed the glass to James. "What happened tonight, Your Grace?"

"Don't call me that! You've called me Devlin for the past ten years."

An amused gleam lit Coates's eyes. Indeed, Coates had been James Devlin's manservant since James had completed his pupilage at Lincoln's Inn and had become a barrister. Coates had found James's new title as a duke quite humorous and loved to tease his master about the strange turn of events over the past two weeks.

"You were supposed to go to Wyndmoor Manor," Coates said.

"I did."

"And that's why you're in such a foul mood?"

"No. My mood is due to a female."

Coates nodded. "That makes sense. Is a disgruntled husband or lover responsible?"

James scowled. He knew he had a reputation when it came to women. Simply put, James loved them. Famed courtesans, bored married ladies, lonely widows, eager female clients . . . society had names for men such as he—rakes, rogues, and womanizers. His free-loving mindset had gotten him into trouble in the past, but he had successfully fought more than one duel with a disgruntled husband. James avoided the marriage-minded ladies of the *ton* like the plague, and he always found delight when uptight matrons ushered their virginal daughters from the room upon seeing him at certain society functions.

But that wasn't what had occurred tonight.

"It's not what you think, Coates. I entered Wyndmoor Manor only to find it occupied."

"Occupied? By whom?"

"An infuriating female who claims she owns the place."

James handed Coates his empty glass. Coates promptly refilled it and handed it back to James who took another swallow.

"But how is it possible that she owns the manor? It took you days to track down the gentleman in Hertfordshire whom the old duke had sold Wyndmoor Manor to, and I was beside you when Sir Redmond Reeves finally signed the deed over to you," Coates pointed out.

It was true. After James had learned that Sir Reeves had been the purchaser, he'd had to search for the man throughout Hertfordshire before finally catching up with him.

"It's not possible. The lovely lady is an imposter."

"She's lovely? I'm beginning to understand why you didn't throw her out," Coates said.

"She claims to be *Mrs.* Sinclair, yet I saw no sign of a husband, only an elderly, female servant. If Mrs. Sinclair was married, I would have expected her husband to have come charging down the stairs after me."

"She could be a widow."

"A widow or an accomplished actress or both."

"You think she lied about owning Wyndmoor Manor?" Coates asked.

"I do. And if by chance she presents me with a deed, I'll be able to tell if it is a forgery."

"What will you do either way?"

An image of Bella Sinclair crystallized in James's mind. Large green eyes, delicately carved facial bones, full lips, and a mass of dark auburn hair that shimmered in the candle-light. She had been wearing her nightgown and although the white cotton had covered every inch of her body from her neck to her wrists to the tips of her bare toes, he'd have to be a monk not to notice she was voluptuously curved. Her full breasts had burned through his shirt when he had pressed against her.

But she was no dainty damsel eager for his affection or at-tention. If he hadn't seen her shadow flicker through the window, she would have happily cracked his skull open with the fireplace poker she had wielded.

Of one thing he was certain—Bella Sinclair was full of spirit and challenge.

And James Devlin loved a challenge even more than he loved women. The combination of the two was irresistible.

The truth was he would have insisted she leave, but then the old woman had descended the stairs and a flash of fear had shone in Bella Sinclair's jade eyes. She had pleaded with him not to harm the servant, and James's firm resolve to fight with the bewitching woman before him had thawed. He wasn't a monster to take advantage of a female's fear.

But neither was he willing to walk away from the manor he had gone to such lengths to obtain.

"Well? What will you do?" Coates asked.

"First thing tomorrow morning ready the carriage. I'm re-turning to Wyndmoor Manor."

Chapter 3

The following morning, Bella pushed aside the black mourning gown in her wardrobe and chose a walking dress with a muslin overskirt of emerald green. She refused to wear black in her own home when she felt no grief, only a great sense of relief to be rid of a pitiless tyrant. She had no plans to venture into St. Albans and act the grieving widow, and the walking dress was her favorite—not only because the deep color matched her eyes, but because it was one of the few dresses that she had owned before her marriage.

Roger had been obsessed with his wife's clothing and had chosen each of her gowns. She had not been permitted to select accessories, not even a pair of gloves, without his permission.

After Harriet brushed her hair and arranged it in a knot at her nape, Bella made her way to the breakfast room. She finished her toast and was sipping a cup of tea when she heard the sound of a coach traveling up the graveled drive. Bella rose and rushed to the window overlooking the front of the house.

An impressive black-lacquered coach and team of six came to a stop before the fountain. It was a resplendent conveyance, emblazoned with the crest of the Duke of Blackwood. The matching team of horseflesh stood obediently, their sleek muscles gleaming beneath the morning sun. A liveried footman hopped down and opened the door. The handsome, dark-haired devil of last night alighted and strode confidently up the front steps.

Seconds later the door knocker sounded.

Sweet Lord! He really is a duke!

She felt momentary panic as her mind jumped to the startling truth—he hadn't lied last evening.

Harriet's footfalls echoed off the marble vestibule. Composing her features, Bella turned.

"He's here," Harriet said, holding out a card. "What do you want me to tell him?"

Bella reached out and took the gold embossed card of the Duke of Blackwood. Her stomach churned with anxiety.

"Please put him in the drawing room," Bella said.

Harriet's brow furrowed. "You'd best be careful, Bella. My instincts tell me he's not a man to be trifled with. Do you want me to stay outside the door?"

Bella touched her sleeve. Harriet was willing to stand outside the door to protect her. *Just like she had with Roger, only nothing could have saved her from her spouse.* "That won't be necessary, Harriet. I have the documents. I can handle him."

Minutes later, Bella made her way to the drawing room. Straightening her spine, she opened the door.

Blackwood was standing at a large window beside a potted palm, looking out at the gardens below, as she entered the room. Hearing the door, he turned.

Unlike their first encounter, today he was immaculately dressed in a well-tailored coat of navy superfine with buff-colored trousers and highly polished black Hessians. In the light of the day, he appeared even taller, and the cut of his coat emphasized his broad shoulders. A lock of black hair fell a little forward onto his forehead, giving him a rakish appearance. But the intense indigo eyes that studied her spoke of a firm inner strength that told her this was no dandy or town fop. He had an air of authority and the appearance of one who demanded instant obedience.

In short, he looked every inch a formidable duke.

He bowed. "Mrs. Sinclair. Shall I properly introduce myself this morning?"

She curtsied. "At least you were gracious enough to knock."

His full lips curved in a smile. "I decided against using my key. I was afraid of being attacked with another sharp fireplace implement."

"Tempting, *Your Grace*."

To her surprise, his mouth quirked with humor. "I'm shocked to hear you address me by my title, Mrs. Sinclair. Shall we dismiss with the formalities then?"

She nodded curtly. "Let us speak plainly."

"Very well. Wyndmoor Manor belongs to me. I have the documents to prove it." He reached for a black leather bag on a nearby settee.

The drawing room, along with most of the house, had come furnished when she purchased it from Sir Reeves. It had been an added incentive since—along with his fortune— Roger had bequeathed all their furniture to the church. Bella had left her marital home with only the pieces that had been in her bedchamber and those that she and Harriet had had the foresight to hide.

Blackwood opened the bag and withdrew a piece of paper, which he offered to her. "This is the deed to the manor, which is officially in my name."

She took it with a surprisingly steady hand and gazed at the official-looking document. The letters blurred before her. A solitary thought crossed her mind—fate was cruel indeed to bring another man to her doorstep intent on wielding power and authority over her, this time to force her from her home.

She thrust the paper back at him. "This document means nothing to me."

"Where is your husband, Mrs. Sinclair?"

The question took her off guard. "He's unavailable."

"You're a widow then? Have you nowhere else to go?"

She lifted her chin. "I don't need anywhere else to go. This is my home."

"Show me your deed."

She went to a rosewood sofa table, opened a slim drawer, and withdrew a piece of paper. "I truly did not believe you would show today, but nonetheless, I am prepared." She handed the document to him.

He studied the deed carefully, and then held it up to the light from the window.

"What are you doing?" she asked.

"Checking to see if it is a forgery."

"A forgery!"

"Quite frankly, yes."

"My deed is true. Yours is the forgery," she insisted.

"Sir Redmond Reeves made no mention of you," he said.

"I don't believe you."

"If your deed is true, and I'm not admitting that it is, then it seems we were both played as fools. You purchased the property from Sir Redmond Reeves three days prior to me," Blackwood said.

"Are you saying Sir Reeves sold Wyndmoor Manor to both of us?" she asked incredulously.

"I am."

"Why would he do that?"

"He could be a swindler. A thief. He may not even be a knight. Perhaps there are others out there with deeds as well," he said.

Others? Her heart beat rapidly.

Rancor sharpened her voice. "But you said yourself, I

purchased it three days before you from Sir Reeves. I am the rightful owner and yours is the invalid deed."

"Not in the eyes of the law."

"Whatever do you mean?"

"The rightful owner is the first to record the deed," Blackwood said. "I recorded the deed with the Hertfordshire Registrar the day I purchased the manor. There was no mention of your deed in the books, and I carefully examined them. I questioned the clerk as well, and he was unaware of another owner or resident. So you see the legality of my deed is no longer in question."

A cold knot formed in Bella's stomach. She'd had no idea she was expected to record the deed. She had believed all was legal when Sir Reeves had scrawled his signature on the deed and handed it to her. But this man, this duke, was trying to steal her home from beneath her based on a legal technicality that was ethically wrong. She refused to be bullied by him.

She had purchased Wyndmoor Manor first!

Bella stalked forward, glaring up at him. "For someone who claims to have been a barrister for over ten years, you were duped alongside me."

He flinched, and she suspected she had struck a nerve.

"There is a simple way to resolve our dilemma," he said. "We have to find Redmond Reeves. He told me he planned on departing Hertfordshire when he sold me the place. Nonetheless, one of the barristers with whom I share my chambers has access to some of the best investigators in the business. I will retain his services to search for Reeves straightaway and see that your money is returned. If he is not found or has spent the money, I will personally reimburse you."

"Why would you do that?" she asked.

"This manor has great significance to me. It belonged to my father, the old duke, before he recently sold it to Reeves before his death. I intend to reclaim it. That being said, I do not believe it will be difficult for the investigator to locate

Reeves. He cannot have gone far, and I will ensure he returns your money."

Bella did not like the direction he was taking. "To the contrary, Sir Reeves has run off with *your* money. You should locate him and argue the matter with him."

He shook his head. "I do apologize for frightening you last night. I've noticed you have only one servant here, an elderly woman. I will instruct my servants to assist yours in packing your things." He looked around haughtily as if he were an appraiser at a foreclosure sale. "I trust it will not take longer than a week. I'm perfectly willing to sleep at the Twin Rams Inn until Reeves is found and your belongings packed."

She glared at him with burning, reproachful eyes. He had her future meticulously planned and probably never once doubted her cooperation.

Just like Roger.

Were all men so selfish and manipulative?

Fury almost choked her, and her breaths came in ragged gasps. She had spent too many years living in fear, capitulating to the whims of a cruel, controlling man, to fall victim once again. She wanted peace, the freedom to run her own life and resume her writing ambitions, and this isolated country manor offered her the perfect respite.

Every curve of her body spoke defiance as she pointed to the empty stone fireplace. "You can burn your document before you leave. It means nothing to me. *I* purchased Wyndmoor Manor first. *I* moved in first. *I* am the rightful owner. You may have recently inherited your title, but you are no gentleman. You are nothing more than a bully trying to oust a widow from her home. I trust you can see yourself out, *Your Grace.*"

But the Duke of Blackwood, as he now was, stood unmoving. His eyes narrowed, and a muscle flicked angrily at his jaw.

His voice, though quiet, had an ominous quality. "I think not, Mrs. Sinclair. You are the one that must leave. I had planned on acting the gentleman by residing elsewhere until the matter is resolved in consideration of your reputation. I have since changed my mind. I intend to live here until that time."

"You're insane! I'm living here. You are now a duke. Surely you have vast estates to choose from in the country and in London." She was aware of the faint thread of hysteria in her own voice.

"Yes, that's true. But as I explained, I intend to reclaim this place. Now I'll ask you again, do you have anywhere else to go? What of the home you shared with your husband? His family?"

She felt icy fingers travel up her spine. The thought of returning to Plymouth and facing the suspicions and hatred of its townsfolk made her gut clench. "I'm not leaving."

They glared at each other across a sudden angry silence.

"Then you will have to reside with me until we locate Reeves and retrieve your money," he said. "Do you truly wish to live with a bachelor? Your reputation will be shredded beyond repair."

Little did he know, Roger had already successfully destroyed her reputation. Since she never planned to marry again, she cared naught for society's cruel and unjust opinions.

She met his gaze without flinching. "As I said, you may have inherited a dukedom, but you are no gentleman."

He stepped forward, appearing tall, broad, and compellingly male. His eyes traveled her face, and he leaned close—so very close—yet he did not touch her. She raised her chin, her eyes flashing with outrage. Then he reached out to finger a wayward auburn curl resting on her cheek, twisting it leisurely between his fingers.

Her heart hammered in her chest. She could smell a hint of sandalwood in his cologne and feel his warm breath on her cheek. She wanted to slap his hand away, resist his unexpected touch, but a ripple of awareness passed through her limbs, upsetting her balance.

Raising her eyes, she was struck by his sardonic gaze, full of challenge and amusement, as if he enjoyed her struggle to maintain her composure and *knew* his effect on her senses. Knew he exuded a potent sensuality.

She pulled away, momentarily abashed.

"Perhaps you're right," he said, "and I'm no gentleman. I've always had a weakness for the fair sex. I seem to find most attractive women irresistible, even widows with tongues that can clip tin. Who's to say I won't behave ungentlemanly and pay a nightly visit to your bedchamber should we live under the same roof?"

Shock and embarrassment yielded quickly to fury. "Bastard!" she cursed, not caring how unladylike she sounded. "If you so much as come near my bedchamber, you'll find me armed with the poker—and I won't waste my efforts on your skull!"

Grasping her skirts, she spun on her heel and slammed the door on her way out.

Chapter 4

What was it about the woman that made James's iron-clad control slip? Had he actually threatened to come to her bedchamber? In all his years of debauchery, he had never forced himself on a woman. It had never been necessary. Bella Sinclair had rightfully called him a bastard.

And until recently, he'd believed the same of himself.

James sighed as he stood in the center of the drawing room. Bella Sinclair was a beautiful woman with a glorious shade of auburn hair that matched her volatile temper. When she'd entered the drawing room, head held high, dressed in a gown that accentuated her generous curves, his blood had pounded in his veins. Memories of the night before returned, and he recalled her dark red tresses loose about her shoulders, whereas today her hair was bound in a tight knot. His fingers had itched to pull the pins from her hair and see the true color in the sunlight. Her gown had enhanced her magnificent green eyes, and he suspected she had carefully chosen her attire.

James knew women, knew all their ploys and virtues, and Bella Sinclair had walked into the room with every intention of throwing him off balance.

She had succeeded.

Bloody hell.

He had to put a stop to his carnal thoughts and consider her as an adversary barring him from what he coveted. She was a female, no different from any other, and James had yet to encounter a woman he couldn't charm and seduce. How difficult could it be to convince her to leave Wyndmoor Manor?

Yet he was not so foolish as to dismiss her entirely. James had always been professional, but aggressive in the courtroom when dealing with his adversaries. It didn't matter that he was now a duke and a member of the House of Lords. His legal training, his way of life, was an intrinsic part of his nature.

She was a widow, and when he had asked about her previous home and husband, he detected a momentary flicker of fear in her eyes. She'd been quick to conceal it, and another man may have missed the telling signs—her quick gasp, the rapid beat of her pulse at the base of her throat, the slight clenching of her fingers beside her skirts—but not James.

His instincts were well-honed from dealing with a wide swath of humanity—both victim and perpetrator. As a skilled cross-examiner, he had learned to carefully observe witnesses on the stand and not only to listen to the words that came from their lips, but to look for their physical responses.

He had offered to pay Bella Sinclair from his own pocket should Redmond Reeves be found fundless. He had initially accounted her adamant rejection of his offer as hotheaded anger and sheer stubbornness, but his gut told him there was more.

So what was the lovely widow hiding? A married lover, a hostile relationship with a meddling mother-in-law, or an overly aggressive creditor?

James had never been one to enjoy investigative research, yet he could think of nothing more scintillating than digging through layer after layer until he discovered all of Bella Sinclair's secrets. He was, after all, a seasoned barrister and a notorious lover—and, when he chose to combine his skills, he could be an expert manipulator. If money could not get her to quit the place, then he would woo her into revealing her secrets. Whatever trivial problem she was hiding, he would use to his advantage.

His seduction must be systematic, methodical, and well-planned, his emotions tightly reined the entire time. Just like a trial, the jury must never see his inner turmoil, only a calm, confident barrister in control of his emotions and the courtroom proceedings, no matter what unethical tactics an opponent attempted or what surprising testimony a witness blurted out on the stand.

Confident with his scheme, James chose a chair by the stone fireplace and sat. He studied the drawing room and soon childhood memories returned. There were notable differences in the décor since his last visit years ago. Gone were the Grecian-style furnishings and Wilton carpet. The wallpaper had been changed to a Chinese motif of winding bamboo, and an Oriental carpet covered the floor, yet the room struck a familiar chord in his chest.

Even though he had inherited a vast amount of property throughout the country and a splendid London mansion, this small manor was an inner anchor, a place where he could escape and feel as if he truly deserved the dukedom recently bestowed upon him. The truth was he felt like a fraud usurping his half brother, Gregory, after all these years.

Only at Wyndmoor Manor had James felt like the old duke's son.

Once a year until he had attended Eton, the duke would send a coach for James at the boarding school where he had resided and bring him to Wyndmoor. Here father and son would hunt, fish, and swim together. No grandmother, no Gregory, just James and the duke. The staff had been kind, and the word "bastard" had never been whispered in its halls. A full week later it would end, and the coach would return James to school.

So why hadn't the old duke publicly accepted him as his son? According to his grandmother, his father had confessed on his death bed that James was his legitimate child. Then why had he not claimed James during his lifetime? Instead James had spent his youth ostracized by his family, spending Christmas dinners at the homes of friends kind enough to share their tables with a duke's bastard son.

James had never been one to wallow in self-pity, and he had overcome his need of familial acceptance years ago. He had been driven to succeed, determined never to depend on handouts from his aristocratic grandmother. She, alongside his own father, wanted nothing to do with him publicly. So James had carved his own future and entered his pupilage at Lincoln's Inn. He had found his calling as a barrister, and the three other barristers he shared his chambers with were more like true brothers to James than Gregory had ever been.

The duke was now dead, and although James had been stunned by his grandmother's announcement, he was prepared to inherit what he had believed belonged to Gregory all along. It had been two weeks since his father's death, two weeks since the dowager duchess had confronted him in the Old Bailey, and James had yet to speak with Gregory.

After the funeral, Gregory had immediately left London to visit a maternal aunt and no doubt deal with the astonishing news of his loss of the dukedom in private. James had not pursued him. They would both return to London soon enough to face each other.

James had left his grandmother at the London mansion and had departed to track down Redmond Reeves and settle the matter of Wyndmoor Manor. He'd had every intention of purchasing the property quickly and returning to London within the week, but then he hadn't counted on confronting Bella Sinclair.

His lips curved in a smile. There was no question that the

lady was hiding secrets. It had been a long time since James had felt challenged by a woman, and a country widow like Bella Sinclair did not stand a chance against him. He estimated she would be out of the house and his life in a week's time.

Bella paced her bedchamber, tucking in the loose curl of hair that had escaped her knot and trying not to think of how Blackwood had touched the strands moments ago in the drawing room.

"Thank goodness you prefer this smaller chamber, luv. At least there's no need to fight over the master's chambers," Harriet said as she folded Bella's clothes and tucked them in the wardrobe.

"He's fortunate indeed I chose this room." Bella had fallen in love with the rose-hued wallpaper and canopied bed. Across from the master's chambers, it faced the back of the house, and she had a splendid view of the sun rising over the back gardens.

"I agree. Knowing how determined you can be if you had chosen the other room, I suspect you'd both be sleeping in it now," Harriet said.

Bella stopped pacing and whirled around. "Harriet! As if I would ever consider sharing a meal with that man, let alone a room!"

"He's a handsome one, he is," Harriet said.

"So was Roger, remember?"

Harriet's brow pulled into an affronted frown. "Do not believe for one instant that all men are like your deceased husband in disposition. As for looks, Roger was twenty years your senior and fair-haired. The duke looks nothing like him and can only be in his early thirties—"

"Outer appearances aren't everything. He shares his same black heart." Bella didn't want to think of Blackwood as handsome. His dark hair, deep blue eyes, and strong profile could only be regarded as haughty and stubborn.

Liar, her inner voice cried out. The mere touch of the duke's hand in her hair had sent an unwelcome surge of excitement through her. And when his breath fanned her face, her skin had tingled uncomfortably. He was a dangerous man—one who wielded both power and virility to his advantage.

"What makes you think he has a black heart?" Harriet asked.

"He all but ordered me out. When I refused to do his bidding, he insisted on staying here. He also claims he's legally entitled to Wyndmoor because he recorded the deed even though I was first to purchase the place and first to move in."

"Perhaps you should seek the services of a barrister, but I doubt there is one in the village. We may have to travel to London," Harriet said.

Bella bit her bottom lip. "I know it's a good idea, but the matter cannot go to court. Should my character arise, people may question the circumstances surrounding Roger's death. They may look into his unsavory business ventures. What if Blackwood went to Plymouth to question people about me?"

Harriet stepped close and touched her shoulder. "Don't fret, Bella. You would only be seeking a legal opinion to be certain he's telling the truth. Besides, Blackwood's a duke. Surely he has responsibilities in London? Mayhap he won't want to stay here long."

"He was a barrister in London, too," Bella added. "I am betting the country life will bore him to tears. We, on the other hand, have lived in the country for most of our lives." Plymouth was a shipping town, but still far from the exciting pace of London.

Harriet's brow furrowed. "If he thinks the country boring, then why would he bother to buy the place?"

"He claims fond memories of the manor as it belonged to his late father. But I'm certain he hadn't a hand in caring for the place. How long will it take before he expires of boredom? Before he misses the challenge and excitement of London, the Season, and his legal cases?"

Harriet measured Bella with an appraising look. "If he's looking for a challenge, then he best prepare to battle you."

Chapter 5

Bella decided she should go about the rest of her day as if the duke had never arrived. She had scheduled interviews to meet with a local cook, a parlor maid, a head gardener, and most importantly, a steward. Harriet would oversee the staff as head housekeeper. As Bella had no plans to entertain, she decided to postpone hiring a butler.

Bella left her room, straightened her shoulders, and marched down the stairs. There was no sign of Blackwood, but a second coach had arrived with more of his belongings; his servants were busy carrying trunks from the coach into the house.

The duke had arrived with five servants in all, and they presented themselves courteously, although not as if she was the lady of the house. She learned Coates was Blackwood's manservant, and he was clearly in charge, ordering the two footmen and the driver to carry the duke's belongings to the master's chambers. The fifth was a small scrap of a boy with red hair and freckles named Bobby, who was the stable boy and responsible for Blackwood's prized horses.

The amount of baggage was substantial, and the men took turns passing trunks to each other and up the stairs like busy ants.

Coates bowed. "Pardon the intrusion, Mrs. Sinclair. We shall not be much longer. Most of the baggage is for the master's chambers."

Bella forced a smile, feeling as if her face would crack from the effort. "I'm sure His Grace has found his room *temporarily* suitable."

"I'm certain, Mrs. Sinclair," Coates responded. If the man heard her sarcasm, he showed no outward reaction.

The door knocker rattled, drawing her attention. The door remained open as the duke's servants continued to unload the coach, and a portly man with fleshy jowls stood on the front step, his brown eyes wide as he noted the activity.

"Good afternoon. My name is Sigmund Gibbs, and I'm here to apply for the position of steward. I had no idea residents would be moving in today."

"Thank you for arriving on time, Mr. Gibbs," Bella said. "I'm Mrs. Sinclair, the owner of the manor, and the place is in need of a steward."

Ignoring Coates's inquisitive gaze, she steered Sigmund Gibbs around a particularly large trunk and into the drawing room. Motioning for him to take a seat on a leather chair, she sat on the settee opposite him.

Folding her hands in her lap, she looked at the man expectantly. "Tell me, have you experience as a steward, Mr. Gibbs?"

He nodded, and the folds of skin above his tightly tied cravat reminded her of an elephant's wrinkled hide. "I've some, but not for a manor as grand as Wyndmoor."

Bella frowned. Wyndmoor Manor was small compared to most country estates. The hundred acres surrounding it were beautiful and had been meticulously kept, but there were those estates that boasted thousands of acres with many tenants to oversee. The size of Wyndmoor was one of the reasons Bella had been drawn to it. It was small enough to manage and with the rents from Wyndmoor's tenants she could afford its upkeep.

"Tell me exactly what experience you do have."

"Well, I've—"

The door to the drawing room burst open and in strode Blackwood. His well-groomed appearance exuded masculinity and authority at once, and a powerful swirl of energy surrounded him.

"What's this I'm told, you are interviewing for the position of steward?"

She feigned a smile, and remained seated. "I am. Wyndmoor Manor is in need of a steward unless, of course, you are volunteering for the position, Your Grace."

He laughed, and the lively twinkle in his blue eyes only incensed her more. "I would, my dear, but the manor already has a steward."

Sigmund Gibbs's jaw dropped, and he jumped to his feet. "Your lord . . . I mean Your Grace, I meant no disrespect."

"Sit down, Mr. Gibbs," Bella said. "His Grace is mistaken. There is no steward."

"Oh, but there is, Mrs. Sinclair," Blackwood drawled in a deep-timbered voice. "Gideon Jacobson has been Wyndmoor Manor's steward for twenty-six years."

She grit her teeth. "May I have a word with you in private, Your Grace?"

"Of course." He turned to Mr. Gibbs. "Thank you for coming today. We will send word to you should another position become available."

Sigmund Gibbs bowed to Blackwood and nearly tripped over his own feet in his haste to leave the room. The door closed on his way out.

How dare he! she thought.

She whirled to him. "I meant for us to speak privately in another room."

He sat on the arm of the settee, his long legs crossed at his booted feet. "I do believe we got off on the wrong foot. Please call me James. I find the title tedious."

She eyed him suspiciously. "That would be most improper."

He arched a dark eyebrow, not bothering to hide his amusement. "And living together is proper? You are full of contradictions, Bella."

"It's Mrs. Sinclair."

"That's a dreadful waste. Bella is such a beautiful name. It fits you."

He gave her a smile that sent her pulses racing. She was struck by how devastatingly handsome he truly was, and combined with his flattering words, the man could be utterly charming when he chose. She imagined the women of London flocked to him in droves. An uneasiness rose in her that she fought to hide.

What on earth was his game?

Her eyes narrowed. "Are you trying to distract me from the topic at hand?"

"Is it working?"

"It is not. As mistress here, I am in charge of the servants."

"That is debatable." He held up a hand to stop her from arguing further. "However, I only ask that you hear me out before passing judgment. The position of steward is most important. I find it difficult to believe any other would have the same number of years as experience. Gideon Jacobson loved this place until Redmond Reeves unjustly dismissed him. As I said, it was Jacobson's home for twenty-six years. Can you say the same for your Mr. Gibbs?"

She could not. From what she had heard the man barely had any experience.

She crossed her arms over her chest. "You have already brought in five of your servants. I only have Harriet. I refuse to have every other servant under your influence."

He waved a hand dismissively. "Fine. I assume there were others you were planning on retaining. I'll leave them up to you."

She was surprised by his easy manner. "Thank you, Your Grace."

"It's James, remember?" He stood to leave, then turned. "By the way, will you dine with me this evening?"

He *was* trying to charm her. "There's no cook."

He winked. "Then hire one today."

James did not have time to consider whether Bella would accept his dinner invitation. As soon as he stepped out of the drawing room, Coates sought him out to tell him his fellow barristers had arrived and were waiting for him in the library.

James heard their voices as he walked down the hall. He had invited his friends to visit Wyndmoor Manor for a short holiday before he had left for Hertfordshire. James had been under the mistaken impression that the business of purchasing the country property would go smoothly, and he had looked forward to spending time with his friends away from their chambers and their hectic dockets. He had not expected a merry chase throughout Hertfordshire, searching for Sir Redmond Reeves to sell him Wyndmoor Manor.

As soon as James opened the library door, two of his colleagues, Anthony Stevens and Brent Stone, rose to greet him.

"Hello, Devlin," Anthony drawled. "Or should we call you 'Duke'?"

James rolled his eyes. His friends had always referred to him by his surname, Devlin, and he had no desire for them to start addressing him by his new title.

"Don't even jest about it. It's bad enough that I will have to leave Lincoln's Inn." James knew it to be true. He couldn't handle the vast responsibilities he had inherited, sit in the House of Lords, and continue to practice as a barrister.

"Where's Jack?" James asked.

Jack Harding was the fourth barrister in their chambers and the most successful in the courtroom. Known as the smooth-talking "jury master," Jack was the only married barrister in their chambers, having wed his pupilmaster's beautiful daughter, Evelyn Darlington, five years ago.

"Jack's with Evie. He has an upcoming trial and they plan to arrive as soon as he's free," Anthony said.

"It will be the first time they'll leave little Phillip to travel together. I suspect their new nanny will have her hands full with that mischievous three-year-old boy," Brent said.

James laughed. "Let's drink a toast to your arrival then." He went to a sideboard, poured three glasses of whiskey, and handed them out. "I'm glad you're both here. I need some advice."

Anthony and Brent lowered their glasses.

"What's amiss?" they asked in unison.

James sipped his whiskey before answering. "I arrived here only to find the place occupied. A sharp-tongued widow who claims she purchased the property three days prior to me from the same man, a Sir Redmond Reeves."

"Have you seen her deed?" Anthony asked.

James nodded. "I have, and as far as I can tell it is not a forgery."

"I have a bad feeling about this," Brent said. "As a barrister, I've heard of it, of course. With the increase of population in debtors' prison, swindlers and thieves have grown desperate and bold. There are others out there selling properties to numerous owners in short amounts of time then fleeing before they can be held accountable."

"I've assumed as much," James said dryly.

"I take it you already recorded the deed?" Anthony asked.

"I did. She did not."

Anthony shrugged. "Then technically the place is yours."

"Wait," Brent said. "She purchased it first, you say?"

"By only three days," James said.

"But she was also first to occupy the manor?" Brent asked.

"Yes."

"Then the matter may not be so cut and dried. She may have an arguable case. What of the old adage possession is nine tenths of the law? If I was her barrister, I would paint her as a sympathetic widow and argue she has the winning side. It would be up to a judge and a jury to decide. Quite simply, there is a possibility, albeit small, that you could lose," Brent said.

Anthony frowned in exasperation as he turned to Brent. "You tend to favor the lady?"

"I'm only giving a legal opinion. Yours tends to be skewed against women," Brent said.

Anthony laughed bitterly. "What the devil do you know about women? You're celibate, for Christ's sake."

Brent's lips thinned with irritation. "Your legal practice has turned you into a jaded man, Anthony. One day a woman will get the best of you."

"Sod off, Brent," Anthony growled.

James rolled his eyes. Even though Brent and Anthony were longtime friends they often mercilessly baited each other.

"You two bicker like old magpies. I don't desire fisticuffs on your first day here." James refilled their glasses, leaned against the sideboard, and eyed the pair.

Anthony was a tall, muscular man with massive shoulders. When not in chambers, he spent his free time at Gentleman Jackson's. An experienced pugilist, Anthony's size did not hinder him in the ring, and James had witnessed Anthony's agility and fast footwork firsthand as he beat a seasoned boxer in the first round.

As for Brent's comment that Anthony was jaded when it came to women, it was true. Anthony specialized in marital matters and had successfully obtained what few barristers dared attempt—the highly desirable divorce. Requiring an Act of Parliament, divorce was close to impossible to obtain despite the fact that marital strife was commonplace among the *beau monde*.

But Anthony had managed to obtain divorces for three wealthy, titled men—all by proving the adultery of the wives. Anthony had become an overnight success, one of the richest barristers in Lincoln's Inn, but the dark side of his practice had a price. Anthony had a hard, cutthroat manner about him, and he scoffed at the notion of love.

Brent Stone, on the other hand, was cut from entirely different cloth. His tawny hair and blue eyes had always attracted attention from females. Yet Brent showed little interest in women. His practice focused on obtaining letters patent for wealthy and oftentimes eccentric inventors. Brent rarely set foot in a courtroom and spent long hours drafting patent claims in their chambers at Lincoln's Inn. To James it seemed like a tedious, unbearable existence, but Brent thrived upon it.

James had never seen nor heard of Brent with a woman. The man claimed to prefer the fair sex, but as far as James was aware, Brent had never had a mistress or lover. At times the difference in their approach strained their friendship, as James had numerous affairs without commitment, and Brent claimed to be searching for a lady with whom he could have a long-lasting relationship.

James's thoughts returned to his own predicament, and he considered Brent's argument in favor of Bella Sinclair.

Bella could take the matter to court. Any barrister worth his salt understood that trying a case before a jury could be as unpredictable as the gaming tables. Wyndmoor Manor was in the jurisdiction of Hertfordshire, and as such any trial would be held here, far from the Old Bailey and London where James had practiced. He was familiar with every judge at the Old Bailey, their procedural likes and dislikes. But in Hertfordshire, he was an outsider, and a sympathetic judge or jury could find in the lady's favor.

"You said she was a sharp-tongued widow. Is she an eyesore?" Anthony asked.

"No," James said. "She's stunning, a true beauty."

There was an awkward silence.

"You've never had a problem with the ladies in the past," Anthony said.

"Don't listen to him," Brent said. "You may anger the lady if you treat her like a common affair."

Anthony's voice held a note of impatience. "Then use your newfound influence as duke. What judge or jury in these godforsaken hinterlands would find against a duke? Bribe the judge if you have to. I doubt it would be difficult. A few hunting outings here at Wyndmoor ought to do it."

"Is that how you practice?" Brent inquired of Anthony. "Not everyone can be bribed or coerced." Brent looked to James. "Your solution may be as simple as reimbursing her for the property."

"I already offered to pay her should Sir Redmond Reeves be found and all the money spent. She refused," James said.

"Then you must find another way," Brent said.

"There is something else. I suspect Mrs. Sinclair is hiding a secret, something involving her past," James said.

"Use it to your advantage," Anthony said.

"I intend to. Your investigator, the one that Jack had used in the past to aid Evelyn, do you still use him?" Jack asked Anthony.

Anthony's face brightened at the suggestion. "He's a clever Armenian by the name of Armen Papazian; he's never failed me in the past."

Jack knew Anthony used the investigator to unearth the secret liaisons of the wives of his clients. Anthony could be ruthless in the courtroom, and he had no qualms about bringing in a string of male lovers to attest to a wife's adultery.

"It's not just the woman I want him to look into. I need to track down Sir Redmond Reeves as well. How fast can your investigator get here?" James asked.

"I'll send for him immediately," Anthony said. "If there's something in your widow's past that you can use, he'll find it."

Chapter 6

"I do hope you'll like your positions at Wyndmoor Manor."
Bella stood in the kitchen, addressing the new servants she
had hired. A parlor maid, a head gardener, and a new cook
stood obediently in a row, hands folded before them.

"I look forward to your braised ham and pastries," Bella
said to the plump, middle-aged cook.

Mrs. O'Brien bobbed a curtsy. "Thank you, Mrs. Sinclair."

As Bella left the new servants to settle in, she breathed a
sigh of relief. Although St. Albans was close to Wyndmoor
Manor, it had been challenging to find a competent cook willing to apply for the position. Bella had learned that Sir Reeves
had been demanding with his palate, and during his short
duration as master of the place, he had gone through no less
than three cooks.

Still, Bella felt elated to complete the task. During her marriage, she had never been permitted to hire a single servant.
Other than Harriet, Roger had insisted upon complete domin-
ion over the staff and they had been loyal only to him. Any
disobedience by his young, headstrong wife had immediately
been reported to her husband. Bella had quickly learned to be
circumspect.

As she made her way from the kitchen, she decided upon a walk and some fresh air. It was late afternoon, her favorite part of the day to write. Thoughts of her current political piece on social reform and the recent Cotton Factories Regulation Act ran through her mind. This is what she had desired, freedom to pen her articles in the hopes of one day getting published.

Stopping to retrieve her notebook and a pencil, she was thankful there was no sign of the duke or his staff. She reached the vestibule when the sounds of male laughter brought her to an abrupt stop.

She recognized the rich timbre of Blackwood's voice coming from the library. *Leave him to his business,* she thought, yet an overwhelming curiosity had her walking down the hallway toward the library. Wyndmoor Manor was *her* home.

Why shouldn't she know who was present?

Before she could knock, the library door opened, and Blackwood stepped out. He was followed by two well-dressed men.

A gleam of interest lit his cobalt eyes when he spotted her. "Mrs. Sinclair. You are just the lady I was speaking of."

Bella stiffened, alarmed to have been the topic of conversation among the duke and the two strange men.

"May I introduce my good friends and fellow legal colleagues, Mr. Anthony Stevens and Mr. Brent Stone," Blackwood said.

The fair-haired man stepped forward first and bowed. "I'm Mr. Stone, and it is a pleasure to meet you."

Bella was momentarily speechless as she gazed into a pair of crystal-blue eyes in a startlingly handsome face. Brent Stone's high cheekbones and chiseled nose were so symmetrical, so perfect, it was as if he were a flesh-and-blood model for one of Michelangelo's marble carvings.

Blackwood cleared his throat and drew her attention. His eyes were narrowed, his lips a thin line, and she wondered why he suddenly appeared annoyed.

The tallest of the three men spoke up. "The duke told us about you, Mrs. Sinclair, but I didn't quite believe him until now."

She looked up at Anthony Stevens, and an involuntary tremor passed down her spine. He was a large, broad-shouldered man, with bold features and shortly cropped dark hair, but it wasn't his size that intimidated her, rather the hard look in his pitch-black eyes that sent a warning. She suppressed the urge to cross herself.

For a brief instant, she wondered if Anthony had a wife or a lover and if those black eyes bore the same look as Roger's had when he ill-treated her, but then she mentally shook herself. Roger had appeared charming and kind to outsiders; this man gave the appearance of a scorpion with his tail raised ready to strike.

He's baiting me, wanting me to cower beneath his glare, Bella thought. *Little does he know, I refuse to be intimidated by a man. My years with Roger are over.*

She tilted her head to the side and smiled. "I can only imagine what His Grace has told you about my presence here. It seems I am in need of a barrister myself. Perhaps you could recommend one for me, Mr. Stevens."

There was an awkward silence; then Anthony Stevens released a sharp bark of laughter. "By God, she does have spirit, Devlin! We best be on our way before one of us offers her our own legal services."

They made their way to the vestibule, and Coates retrieved their coats and hats.

"We are staying at the Twin Rams should you need us, James," Brent Stone said.

Blackwood smiled. "I would offer you both lodgings here—"

"That would be improper," Brent said.

"Yes, I suppose. Mrs. Sinclair may feel obligated to share a residence with one bachelor, but to add two more would be enough to send any lady into hysterics," Blackwood said dryly.

"There's no need to be rude," Brent said, bowing politely to Bella. "It was a pleasure, Mrs. Sinclair. We are expecting our remaining colleague and his wife to arrive in a few days. I think you would get along nicely with her."

Bella smiled up at the handsome barrister and found herself saying, "I look forward to meeting her, Mr. Stone."

The pair departed and she was left alone with Blackwood.

"I'm surprised," he said after he closed the door and turned to her, "that you have charmed them."

"Are you?"

"Anthony Stevens doesn't usually find females clever. And most women find him . . . how shall I phrase it . . . quite frightful."

She looked at him with mock innocence. "Indeed. I did not find him frightful at all."

"And as for Brent Stone, he may very well be your new champion."

"He seems an agreeable gentleman."

His gaze pierced the distance between them. "You find Mr. Stone attractive?"

"Whatever makes you believe that?" she asked.

He shrugged. "A guess is all. Where were you headed, by the way?"

"I was going for a walk."

"Splendid. There are a few matters I'd like to discuss with you. May I join you?"

She hesitated. She did not want to spend more time with him than necessary, yet if they were to resolve matters between them they needed to speak. She placed her notebook and pencil on a pedestal table beside a vase of fresh flowers and faced him. "That would be fine."

He opened the door. "Do you wish to fetch your cloak?"

"There's no need. The weather is pleasant enough."

He grinned, held the door wide, and stepped aside.

Her heart skipped a beat. His smile softened his chiseled features, and she found herself stealing glances at his profile beneath lowered lashes.

They descended the front steps and strolled past the fountain. The flagstone path led to the formal gardens with its box hedges, blooming azaleas, and floral borders. Spring had arrived, and the sky was a brilliant blue with a few puffs of cloud. Bella raised her face, and the afternoon sun warmed her cheeks. A hawk soared above, precise and mindless, a part of things. How she envied its blissful freedom.

"Tell me how you first came to see Wyndmoor Manor," he asked.

"There's not much to tell, Your Grace. I was passing through St. Albans when I spotted the place. We stopped at the Twin Rams, and when I inquired I learned the property was for sale."

"Must we be so formal? Please call me James. No matter the circumstances, we are living together. Besides, the title is new to me."

He insisted she call him James, but use of his Christian name was horribly improper despite the fact that they were sharing a residence. She didn't want to think of him as James. It was one step closer to thinking of him as a man rather an aristocrat who desired to drive her out of her new home.

At her hesitation, he said, "It is not much to ask, and if we are in public, then you may certainly address me by my title."

She could hardly refuse without sounding churlish or intimidated, and she didn't want to appear either. "Only when we are in private then."

They headed away from the house and the formal gardens and crossed an open grassy field dotted with wildflowers of every color of the rainbow. The air was heady with the fragrant scent of their perfume. Succumbing to a fanciful impulse, she stopped and picked a handful of the delicate-looking blooms.

They walked for some time before stepping onto a tree-lined path with sun-shot leaves that arched overhead. It was a warm May afternoon and the foliage provided refreshing shade. Blackwood knew where he was headed and soon the sounds of a nearby brook could be heard above the chirping birds.

They cleared the trees and she realized it was not a brook but a stream with a small waterfall. She gasped as a pair of swans floated past, their pristine white feathers and curved necks as graceful as ballet dancers. The lovely vista beyond the stream was a picture of treetops and rolling hills that had enthralled her the first time she had laid eyes on the land.

When Bella had offered to buy the property from Sir Reeves, she had pictured herself venturing out into the closest town of St. Albans. Before her marriage, she had enjoyed strolling through Plymouth's shopping district and discreetly observing people. She had scribbled notes about their mannerisms and speech and had poured every detail into her writing.

Her father had encouraged her ambitions. He had loved books of all kinds, especially those of history and politics, and her childhood home had been cluttered with newspaper clippings and books on foreign affairs and domestic social reform. Over the years she grew to find the topic of social reform fascinating. The strife of the poverty-stricken and laborers in London had caught her interest. She'd researched the child labor laws and the increase in crime from the destitute and oftentimes injured soldiers that had returned from Waterloo, and she had started writing her own articles.

Then one day Roger Sinclair had visited her father and expressed interest in Bella. He had been respectful and reserved, and when Bella had mentioned her own ambitions to submit her work to the London newspapers in hopes of getting published, Roger had nodded with feigned enthusiasm. It was her first taste of his remarkable talent for deception.

Soon after her marriage, Roger had found her addressing an envelope to *The London Gazette.* He had ripped her work out of her hands and torn it into pieces. "No wife of mine will ever engage in such unacceptable activities," Roger had spat. Writing and politics, he insisted, were for men. When Bella had argued, Roger had immediately threatened, "Harriet is old and slow. Servants should be useful. I've a mind to cut her without a reference."

Roger had known quite well that at Harriet's age she would never find new employment and would starve, and Bella would do anything to protect her. With no more than a curt slash of his hand, Roger had destroyed her aspirations as a writer. He had been an adept liar, and he had woven tales of his wife's "fragile mental state" until people eyed her warily on the seldom occasions she had been seen. Some had even offered Roger their admiration for not committing his mad wife to an asylum.

She was now a widow and the owner of Wyndmoor Manor. She could pen political articles or even short love stories that struck her fancy and, under the guise of a pseudonym, send them to any London newspaper or publisher of her choosing. The people of Hertfordshire had no knowledge of her past—a fact that added to Wyndmoor's charm—and she was free to join a poetry group, a book discussion group, or the church choir, and even attend the occasional afternoon tea or country fair.

After seven tumultuous years bound to a cruel spouse, she could peacefully spend the rest of her life here, and it had seemed as if fate had finally smiled upon her.

Or so she had thought.

She glanced at the man beside her. With his compelling blue

eyes, his firm features, and the confident set of his shoulders, he exuded masculinity and command.

He shed his jacket and spread it out on the grassy bank. "Shall we?"

Gathering her skirts, she sat and placed the wildflowers on her lap. He sat beside her, stretching his long legs out before him.

"I've told you about my reasons for wanting Wyndmoor Manor, but I am uncertain as to yours. Why do you insist on keeping it?" he asked.

"Because it's mine," she said. *Because no man will ever dictate my desires again.*

His brow furrowed. "You do realize the longer you stay here with me, the more damage to your reputation."

"I'm a widow, remember?" she retorted.

"No matter. We cannot reside together indefinitely."

He picked up a flat stone by the bank and turned it around his fingers. Then in one sweeping motion, he threw it toward the lake and watched as it skipped across the water's surface like a jumping bean before finally sinking with a soft splash.

"Were you serous about seeking legal advice?" he asked.

She raised her chin a notch. "Yes. I plan on hiring my own barrister."

"You mean a solicitor. There is a difference. If the solicitor finds the matter needs to be resolved by a judge and jury, he contacts a barrister who alone handles matters in the court-room."

She knew there were differences, of course, but she hadn't truly understood their functions. She had never needed to avail herself of the legal system before.

"You do realize you would be up against an experienced legal professional?" he asked.

"Yes."

"I always win in the courtroom, Bella." There was a spark

of some indefinable emotion in his eyes. Anticipated challenge, perhaps?

She remained silent, but his words echoed in her head, tormenting her mind. *I always win in the courtroom.*

Life had taught her only the strong survived. But would it truly come to that?

Chapter 7

"I know very little about you other than the fact that you are a widow. Were you born in Hertfordshire?" Blackwood asked.

Bella leaned back on her hands in the soft grass. "No. I was born in London, but my father moved to the country when I was seven. We settled in Plymouth when I was sixteen, and I was married a year later."

"Did you remain in Plymouth after your marriage?"

"Yes."

"I'm an admirer of the architect John Rennie's work on the mile-long Breakwater in Plymouth Sound. Did your husband work on the project or on the dockyards?"

Her heart skipped a beat. How much to tell? Blackwood was proving to be intelligent and intuitive. Years of experience hiding her inner thoughts from her husband had taught Bella to be forthright with the basics while concealing the heart of the matter. Bella dare not reveal the extent of Roger's greed.

Treason, her inner voice cried out. When Roger's business ventures had failed to produce a lucrative profit, he had turned to illicit, illegal activities.

Making a show of arranging the wildflowers on her lap, she chose her words carefully. "Roger was a merchant; his livelihood was import and export. Mostly timber, coal, barley, and grain."

"How long were you married?"

"Seven years."

"Do you miss him then?"

She stayed silent, again uncertain what answer to give. Miss Roger? She gave thanks for every day that his shadow failed to cross the threshold of her bedchamber.

"I've come to accept his passing," she finally answered.

Blackwood picked up another flat stone and rubbed it between his thumb and forefinger.

"Are your parents alive?"

She knew he was prying for information. He wanted to know if she had family she could reside with should he succeed in his plans of eviction. "No," she said. "My mother died when I was an infant, and I am an only child. My father died in a carriage accident soon after I was married."

"You must have been distraught. I'm sorry for your loss."

The sincerity in his tone made her speak. "Father was a wonderful, loving parent, and I am grateful that God gifted me with him for as long as he did."

Blackwood threw the stone in his hand and it skipped across the water's surface four times. She turned to look at him then and was surprised to see some unfathomable emotion—pain? Regret?—in his eyes.

"You must have fond memories of your parents," she said. "You had mentioned that Wyndmoor Manor reminded you of your family."

"I never knew my mother. She was a parlor maid who caught the eye of my father, the old duke, when she was in service to the family. She died when I was born. I grew up believing I was illegitimate, and I was never officially acknowledged by my father," he said coolly. "I have a half brother who, until weeks ago, believed he was the heir and treated me with as much brotherly love as one does a stray dog, and a grandmother who is a rigid dowager duchess whose only redeeming quality was to pay for my boarding school as a boy and my education at Eton years later."

He plucked another stone from the ground. His fingers, long and tapered, caressed the smooth surface.

She was as stunned by his speech as the light bitterness in his tone. She had not expected such a story from him. He appeared so confident, so sure of his rightful place in the world.

One question plagued her: If he was illegitimate, then how on earth could he have inherited a dukedom?

As if reading her thoughts, he said, "It turned out that I was not the illegitimate son but the proper heir all along. Too bad I spent a lifetime ostracized by my family as the bastard."

A frisson of pity rose in her breast. Bella didn't know why she felt sorry for him. James Devlin was now a duke, with great wealth and power at his fingertips. Yet he had never known a mother's love or a father's loyalty. Bella's father had loved her unconditionally and it was those treasured memories that had allowed her to survive the horrors of her marriage.

She didn't want to know more about James Devlin, truly she didn't. She did not want him to become a person to her, rather than a demanding, spoiled aristocrat. But the truth was, he wasn't spoiled and had known true hardship. There was an air of isolation about him that tugged at the core of compassion inside her.

He was rejected, just like me. Only I was betrayed by a brutish, selfish husband, and he was betrayed by his family.

"How did you become a barrister?" she found herself asking.

"I could not fathom a life of begging for every shilling as the illegitimate offspring in order to survive. After Eton I attended Oxford, where I met students who desired to enter one of the four Inns of Court and find willing pupilmasters. I was accepted into Lincoln's Inn. After I became a barrister, I joined the chambers of my colleagues whom you met today.

I was quite successful and had no need to ever request anything from my family again."

Never had she suspected he was a self-made man. She assumed all of the nobility were handed a fortune and never had to toil a day in their lives.

"Why do you insist on reclaiming Wyndmoor Manor? If you have no fond feelings for your family, then why on earth would you seek to reclaim the country estate?" Bella asked.

"It was the only place the old duke treated me as his son. I know the land like the back of my hand. I feel at home here. Can you say the same?"

She looked at the stream, the twin swans, and the peacefulness of the landscape. "Yes, I feel safe here."

They sat in silence, observing the view; then he rose to his feet and offered her his hand.

She placed her hand in his and felt the warmth of his fingers as they wrapped around hers. Slowly he pulled her to her feet.

A wan shaft of sun struck his hair and it gleamed like ebony. His strong features held a certain sensuality that she now realized was not entirely arrogance, but pride.

Nervous beneath his steady gaze, she lowered her eyes to the stone he still held in his hand. "How do you manage to throw the stones so far?"

He looked surprised, then laughed. "It's simple. You need to find a flat stone, preferably one with a smooth surface."

He reached down and plucked another stone from the bank, then showed her how to hold it. Standing behind her, he held her arm and imitated the proper throwing motion. She felt a tremor as the front of his body grazed the back of hers.

He leaned down until his mouth was close to her ear. "You try now. Throw the stone."

Her flesh prickled at the nearness of his touch, and she

raised her arm to throw. The stone bounced off the water's surface once before sinking. "Yours bounced four times!"

"It takes practice. I used to come here as a boy, skipping stones for hours."

She made several more attempts, succeeding in bouncing the stone twice. "I don't believe I shall ever be able to compete with you." As soon as the words left her mouth, she realized they may be incorrectly interpreted to imply their property battle ahead.

He turned her by the shoulders, and she was suddenly looking into his indigo eyes.

"I didn't mean it that way," she said softly.

His gaze searched hers before dropping to her lips. "I know."

"I should head back."

His eyes darkened, and he reached out to cup the side of her face with his hand. "No," he said softly. "Not yet, Bella."

Whatever rational thought she had flew from her mind as his head slowly lowered. Then his mouth covered hers in a kiss as tender and light as a summer breeze. For several heart-beats he simply shared her breath. Then his lips brushed hers, back and forth, and he traced her full bottom lip with the sweep of his tongue. Her response was shameless, instant and total. A wild surge of pleasure spiraled through her.

Her lips parted of their own accord, and his tongue slid into her mouth. His kiss was skilled and seductive, coaxing and encouraging her response. Tentative at first, she met his tongue with her own, and her heart fluttered wildly in her breast. Then his kiss changed, became more demanding. He turned her head to one side as he plundered her mouth, send-ing fire through every nerve in her body.

Never had she been kissed like this by a man. Her experi-ence was limited to Roger, and he had been demanding and hurtful. His affections had been a brutal performance of dominance. He had never been concerned for her pleasure, only her capitulation. She had learned early on to tamp down her defiance, or he would prolong his torment.

But James. He didn't touch her with anything but his lips and the hand cradling her face. She was free to step away should she wish to. Only she did not.

For the first time in her life, she felt true lust. It was a heady emotion, a dangerous weapon in this battle of wills. A small warning voice cried out in the back of her mind that if she allowed him to treat her like a common dalliance she would lose whatever footing she had at Wyndmoor Manor. Yet, this rising passion could not be denied. How could a kiss be this potent, trigger such primitive yearnings?

Leaning forward an inch, she brushed against the harness of his chest, felt the warmth of his body, and inhaled the alluring scent of his cologne, sandalwood and cloves.

A groan rumbled from deep in his throat. His lifted his head, his dark eyebrows slanted in a frown, and looked down at her.

"I hadn't expected that," he said.

"The kiss?"

"No, your response."

Enthralled by the gleam of desire she saw in his eyes, she tried to still the wild pounding of her heart. "It was a mistake."

He laughed hoarsely. "Living together is a mistake, but neither of us is inclined to change our minds, are we?"

She shook her head.

He sighed, then reached for his jacket. "Shall we go back, then?"

He waited for her to pick up her discarded wildflowers, and they headed back to the house in silence.

Bella's brain was in tumult as she hurried to keep pace with his long stride. What had come over her? Not only had she allowed him the liberty of a kiss, she had *enjoyed* it. The Duke of Blackwood was a complex man, and the fervent passion she had experienced in his arms alternately thrilled and frightened her. This attraction, this lust was entirely new—a first for Bella—exciting, yes, but also utterly dangerous.

He stopped to help her over a fallen log, and his fingers grasped hers. Their eyes locked, their breathing came in unison, and the tingling in the pit of her stomach was quick to return. She must avoid being alone with him in the days to come, but how could she accomplish such a task when they shared a residence?

She was still contemplating the question when they approached the stables, and a boy with bright red hair and a gap-toothed smile waved and called out for Blackwood.

"Coates mentioned the lad is your stable boy," Bella said.

"Bobby may only be twelve years old, but he's quick, intelligent and exceptional with the horses. He keeps an immaculate stable, and he will care for your mare as well as my horses. Anything you require in the stables, you have only to ask."

"I shall keep that in mind, Your Grace."

He stopped and looked down at her. "It's James, remember?" he said, with a grin.

Her heart gave a little lurch.

He bowed. "The boy needs to speak with me. Until another time?"

She bobbed a quick curtsy and fled to the house.

James watched as Bella hurried into the house. He should be pleased that his plans were falling into place. But he hadn't counted on the sweetness of Bella's lips, her evocative response to his touch. And when she had capitulated to her desires and kissed him back, his heartbeat had skyrocketed and his arousal had been swift. He'd wanted to get closer to her, crush her lush curves against him, and discover if her auburn hair smelled like the vibrant wildflowers that she had picked.

He had ended the kiss only to find that when she raised her

lids, she gazed up at him in wonder, like an innocent, inexperienced girl who longed to have him reveal the mysteries of sex. But how could that be? She had been married for seven years. Either she was a consummate actress or . . . or what?

He shook his head at his folly. Perhaps the problem lay with him. How long had it been since his last conquest?

Over the past months his docket at Lincoln's Inn had been taxing, and then the dowager duchess had resurfaced in his life. Since then James had been consumed with the news of his unexpected inheritance. And no matter how much he had told himself his father's rejection had meant little to him as a man, the old duke's passing had left a permanent sorrow and heaviness in James's chest.

It was entirely reasonable to assume his ardent response toward Bella Sinclair was due to the recent pressure in his life and the fact that he had gone too long without female companionship. Unlike his colleague Brent Stone, James was not accustomed to even short stints of celibacy.

As for his telling speech by the stream, he hadn't meant to reveal his entire family history—only that he had inherited the dukedom. But the sadness in Bella's eyes when she spoke of her father's passing had made him want to speak of his own parent. The irony was not lost on him. He had always been adept at getting a witness to confess on the stand, not the other way around.

There had to be a solution to this dilemma. He would win— he didn't doubt himself—yet he found himself thinking of her. Reeves would eventually be found, and if the thief had spent all their money, then James would offer to pay Bella from his own pockets. If only she would accept the money and quit the place, then he never need be tempted by her again.

It was a good solid plan. She was merely a woman, no different from the countless other females whom he had entertained. He had a clear sense of himself and understood his current fascination with Bella Sinclair was due entirely to the fact that she was an irresistible challenge on two fronts—to bed her *and* to win against her in their battle over property ownership. He must maintain his focus, and not let the widow, no matter how alluring she was, distract him from his goal.

Chapter 8

"The duke requested you join him downstairs for the evening meal."

Bella sat at a mahogany writing table in the corner of her bedchamber. Her notebook was open before her, the page blank. Whatever aspirations she'd had for writing had vanished for the day. She turned to see Harriet standing in the doorway, a look of expectation on the older woman's face.

"Kindly give the duke my apologies and tell the new cook, Mrs. O'Brien, to prepare a dinner tray to be brought to my bedchamber," Bella said.

Bella was tired from today's events, and sitting across the table from Blackwood was the last thing she desired. Besieged by confusing emotions, she sought the comforting solitude of her room.

"He'll want to hear it from you," Harriet said.

Bella sighed. "I'll write a note and have it delivered to him then."

Harriet stepped into the room and shut the door. "You must meet him on equal footing, Bella. It is *your* house and you should dine downstairs rather than cloister yourself in your bedchamber."

Bella raised her hand and stood. "Not tonight, Harriet. I spent enough time in his presence this afternoon."

Harriet sat on the window seat and patted the cushion beside her. "Sit, Bella."

Bella sighed and sat beside the elder woman. Harriet's wizened eyes traveled Bella's face as if looking for something amiss. "Tell me what happened."

Bella bit her bottom lip, then blurted out, "He kissed me."

Harriet's face brightened. "Indeed. How was it?"

How was it? It was a kiss Bella wouldn't easily forget. Just thinking of his lips brushing hers was enough to make the blood rush through her veins.

His first day here and she had fallen victim to his charm, had actually *kissed* him back. She had been overcome by the beauty of the landscape, the comforting warmth of the sun, and the virile man stretched out on the bank beside her. She had been entranced by the bitter sadness of his face—however brief the flicker of emotion—when he had mentioned his family's abandonment. And when his arms had wrapped around her as he had demonstrated how to skip a stone, she had been foolishly swept away by an awakening yearning.

He was a skilled kisser, and no doubt a skilled lover. She couldn't help but wonder—what would it be like to bed the duke? Her experience was limited to Roger, and based on James's kiss alone she suspected the experience would be vastly different.

But Blackwood's motives were questionable. He was devastatingly attractive and unscrupulous enough to take any woman. Combined with his title, she suspected females would be attracted to him in droves. Bella was nothing more than his opponent.

So why kiss her?

Harriet frowned, her eyes level under drawn brows. "Did the duke hurt you?"

Hurt her? Heavens, no.

James hadn't even held her as he kissed her. It had been marvelous, gentle, and thrilling, and the degree to which she had responded stunned her. She could never admit, even to Harriet, that it had been *he* who had broken their kiss.

"No, he did not hurt me," Bella said. "Yet he is trying to manipulate me. He wants me gone from Wyndmoor Manor."

"You may be right. But how was the kiss?"

Harriet could be as tenacious as a terrier when she sought information.

"It was pleasant," Bella answered.

Harriet eyed her as she had when Bella had stolen a sweet from the pantry. "You feared he'd be like Roger? You shouldn't. Roger was nothing but a sick bastard, he was."

Bella's gut clenched just thinking of her deceased husband's sexual attentions. Roger had only approached her after he had drunk no less than four tankards of ale. He had been mean without alcohol, but combined with spirits he was downright cruel.

It was then that he'd demand his marital rights. He'd douse the fireplace, insist she disrobe before him and stand still in the center of their bedchamber. She'd often tremble from the cold and dread, knowing what was to follow. As a young bride, she had been horrified to discover that he needed to inflict pain and fear in order to stimulate himself.

Bella was prideful by nature, and she had glared up at Roger in hatred. Often his frustration and ire would take control, and he would wrench her arm, push her to the floor before him, and strike her. After the first months of their marriage, he was unable to perform sexually, and he'd viciously berate her, repeatedly ranting that she was inadequate as a woman and not worthy to be his wife. She had prayed his visits to her bedchamber would stop, but to no avail. Her only consolation was he'd not been able to bed her.

She'd soon heard of whispers from the servants that Roger had whores enter through the kitchen door. Rumors abounded that the women were skilled at dominating Roger, inflicting pain upon him. That he'd *paid* to be whipped with his own riding crop.

Bella had been shocked, for Roger had always seemed to thrive on enforcing his power over her, whether by isolating her on the estate grounds or coming to her bedchamber. If only she had known of his sick deviancy, she would have gladly offered to whip him for free.

Harriet reached out and took Bella's hands in hers. "What I'm saying, luv, is that there is nothing wrong with you as a woman. I always worried your husband's sickness and belittling had wounded you more than any physical abuse. Despite the circumstances that brought the duke here, I'm glad he kissed you. A little attention from a handsome man like Blackwood proves my point. Not all men are like Roger."

"What about our fight over the manor?" Bella said.

"One kiss doesn't mean you're handing it over to him," Harriet said.

Bella kept her features deceptively composed. "I do not trust him." *I do not trust myself with him,* she thought. Any more attention from James could put her future plans at perilous risk.

James sat at the head of the table in the formal dining room as the footman delivered the first course. The new cook, the servant Bella had hired, had prepared a delicious turtle soup.

Even after Coates had handed him the note from Bella, James had decided to remain and dine at the manor rather than at the Twin Rams Inn. He needed to stake his claim, both with the servants and the striking woman upstairs.

Which led James to thinking about Bella Sinclair for the hundredth time that evening. He wondered what she was eating, and if she was dressed in the same pristine nightgown that covered every inch of her body down to her pretty feet that she had worn the first time he had seen her.

Was she sitting in bed enjoying the same soup or eating cold roast beef instead? And why did he give a damn what she was consuming? Except the thought of her in bed doing anything made him feel hot and heavy all over again.

One kiss. One kiss and he felt like a randy schoolboy with his hand caught beneath a girl's skirt.

He dropped the spoon and it slid into the soup. This wouldn't do. He'd have to get out despite his intentions. He threw his napkin on the table and rose. He would go to the Twin Rams, where strong spirits, a lively conversation with Anthony and Brent, and maybe the coy smile of a willing barmaid could distract his mind from the woman who slept under his roof.

Sleep eluded Bella that night. Her blood soared with un-bidden memories, and her mind relived the velvet warmth of James's kiss. The gentle persuasiveness of his lips had been as unexpected as her lustful response. She raised her finger-tips to her own lips and imagined his perfect, firm mouth exploring hers.

It was well past midnight and her bedcovers were a tangled mess from her fitful tossing and turning. In the quiet solitude of her room, her thoughts ran free. She was helpless to stop herself from pondering the scandalous. What would it feel like to have him kiss more of her skin?

She fantasized about just that—his lips urgent and exploratory, searing her neck, her shoulders. He would leisurely lavish attention on her breasts, her nipples firming instantly under his touch. His touch arousing, but never painful. His tongue would lick a path down her ribs to her stomach, his hands roving lower still, to the pulsing ache between her thighs.

A moan slipped through her lips. She sat up and pushed the twisted covers aside. Scrambling to her feet, she flung the window open wide and inhaled deeply, hoping the cool night air would quench her overheated skin.

What had overcome her? James Devlin had come to Wyndmoor Manor and in a day he had succeeded in driving all logic and caution from her head. She was twenty-four years old, a widow of a seven-year marriage, and she had never truly experienced passion. For the first time, she suffered the dull ache of desire at the thought of a man.

But why in heaven's name did it have to be for *this* man? She was a nuisance to him, and he had clearly stated his intentions toward her.

I always win in the courtroom.

She gripped the windowsill, her body suddenly engulfed in weariness and despair. Her eyes burned dryly from sleeplessness. She needed to sleep for whatever hours were left of the night. She needed to be prepared to face him tomorrow.

Harriet had always fixed her a cup of warm milk laced with brandy when she had difficulty sleeping after Roger had left her room. Bella's hand reached for the bell pull, but she hesitated.

She didn't want to wake the old woman. There was no longer the risk that she would run into Roger walking the halls at night. The first and last time that had occurred, Roger had flown into a jealous rage and had accused her of meeting a lover. He had locked her in her room for a week. Even Harriet was prohibited from attending to her. Bella had almost gone mad, and she had never again ventured out at night without Harriet beside her.

But life was different now. Harriet had overheard Blackwood tell his manservant that he was going out after dinner to the Twin Rams to meet his friends and would not return until late. Bella could go downstairs, fix herself a cup of warm milk, and even wander the halls if she chose. She could relive the first night she had slept in the house, oblivious of Blackwood's impending claim.

Lifting a bedside candle, she opened the door. She was at the top of the stairs when a trill of feminine laughter echoed off the marble vestibule. Then came a distinct male laugh that Bella knew belonged to Blackwood.

She froze, like a bird that had flown into a stone wall.

How dare he!

She had just lain restless, burning with her first taste of desire because of his kiss, and he was returning to *her* house from a night of drinking and carousing with a woman.

Bella rushed down the stairs to see Blackwood hand his hat and a woman's cloak to Coates, who, in turn, nodded when he spotted Bella clutching the balustrade, then discreetly disappeared.

The woman's hand rested on Blackwood's sleeve, her golden hair swept up in an elegant coiffure, her blue eyes exotically slanted like those of a Persian cat. She was stunning, and Bella suspected she was an expensive Cyprian that only a duke could afford.

Bella's spine stiffened. If Blackwood thought he could bring this type of woman into the house he was gravely mistaken.

Blackwood and his ladybird looked to her. "Bella," he drawled. "I hadn't suspected you were a night owl."

She lifted her chin and boldly met his eyes. "Get out. I don't care that you are a duke or a barrister or if you were first to record the deed. I won't stand by and permit you to bring women here. Go back to the Twin Rams and rent a room," she ordered in a voice that brooked no argument.

To her dismay, a chuckle rumbled from his throat. "I warned you about sharing a residence with a bachelor. It's not too late to reconsider," he said.

Bella's breaths came in ragged gasps. "Don't you dare mock me, Your Grace."

Amusement lurked in his eyes. "Don't tell me that we're back to rigid formality again."

The blonde pursed her lips at Blackwood, her eyes flashing a gentle but firm warning. "Stop instigating, James, and introduce me."

James. The woman had called him James.

Her familiar manner and use of his Christian name suggested that she was no random trollop he had brought home for the evening, but someone with whom he shared a relationship. A longtime mistress, perhaps?

The nauseating sinking in the pit of her stomach was as confusing as it was distressing.

"If you insist. Although I admit her reaction is highly amusing." James made a sweeping motion with his hand. "Bella, may I introduce Lady Evelyn Harding, the wife of my good friend and legal colleague, Jack Harding."

Lady Evelyn stepped forward and smiled. "It is a pleasure to meet you. I do apologize for the late hour. My husband and I hadn't planned on visiting until several days from now, but his trial was postponed and we decided to arrive straightaway. We would have arrived hours ago at a decent time, but our coach threw a wheel. We were stranded on the road until, as luck would have it, James was returning home from the Twin Rams and spotted us. My husband is seeing to the horses in the stable as we speak. I had hoped we'd only have to disturb the young stable lad from his sleep."

Bella blinked and gazed at the smiling blonde. It was then that she noticed her fine traveling gown of violet silk with lace trimming and black kid gloves. Blackwood had called her "Lady Evelyn," which could only mean the woman was the daughter of an aristocrat who had kept her courtesy title upon her marriage to a commoner. A nervous fluttering began low in Bella's stomach.

"I do believe you owe Lady Harding an apology," James said.

"Don't be daft, James," Lady Evelyn admonished. "Mrs. Sinclair owes me no such thing. It's perfectly understandable for her to question the arrival of a strange woman with a bachelor in the dead of the night in her home."

Bella did not miss the insightful words at the end of Lady Evelyn's speech. She had referred to the manor as Bella's home.

Could it have been an accidental slip? Or can she be an ally?

Bella felt her face redden as she looked to the lady. "He's correct. Please forgive my rush to judgment and rudeness, Lady Evelyn. I would be honored to have you and Mr. Harding as guests at Wyndmoor."

"Thank you for your kindness," Lady Evelyn said.

Bella glanced down at her attire, at once conscious of her nightdress, wrapper, and bare feet. She couldn't very well escort Lady Evelyn and her husband to the guestroom dressed as she was.

"If His Grace would be so kind as to escort Lady Evelyn to the drawing room, I shall see that a room is prepared," Bella said.

James grinned. "Excellent idea. I do believe your senses have returned."

Bella bit back a scalding retort, not wanting to further spar with him. She had already behaved foolishly enough for one evening. She waited until the pair made their way around the corner and out of sight. Only then did Bella sprint up the stairs to awaken the staff and prepare for their unexpected guests.

Evelyn Harding was pleasantly surprised when James escorted her not to the drawing room, but to the library instead. She was the daughter of an earl, but before her father inherited his title, he had been a barrister and lecturer at Oxford. Evelyn had spent her childhood at Lincoln's Inn surrounded by books and listening to fascinating legal arguments.

She roamed the library, her fingers passing over the colorful spines of the volumes on the mahogany shelves. The comforting smell of books and well-oiled leather furniture surrounded her. With his back to her, James poured a whiskey from a sideboard.

"Were all these books here when you arrived?" Evelyn asked.

James turned and sipped his whiskey. "Yes, it seems my father no longer had a use for them, and the man he sold the manor to, a Sir Redmond Reeves, sold the place with the furnishings, including the books, intact." James pointed to one of the shelves. "I brought those legal volumes with me from chambers."

Evelyn had known all the barristers in her husband's chambers for five years. There was Brent Stone, with his tawny mane and striking looks, but whose unfathomable blue eyes seemed to hold long-buried secrets. And Anthony Stevens, whose pugilist pastime and controversial area of legal practice had sculpted him into a hard, jaded man. But as for James Devlin—the new Duke of Blackwood—she had always found him the most controversial. She was aware of his reputation with women, and Evelyn vividly recalled her first encounter with him before she had married.

She had run into James at Lincoln's Inn when she was seeking out Jack Harding's legal representation. James had flirted outrageously with her in the doorway of chambers, and had tried to tempt her into switching barristers, insisting he was the most competent. His antics had made her laugh, and when she'd refused him, he'd merely shrugged, tipped his hat, and wished her luck with her legal endeavors on his way out the door.

She had never approved of James's lifestyle—his lovers or his liaisons with the willing wives of his clients. But since Evelyn had married, James had always treated her with the utmost respect. Evelyn had grown to care for him, as well as the other two barristers in their chambers, Anthony and Brent, as friends.

"How's Phillip? I promised your boy a pony when I return," James said.

When it came to Evelyn's three-year-old son, Phillip, James was a beloved uncle. "You spoil him," she said.

"I take my job as an uncle seriously."

Evelyn sighed. "Phillip's as precocious as ever. But it's the first time Jack and I have left him, and I miss him terribly already. He adores you, you know."

"Don't give me too much credit. It's quite enjoyable to act the doting uncle knowing I get to hand the boy over to his parents at the end of the day."

"Hmm." Evelyn wasn't fooled. James did have a knack with children. Perhaps it was his devil-may-care attitude.

But tonight James had behaved strangely. James had spoken with them in the carriage ride about the unexpected appearance of the widow at the manor, and Evelyn knew he wanted Bella Sinclair to rescind her claim to Wyndmoor. Then Bella had marched down the stairs and confronted James. His reaction had seemed unperturbed, yet behind his façade of amusement, Evelyn had been surprised to sense an undercurrent of tension in him around the beautiful widow.

I warned you about sharing a residence with a bachelor. It's not too late to reconsider, he had told Bella.

Bella had eyed him with challenge, and the sparks between the pair had flashed.

In all her time, Evelyn had never known James Devlin unable to win over a woman he had set out to charm. He enjoyed his freedom and avoided emotional commitment like the plague. There had been women who sought more from him than to share his bed, women who had claimed to love him, but he had been quick to break off those affairs. Bachelorhood, he often said, was the epitome of freedom. Why ruin it with marriage and children?

He rarely spoke of his past or his family. His mother had died in childbirth, and—prior to recent revelations at least—it had been common knowledge that he was the illegitimate son of the Duke of Blackwood. The dowager duchess had paid for his education and housing as a boy, but apparently that had been the extent of her sense of duty toward him.

His father had spent only one week a year with James in his youth, and Evelyn understood that was the reason James wanted to hold on to Wyndmoor Manor. "How would you feel if your father had only acknowledged you and shown you affection for one week a year, and ignored you the rest of the time?" Jack had asked her. Evelyn had only known unconditional love from her father, and couldn't fathom how she would feel if her sole parent had rejected her.

Despite his past, James had made his own way as a man and had done quite well in his chosen profession. But he had learned the lessons of his youth, and he had erected emotional barriers like a suit of armor.

So what was going on with Bella Sinclair? Had James finally met his match? She watched as James leaned against the windowsill and sipped his whiskey.

"Have you made any progress with Mrs. Sinclair?" Evelyn asked.

"Do you mean with her leaving?"

"She was first to buy, James. She may have a legal argument," Evelyn said.

"You sound like Brent."

"I take it Brent Stone took her side?"

"I'm not surprised either of you would side with a woman," James drawled.

"You should show more compassion. She lost her husband."

"Yes, about that. Something doesn't add up. I asked Anthony to send for his investigator," James said.

"You mean to investigate her?" Evelyn asked incredulously.

"Don't sound so shocked, Evelyn. You know how barristers work. We must know all the facts."

"Yes, but this isn't just one of your criminal cases. She's just as innocent as you. Neither of you knew you were being swindled by the seller," Evelyn pointed out.

There was a low knock on the door. A glint of anticipation lit James's indigo eyes before his gaze shuttered. A maid entered and announced the guest chamber had been prepared. Behind her walked in Evelyn's husband, Jack Harding. But what was it Evelyn had seen in James's face? If she didn't know any better she'd have sworn she saw disappointment that Bella Sinclair hadn't personally made an appearance.

Interesting, Evelyn mused.

Then her husband approached, and Evelyn stood to greet him. With his light brown hair, green eyes, and quick smile, she had been in love with Jack Harding since he had entered her father's chambers as a pupil when she was twelve.

"How's the coach?" she asked him.

"The wheel needs a blacksmith."

"There's a good one in St. Albans. We can call upon him tomorrow. You are welcome to stay at Wyndmoor for as long as you wish," James told them.

Jack Harding looked about the room. "The library is perfect. You know how much my wife loves books."

"Yes, I suspect she'll be using them to research some arcane property laws," James said dryly.

Her husband chuckled and squeezed Evelyn's hand. "If that's what Evie sets her mind to, you won't be able to stop her."

Chapter 9

The arrival of Lady Evelyn Harding turned out to be fortuitous for Bella. After only three days, word of the new duke's arrival had traveled rapidly through the closest town of St. Albans. Bella had anticipated a ripple of scandal when people learned that a bachelor inhabited the same residence as a widow, but to her astonishment, many thought the married Lady Evelyn a proper chaperone for Bella. But Bella was most grateful for the Hardings' company, not only because they were a distraction for Blackwood—who spent much of his time with his three fellow barristers—but because she found Evelyn Harding genuinely friendly.

Bella had gone out of her way to avoid Blackwood, and she had kept busy unpacking her trunks and learning how to run the household. Yet by the end of the third day, Bella had run out of tasks and realized she needed to take a new tactic. Blackwood wasn't leaving or expiring from boredom in the country. She had to learn more about him, and she hoped Evelyn would be able to enlighten her.

With that thought in mind, Bella had searched the house to ask Evelyn to join her for tea when her husband, Jack Harding, informed Bella that Evelyn had been ensconced in the library for most of the afternoon. He smiled, shrugged his shoulders, and said, "She can't resist those books."

Bella knocked softly and opened the library door. Evelyn sat behind a massive oak desk, a stack of open books spread out before her. Light streamed in from the large window behind the desk, turning her hair to a luminous gold.

Bella closed the door and approached. "I apologize for disturbing you, my lady. Would you like to join me for tea on the terrace?"

Evelyn looked up. "Please call me Evelyn. May I call you Bella?"

"Yes, please."

"You have been nothing but kind to us since our arrival, and I'm grateful. You must understand, however, that my husband and I do not keep secrets from each other, and I'm aware of the situation between you and James. I take an interest in all my husband's friends and have grown quite fond of them," Evelyn said.

Disquieting thoughts raced through Bella's mind. Had she made a mistake in approaching Evelyn Harding?

"I understand," Bella said in a low, composed voice.

Evelyn leaned across the desk and a thoughtful smile curved her mouth. "That does not stop me from making my own judgments. Your position may not be as precarious as he would have you believe."

Surprised and more uncertain than before, Bella asked, "You mean the duke?"

"I do."

"I assume you are speaking of our dispute over ownership of this property."

"I am."

"Blackwood claims the legality of his deed is not in question because he was first to record the deed despite the fact that I purchased the property first and moved in days prior to him," Bella said.

"I'm quite proficient at reading and interpreting case law, even the arcane property statutes, and I have discovered one court that was divided on the issue. Most courts have held that the first to record the deed is the owner; one held for the first to purchase and possess. Every case is fact specific, you see."

Bella approached the desk and looked over Evelyn's shoulder. Even though Bella was well read, the thick text of the legal volumes was baffling, with many of the words in Latin. It was like an indecipherable code.

"How can you understand what you are reading?" Bella asked.

Evelyn chuckled and turned in her chair to look up at Bella. "I am the daughter of a longtime barrister."

"I thought you were the daughter of an aristocrat."

"It wasn't until years later that my father inherited my uncle's earldom. For most of my life, my father was a revered Master of the Bench—otherwise known as a Bencher—at Lincoln's Inn. I spent my youth roaming around the Inn and my father's chambers, listening to him lecture his pupils on the topics of contracts, torts, and criminal law. Father has since retired from Lincoln's Inn, but he never lost his love of teaching and still lectures at Oxford. James and the others call me 'Lady Evelyn' in honor of my father."

"Your father mentored others to become barristers?"

"Oh, yes. My husband and James Devlin were just two of his many pupils."

"Is that how you met Mr. Harding?"

"I was a skinny twelve-year-old girl when Jack Harding became my father's pupil, but I adored him the first time I set eyes on him. He's always been a charmer."

An image of Jack Harding rose in Bella's mind: tall and lean with green eyes and an easy grin. She could imagine Evelyn's fascination with the handsome barrister.

"It wasn't until a decade later that I encountered Jack again, only I believed I was in love with another, a scholar and my father's Fellow at the University, who was under suspicion for murdering the Drury Lane actress Bess Whitfield."

Stunned, Bella could only stare. News of the notorious Bess Whitfield's murder had reached even the residents of Plymouth far from the London theater district.

"I needed a competent criminal barrister to represent my anticipated betrothed, and Jack Harding is one of the best," Evelyn explained. "Needless to say, my youthful infatuation for Jack blossomed, and I realized I was wrong about the scholar. Jack and I married soon after Bess Whitfield's true murderer was unearthed. We have since been blessed with our three-year-old son."

"You are both fortunate indeed to have each other."

Evelyn tilted her head to the side and regarded Bella curiously. "James told me you were married for seven years. You must be distraught."

"It was not a love match." Bella regretted the words the moment they left her lips. Why had she spoken so honestly?

"I've known many friends that have married out of duty. There is no shame in it. I take it you see Wyndmoor Manor as a fresh start."

"May I speak plainly?"

"Of course."

"I have always yearned to write, yet my husband never understood and did everything in his power to stop me. Wyndmoor Manor is indeed a fresh start for I am finally free to pursue my dreams of publication and write my stories and articles, despite the fact that some would disapprove of a female author. Can you understand?"

A sudden light glinted in Evelyn's eyes, and she stood and eagerly clasped Bella's hands. "I understand only too well. For years I longed to be a barrister. Oh, to experience striding into the Old Bailey and arguing a case before a jury. It makes gooseflesh rise on my arms. But as a woman, I am not permitted to be called to the bar."

Evelyn Harding's enthusiasm was contagious. They were kindred spirits. Women whose talents and longings were bound by rigid rules—whether established by social mores, universities, or the commands of stern spouses.

"It's not just novels that I long to write," Bella blurted out. "I have submitted a political article to the *Times* using a male pseudonym."

Evelyn clasped her hands to her chest. "Wonderful! If Wyndmoor Manor and your status as widow provide the security and freedom to pursue your dreams, then you must fight for the place and your happiness. You need to retain a solicitor about your dispute of ownership. There's no guarantee you will win, but you deserve representation. I can recommend a solicitor, but you will have to travel to London."

"Why are you helping me?" Bella asked. "Blackwood is your husband's friend."

"James may be a friend, but he knows quite well that I cannot stand by and allow him to bully an innocent widow."

"He has offered to pay me for Wyndmoor Manor if the seller Sir Reeves is found and all our monies spent," Bella said.

"Will you accept his offer?" Evelyn asked.

"I will not. He cannot get rid of me so easily."

A look of mischief crossed Lady Evelyn's face. "Good. James deserves to be challenged by a woman."

"And your husband?" Bella asked. "How would he feel about your helping me?"

Evelyn responded without hesitation. "Jack understands me."

What would it be like to have such devotion from a man? To have the confidence to do what you felt was right, without the fear of disapproval? Bella couldn't fathom it. When she had stumbled upon one of Roger's questionable business ventures—even those that involved treason—and confronted him, he had immediately responded with threats. "Harriet is old, her bones are brittle, she could easily suffer a fall," Roger had spat, a wicked gleam in his eye.

A knock sounded on the door, and Harriet entered. "Pardon, Bella. A gentleman caller has arrived asking for the duke. Coates left the man's calling card on the vestibule table before leading him to the drawing room and summoning Blackwood. I do believe the gentleman's identity may be of interest to you." Harriet stepped forward and held out a card.

Bella reached for the card, her brow furrowed and she read out loud, "Armen Papazian, Investigative Services." She glanced at Harriet in confusion. "I do not know this man."

Evelyn spoke up. "He is the investigator James hired to find Sir Reeves and look into a few other matters."

A few other matters? Bella knew, with certainty, James was investigating *her.* Dear Lord, what if he learned the truth, learned everything . . . ?

Bella turned to Lady Evelyn. "Please excuse me. Perhaps we can have tea on the terrace another time?"

Evelyn smiled warmly. "That would be lovely."

Not wasting another moment, Bella turned on her heel and rushed from the library.

James had just seen Investigator Papazian out and was closing the door when Bella came rushing into the vestibule.

"I was informed there was a guest. An investigator," Bella said.

Her cheeks were flushed. Her eyes bright slashes of jade in her oval face. As always of late, a frisson of excitement thrummed in his veins when she entered a room. They had resided under the same roof for less than one week, and even though she went to great lengths to avoid him, he had kept an eye on her as she'd busied herself organizing the servants and unpacking and placing her own belongings.

James's gaze lowered to the calling card clasped in Bella's hand. "I must remind Coates to exercise discretion when I have a visitor."

"Why was the investigator here?" she asked.

"Upon inquiry of the patrons of the Twin Rams, I learned that Sir Reeves had left the village immediately after he sold me Wyndmoor Manor. My investigator has located Reeves, and I'm on my way to see him."

"Now?"

"I see no need to wait to question Reeves," he said.

"I'm going with you," she said matter-of-factly.

James shook his head. "It is not a good idea. Reeves is staying at the Black Hound, a rundown posting inn on the outskirts of Hertfordshire."

She met his gaze without flinching. "I'm going. The man owes me an explanation."

His lips parted in a curved, stiff smile. "The Black Hound is a bawdy, boisterous establishment. It certainly is no place for a lady."

She answered in a rush of words. "If Sir Reeves is there, then nothing can keep me away. I am just as much his victim as you, and I have a right to confront him face-to-face."

"I will confront him for us both. Or do you not trust me?"

"You have yet to exhibit trustworthy behavior."

His temper inexplicably flared. "Are you always this argumentative?"

"Since you present no logical reason for me not to accompany you, then yes."

"Fine," he snapped. "But don't say I didn't warn you."

His gaze raked her from head to toe, noting her cream gown with its rounded bodice. It was hardly scandalous, nothing close to the plunging bodices of the London females of his acquaintance, but the smooth silk accentuated the nubile curves beneath her dress, and the cream color heightened the translucence of her face and neck.

As a barrister whose practice occasionally involved criminal cases, James had met with clients in unsavory establishments throughout the London rookeries, but never with a beautiful lady in tow. His gut clenched as an image crystallized in his mind of the patrons of the Black Hound gawking when Bella Sinclair walked through the door.

His thoughts raced headlong, and anger toward Sir Redmond Reeves rippled along his spine. *Damn him,* James thought, *for thrusting us into this predicament.*

His voice was cold when he spoke. "You'll need to change. Do you own a darker gown?"

"I have a mourning gown."

It was on the tip of his tongue to ask why, as a widow of less than a year, she never wore it. Instead, he said, "Good. And fetch a cloak, something that covers you from the neck down."

She opened her mouth to argue but, spotting a parlor maid and one of the footmen staring from around the corner, thought better of it. They were making quite the spectacle for all the servants to overhear—both hers and his.

She took a deep breath, her green eyes blazing with determination. "I'll be but a moment, Your Grace." With a swish of her skirts, she made for the stairs.

James watched as she ascended, her hips swaying with each step.

Magnificent. Despite his anger at having to escort her to the Black Hound against his better judgment, her defiance was a challenge, a novel experience that drew him like a lodestone. He wondered what her reaction would be if she knew just how much her rebelliousness attracted him.

James was waiting beside the carriage when Bella came out of the house. Satisfied with the demure cut of her black dress, he said, "I approve of the dress, but where is your cloak?"

As if on cue, Harriet came out of the house, a dark cloak draped across her arm.

"It's too warm to wear it," Bella said. "I thought to carry it with me until we arrive at the Black Hound."

"I don't suppose you can convince her to stay here?" James asked Harriet.

The old woman's brows drew downward in a frown. "I've tried, Your Grace. But she has a stubborn streak."

Stubborn streak indeed, James mused.

Of all the women he had known, every one would have happily stayed in the safety of her home and allowed James to confront Sir Reeves at the Black Hound on his own. Further still, the women of his past would have gladly taken the money James offered for Wyndmoor Manor without a second thought and gone on to spend it lavishly on an opulent lifestyle.

But Bella Sinclair was different.

Despite the odds of feuding with a man, a barrister and duke to boot, she refused to be cowed. He should be annoyed, but as each day passed, he became more intrigued.

"Where's your carriage?" Bella asked.

"The investigator lent me his in exchange for mine. I had no desire for the patrons of the Black Hound to get a look at the ducal crest on the side of my carriage."

A footman opened the carriage door and the step was lowered. Bella climbed in, and James settled on the bench across from her. The late-afternoon sun streamed in through the windows, and her auburn hair gleamed deep mahogany and rich red.

She shifted on the soft leather seat, watching out the window as Harriet went into the house and shut the door. Keeping her gaze averted, she sat straight and folded her hands in her lap, clearly determined to ignore him for the duration of the trip just as she had avoided him during the past three days.

Her behavior irked him. He wasn't used to being ignored by a woman, especially one who had tantalized him after only one kiss. A devilish part of him wanted to upset her composure. He stretched his long legs, brushing her skirts.

She started, and the heavy lashes that shadowed her cheeks flew up. Their eyes met, and she colored.

Ah, she wasn't as immune as she would have him believe. Only now she appeared nervous, biting her bottom lip, and growing increasingly uneasy under the heat of his gaze. He didn't want that either. Truth be told, he admired her bravery. She would never play the dreaded damsel in distress that many women had thought he would find attractive. A woman like Bella, if she allowed herself, would be full of passion in the bedroom. Where he'd thought he'd find satisfaction in her nervousness, instead he now longed to see her unwavering courage return.

What had addled his brains?

Annoyed with his thoughts, James banged on the roof. The horses set off with a jingle of harness and the carriage lurched, before settling into a steady pace across the graveled drive.

James leaned back on the bench. "When we get to the Black Hound and find Reeves, let me speak first."

She regarded him with a speculative gaze. "Why?"

"I don't know what type of criminals he's consorting with."

Her eyes grew wide. "You think Sir Reeves consorts with criminals?"

"Don't be so naïve, Bella. Redmond Reeves *is* a criminal."

"But still—"

"Is your safety of no concern to you?" his voice grated harshly. "There's only one reason for a beautiful woman to be present in such an establishment."

Her lips parted in surprise, and he suspected she was more shocked that he had called her beautiful than that he had suggested the Black Hound's customers would think her a prostitute.

Had her husband never told her she was beautiful?

Not for the first time James sensed her marriage with the deceased Mr. Sinclair had been intimately unsatisfactory. Whether the man had been a simpleton or a selfish bastard,

James could only guess. What James knew for certain was that Bella's innocent yet sensual reaction to his kiss would forever be imprinted on his mind.

A foreign stab of protectiveness pierced his chest.

They rode in silence for the remainder of the journey until the swaying of the carriage slowed upon a section of the cobbled road that had fallen into disrepair. With a creak of the harness, the wheels of the carriage hit a rut with a teeth-jarring bounce, and Bella was jolted from her seat and thrown atop him. James grasped her about the waist at the same time she reached out to clutch his thigh, and they nearly bumped heads.

A glance down at her small hand on his upper thigh caused the temperature in the carriage to rise twenty degrees. An erotic image focused in his mind of Bella touching him without the barrier of clothing.

"Oh!" she cried out.

"Easy, Bella."

Realizing where she grasped him, she pulled her hand back as if she had clutched a scalding hot poker. She leaped off him, reseated herself, and smoothed her skirts.

Just then, the carriage came to a full stop. James glanced out the window. His arousal instantly cooled, and his gaze narrowed on the inn across the street. "We've arrived."

Chapter 10

The sign for the Black Hound creaked on its rusty chains above the door. The posting inn was at a crossroads, where travelers on their way to London or through the villages of Hertfordshire might be unfortunate enough to stop.

Bella had spent her married years in Plymouth and was aware of the many taverns the sailors, fishermen, dockworkers, and prostitutes frequented, but she had never set foot in one of those establishments.

Night had descended, and thick clouds obscured a hazy moon that seemed to hang precariously on a curtain of black velvet. Fog furled around the crumbling stone walls of what looked more like a dockside whorehouse than a frequented inn. One of the inn's shutters hung askew on its hinges, and coarse male laughter spilled into the street. Two men leaned against the posts just outside the door smoking, their eyes red from too much gin, their jaws unshaven. They turned to stare at James and Bella as they passed, and she lifted the hem of her skirt to avoid the debris of broken bottles and horse dung.

James opened the door and ushered her inside. A thick cloud of smoke stung her eyes and swirled above to hang in the rafters in a heavy cloud. A long bar with stools ran the length of one wall, and an assortment of tables and chairs jammed the floor. The tavern was crowded with laborers, farmers, and local tradesmen, whose voices and laughter resounded in the small space. Barmaids scurried through the room, tankards of ale or cups of gin balanced on their trays. A handful of other women lingered at the occupied tables, and judging by their rouged lips, brazen smiles, and low-necked dresses, Bella suspected they earned their living selling their bodies to travelers who passed through the inn.

The door closed behind them, and Bella's heart hammered in her chest. The pungent stench of sweat, boiled cabbage, and smoke made bile rise up in her throat.

James put her hand on his sleeve and wove his way to the bar. They passed a table of men holding cards, who eyed Bella with lascivious interest. One of the players, a drunken man with a bald head and a black patch covering one eye, leered at her, his lips twisting into a fearful grimace.

Repulsed, Bella inched closer to James and tightened her grip on his sleeve. He pulled out an empty bar stool. "Sit until I can spot Reeves."

The bartender approached, and James ordered two cups of ale. Turning his back to the bar, he surveyed the room above the rim of his tankard.

"I don't see him," she said.

"I've no doubt he's here."

As Bella scanned the common room, the door opened and a group of eight men entered. Dressed in mended corduroy jackets and patched trousers, they looked like farmers passing through with their goods. They made their way to an empty table in the center of the room. One of them held back. He was dressed differently in simple trousers and a blue cotton shirt, which proclaimed he was not with the group of farmers, but nonetheless, his attire was nondescript enough to fit in with the other bar patrons. He wore a hat with its curled brim pulled down, but something about his manner-isms and stance was disturbingly familiar. . . .

"I see Reeves," James said, interrupting her thoughts.

Bella's head turned to follow his stare and all thoughts of the stranger were forgotten as she too spotted Reeves in the corner, his back to them. She slid from the stool and followed James closely as he elbowed his way through the crowd. He grasped the man firmly on the shoulder from behind.

Reeves jumped and whirled around. "What the hell—"

Clearly deep into his cups, it took him several seconds before his eyes widened in recognition. His attire was slovenly, his shirtfront stained, with missing buttons. His bloodshot eyes traveled from James to Bella before returning to James. Bella couldn't fathom he was the same man who had sold her Wyndmoor Manor. Sir Redmond Reeves had presented himself with a dapper top hat and cane accompanied by a sense of snobbery so frequently associated with a man of his rank. This Sir Reeves before her looked like a criminal drunkard from the rookeries.

"Your Grace," Reeves said. "What an unexpected surprise."

James led Bella around and held a chair for her, taking for himself the one across from Reeves.

"Did you honestly believe you could get away with such a scheme?" James asked.

"Whatever do you mean?" Reeves asked.

"Apologize to the lady." James's voice, though quiet, had an ominous quality.

Bella spoke up. "Why would you do such a thing as to sell the same property twice?"

"I fell upon bad times," Reeves whined.

"That's your excuse?" James said.

"You must understand," Reeves pleaded. "I had a solid streak of luck at the gaming tables when I was last in London. I was at the same table as the old Duke of Blackwood when he said that he wanted to sell a property in Hertfordshire. I was up a bloody fortune at the time, and I thought it a good investment. Afterwards, my luck at the tables changed, and I was hounded by a bloodthirsty moneylender. Rather than lose an arm, I sold Wyndmoor Manor to the widow here."

"Then what possessed you to sell it to Blackwood, too?" Bella asked.

"I thought it would be sufficient to cover my debts, but the damned moneylender demanded so much in interest! Then you came around," Reeves said, pointing to James. "You wanted the place so badly and quickly too . . . and, well, the idea came to me to sell it again, and I prepared another deed. I figured the lady would leave when confronted by a duke."

"You thought wrong!" Bella cried out.

"Where's the money?" James asked.

"I don't have it!"

James's eyes narrowed to slits. "You're lying."

"I'm not. I swear to it. I had to pay the moneylender," Reeves said.

"You're coming with me to be tried for fraud. But first you owe the lady an apology," James said tersely.

Reeves's beady eyes shifted to Bella. "A female that looks like her can work off her debt. I can't!"

A low growl erupted from James's throat. He stood and dragged Reeves up by his shirtfront. "I'll personally see to it that you rot in jail."

Panicking, Reeves grasped his tankard of ale, and drew back his arm, but James ducked and it sailed through the air, hitting a burly man with a torn jacket at the next table.

The man jumped to his feet, his face a menacing mask of rage. "You son of a bitch!" Tall and broad-shouldered, he carried perhaps twice Reeves's weight. In one powerful move, he overturned his table and lunged for the smaller man.

Within seconds, the crowded room burst into pandemonium. Chairs scraped across the wooden floor, and fists flew in a blur. Bella was swallowed up by the crowd as prostitutes shrieked, glass bottles shattered, and the sounds of flesh pummeling flesh surrounded her. A man reached out to grasp her waist. She kicked his shins and he released her with a grunt.

"James!" Bella shouted.

She lost sight of James amongst the throng, and panic welled in her throat.

A solid hand like a steel band clasped her arm. She whirled, intent on landing another kick, when a deep, powerful voice stopped her. "This way, Bella!"

James's eyes were fierce as he led her toward a back door. He fought his way as they went, dodging fists and landing punches. She spotted Sir Reeves sprawled on the floor, his nose bloody. James pushed through the rear door onto a cobbled lane.

She gulped in the fresh night air. It was dim, without torches or gas lamps, and her eyes had to adjust from the bright, smoky interior of the inn to the dark back alley. Bella bent forward at the waist, breathing heavily.

She heard the scrape of booted feet and jerked around to make out a shadow of a man smoking a cheroot, leaning against the building. The smoke wafted to her like a slithering snake. The distinctive acrid odor of the tobacco triggered a sickening memory of Roger circling her, a cheroot in his hand, as she had stood shivering and naked in her bedchamber.

The stranger did not approach, and in the dim light she could make out the hat with its curled brim. Without a doubt she knew he was the same man she had spotted inside the bar. The clouds parted and a faint shaft of moonlight illuminated the side of his face, revealing a glimmer of fair hair.

Bella's breath stalled in her throat.

It couldn't be!

Roger arisen from the grave?

Impossible. She was hallucinating after the violent experience of her first bar brawl. She took a deep breath, forcing the panic at bay. It had been months since Roger's death; she refused to allow his foul memory to haunt her.

"Are you all right?" James asked.

"Yes."

"Let's get back to the carriage."

She couldn't agree more. He led her across the street to where the carriage awaited. The driver hopped down when he saw them and opened the door.

"Hurry and let's be on our way," James told the driver. "The lady isn't well."

James lifted her into the carriage and settled beside her. It was only after the carriage started on their journey home that she realized she was shivering. He gathered her into his arms, and her cheek rested against his broad shoulder. For several long minutes, he simply held her.

"You're safe now," he whispered in her ear. "I won't let anything happen to you."

Tears welled in her eyes. She would have sold her soul to have a man speak such words to her months ago, to take away the constant fear and worry she had experienced both before and after Roger's death. Then she remembered who held her and why she was where she was.

"I'm fine now," she said, trying to sound calm.

He didn't release her, and she didn't push away. His linen shirt caressed her soft cheek, and the protectiveness of his strong arms felt blessedly good. His spicy, masculine scent was exhilarating, unlike the foul odor of smoke and un-washed, perspiring bodies that permeated the Black Hound.

"I'm sorry about Reeves," he said. "I had hoped he hadn't spent all of the money."

Lifting her face from his shoulder, she looked up at him. "Were you serious about seeking his arrest?"

James's eyes held a sheen of purpose. "I still am. I intend to contact the local magistrate. If by some miracle Reeves is not imprisoned, then I'll go after him myself. He won't get away unscathed."

Despite the warmth of his arms, a cold wave entered the

carriage, and she actually felt a ribbon of sympathy for Sir Reeves.

Blackwood's unaccustomed to losing, and he's never been swindled before.

He was a confident man, used to getting his way once he set his mind to a task. She did not doubt that he was a successful barrister, shrewd and determined. Hadn't he escaped a life of dependency on his family? If James Devlin hadn't been in such a hurry to purchase Wyndmoor Manor, Bella suspected he would have caught on to Sir Reeves's ruse.

"I would never have forgiven myself if you were hurt," he said.

"I insisted on coming, remember?"

"It doesn't matter. I'm responsible."

"No man is responsible for me."

"I beg to differ," he said. "You placed yourself in my care the moment you agreed to share a residence with me."

She studied him beneath lowered lashes. Light from the lamps on the sides of the carriage illuminated his incredible blue eyes. His look was intense, as if she were one of the many beautiful ladies that must have flocked around him in London.

"Do you always get what you want, Your Grace?"

"It's James, and yes."

"How boring."

"Indeed."

Reaching out, he traced the edge of her cloak, where the tie rested against her throat. Then with his hand, he caressed her cheek and ran the pad of his thumb across her full bottom lip.

Her hand rested on his muscular chest, and she could feel the strong, steady beat of his heart through his shirt. The longing to slip her fingers beneath the fine linen and caress his skin simmered in her blood. Breathlessly, she watched him lower his head to capture her lips.

His kiss was swift and passionate. She unfurled for him, like an eager flower at the first touch of dawn. She parted her lips and his tongue swept inside, tasting and touching all she offered. She nestled closer to the blissful warmth and hardness of his body in wonder as desire flooded her limbs. So this was passion, what all the silly young girls had tittered about at the garden parties she had attended as an innocent seventeen-year-old. This was what she had never experienced during her marriage.

He lifted his head and trailed his lips along the slope of her neck, then licked the shell of her ear. She gasped, her fingers curling in his shirt.

"You taste of strawberries and woman," he murmured, "and I have a strong weakness for strawberries. What am I going to do with you?"

You can keep kissing me, she thought. Then she stretched up and kissed him instead. Her fingers speared through his thick, dark hair, and he moaned.

His hand outlined the circle of her breast. Her breath caught, and her nipples firmed. His fingers traced her nipples through the muslin of her gown, his touch light and painfully teasing. Ripples of wanting ran through her, pooling low in her belly. Just as it had been at the lake, all logic and reason fled and her senses reeled. They were alone in a carriage. His strong arms cradled her safely. It was pointless to resist his seductive, leisurely expertise when she had no desire to escape his embrace.

She arched into his touch, and his hand slipped inside her bodice to caress a sensitive swollen nipple. His palm was fiery hot, as hot as she felt. His other hand moved to her waist and pulled her close. Tearing his lips from hers, he kissed a path down her throat and licked the swell of her breasts above the fabric of her dress. *Sweet heaven!* His breath was warm and moist. Her heart thundered in her ears, and it felt as if her body were melting against his.

The sway of the carriage changed to a stop-and-go motion, but she paid no heed until James lifted his head.

"We're home," he said.

Home. What an unusual choice of words for him to use. Bewildered, she glanced at his face, and was struck by his expression. His indigo eyes blazed with unmistakable lust and another emotion—something akin to fierce determination.

"My offer still stands, Bella," he said, his voice gruff. "I'll reimburse you for whatever you paid Reeves."

His words struck her like a bucket of ice water across her heated skin. She withdrew from his arms, moving as far from him as the bench allowed, and pulled together her scattered thoughts.

What on earth had she been thinking to kiss him like that? He was battling lust, yes, but nothing more. He hadn't forgotten their dispute, and had chosen the precise moment to fling his offer in her face. Whereas—to her complete and utter shame—she had been caught up in passion.

He is a successful barrister and practiced seducer, she reminded herself. *Masterful persuasion is his style, no matter the methods used.*

Fury simmered in her blood. Fury at herself and the coldhearted man sitting beside her.

"Wyndmoor Manor is not for sale, Your Grace. And neither am I."

Not waiting for assistance, she gathered her skirts, flung the carriage door open, and jumped down on her own. Head held regally high, she marched into the house.

James watched as she slammed the front door behind her.

Bella Sinclair was proud. It was why she had insisted on accompanying him to the Black Hound to face Sir Reeves tonight. It was why she refused his offer of reimbursement and insisted on fighting a duke. It was why she had purchased an isolated country property rather than travel to London.

Yet she hadn't fought him in the carriage. She had capitulated to his expertise with a fiery passion that had surprised him. He had been in control—or so he had thought—until she had pulled his head down to deepen the kiss.

Thereafter, his prized control had been sorely strained.

He wanted to make love to Bella with a yearning that was staggering. Thoughts of property deeds had nothing to do with his lust. He recalled the tantalizing ripeness of her breast filling his hand—the weight, the perfect smooth skin, the pebble-hard nipple that made his mouth water—and he felt a hunger so fervent that it weakened his resolve. His plan to woo her, to seduce her and bend her to his will, was at risk from his own weakness. He forced himself back from the unbridled hunger, for he was all too aware of what emotional trap lay there.

A trap that, no matter how delectable the woman, he had no intention of falling into.

Chapter 11

Bella woke the following morning with newfound determination. She had planned on meeting Wyndmoor's tenants soon after arriving at the manor, but when the Duke of Blackwood's shadow had darkened her doorstep she had been distracted by his legal claim. She had made a mistake. There was no better way to establish her position than to present herself to the tenant farmers as the new owner.

Last night's debacle at the Black Hound had proved that the stakes were higher than ever. She hadn't realized what a formidable opponent James truly was. If his kiss was sufficient to raise her passion, then he held a power over her that she must never allow to be unleashed. He cared only for the property, not the country widow that accompanied it.

Donning her riding habit, Bella made a quick stop to the kitchens to seek directions to the tenant farms and to gather a basket of fresh sweet rolls before heading to the stables. The young, red-haired lad was busy polishing tack.

"Would you please saddle my mare, Bobby?"

"Aye, my lady." He reached for a side saddle that hung on the stable wall, then went for her horse.

"Where are you headed this morning?" A deep male voice spoke behind her.

Bella jumped. She whirled to spot James in the far corner of the stables, holding the reins of an enormous black stallion. He walked forward, his gaze lazily appraising her.

Memories of last night came back to her in a rush. She recalled resting her cheek against his broad shoulder, the strength of his arms as he held her after the frightful bar brawl. Then there had been his passionate kisses and his tantalizing touch on her breast.

Heat stole into her face along with renewed humiliation. His practiced seduction had been carried out with expertise. His kiss, his caress had upset her balance, and she had eagerly responded. His thoughts, however, had never been far from seeking her gone from Wyndmoor.

Their eyes locked, and the annoyance in her voice was ill-concealed. "My whereabouts are none of your concern, but if you must know, I'm going for a ride."

"By yourself?"

"Yes."

His lips curled into a smile, and she had the distinct impression he knew she was recalling last night's intimacy. His eyes lowered to the basket on her arm. "That smells like fresh baked bread."

She spoke quickly. "I'm picnicking."

"Alone? At nine o'clock in the morning?"

"Fine," she snapped. "I've decided to visit my tenants for the first time."

He brightened. "We must truly have a psychic connection. I planned on doing the same this morning." He reached out to lift the checked fabric covering the basket she carried and peeked inside. His stomach grumbled loudly. "Your rolls do smell delicious. You will certainly be greeted more enthusiastically than I will."

She slapped his hand. "You should have eaten breakfast with the Hardings."

"I have an idea. Since we both planned on the same destination, let us travel together," he said, seeming very pleased with himself.

"I don't suppose you can alter your plans and go another day?" she said.

He grinned. "Not a chance."

She wanted to stomp her foot and scream in frustration. He'd had no intention of visiting Wyndmoor's tenants today. By the look of his tousled hair and the fresh scent of pine emanating from him, he had missed breakfast in order to ride.

Bobby led her mare to the mounting block and held the reins. She went to the block, intent on mounting her own horse, but James was by her side in a flash.

"Allow me."

Before she could respond, his strong hands spanned her waist, and he lifted her onto the mare's back. He lingered moments more than necessary, and her heart hammered against her ribs at his touch. Sitting side-saddle, she adjusted the basket on her skirts and looked into his eyes.

"Last night was a mistake. Your efforts are in vain."

He arched a brow. "Please enlighten me as to what efforts you refer to."

"I won't be charmed or seduced into leaving."

His hand covered his chest. "You offend me. Here I was thinking I was being polite." He didn't look or sound offended, not even slightly disturbed by her comment—rather he appeared like a man who eagerly anticipated the rare opponent who would dare throw down the gauntlet in challenge.

James mounted his horse, and she couldn't help but admire the animal. Large, with a shiny, black coat and sleek muscles, it was a perfect fit for its rider.

James ran his hand down the stallion's velvety muzzle. "His name is Maximus, and he was a racing champion until he retired this year. I rode him from London and had him stabled at the Twin Rams. Keeping Maximus in the city seemed a waste as he needs a good run each day."

"He's stunning," she said.

"He's temperamental and can be dangerous."

Just like his master, she mused.

She glanced at Blackwood's buff riding breeches and the thick muscles on his thighs as he controlled the powerful stallion. He'd chosen not to wear a riding coat, and his tailored white shirt hugged his broad shoulders like a second skin.

They rode their horses side by side through the meadow of wildflowers they had passed days ago, and the air was fragrant with honeysuckle and gardenia. James led her east toward the tenant farms. The sun shone brightly on fruit trees, their boughs bursting with flowers that would soon bear peaches, pears, and apples. They passed grazing pastures where sheep roamed freely.

Soon the cottages of the tenant farmers came into view. In total, there were five tenant families who farmed the one-hundred-acre property. As James and Bella rode close, the families came out of their homes. A handful of children played outside, some throwing a stick for a large dog to fetch and others kicking a ball. When they spotted James, they ran forward, their faces smiling and animated.

"Blackwood! Blackwood!" the children shouted as they reached out to pet his horse.

James laughed and jumped down from his horse to embrace the youths. He placed the smallest of the children atop his shoulders, and took the stick from another and threw it for the dog to retrieve.

To Bella's astonishment, James knew all the children's names and personally greeted each of the tenants.

How many times has he been here?

As if reading her thoughts, he said, "I spent summers here as a boy, remember?"

"But the children. How do you know their names?"

He winked, and lowered the child atop his shoulders to the ground. "I've come every day for the past week."

Oh, she wanted to wipe the smug look off his face, but at the same time she was surprised he would take such a keen interest in the tenants. Roger had owned a much larger estate, and he had never bothered to know the tenants' names or play with their children. He had only been concerned with the timeliness of the rents to support his lavish lifestyle and fondness for fine wine.

Three tenants with calloused hands and weathered faces as dark as tanned leather conversed with James about which fields would be left fallow and which crops were planned for the summer's harvest.

They believe he is the true master of Wyndmoor! She felt uncertain, not knowing how to broach the subject, but it was James who came to her aid. "May I introduce, Mrs. Sinclair. We both claim ownership to Wyndmoor, but hope the decision will be made soon."

The farmers looked at Bella, then to James. "Begging yer pardon, Yer Grace, but we are all grateful that Sir Reeves is no longer the owner. 'E wasnna 'ere more than days and 'e said 'e'd be raisin' the rents. Yer father, the old duke, never much came out 'ere, but 'e was fair and never raised the rents as much as Sir Reeves 'ad planned."

"Whoever is master here, neither of us shall raise the rents," James said.

Rather than feel outrage that he had spoken for her, Bella nodded in agreement. "He speaks the truth."

Just then a girl no more than six with curly gold locks came up to Bella and peered at her basket.

Bella bent down on one knee and lifted the checked fabric. "Would you like a roll?"

The child's brown eyes widened with uncertainty. She nibbled her bottom lip before she tentatively reached out for a roll. Taking a small bite, she looked at Bella. "Yer pretty. Are ye 'is wife?"

Bella's lips curved into a smile. "No. We are not married."

"But yer with 'im?"

"Only for today." Bella glanced at the group of women standing outside the doorway of one of the cottages. They watched the scene with wide-eyed interest. "Which one is your mum?" Bella asked.

The girl pointed to one of the women in the middle of the group.

Bella went over to the women and introduced herself. The wives were reserved, uncertain of Bella's position. Bella attempted to put them at ease.

"Is there anything that you need from Wyndmoor's master?" Bella asked.

The child's mother looked at the others before speaking up. "Our roofs are in need of repair, but 'is lordship 'as provided the funds from 'is own pockets after 'is first visit 'ere."

"'E's buildin' an extra cottage as well," another woman piped up. "Two of our families live together, but with Justine givin' birth to 'er fifth, it's crowded, it is."

Bella was stunned by James's generosity. She told herself he wasn't being generous, just overly confident that he would be victorious over the battle of ownership of the land. Yet she would have to be blind not to see the admiration and respect for the new Duke of Blackwood stamped on the faces of Wyndmoor's hardworking tenants.

James approached, holding the reins of both Maximus and her mare. He grinned at her with a cheerful smile that made her heart flutter. "Shall we return?"

"Of course."

Before she could mount her horse, the little girl ran forward, her blond locks bouncing. She motioned for Bella to lean down, and she whispered in her ear. "My mum says if ye marry 'im, ye can stay."

* * *

Upon Bella's return, Evelyn was waiting for her to go on a shopping excursion. Bella could barely contain her excitement. It felt like eons since she had shopped for her own clothing; Roger had taken perverse delight in picking gowns that he knew she disliked. Bella hurried to change from her riding habit into a mourning gown appropriate for a widow of less than a year and met Evelyn outside.

Their first destination was a reputable dress shop in St. Albans. Unlike the snobby French courtiers in London, the dressmaker, Mrs. Fisher, was a sturdy Englishwoman with a welcoming smile. Racks of dresses lined the walls of the small shop, easels held sketches of new designs, and tables were laden with an array of chemises, stockings, fans, parasols, and gloves.

Evelyn pointed to an amethyst dress on a mannequin in the corner. "You will look ravishing in this! The color will bring out the green in your eyes."

Bella reached out to touch the fine silk, and a thrill raced down her spine. "It's lovely."

Evelyn eyed Bella's gown. "I've noticed you do not wear black at home. 'Tis a shame you feel the need to wear it out."

Bella hated the mourning gown and would have been overjoyed to see it burned. Even though Evelyn knew Bella's marriage had not been a love match, members of the town believed her to be a grieving widow, and Bella had no wish to correct the misconception.

"Roger has not yet been gone a year," Bella said.

Evelyn smiled easily. "I was never a stickler for propriety."

Thank goodness, Bella thought. She enjoyed Evelyn Harding's company; her straightforward, nonjudgmental outlook on life was a refreshing change. Evelyn and her husband would soon return to London, and Bella would be sad to see Evelyn depart. Bella had not been permitted a friend for years, another way her husband had isolated her, and she hadn't realized how much she had missed female companionship.

Mrs. Fisher approached with a stack of sketches in her arms, and Bella pointed to the mannequin. "I'd like to be fitted with this one."

The women were led to the back of the shop, past tall shelves stacked with bolts of cloth. Silks, satins, muslins, and linens spilled onto the floor in a splendid burst of color like an artist's palette. Beyond the stocks of fabric they entered a tiny back room cluttered with baskets of sewing materials and discarded bits of cloth strewn about the floor. The dressmaker helped Bella remove her gown and try on the amethyst silk. Bella stepped onto a pedestal and gazed in the cheval glass mirror.

She blinked, scarcely recognizing her reflection. A low neckline with tight under sleeves emphasized the swell of her breasts. A band of ruched silk detail trimmed the hem and matched the lining of a long, embroidered stole.

Mrs. Fisher pulled the tape measure from around her neck and measured Bella's waist and hips. "You look exquisite. The amethyst suits your fair skin and highlights the red in your hair."

The shop's bells chimed, announcing the arrival of a new customer.

"Pardon, I'll be but a moment." Mrs. Fisher put down her tape and rushed from the room.

Evelyn walked close and looked at Bella's reflection in the mirror. "James will fall at your feet. Before long, he'll gift you with Wyndmoor."

Bella's cheeks burned in remembrance of James's bone-melting kisses and her fierce, eager response to his intimate caress. "I don't believe it. He has shown no signs of relenting. I fear I need the name of the solicitor in London you had mentioned."

"I'll give it to you, of course. But know this—deep down James is not a bad man."

Bella thought of Wyndmoor's tenants. James had promised not to raise their rents and to spend his own funds to repair their roofs and build a new cottage. She thought of him fighting their way out of the violent bar brawl at the Black Hound and the strength and warmth of his arms as he held her in the carriage. Had his comfort been a ruse to gain her trust? Or had he truly been concerned for her well-being?

"Of all my husband's friends, I am the closest to James," Evelyn said. "I know him well, and he acts differently around you."

"Whatever do you mean?" Bella asked.

"When you walk into the room, his attention is riveted. You are beautiful, yes, but James has had his fair share of beautiful women throwing themselves at him. You challenge him, Bella, and it is driving him to distraction, making him helpless. You oppose him on two fronts, your claim to Wyndmoor Manor and your resistance to his charms."

"It has been less than a week," Bella pointed out.

Evelyn waved a hand dismissively. "Any other woman would have tumbled headlong into his bed after two days' time. But you have managed to resist him entirely."

Not entirely, Bella thought. "It's not me he wants, but the manor, and he foolishly believes seduction is the way to get me to relinquish the property."

Evelyn regarded her thoughtfully. "No, you're wrong. He may have started out believing that nonsense, but he is drawn to you and it is playing havoc with his plans."

A thrill raced down Bella's spine. James Devlin drawn to her? It felt delicious and wonderful to have such a virile, masculine man find her attractive. Roger's berating had made her feel inadequate as a woman.

On impulse, Bella stepped down from the pedestal and picked up a pair of black silk hose and frilly garters from one of the baskets. The hose were completely sheer and light as butterfly wings. Roger had never allowed such sensual undergarments. He had preferred she wear wool hose, even in the heat of the summer.

When the dressmaker returned, Evelyn held out the black silk. "I'll take these along with the dress. When will it be ready?"

"The dress needs very little tailoring. You're as slender as a reed, and I certainly do not need to let out any of the seams as I must for many of my customers. A nip here and a tuck there ought to suffice."

"I want to visit the haberdashery for my husband," Evelyn said. "Will the dress be ready by the time we return?"

"I'll work on it straightaway, my lady," the dressmaker said.

Bella and Evelyn left the shop and walked arm in arm to the haberdashery. Shoppers strolled down the street, stopping to look at displays of merchandise in the windows. Bells chimed as shop doors opened and closed. They passed a toy store, and a small child tugged on his mother's sleeve and pointed to a hand-carved wooded train in the window.

For years Bella had longed to casually stroll the shopping district of Plymouth without strange stares and whispers behind her back, and most certainly, without the fear of her husband's wrath upon her return home.

The redolent aroma of fresh baked bread wafted from a bakery across the street. Bella strained to read the shop's small, hand-printed sign when she spotted the man outside the door. A sudden image of the fair-haired smoker outside the Black Hound came to her.

He was looking at them, Bella realized with alarm, but when he realized she returned his stare, he averted his gaze. Unlike the man in the Black Hound, he was dressed in a fine frock coat with a flared skirt and a tall-crowned hat, and from this distance she could not make out his hair color, yet she could swear it was flaxen. He held a cheroot in his gloved hand. Icy fingers trickled down her spine.

Was the same man following her?

Nonsense. She had stayed to watch as the last shovel of dirt had covered Roger's grave. Her imagination was running wild, a result of years living in fear with a demented fair-haired man.

Bella trailed behind Evelyn as she opened the door to the haberdashery. She wandered around the shop aimlessly, her mind a mixture of anxiety and confusion as she picked up cravats from a table and put them down without really seeing them. She resisted the urge to look out the shop's bay window and see if the man was still outside the bakery.

A half hour later, Evelyn spotted a beaver hat with a wide brim and held it up for Bella. "This is perfect for Jack. Let's pick up your dress and go home. I want to see the sparks fly when James spots you wearing it."

Chapter 12

Bella returned from St. Albans to learn from Coates that a letter had arrived. Handing her packages to Harriet, Bella went to the small table in the center of the vestibule and picked up the envelope. Her heart pounded in anticipation when she saw the return address was from the *Times*.

It had arrived! Had the editor liked her political article?

Bella held the envelope in her hand, trying to judge by the weight and thickness whether it was a rejection or an acceptance. She held it up to the light. Nothing.

Slipping the envelope into her skirt pocket, she rushed to the library, where she intended to rip it open and read it in private. She burst into the room and stopped short at the sight of James seated behind the massive oak desk. Bobby sat beside him with an open book between them.

"Pardon my interruption," she said, startled. "I had no idea the library was occupied."

James leaned back in his chair and grinned. "Nonsense. You are not interrupting."

"The duke is tutoring me in Latin," Bobby said.

Bella frowned, bewildered. "Latin?" Why would a duke's stable boy need to learn Latin?

"I want to be a barrister just like Blackwood," Bobby said.

"The duke has been tutoring me for over a year now, ever since I came into service for him. He says I'm too smart to remain in the stables forever." Bobby's face lit with idol worship as he looked at James. "We are preparing for a mock court."

"A mock court?" she asked.

"You're just in time, Bella. For us to successfully conduct Bobby's first mock court, we need more than two people."

"I'm not certain I'm suited for—"

"It's simple," James said. "A mock court is a practice courtroom procedure, only Bobby acts as the barrister and we act as his witnesses."

She eyed him speculatively. "Don't you need a judge?"

"How astute you are, Bella. And you had claimed to know little of the legal system."

"Even a layperson knows a judge is required, Your Grace."

"Well then, we are fortunate indeed that my colleague Anthony Stevens has not yet returned to London and is in the billiard room as we speak."

"There is no billiard room at Wyndmoor," she pointed out.

There was a trace of humor around his mouth and near his eyes. "Have I forgotten to mention that I had a snooker table delivered this morning while you were out shopping with Lady Evelyn? You needn't fear. I purchased it with my own funds."

She arched an eyebrow. "'Tis a shame you will have to leave it behind when you return to London yourself."

A smile remained on his extremely handsome face, and a humorous gleam lit his cobalt eyes.

She knew he was enjoying himself, enjoying their banter. The trouble was so was *she*.

"Bobby, go fetch Mr. Stevens and tell him we are in need of a judge," James said.

Seemingly oblivious to the tension in the room, Bobby departed.

"I do enjoy you, Bella," James said.

His voice, deep and sensual, sent a ripple of awareness through her. "I'm glad I can entertain you, Your Grace."

She regretted the words as soon as they left her lips, for his eyes raked her form as if she wasn't fully dressed, but naked for his pleasure.

The door opened and Anthony Stevens arrived with Bobby.

"A pleasure to see you again, Mrs. Sinclair." Anthony's pitch-black eyes studied Bella. "I was told you are in need of a judge." Anthony started forward, and Bella noticed that despite his tall, broad-shouldered frame, the barrister moved like a panther across the room.

James rose; Anthony occupied the chair behind the desk.

"Anthony sits in the judge's perch." James moved a small chair beside the desk. "And this is the witness stand, where you are to sit as the first witness." He held the chair for Bella.

"What am I to do?" she asked.

"Pretend I am on trial for a crime," James said. "Let's say theft and burglary, which occurred two months prior."

"That will not be difficult."

"Good. You are to play my lover."

"I will not!"

"You are *acting,* Bella. This is for educational purposes, remember? To help Bobby."

Bella liked Bobby, and from the excited, eager look on his young face, she could not refuse without disappointing the lad.

By the mischievous grin on James's face, he knew it as well.

Evelyn's words came back to Bella: *You challenge him, Bella, and it is driving him to distraction, making him helpless.* Bella smiled a secret smile. She'd love to drive James to distraction and make him helpless right now.

Bella nodded her consent. "All right, Your Grace. We shall be lovers. For Bobby."

From the judge's perch, Anthony Stevens chuckled.

James's smile cracked a bit. "As I was saying. I'm on trial for theft and burglary. As my lover, you are my alibi at the time of the crime. Bobby is my defense barrister."

"He is not the Crown's prosecution?"

"No. As defense barristers, our job is to present the best possible defense for our clients and to ensure a fair trial against the Crown's prosecution. Bobby is to obtain testimony showing that we were together at the time of the crime. You are Mrs. Lovelace, and I am Mr. Smith."

Bella sat up straight and folded her hands in her lap. "Very well. I'm ready."

Bobby walked up to the mock witness stand and cleared his throat. "Mrs. Lovelace, is it true you are Mr. Smith's lover?"

James jumped to his feet. "Remember what I taught you, Bobby. You are not permitted to ask leading questions on direct examination of your own witness. Leading questions are allowed on cross-examination only. A good prosecutor would object."

"I'm sorry. I forgot," Bobby said.

"It's all right, lad," James said. "Think of another way to ask the same question of your witness."

Bobby cleared his throat again and looked at Bella. "Mrs. Lovelace, what is your relationship with the accused, Mr. Smith?"

"We are lovers," Bella answered. "We have engaged in all types of sordid and lustful acts."

"I see," Bobby said. "And as lovers, how much time do you spend together?"

Bella batted her lashes. "Ah, well, we used to spend every night together. But I'm afraid Mr. Smith's performance has declined over the past three weeks. To be delicate about it, his advanced age has affected his manhood's performance, you see, and as a woman of great appetites and urges, I've had to supplement my bed sport with younger, more virile men."

There was a roar of laughter from Anthony Stevens.

Bobby stared, agape.

"You're diverging from your script," James snapped.

Bella gave him a look of pure innocence. "I wasn't aware of any script, merely that we are lovers."

Anthony pounded his fist on the desk. "Let her be, James. Her speech is perfect, just the sort of unexpected and damaging testimony barristers are often faced with from their own witnesses on the stand. It's a good exercise for Bobby. See how the lad handles it."

Bobby snapped to attention and continued with his line of questioning. "So your testimony is that you have taken other lovers because of Mr. Smith's"—Bobby pointed to James—"lack of performance?"

"Oh, yes," Bella said.

James looked like he wanted to throttle her.

Perfect.

If a challenge could unnerve and distract him, then she needed every advantage.

"But your testimony is that you have only recently taken other lovers over the past three weeks, correct?" Bobby asked.

"Yes."

"And the alleged crime had occurred two months ago. So were you with Mr. Smith that night?"

"Yes, I must have been."

"Bravo!" Anthony Stevens shouted. "See how well you turned Mrs. Lovelace's damaging testimony around? You still showed that she is a solid alibi for your client."

Bobby's face spread into a smile like a child given a new toy. "I hope to be half as good a barrister as both of you one day," Bobby told James and Anthony.

James slapped Bobby on the back. The lad departed with Anthony, leaving Bella alone with James in the library.

"You tutor Bobby. Why?" Bella asked him.

"You mean why would I waste my time on a servant?" James said.

"I didn't mean to imply—"

"Bobby's a bastard whose father never gave a fig about him. I believe the status of one's birth shouldn't dictate his life. He's a bright boy with a lot of potential."

"You see yourself in the lad."

James shrugged nonchalantly. "I suppose."

Bella wasn't fooled. He had to feel greatly on the matter to take the time to tutor the boy. Was he reminded of his own father's abandonment?

"I'd like to help," she said. "I'm not fluent in Latin, but I am a solid writer. I can tutor Bobby in grammar."

"You are full of surprises, Bella. What do you write?"

The letter from the *Times* was still in her skirt pocket. She had briefly forgotten about it when she had walked in the library, but now the urge to tear it open and read the editor's response was overwhelming.

He was studying her intently, as if her response meant a great deal to him, and she found herself wanting desperately to confess her secret. What was it about this man that unnerved her so?

He took a step closer. "You're fidgeting. I've had years of practice reading witnesses' physical responses, and I suspect there is something of the utmost importance you are bursting with the need to tell me. Please do not leave me in a state of suspense."

She stared into the blue enigma of his eyes and wondered if he knew the effect he had on her. Taking a breath, she spoke in as reasonable a voice as she could manage. "I've written a political piece and submitted it to the *Times*."

"On what topic?"

"The Cotton Factories Regulation Act that was passed on February seventh of this year. The act sets forth that children aged nine to sixteen years are limited to working twelve hours per day—seventy-two hours per week. No system was devised, however, to enforce the Act."

"Go on," he said.

At the eager gleam of interest in his eyes, she gained confidence to continue. "My article points out that there is not much difference between this act and the Factory Act of 1802. The working hours imposed on our young children are abominable. Without the benefit of schooling, the children will never better themselves and will continue to be slaves to the factory owners. Most importantly, without governmental inspections to enforce conditions or internal supervision to ensure the laws are followed, how can parliament expect any factory owner to follow the law?"

"Fascinating," he said. "Utterly fascinating."

She eyed him warily. "The truth is I've never been published."

"So?"

"You do not think it inappropriate for a woman to write such a political piece?"

"To the contrary, I think it commendable," he said. "I also find the fact that you had the courage to submit your work to the *Times* admirable. Many writers are plagued by self-doubt and rarely send out their work for fear of rejection or criticism. So you must tell me, did they agree to publish it?"

She felt a thrill of joy at his words. Whatever hesitation she had felt at reading the letter in his presence vanished. She pulled the envelope out of her pocket. "I received the editor's response today, but haven't opened it yet."

"Well? What are you waiting for?"

"I had hoped to read it in private."

"I shall leave at once," he said.

"No. Stay. If it is a rejection, I'd like to share a drink with someone."

His voice was calm, his gaze steady. "I have faith in you."

She tore open the envelope and read out loud.

Dear Mr. Adams,

Upon reading your submission, we would like to publish your article in our opinion section. I am enclosing a draft in the amount of ten shillings, our standard payment for a first article. We would also be interested in seeing any future opinion pieces. It is my understanding that your health prohibits you from traveling to our London office. Kindly advise in writing if pursuing an arrangement with our newspaper would be open to discussion.

Ludlow Harper, Editor-In-Chief

"It sold!" Without thinking, she threw herself in his arms and kissed him on the cheek. As she stepped to move back, his arms tightened around her, and he held her against him. Her breath caught in her throat at the hardness and warmth of his embrace.

But just as quickly he released her and looked into her eyes. "The only surprising item in that letter is the use of your pen name, Mr. Adams. As a professional writer, could you not think of something more creative?" he asked.

"Such as?"

"Mr. Roundbottom or Mr. Beeswax or Mr. Longtooth comes to mind."

She giggled.

"How about a celebratory toast?" he asked.

"Yes, that sounds lovely."

James went to a sideboard in the corner of the room.

Bella watched as he poured two glasses of amber-colored alcohol. He wasn't wearing a jacket, and the taut line of his shoulders strained against his white shirt. She was acutely conscious of his tall frame, his movements both graceful and virile. Even his hands were beautiful, long-fingered and strong. She remembered his hands and the way they had made her tremble as they explored the hollows of her back, her waist . . . her breast.

He turned and handed her a glass. "A toast," he said. "To your first of many publication credits."

She looked at the glass. "What is it?"

"Fine scotch whiskey. Try it."

She took a sip. The alcohol burned her throat and every inch of her esophagus on the way down. She sputtered and coughed.

He laughed a deep rich sound. "I apologize. I did not bring any champagne with me from London."

"No matter. I'm celebrating!" A warm glow flowed through her; whether it was from the whiskey or her current happiness she couldn't tell. She knew only that she was blissfully happy, fully alive, and she was sharing the moment with a handsome duke who had surprised her with his words of praise and encouragement.

"Did your late husband know you were a writer?" James asked.

"Yes, but he did not approve."

"Then he was a fool."

Her pulse leapt at his words. Never had she expected a man to approve of her writing endeavors.

"While you are in a celebratory mood," he said, "there's something else I'd like to discuss with you."

"Please tell me you will not ruin the moment by bringing up property ownership."

He grimaced in good humor. "I wouldn't dare. The old duke hosted an annual fair during the first week of June for Wyndmoor's tenants and servants. It was the only holiday for them other than Christmas. The servants may be new, but they have been working hard, and I'd like to follow the tradition."

"Which servants? Yours or mine?"

"Both, my dear. In addition, my colleagues and the Hardings must return to London. They are busy barristers with full dockets. Their brief visit, no matter how delightful, must end. I would like to host the fair at the end of the week before their departure."

She eyed him above the rim of her glass. "Don't you also have your own cases waiting in London? From what you said, your claim to the title was unexpected."

"Anthony, Brent, and Jack have agreed to take on my case-load and ease the transition for my former clients. But truth be told, I had thought to return to London by now."

If it wasn't for her remained unspoken.

At her silence, he prodded, "Come now, Bella. We could all benefit from a day of games and fresh air."

"I suppose you are correct, Your Grace. The servants have been working hard."

"Shall we agree upon a temporary truce for the games then?"

She found herself smiling. "Yes. A truce."

"You should have been there! Bella called James's man-hood into question. She even went so far as to say his 'ad-vanced age' affected his sexual performance," Anthony said.

Brent let out a bark of laughter. "I'd pay to have been a fly on the wall."

"I was also in the billiard room with Anthony. Why didn't you summon me to be the judge for your mock court?" Jack asked.

James glared at his friends. He had met Anthony, Brent, and Jack at the Twin Rams that night, and James had known the moment he set foot in the tavern he would be fodder for their teasing.

A barmaid sidled over and hovered near Brent Stone. She smiled coyly at him and brushed her large breasts against his sleeve. Brent barely glanced at her, and said, "Four tankards of your best ale."

For years James had thought women's attention to Brent a waste, until he realized his friend was not as uninterested as he appeared. The signs—a tenseness of Brent's jaw and a quick sideways glance at the barmaid—were slight and one needed a keen eye to catch them. There was a mysterious element to Brent Stone. A dangerous undercurrent that he suppressed behind his façade of hardworking patent barrister. Whenever anyone brought up Brent's past, he would immediately clam up. James had never minded as he never wanted to speak of his own past.

The tankards were delivered, and Brent spoke up. "I never thought the day would come. A woman James Devlin can't seduce."

"More than that," Anthony said. "She has a splendid sense of humor, and she stands up to him."

"Evelyn is quite enamored of Bella," Jack said. "My wife says Bella remains adamant about her ownership of the property."

James shot Jack Harding a dark look. "Your wife would represent her in court if she could," he said dryly.

Jack turned his smile up a notch. "She'd probably be victorious, too."

James raised his tankard and drank. He wasn't surprised that Jack supported his wife. Evelyn was friendly by nature, but what James hadn't anticipated was Bella's genuine warmth and hospitality toward Evelyn.

After that first night, when Bella had stormed down the stairs and accused James of bringing a ladybird into the house, she had instantly changed her behavior and had welcomed the Hardings with open arms even though they were close acquaintances of James's. Bella wasn't the cold, bitter widow he had initially thought. In fact, nothing about her was what he had initially believed.

"I warned you not to treat her like one of your London doxies," Brent said.

"She has a spine," Anthony said. "If I could stay and witness the outcome of this battle of wills between you two, I would. Unfortunately, Lord Stafford is disgruntled by his conspiring wife and mother-in-law, and I must return to chambers and work on his marital dilemmas."

"Good grief, Anthony. Why do you insist on practicing the type of law you do?" Brent muttered.

Anthony turned hard eyes on Brent. "I told you before. I enjoy it."

Anthony's clipped tone, massive size, and menacing expression spoke volumes, but Brent wasn't the least disturbed.

"Don't be an ass, Anthony," Brent said. "How can you enjoy the strife between squabbling spouses? You should stop before your disgruntled clients drive you completely mad."

James spoke up before the bickering between two friends turned into a full-blown fight. "We're holding an annual fair this Friday at Wyndmoor."

Three pairs of eyes turned to him.

"I thought to celebrate with my friends before you leave, and the spring fair was a tradition of the old duke's," James said.

"And Bella agreed?" Jack asked.

James shrugged. "I mentioned it when she was in a celebratory mood."

"Pray tell us, what was she celebrating?" Jack asked.

"She sold a political piece to the *Times,*" James said.

Brent leaned forward in his seat. "She's a writer?"

"Yes, a *professional* writer, now," James found himself saying.

"The *Times,* you say? I know the editor. His hide is as tough as a rhinoceros. It's quite an accomplishment on her part," Anthony said.

A vivid image came to James of Bella tearing open the envelope and the joy written on her face after reading the news, and then, as she threw herself into his arms. Suddenly, it had felt like a blazing-hot August afternoon. But even more dangerous than her luscious curves pressed against his body had been her jovial laughter and delight over her first sale of her work. When she had lifted her face and revealed her dazzling smile, he had felt her happiness as if it were his own.

He had wanted her dream to become a reality, and it had taken every ounce of willpower not to pick her up and twirl her about.

Ridiculous.

Why should he care? Was he losing his edge, his firm resolve, when it came to Bella?

"She's determined and intelligent? You best rethink your plans, James," Brent warned.

"You had said she's guarded about her past," Anthony said. "You wanted Investigator Papazian to look into the matter. Has the man unearthed anything?"

"I have an appointment with the man after the fair. His note said there were items to discuss," James said.

"I'd be curious as to what a country widow could be hiding," Anthony said.

James drew his lips in thoughtfully. "So am I."

Chapter 13

The morning of the fair dawned bright and sunny. Bella stood on the lawn, looking forward to watching the wide array of games that she and the staff had arranged at the duke's request.

A large washtub filled with water, which would later be used to bob for apples, sat on the far side of the lawn. Four empty wheelbarrows stood ready for races; there would also be footraces, sack races, and even a race to climb a pole greased with duck fat. A table had been set up outside, and Mrs. O'Brien had outdone herself with a wide array of sweet rolls and puddings. Pitchers of lemonade were poised to quench the thirst of the participants of the games.

Harriet and the wives of the tenant farmers sat beneath a large oak conversing; others, servants and the male farmers, prepared to join the games. One of the footmen leaned against the refreshment table, playing a Scottish tune on a hand-made flute.

A burst of laughter and a flash of white at the corner of her eye drew Bella's attention.

A shuttlecock whirled through the air and landed at Bobby's feet. "I'll never learn!" Bobby shouted, waving his small racket in the air.

"Let me show you, lad," James said as he loped over to the boy and demonstrated how to swing his battledore to hit the elusive shuttlecock.

Bella's gaze turned to James. He was once again dressed casually in his shirt and breeches, and it occurred to her that other than when he had first arrived in his crested carriage, he rarely wore formal attire. The top two buttons of his shirt were undone, revealing a sprinkling of hair at the V of his open collar. A lock of dark hair fell over his forehead as he leaned forward to patiently instruct Bobby in the fine art of how to hit a shuttlecock with the small racket.

After several attempts, Bobby threw the shuttlecock high in the air and successfully hit it with his racket. The boy jumped up and down with glee, and James's blue eyes twinkled with delight.

Bella's heart did a little jump. She couldn't help but acknowledge the duke was a finely made man. He had an innately captivating presence, and as that was combined with his devastatingly good looks, she understood why many society women found him deliciously appealing.

Three more boys ran up to James, and she recognized them as the children of the tenant farmers. James handed each of them rackets and proceeded to teach them how to play. The fact that the children batted at the shuttlecocks without the slightest hint of talent did not dissuade James in the least. He was easygoing and good-natured, and he seemed to genuinely enjoy himself.

She should have known he would be good with children. Over the course of the week, every single one of her negative beliefs about the Duke of Blackwood had been shattered.

He wasn't a typical aristocrat, born into a life of leisure and luxury. To the contrary, he had been raised to believe he was a bastard and had been treated abominably by his own family, only to overcome great odds and become a successful, self-made man. He was a selfish and greedy barrister, she had thought, yet he'd agreed to build a new cottage for Wynd-moor's tenants and repair their roofs with funds from his own pocket. He had taken an illegitimate boy off the streets and under his wing and had employed him. But James hadn't stopped there; he tutored the boy to follow in his footsteps in the hope that one day he would become a barrister.

Most shocking of all, he hadn't mocked her when she had told him of her writing ambitions, but had praised her efforts, going so far as to call her courageous for submitting her work; and he had celebrated alongside her when she had sold her first piece. After Roger, never had she suspected a man could be supportive of her writing.

The duke's friends arrived, their arms full of sporting equipment, and joined the festivities. A game of lawn bowls started on the far patch of lawn. Bella watched as Brent Stone and Anthony Stevens paired off against the duke and Jack Harding.

Each team received its own color bowls, brown or yellow, and the smaller white "jack" was thrown. After their first bowl, Brent and Jack went for their respective teams, their bowls stopping close to each other. Anthony went next, his brown bowl just grazing the jack and resting right beside it. At James's turn, he knocked his opponent's bowl away from the jack to score a point. Jack cheered and slapped James on the back. Anthony and Brent scowled, then laughed and issued cocky challenges full of male bravado as they retrieved their bowls to continue the game.

Bella's father had once said that one could discern much about a man's character by the type of friends he kept. The duke's friends, even the daunting and intimidating Anthony Stevens, were respectful toward her. All were successful barristers and loyal to each other. Only Jack Harding was married, and if the choice of his spouse reflected upon his character, then he was an upstanding man to have won the heart of the delightful Lady Evelyn.

Evelyn joined Bella on the lawn. "What a wonderful spring day for us to enjoy."

Bella looked up at the cloudless sky. Sun bathed the lawn with dazzling light and warmth. It was as if James had ordered the pleasant weather and Mother Nature had gladly obliged.

Shouts from the lawn sounded, and the women turned to see that two of the yellow bowls were closest to the white jack.

"Look! Jack and the duke earned two more points!" Evelyn cried out, cheering enthusiastically for her husband.

An odd twinge of jealousy stirred inside Bella. *Lady Evelyn truly adores her husband and her happiness is clearly written on her face for all to see.*

Bella had once been a naïve young woman who believed in the fairytale of the knight in shining armor proclaiming undying love for his lady. Then Bella had the misfortune of marrying Roger Sinclair, and her illusions had crumbled around her like a poorly built cottage during a windstorm. She had never desired to remarry after Roger; she had no longer believed in a perfect union between a man and a woman. But gazing at Evelyn Harding, she realized perhaps she was wrong. . . .

The men shouted as a goal was made, and Bella's attention returned to the game. The truth was she was mesmerized by this fun-loving side of James. His intelligent eyes shone with pleasure, and he encouraged the servants to join in on the game. He had once confessed that Wyndmoor Manor was where he could be himself, where he truly felt like the duke's son, and she could see it now in his relaxed demeanor.

An instant's squeezing guilt pierced her chest. She was the only obstacle in his way. . . .

She made to turn when he spotted her.

"Bella, you are just the person I was looking for." He walked toward her and extended his hand. "We need another player for the leg races."

She placed her hand in his. "Leg races?"

"It's simple," he said, holding up a shoelace. "We tie one leg of each partner together and race to the finish line. Evelyn will surely partner with her husband, leaving me the odd man out. What do you say?"

Bella was caught off guard by his cheery smile. "I'm not very good at physical sports. Perhaps another partner will do you justice—"

"Nonsense."

"Do join us, Bella," Evelyn encouraged. "It will be such fun."

Before Bella could think of another response, James knelt and lifted the hem of her skirt a demure inch. He proceeded to wrap the shoelace around her ankle, securing it to his own. Guiding her to a chalked line in the grass, they lined up beside four other pairs of contestants.

Coates waved a flag and they were off.

Three steps in to the race, Jack and Evelyn fell to their right and a pair of servants stumbled to their left. Bella giggled as they struggled to find a rhythm to their steps. James's arm went around her waist, and his warmth enveloped her. She was conscious of the occasional jolt of his muscular thigh brushing her hip, and her skin prickled pleasurably. She was filled with a strange excitement as the thrill of competition raced through her, and they hobbled closer to the finish line.

"We're almost there!" he shouted.

They stumbled through the finish line and fell together, Bella somehow landing on top of James.

"Oh!" she cried out.

Every inch of his body was solid beneath hers. She was aware of his strength and the heat of his flesh. Her heart jolted, and her breasts tingled against the fabric of her dress. Their position was horribly improper, but he was laughing, a rich pleasant sound. She felt the rumbling of his chest beneath hers, and with a giddy sense of pleasure, she too broke into laughter.

He rose awkwardly, helped her to her feet, and untied the lacing at their ankles.

"We won!" She smiled up at him.

He reached out to pluck a blade of grass from her hair. "Indeed. I had no doubt."

His gaze was soft as a caress, and she struggled to restrain the dizzying current racing through her. A sensuous light passed between them, like a warm, topical breeze across her skin.

Bobby's voice broke the moment. "Time to climb the greased pole!"

The lad's face flushed with eagerness, and Bella glanced up at James. "You should know the ladies are placing wagers on which man will reach the top first, Your Grace."

James grinned. "I'm a sure win." He raised her hand and brushed his lips across her fingers. She inhaled sharply, a rush of warmth flashing over her. He lifted his head, his compelling blue eyes studying her. "Thank you for partnering with me, Bella."

He turned on his heel and jogged to the pole with Bobby by his side. Bella stared at his back, her heart thumping uncomfortably. She was weakening toward him. Nothing had changed regarding their property battle, and yet it was pointless to deny her attraction to him. Her growing feelings had nothing to do with logic or reason.

It was madness on her part, pure madness.

She stood as if in a daze and waited until her quickened pulse returned to normal, then wandered to the refreshment table. Picking up an empty pitcher, she decided to return to the house. She needed privacy, time alone to think and calm her nerves. She wove her way through the house and to the kitchen and was refilling the pitcher with fresh lemonade when the scrape of footsteps on the tiles made her turn.

Harriet entered the kitchen. "You should be outside enjoying yourself."

"I saw no need to bother the servants," Bella said, "and the children need more lemonade."

Harriet's shrewd eyes studied Bella's face. "You are avoiding him."

Bella's chin rose. "I am not." She realized as soon as the words left her lips that inquiring about whom Harriet referred to had never occurred to her.

"The duke is not hiding, but seems to be thoroughly enjoying himself," Harriet said.

Bella experienced a sudden bitterness and frustration. As the days passed, James seemed to be enjoying time with his friends and the country life, while she was consumed with thoughts of the property dispute—or worse—thoughts of him.

"He must be confident in his victory over me. Why else do you think he is so at ease?" Bella said.

"You seek my opinion?" Harriet asked.

"I do."

Harriet stepped close to touch Bella's sleeve. "My opinion is that Blackwood is a handsome and charming man who is shrewdly intelligent and who wields the power of a dukedom. He's accustomed to women swaying at his feet and has never had to work hard to seduce one into his arms. The combination of looks and power make him a worthy opponent, but what makes him a *dangerous* opponent is the challenge you pose."

"Because I will not hand over the property on a bloody platter?" Bella said.

"No. Because you are as unattainable as the place. He wants you, Bella. Just as fiercely as he wants Wyndmoor."

"How on earth do you know that?"

"I was young once, and there were men in my life. I know when a man lusts after a woman."

"Harriet!"

Harriet took the pitcher from Bella's limp hands and set it

on the table. "Don't look so shocked. Blackwood desires you. A blind woman could see it."

"If what you say is true, then what would you have me do to be rid of him?"

"I don't believe the answer to our problems is to get rid of the man. To the contrary, the answer just might be to draw him closer, encourage his affections—"

Bella eyed her incredulously. "Are you suggesting I seduce him?"

"Not seduce him, Bella. But encourage his amorous feelings."

"You think if I bed him, he will hand the place over in gratitude?"

Harriet's lips thinned. "I'm not speaking of a passing lustful affair, but a more permanent position."

"You mean marriage? He is a duke. He can marry any titled debutante or heiress he wishes. Women will flock to him upon his return to London."

"But he is here now, luv, and by the looks of him the only woman who has caught his eye is you."

"Lust is not love," Bella argued. "I refuse to be any man's mistress, and I swore never to marry again after Roger."

Harriet squeezed Bella's hand. "That's just it. Roger was a bad man, a rotten man, and I'd hate to see you avoid remarrying because of him. You are beautiful and good-hearted and too young to spend the rest of your days alone. You deserve a good man, someone you can share your life with and have a family with."

"Do you honestly believe the duke is a good man?"

"I do. Both the servants and the tenant farmers are fond of him. And unlike Roger, the duke has never suggested that I leave, even though at my advanced age he could have insisted upon my dismissal."

At Bella's silence, Harriet pressed on. "Think about it, Bella. You could keep Wyndmoor Manor, be a *duchess*."

Bella should have found the thought of marriage abhorrent, but for a brief instant, she allowed herself to consider the notion. Could Harriet be right about James? Could the memory of her seven dismal years spent as Roger's wife be erased—or, at the least, diminished? As the Duke of Blackwood's wife, she could keep Wyndmoor and have financial security.

Then reality intruded. From everything she knew and had heard, James was a rogue, a womanizer who had only recently come into his title. He was in no rush to the altar. And if by some miracle he was looking for a wife, the untitled widow of a Plymouth businessman would hardly be his first choice.

Bella embraced her maid. "Oh, Harriet. You pose the impossible and are ever the dreamer." She picked up the full pitcher and made for the door. "I need to return. The children are waiting for their lemonade."

"You'll think about what I said?" Harriet asked.

"I will." How could she not? Observing James today had allowed Bella to see him in yet another light—which she knew was perilous for her heart, because she found herself yearning for deeply buried desires and dreams long forgotten.

Chapter 14

Hours later, the games were over and everyone sat on blankets spread out on the lawn enjoying lemonade and sweet rolls. James and his fellow barristers told jokes and laughed with Bobby and the other children.

The heat of the afternoon sun ebbed, and Harriet and Mrs. O'Brien directed the servants to carry the plates and cups inside. Soon after, a large coach and team of six arrived and stood ready in the drive to return the duke's friends to London.

"It's been a pleasure," Brent Stone said, bowing politely to Bella.

An odd amusement flashed in Anthony Stevens's obsidian eyes. "I'm certain we will see each other again, Mrs. Sinclair."

Bella curtsied. She had no intention of seeing Anthony Stevens again and had no idea as to what the tall barrister referred. The only trip Bella planned to London would be to meet with the solicitor Evelyn had recommended.

Evelyn stepped forward to embrace Bella warmly and whispered in her ear, "Please contact me when you are in London."

"I promise," Bella whispered back.

Evelyn's husband helped her into the coach, and the footman shut the door. With a low whistle from the driver, the wheels of the coach crunched over the graveled drive. James waved to his friends from the front steps when Bella turned to enter the house.

"Bella," he called out, "will you walk with me? There's something of interest I want to show you."

At his sudden, arresting smile, she felt a moment's uncertainty. Harriet's words rushed back to her.

Encourage his amorous feelings. You could keep Wyndmoor Manor, be a duchess.

Could she do it? Looking into his handsome face, her pulse quickened at the idea of marrying him, of knowing him intimately as a man.

He must have mistaken her hesitation as a refusal for he walked forward and said, "It will take but a moment."

"All right." She walked down the front steps and they headed down the graveled drive, but instead of following the path to the gardens, he turned toward the stables.

"Where are we going?"

"You'll see. It's a surprise."

Her curiosity piqued.

The sun was descending, a brilliant orange ball in a painted sky of pinks, grays, and blues. Gently sloping lawns and a field of buttercups dotted the country landscape. They came to the stables, and she thought he meant to go inside, but instead he led her around the perimeter of the building to the back.

A strange-looking contraption rested against an oak tree. Consisting of a curved wooden frame, it had two large in-line wooden wheels and a wide handlebar assembly in the front.

"It's a swiftwalker!" she cried out.

"You've seen one?" he asked, clearly surprised.

"Not in person, but I've seen a sketch in the newspaper. The article said they are all the rage and the dandies are riding them in London. They are even calling them *dandy horses.*"

He chuckled. "It's all true, but its proper name is a velocipede."

She approached the velocipede and ran her hand down the wood frame. "How does one ride it?"

"This one was made for a shorter man, but I can still show you." He straddled the frame and held on to both ends of the handlebar while his feet touched the ground. He pushed along the ground with his feet, and as he pivoted the handlebar, the front wheel turned and allowed him to steer. Then he started to run, increasing his speed. She clapped and burst out laughing.

He stopped beside her.

"Where did you find it?" she asked.

"It belonged to Reeves. Bobby found it mounted on the back wall of the stables." He pointed to an etching on the frame. "This particular one bears the mark of its inventor, Denis Johnson, a London coachmaker. Brent Stone obtained the letters patent for the man last December."

Bella's lips twitched. "I can just imagine Sir Reeves riding it in London, strutting around like a peacock and showing off."

James rolled his eyes. "Such an unsavory image." His smile changed and he looked at her in earnest. "Do you want to ride it?"

She did and desperately. But how would she straddle it with her skirts?

As if reading her mind, his gaze traveled her morning dress. "Don't worry about your skirts. We're behind the stables and no one can see. You're free to ride."

"But you're here."

He winked. "I promise to look away. Go ahead. Try it."

She lifted her skirts and swung her right leg over the frame. The tips of her toes reached the ground. She pushed off and began walking, slowly at first, then faster.

"Don't forget to steer!" James said as she came perilously close to riding into the oak tree.

"You said you wouldn't look!"

"I'm not looking at your legs, just your form."

The statement seemed so ridiculous she laughed. She didn't stop riding, however, and kept her speed. It was daring and fun and he shouted out words of encouragement. She rode in a large circle behind the stables for a full ten minutes until her legs tired, and she dismounted and rested the velocipede against the oak.

She was breathless and flushed, and yet she felt as joyfully buoyant as a child on Christmas morning. James was the most exciting man she had ever known, and her already vulnerable feelings toward him were intensifying.

"I knew a woman courageous enough to write and sell her work would be daring enough to ride a velocipede," he said, with his irresistible grin.

His words and nearness made her senses spin. She licked her bottom lip, and his gaze dropped to her mouth. "I find myself daring to try new things of late," she said.

Awareness passed between them, like the crackle in the air before lightning strikes. His eyes darkened to sapphire, and he pulled her into his arms and kissed her. His mouth covered hers hungrily. She wound her arms about his neck, and kissed him back, lingering, savoring every moment. This was what she wanted, what felt right.

He must have felt it too because his kiss, his very taste and essence, felt different.

His hands were everywhere at once—in the hollow of her back, at the curve of her waist, and higher still to cup her breast. When his thumb grazed her hardening nipple through the thin fabric of her gown, she gasped and drew herself closer. The scent of the outdoors on his skin, the warmth of his palm on her breast, and the velvet stroke of his tongue spun a magical web of raw need and sweet desire, which she knew had the power to bury and replace the dreaded memories of Roger's sordid touch.

Her blood pounded, her muscles tensed, her body aching

and battling the remnants of her self-control for a taste of what he offered.

He understood. She saw it in his eyes when he lifted his head, his hands cradling her face. "There's something I must ask you, Bella. I was uncertain at first with our fight over the property, but no longer. Such an arrangement will solve our dilemma."

Harriet was right! He's going to propose!

He kissed her forehead, her cheek, the nape of her neck. "We both want each other, darling. There's no denying the attraction and passion between us. You can stay at Wyndmoor for as long as you wish to remain."

His tongue flicked the sensitive shell of her ear, and a delicious shudder heated her body.

"You needn't worry about finances. All will be taken care of, your clothes, your carriage, the servants." He emphasized each word with the brush of his lips across her collarbone. "I have business I must regularly attend to in London, of course, but I promise to return often. You needn't fear anything," he murmured. "I know how to prevent an unwanted child."

His lips were wreaking havoc with her senses, and her mind was sluggish to comprehend. *Unwanted child?* What was he saying? She was dimly aware that he hadn't knelt down on one knee, hadn't proposed. Understanding dawned, and with it a simmering anger.

Crestfallen, her smile quickly faded, and she pulled back. "You want me to be your mistress?"

His brow furrowed. "I never liked that term—"

She pushed him away suddenly and took a step back. Her eyes narrowed, and outrage stiffened her spine. Reaching up, she slapped him.

His expression was taut and derisive. "I take that to be a no."

Why couldn't he be an old, ugly, wrinkled man? Why did he have to be so attractive?

Dark eyebrows slanted in a frown. "You cannot still be pining for your husband," he said. "I know there were no fond feelings between you."

How dare he! "Did Evelyn speak with you?"

"No."

"Then what makes you believe I disliked my husband?"

"I'm quite astute and have drawn my own conclusions regarding the level of passion in your marriage," he said.

"Then your intuition is not as honed as you believe, Your Grace. What I do believe is that your man has been following me. I spotted him when I was shopping in St. Albans. Did you tell him to look into my past as well?"

A fierce shaft of blue fire shot at her before his gaze shuttered. "You're being followed? By whom?"

She had come to suspect the man outside the bakery in St. Albans was James's hired investigator. As for the man at the Black Hound, she had been too distraught after escaping the bar fight and, in hindsight, couldn't be certain they were the same person.

The fury within her now throbbed in her voice. "*I* do not know. I'm certain only that you hired an investigator to look into matters, to look into me."

"You're wrong. The investigator I hired has succeeded only in locating Sir Reeves. I never instructed him to follow you, and he has told me nothing of your marital relationship."

"Your instincts about me remained flawed, Your Grace. I'll never be your mistress or your lover or whatever term it is you do prefer!" Turning on her heel, she fled toward the house.

"You've been spotted," James said.

"That's impossible."

James had met Investigator Armen Papazian in the library. After the disastrous scene with Bella outside the stables, he had learned that she had stormed into her bedchamber and had not come down since. This suited James just fine, he told himself, as he had an appointment to meet with the investigator.

James paced the room. Papazian occupied an armchair by the window. The investigator was a short, but muscularly built man with black, unruly hair and olive-black eyes leveled under drawn brows. The man's features appeared deceptively composed, but James caught the uncanny shrewdness in his gaze.

Anthony Stevens swore the investigator was the best. So successful, in fact, that he had unearthed secret letters between a viscountess and her French lover who had happened to be a general in Napoleon's army. The letters revealed the names of two members of the British army who had aided the French by selling them military secrets. The Regent's top agents had been searching for the letters for two years without success before Papazian found them a month before Waterloo.

"She didn't see me," Papazian insisted. "If she noticed someone else following her, it was another man."

James stopped his pacing. "It makes no sense. Why would someone else be following her?"

"Maybe it has to do with her deceased husband's business ventures."

"Tell me what you've learned."

"Roger Sinclair was a well-respected and wealthy Plymouth businessman. He specialized in importing commodities, mainly grain, barley, coal, and timber. His young wife rarely left home, and upon inquiry of the Plymouth townsfolk, people said she was 'not of sound mind,' and some went so far as to say she had gone mad. They sympathized with Roger over his wife's infirmity and admired that he had not left her."

"That's ludicrous. Bella is far from mad," James said.

"I tracked down Sinclair's former steward. The man was tight-lipped at first, but he's also a drunkard and was easy to bribe with a few guineas. He said Sinclair acted the perfect gentleman outside the home; he regularly attended church and donated generously, but at home, he was a tyrannical bastard and rigid master. He had a jealous and obsessive nature and rarely permitted his wife to leave the house for fear she would cuckold him. There were incidents of beatings, and he had frequently threatened to harm his wife's elderly nursemaid if she defied him."

A flash of pure rage shot down James's spine, and he clenched his fists at his sides.

"There's more," Papazian said. "Despite Roger Sinclair's public persona as avid churchgoer and supporter, he was a greedy bloke and consumed with increasing his fortune. After war with France broke out, Sinclair's trade suffered and he began engaging in questionable activities. He started small, importing French brandy and other embargoed goods, but soon grew emboldened and began exporting guns and ammunition to the French troops. Roger Sinclair's highly treasonous activities were never discovered by the authorities, and he died six months ago when he fell down the stairs while intoxicated and broke his neck."

"The reprobate died an easy death," James said. "The punishment for treason is to be drawn and quartered."

James thought of Sinclair's abominable treatment of Bella, and his blood simmered in his veins. He vividly recalled her excitement upon opening the letter from the *Times*. She had said her husband had not approved of her writing. And then there was her instinctive response to his touch, his kiss. Each time he held her she had molded her body to his, pressed against him with innocent ardor. James had known that her marriage had lacked passion. He had mistakenly thought her spouse had been a blundering fool. But now that James knew Roger Sinclair had abused and isolated her—had used Harriet as a weapon—he marveled that Bella's spirit had not been entirely crushed.

Sinclair deserved to be drawn and quartered alive for his treatment of his wife alone.

James took a deep breath to calm his violent emotions.

"As for whom Mrs. Sinclair spotted watching her," Papazian said, "I assure you again it was not me."

"She claims she saw a man when she was shopping," James pointed out.

"I followed both women the day they ventured into St. Albans, but neither noticed me."

So why would anyone else follow Bella? The thought of her in danger made James's gut clench tight. "We need to determine if it was you she saw."

"How can we do that? You don't plan on asking her, do you? During the length of my career, I've yet to find a woman happy to learn a man had her followed," Papazian said dryly.

"Don't be a fool. I'm going to introduce you as an old friend. Let's say, Tom Jones. If you're the man she spotted, I'll be able to tell from her reaction."

It was a simple matter to arrange. Coates mentioned to the parlor maid—just as Harriet was passing by in the hall—that a neighbor and his wife were paying a visit to greet the new owner of Wyndmoor Manor.

As expected, Harriet rushed to tell her mistress, and Bella entered the library within ten minutes' time.

Both James and Investigator Papazian rose to their feet.

The first thing James noticed was she had been crying. There was a rawness about her beautiful green eyes, the delicate skin of her lids swollen. His stomach knotted.

He wanted to go to her, to gather her in his arms and comfort her. He knew she had expected him to propose marriage rather than that she become his mistress. But marriage was too high a price. There had been women who had sought to marry him after he had achieved his success at Lincoln's Inn.

He had never considered proposing to any of them. He coveted his freedom, his bachelorhood. Marriage was to advance one's social status and produce children. Growing up believing he'd been the illegitimate son of a duke, he had always despised the *ton* and never once wanted to join its ranks. And as for children, he liked them—especially young Phillip—but he could not fathom becoming a father himself as his own parent had been mostly absent and disinterested his entire life.

Bella's eyes darted from James to the investigator.

James inclined his head, watching her features. "This is Mr. Jones, an old school friend."

Her brow furrowed. "A school friend? I was told neighbors were visiting."

"Who told you that?" James asked innocently.

Bella's face reddened as she no doubt recalled the source of her knowledge was none other than Harriet's eavesdropping.

James knew her well enough to understand her method of thinking. She was mulling over whether Harriet—at her advanced age—had heard correctly.

But there was no glint of recognition in her eyes as she looked at Investigator Papazian. Clearly, she had never seen the man before.

"Ah, I understand," James said. "You must not believe all the servants' gossip."

Bella's eyes flashed with annoyance before turning to Papazian. "What school did you both attend, Mr. Smith?"

"Eton. We were reminiscing of our youthful days," Papazian lied smoothly.

She smiled politely at the investigator. "I apologize for disturbing you." She curtsied, and the swell of her breasts rose temptingly against the rounded neckline of her gown. The rich browns and reds of her hair contrasted with the ivory skin at her throat.

James tamped down on the stirrings of desire and waited

until the door closed behind Bella before returning his attention to the investigator. "She didn't recognize you."

Papazian shrugged. "I told you."

Sinclair was dead. Then who was following her and why? Had Bella imagined it?

For years she had been under the control of an obsessive and psychotic husband. James himself had tried a case where a wife who had been physically abused for over a decade had finally cracked and stabbed her husband in his sleep.

But Bella didn't fit that type of profile. James's instincts were solid, and he had more than just instinct to rely on where Bella was concerned. Miraculously, her mind and spirit had not been broken by her spouse.

She was intelligent and witty. She had pride and was compassionate and protective of those in her care. He understood pride, as it was all that had held him together during his lonely childhood spurned by his blood kin, and he admired her care of Harriet.

Of all things, Bella Sinclair was certainly not *mad*. If she believed she was being followed, then James had no doubt that it was true.

His heart hammered, and he felt as if his breath was cut off. The physical response was foreign, and with a sense of dread, James recognized it as fear. Fear for Bella.

"Find out who's trailing her and why," he ordered.

Chapter 15

The morning after the fair, Bella rolled over in bed at the soft knock on her door. Harriet entered carrying a breakfast tray and opened the drapes to let in the bright morning sunlight. Bella groaned and covered her face with her pillow.

"You never oversleep, luv," Harriet said, pulling the pillow away.

Bella sat up. Her eyes were swollen and her throat raw. It had been years since she had cried herself to sleep. She had decided long ago that crying over the state of her marriage was not worth the effort; she had refused to shed a tear over Roger.

But last night had been about James.

"I was so certain he would ask me to become his wife, but instead he offered to make me his mistress. I acted like such a fool."

Bella knew she wasn't experienced when it came to men. She had married young and had never had a London Season, whereas James was experienced and worldly. She must have appeared like an immature, lovesick girl. She had allowed herself to dream and resurrect her childish fantasy of the chivalrous knight. As if seven years of misery hadn't beaten the fantasy out of her.

Yet James had made it so easy to fall back into her old ways. He'd been carefree and fun during the fair, and afterwards, when he had shown her the velocipede. He'd called her courageous and daring for writing and selling her work. With a few chosen words of flattery from his lips, she had come close to eagerly handing her deed over to him.

Foolish girl.

"You may have played your cards just right. The duke is not accustomed to women refusing whatever he offers," Harriet said.

"Humph."

"Trust me. You haven't seen the looks of him yet this morning. He's in a foul mood and barking at his dedicated manservant."

"Good. All the servants think him charming; let them see him for who he truly is," Bella snapped.

Harriet removed her riding habit from the wardrobe. "You need fresh air. A pleasant ride in the country will do you good."

Harriet helped her dress, and Bella nibbled toast and sipped her tea before heading straight for the stables.

Bobby wasn't present. Rather than summon the lad, she decided to saddle her own horse. She reached for a bridle hanging from a hook on the stable wall, when an eerily familiar voice froze her hand in midair.

"Hello, Bella."

She whirled around and her heart plummeted in her chest. *Sweet Lord! It's Roger returned from the grave.*

She would have fainted had a vise-like grip not grasped her wrist.

"I see you've forgotten my existence."

Through the roaring din in her ears, his voice was like an echo from an empty tomb. Her head fell back, and she gazed into frightening brown eyes. She opened her mouth to scream, but no sound came out.

He squeezed her wrist painfully, and she snapped to attention. She then noticed the differences. The hair was a darker shade of blond. The shape of the face not oval, but coffin-shaped. The nose, slightly bent as if it had been broken before.

He grinned, and his hard eyes gleamed with distrust, rather than demented obsession.

"Rupert," she whispered.

Roger's twin brother.

"Good, Bella. You haven't forgotten."

"But you died!"

His laughter had a sharp edge. "Is that what Roger told you? We had a disagreement. I can only assume he concocted a story about my demise."

She'd only met Rupert Sinclair once before, and it had been on her wedding day all those years ago. He'd only stayed an hour to wish his brother and new bride well before departing the festivities. Rupert had lived in Somersetshire and apart from his twin since their eighteenth summer until—she was told—he had died of consumption last spring.

Her stomach sank. So what was Rupert doing at Wyndmoor Manor sneaking into the stables?

She wrenched her wrist free. "What do you want?"

"Is that any way to greet your beloved brother-in-law?" he said, his voice heavy with sarcasm.

"Roger's dead. You never came to the funeral."

"Alas, I could not. I was away on business matters and far from Plymouth."

"Why are you here?" she said.

"My twin is dead and some rumors say that you were responsible for his untimely demise."

A ribbon of fear threaded low in her belly. He couldn't know. Could he? "The rumors are lies. Roger fell down the stairs."

His dark eyes were like bits of stone. "I asked a few of his staff. They said he was quarreling with you at the top of the landing. You pushed him down."

"I didn't! He tripped on his own and fell. He was drunk!"

"I wonder if the authorities would believe the same."

"The constable was called, and he concluded rightfully that it was an accident," she insisted.

"But I have a witness that says otherwise."

"Who?"

"Roger's former housekeeper."

"She wasn't there."

Rupert laughed bitterly. "A few shillings and that greedy woman will testify to anything. You would surely languish in prison. What would happen to your beloved nursemaid? Roger told me he often used her as leverage. He enjoyed manipulating and twisting you to his will, Bella." He reached out to tug a wayward curl at her shoulder. "You are even more beautiful than on your wedding day. I can understand my brother's obsession."

Repulsed, she slapped his hand away. "I cannot imagine you have traveled all this way to threaten me. What do you really want, Rupert?"

"It's simple, really. My brother and I were engaged in certain shipping activities—"

"Are you referring to Roger's imports of French brandy, or his illegal exports of guns and ammunition to the French?"

"So you know," he said in a nasty tone. "You always were more intelligent than you let on. I tried to warn Roger, but he was infatuated from the first time he saw you in the village."

Disgust roiled through her. She had found documents that revealed Rupert occasionally had aided Roger with his endeavors, but she had not known to what extent. Looking into his frighteningly similar features, a fierce hatred ran down her spine.

Hatred commingled with a sickening fear.

He turned and it was then that she saw the pistol in his waistband. A shaft of light from the parted stable door glinted off the steel.

She swallowed. "If you're here to find out whether I told anyone of my knowledge, I did not."

"Good, but that's not why I traveled all this way. You were a hard woman to find. I knew you wouldn't remain in Plymouth after Roger had convinced people you were mad, but I was certain you would head for London. I never thought you would buy a country estate until I learned you were living with a man. You wasted no time in finding a benefactor, did you? A duke, no less! I would have filled the position had I known it was open."

"You flatter yourself."

His eyes narrowed to slits. "I've been following you, waiting for the perfect moment to get you alone."

Realization dawned. "It was you in the Black Hound and later in the shopping district." She hadn't lost her mind imagining Roger's ghost.

"Yes. The fight at the bar prevented me from approaching you. As for your excursion in St. Albans, you never separated from your female companion."

"What do you want?"

"Roger kept detailed ledgers of all his business dealings. I want them."

"You can't be serious! Roger kept many, many ledgers."

"We both know he kept two sets of his import/export activities. One for the tax collector to inspect and the other, well, to keep record of his more illicit activities."

Bella knew this. She had stumbled across the second set of books and was reading about Roger's treasonous activities when he had walked in on her. He had never been as furious.

"I don't have his books," she said. "I left Plymouth with only our necessities. The ledgers must still be hidden in the house."

"I purchased the house after you fled. I searched every nook and loose floorboard in the place and came up empty. The ledger isn't there. I suspect Roger hid it in your belongings unbeknownst to you," Rupert said.

"You're jesting."

"The ledger will be simple to find now that you know to look for it. I must have it as it incriminates me as much as it did my twin."

Bitterness spilled over into her voice. "What's to stop me from turning the ledger over to the authorities myself to have *you* sent to prison?"

A lethal calmness lit his eyes. "I'm impressed, but I've thought of that already. Should anything happen to me, I paid a man to drag you before the constable to be tried for my brother's murder and to see to it that your old hag of a nurse-maid suffers in your absence. Find the ledger, give it to me, and you shall never have to set eyes on me again."

Bella felt as if an iron fist tightened around her heart. He would do it, she knew. He could easily bribe Roger's house-keeper to testify to anything he chose. The hint of truth behind the threat made it even more ominous.

Still, the new Bella Sinclair had sworn never to cower to a man again.

She raised her chin. "As you astutely pointed out, there is a duke in residence. Even your paltry threats won't work on him."

"Then I'll have to kill him."

Bella halted. Was he serious? Roger wouldn't have hesi-tated to hurt the Regent himself if the royal had stood in the way of his own greed. "An accident can easily be arranged," she had heard her husband say when speaking of one of his enemies.

But to murder a duke?

Rupert, it appeared, shared not only his twin's looks, but his ruthlessness as well.

Rupert pushed her roughly toward the stable door. "Go. Now. And tell no one you saw me. Especially your duke."

Bella found Harriet hard at work in the larder, checking the stores against her list and instructing one of the maids on how to properly label the jars of jam and vegetables. The maid, relieved at the distraction, scurried out of the room, and Bella drew Harriet into a far corner of the kitchen.

"Where did you store all the trunks?" Bella asked.

"What's all the fuss?" Harriet countered.

"It's imperative we search through everything we took with us from Plymouth."

"Why?"

"I had a run-in with Rupert in the stables," Bella said.

"Roger's twin?" Harriet asked incredulously. "But that's impossible. He died last—"

"No, that was another of Roger's lies. Rupert is very much alive, I assure you."

"Why has Rupert come now?"

"He's seeking one of Roger's business ledgers." Bella needn't specify which one; Harriet knew everything about her former employer. "Rupert couldn't find the ledger in the Plymouth house, and he is certain Roger hid it amongst my belongings. The man won't leave until he has it."

"So? It seems to me that we have the upper hand. Can we not use the ledger against him?"

Anxiety spurted through Bella. "No! That's not an option."

Harriet grasped Bella's hand. "Don't let that scoundrel use me to manipulate you to his will the way Roger did."

"It's not just that," Bella rushed on. "Rupert threatened everyone's safety, even the duke's, and he claims he can bribe Roger's former housekeeper to say I pushed Roger down the stairs." Bella bit her bottom lip. "There's truth to it. When Roger raised his hand to strike me, I did—"

Harriet squeezed her hand. "Bella, stop that nonsense and listen to me. We are under the protection of the Duke of Blackwood."

"We most certainly are *not*. Sharing a residence does not mean the man owes us the slightest shred of protection."

"I've got a good sense of people's characters. Blackwood

wouldn't allow harm to befall you. He's half in love with you. You have the power to make him fall all the way."

"As his *mistress*. Truth be told, Rupert's arrival has awakened me to my folly. I swore never to remarry and put myself under a man's domain. A mistress is no better off—she is lulled into a false sense of independence and security until her benefactor tires of her and casts her aside. The law was written by men and fails to protect women. I'd lose Wyndmoor Manor for certain."

"What about Rupert?" Harriet asked.

"We need to find that ledger."

James understood Investigator Papazian required time to solve the mystery surrounding Bella Sinclair. A successful barrister spent many hours patiently waiting for results, whether from his own investigators or in the hallowed halls of the Old Bailey waiting for witnesses, trials to commence, or for delayed jury verdicts. But this time, James's patience seemed to have abandoned him as strange and disquieting thoughts ran through his mind regarding Bella's safety.

Knowing he needed a distraction, James busied himself with estate matters the entire morning. He met with Gideon Jacobson, the old duke's steward and the man James had urged upon Bella for the position. James locked himself in the library with Jacobson, and together they ensured that the books were in order after Sir Reeves's short but fiscally irresponsible ownership of the place.

After four hours of accounting figures, ink-stained fingers, and strained eyes, James emerged from the library feeling restless and caged within the confines of the house.

James immediately called for Coates. "I'm going for a ride."

Coates took one look at his master's disgruntled features and asked, "Is there a problem I can take care of for you, Your Grace?"

"Nothing a good ride won't solve."

James entered the stables and went to his stallion in the corner stall. Maximus whinnied and repeatedly shook his head.

"Ho, Maximus. What's troubling you, boy?"

James picked up a brush. The young stable boy, Bobby, was nowhere in sight. As he drew near, Maximus snorted and thumped the side of the wood stall.

The other horses whinnied in response; the matching pair of chestnuts reared up, wild-eyed.

James's nerves tensed immediately. He whirled around, simultaneously scanning the stables.

Then he spotted him.

"Christ!"

Bobby lay sprawled face down at the far end of the stable floor. James crouched and gently turned the boy over. The left side of his face was bruised and bloodied. Pieces of hay clung to his red hair and clothing. All of the horses were accounted for in their stables.

There was no question. The boy had been attacked.

James quickly checked for a pulse, relieved when he felt the strong beat beneath his fingers.

Suddenly, James spotted a blur from the corner of his eye. Instinct kicked in, and James rolled to the side just as a dark figure launched at him.

His attacker had a wiry strength. James blocked a fierce punch and they wrestled in the straw when the man raised his fist again, and James spotted a pistol in his grip. James lunged for his arm, and they struggled for control when the pistol fired. A searing pain lanced James's side. Through a haze of red, James saw the man stumble to his feet and flee the stables.

Chapter 16

"Sweet heaven! What was that?" Harriet asked.

Bella's head jerked to the nearest window. "It sounded like a gunshot."

They had been searching the trunks they had brought from Plymouth in a spare bedchamber when the sound of the shot reverberated throughout the room.

Bella jumped to her feet. "Stay in the house until I return."

"But what if it's dangerous?"

Ignoring Harriet, Bella rushed to the top of the landing and down the front stairs. The front door stood open and she sped outside. The duke's manservant, Coates, and two of the footmen were already sprinting across the lawn.

"What happened?" Bella shouted to Coates.

He barely looked her way. "In the stables!"

After a moment's hesitation, she ran after him. As she approached the stable door, James stumbled out carrying Bobby, unconscious in his arms. The boy's head hung to the side, revealing a bloodied face.

As James gingerly handed the boy over to a footman she saw the blood staining the duke's white shirtfront.

The entire right side of his shirt was crimson.

Her breath caught. *What has gone on here?*

She ran to his side. "What happened?"

Sapphire eyes held not only pain, but rage. "Bobby was knocked unconscious. I wrestled with his attacker, and I was shot."

Bella's hand fluttered to her breast.

Rupert. It was Rupert who had attacked Bobby and shot James. Air rushed in and out of her lungs like a bellows. She was vaguely aware of the rest of the household gathering around.

"Summon the physician," James instructed another footman. "Bobby took a nasty hit to the head."

Leaning on Coates, James made his way inside. Bella trailed after them, her mind a crazy whirl of fear and dread.

Once inside she found her voice. "The drawing room is closest," she directed Coates. "Lay him on the settee."

It was James who hesitated. "I'll bloody it."

"You've been shot! You think I care as to the state of the upholstery?" she asked incredulously.

He shot her a lopsided grin and sat. "It's only a flesh wound."

Coates helped him unbutton his shirt. Bella winced at the jagged oozing wound. She had seen a man's naked torso, of course. But Roger had been older, and his fondness for sweets and liquor had turned him into a plump, paunchy man. He had been fair and his flesh pale.

But James's chest . . . oh my, it appeared to have been molded of bronze. He shrugged the shirt completely aside, and the fluid, rippling motion of the muscles in his wide shoulders and back fascinated her.

Coates probed the wound, and James hissed in pain.

"Careful! You're hurting him," she blurted.

Coates eyed her. "I need to make certain the ball passed through. Whiskey would help right now."

She rushed to the sideboard and withdrew a crystal decanter and glass. She poured a good amount with a shaky hand and handed the glass to Coates.

Coates took both the glass and the decanter from her. He handed the glass to James, who downed the contents in one swallow. Coates then took the decanter and poured it on the wound.

James's entire body went rigid. Gritting his teeth, he let forth a groan of pain.

"What did you do that for?" Bella asked.

"To kill any infection, of course." Coates spoke as if she was a simpleton.

"I know alcohol kills infections. I meant to ask shouldn't you wait for the local surgeon? The footman left to fetch the man."

"Good," James grunted. "He'll need to clean the wound and put a few stitches in me." His glare sharpened at her. "Then we're going to talk about who was in the stables."

Bella paced her bedchamber awaiting any news. The local surgeon, a man by the name of Dr. Muddleton, had arrived two hours ago and had marched straightaway to the duke's bedchamber and firmly closed the door.

A cold shiver spread over Bella as she thought of James. The rose-hued walls and large window overlooking the rear gardens had always soothed her nerves in the past, but failed to ease the tight knot in her stomach now. She felt like a slashed rope, unraveling thread by thread.

The door opened and Harriet slipped inside. "The stable lad came to and the surgeon believes he'll suffer no ill effects."

"Thank goodness!" Bella said. "And the duke?"

"The surgeon continues to treat him as we speak."

Bella bit her bottom lip until it throbbed like her pulse.

"Rupert is the culprit. Both Bobby and the duke must have walked in on Rupert in the stables. It's all my fault!"

"You must not blame yourself for Rupert's foul deeds. You couldn't have known."

Guilt seared Bella's chest. How could she not feel responsible? Her past had returned to harm those who'd had no hand in Roger and Rupert's treason. The ball may have grazed James, but she had seen the gruesome wound with her own eyes. The flesh was torn and there had been so much blood.

Then there was the risk of infection.

Bella had a vivid memory of one of Roger's tenants who had injured himself pitching hay. The man's thigh had been punctured to the bone. Roger had dismissed the tenant's injuries, saying they were merely superficial and had sent the surgeon away. A day later, the man had developed a raging fever; two days later, he had perished.

Could James suffer the same fate?

She would never recover, would never forgive herself.

A heaviness centered in her chest. At one time she had compared James to Roger. She had thought James selfish and depraved—but he had never exhibited Roger's behavior. Yes, she had been furious that James had assumed she was just as susceptible and amenable to his charms as his prior conquests and would be delighted to become his mistress. He had arrogantly thought he had contrived the perfect solution to their dilemma over the property.

But the truth was he was just as much a victim of Sir Reeves's criminal plot as she. And as for Roger—he would have ruthlessly dispensed of a widow occupying a home he believed rightfully belonged to him. If the woman refused to leave, Roger would not have hesitated to inflict grave harm.

James had never harmed her. The first day he had arrived in his ducal carriage, he had alluded to his base desires and had threatened to visit her bedchamber. She had been appalled and had replied in reckless anger. But she knew now he would never have carried through with the threat. For being raised as the bastard son of an aristocrat, James had more morals than most men of the *beau monde*.

"I overheard Coates in the hall," Harriet said. "They all believe it was a horse thief come to steal the duke's big stallion."

"Maximus? They believe Bobby and the duke walked in on a common horse thief?"

"Aye."

Bella's mind halted. "We must find that ledger."

"They'll search for the criminal. Surely Rupert must be panicked. Perhaps he'll flee and leave us alone," Harriet said.

Bella shook her head. "He wants the ledger too badly."

A knock on the door startled the women.

Harriet opened the door, and Coates stood in the doorway. His expression was taut, his brow creased with worry.

"The duke is asking for you, Mrs. Sinclair."

Bella opened the door of the master bedchamber and quietly stepped inside. The drapes were drawn and the room was dim, save for a handful of candles on the bedside table. The large four-poster was hung with a sheer silk, and Bella could make out Blackwood lying still against the pillows. A stout, middle-aged man was bent over the bed, his face set in deep thought as he tended his patient.

Bella closed the door, and the surgeon straightened at her approach. "I'm Dr. Muddleton. I assume you are Mrs. Sinclair. His Grace asked to speak with you."

"How is he?" Bella asked.

"The ball tore up his side, but it passed through. He's a lucky man as it missed his liver by a hairsbreadth." Dr. Muddleton held up two fingers a hair apart to demonstrate just how close the ball had come to killing Blackwood.

There was a heavy feeling in her stomach, and she forced herself to breathe.

"I dosed him with laudanum before I stitched the wound, but he still would have had a good bit of pain. Strong as an ox, he is. He should be tired from the drug, understand? You must not visit long," Dr. Muddleton instructed.

Bella gathered the courage to ask the question that had been concerning her. "Will His Grace fully recover?"

Although the surgeon wore thick spectacles, she had no trouble seeing the wariness in his eyes. "He's at risk for infection. If he becomes fevered, I'll bring the leeches."

"Leeches?"

"I'll need to bleed him."

At her slight gasp, he said, "I'll return tomorrow." Snapping his black bag shut in a no-nonsense manner, he made for the door.

As soon as the surgeon departed, Bella approached the bed. James appeared to be sleeping. His eyes were closed and his chest rose in an even, rhythmic breathing. Yet his complexion was pale, not the healthy bronze she had grown accustomed to. The dark arch of his eyebrows and eyelashes stood out against the paleness. He was shirtless, a large bandage wrapped about his torso. A sheet covered him from the waist down. Even ill and drugged, she couldn't help but admire his beautifully proportioned body, all lean muscle and sinew.

He took a deep breath, and she hesitated, not wanting to disturb him. She took a step back.

His eyes opened suddenly, and she froze.

"You asked for me, Your Grace," she whispered.

"Come close, Bella. I'm not dead."

She stepped forward, until her skirts brushed the side of the bed.

"Thank you for coming. I want to apologize," he said.

"Apologize? Whatever for?"

"For causing you distress by suggesting a scandalous relationship. You are a true lady and deserve more from a man."

Of all the things she had expected him to say, an apology was not one of them. Her bewildered thoughts veered like quicksilver. He had just had a ball rip into him—all because her brother-in-law was searching for a ledger that should have been destroyed long ago. And James was apologizing to *her?*

She wanted to throw herself at his feet and beg for *his* forgiveness. She had unwittingly embroiled him in Rupert's twisted plot to retrieve a treasonous document that her spouse had been arrogant enough to hide amongst her belongings. For this, he had almost been killed.

She swallowed hard and bit back tears. Reaching out, she clasped his hand. He looked at her, and she could see pain in the incredible blue depths of his eyes.

"There's no need to apologize to me," she said. "You should know that I briefly considered your salacious offer."

He grinned. "Truly? I'm flattered by your honesty."

There was so much more she wanted to confess, but she held her tongue. "The surgeon said I shouldn't overstay my welcome. You must rest."

She tried to pull her hand from his, but his grip tightened.

"Wait. Tell me what's going on, Bella."

At the sudden intensity in his gaze, a sliver of alarm raced down her spine. "What do you mean?"

"A man attacked Bobby, a servant who is little more than a lad. When I found Bobby face down in the straw, I had no warning before the criminal jumped me from behind. I spotted the pistol and we wrestled a good deal for control of the weapon before it discharged and I was shot."

Struggling with her conscience, she spoke with as calm a voice as she could manage. "Harriet overheard from Coates that it was a horse thief."

"Do you believe that?"

"Why wouldn't I?"

"You had said you were being followed. Are you in danger, Bella?"

She chose her words carefully. "I was mistaken about being followed. I spoke hastily."

"There is no need to lie to me. I can help you."

"I thank you for your offer, but there truly is no need for any aid. Besides I thought you wished me gone from Wyndmoor Manor?" she said.

"Maybe I did, but that has nothing to do with your current safety. You must understand that I can help you."

No one could help her. Not even a duke. Her future lay in her own hands. Rupert was not only Roger's brother, but his twin.

Bad seed fallen from the same rotten tree.

"Please do not concern yourself with dangers that do not exist. The surgeon says you must rest to recover."

"Perhaps you're right. I'm feeling quite tired." He released her hand, yet his eyes held a sheen of purpose that frightened her. "But be aware, Bella, that I expect to finish this discussion later."

Chapter 17

Bella tossed in bed that night. At last she fell into a fitful sleep only to wake in a cold sweat from a horrid nightmare that began at her father's funeral. The coffin was lowered into the ground, but at the last moment the lid was raised and the duke—not her father—was resting within the intricate folds of white satin. She had screamed until her voice was a hoarse whisper, yet none of the dozens of mourners seemed to notice, and the lid was closed with an ear-piercing screech.

Heart pounding, Bella opened her eyes wide to stare at the pink canopy above her bed. Gasping in deep breaths of air, she sat up and flung the covers aside.

Something was wrong. She felt it deep in the marrow of her bones. She needed to see James. Now.

Pushing her feet into her slippers, she donned her robe and lit a candle on the end table by the bed. Opening the door, she glanced from side to side. Not surprisingly, the hall was empty in the dead of the night. She slipped from the room and headed for the master's bedchamber, her feet silent on the plush Brussels runner. Light from her single candle cast eerie shadows on the flocked wallpaper, and she shivered. Specters of her nightmare lingered in her mind.

She came to Blackwood's door and slowly opened it.

Coates was asleep in a corner armchair, his chin resting on his chest. James lay in the bed, and even from across the room she could see his labored breathing. She approached the bed and set the candle beside a water pitcher and glass. His eyes were closed, and bright red splotches covered his forehead and cheeks. Reaching out, she touched his forehead.

Sweet Lord, he was scalding hot!

"Coates," she whispered vehemently. "He's burning with fever."

Coates jumped to his feet. "Mrs. Sinclair, what are you doing here?"

"Never mind that," she snapped. "The duke is fevered."

Coates rushed over and at one look at Blackwood, he said, "I'll send for Dr. Muddleton immediately."

"Meanwhile, we must lower the fever with cold compresses," Bella said.

"I'll wake the staff." Coates ran from the room.

Within minutes, the footmen and a maid arrived with basins of cold water and clean cloths. Compresses were applied to James's face and chest.

James muttered in protest, but he never fully woke from his fevered state.

Dr. Muddleton arrived and removed the bandages. Bella stifled a gasp at the sight of the swollen and scarlet flesh inflamed around each of the black stitches. It was her nightmare turned to reality, and the thought that James could die froze in her brain.

The surgeon's face was stark. "The wound is infected and a fever has come upon him. I must bleed him at once." Reaching into his bag, he withdrew a glass jar full of leeches. Their slimy black bodies writhed within the glass.

"Is that necessary?" Bella asked.

Muddleton shot her a scalding look and replied with contempt that forbade any further argument. "Bloodletting balances the humors, and fevers are a result of too much blood. Now, do you call yourself a surgeon, Mrs. Sinclair?"

Coates met Bella's wide-eyed glance, and they shared a look of complete helplessness.

"What else can be done for him?" Coates asked.

"Fevers are difficult beasts to manage. A patient may have moments of lucidity when the fever ebbs and he appears to be on the road to recovery. You must not let your expectations get the better of you, however, as he will continue to have incoherent mumblings when the fever rises, usually in the late afternoon and through the night. He'll require constant care."

Bella spoke up before Coates. "His Grace shall have whatever he needs."

Muddleton tied James's arm until the veins swelled, then cut him with a small blade until two bright lines of blood marred his skin. The surgeon then opened the jar and withdrew a leech, its wormlike body twisting in his fingers.

"I'll have to apply two the first time," Muddleton said. "It will take an hour to breathe the vein and for the leeches to become fully engorged."

Bella's gut twisted and she turned her head, unable to watch as the leeches latched on to James's arm.

James lay in bed, his entire right side throbbing and burning. At times it felt as if a blade were repeatedly being thrust and twisted inside him. "The whiskey doesn't help."

"Dr. Muddleton says it's necessary to treat the infection," Coates said.

"I'm not talking about the infection, dammit. I'm speaking of the pain."

Coates looked appalled at the misunderstanding, and James inwardly cursed himself. It was embarrassing to admit how much he was affected by the pain. He had always believed himself strong in mind and body, able to withstand pain. He enjoyed the vigorous pugilist exercise at Gentleman Jackson's, and he had sparred with seasoned boxers as well as his bulky and rather ruthless colleague, Anthony Stevens. On numerous occasions, James had suffered bloody noses, black eyes, even broken ribs. But *this* pain was far worse than being pummeled by an opponent in a ring. This was a gnawing pain that could not be alleviated by whiskey or laudanum.

"Dr. Muddleton is expected soon, Your Grace. I shall speak with him about a stronger tonic," Coates said.

James watched Coates busy himself about the room. James was familiar enough with his longtime manservant to know that he was anxious. Coates knew his master disliked the formality of being called Your Grace, and Coates never used the title unless in a mocking tone, or in public, or when he was nervous. And whenever Coates could not meet his master's needs, he flitted around immersing himself with mundane tasks.

Coates adjusted drapes that were sufficiently closed, filled a glass of water on the bedside table that was already more than half full, and made to adjust James's pillows.

"What day is it, Coates?"

"It's Sunday afternoon, Your Grace."

James frowned. "I've been in bed for a week now?"

"Yes."

"Have they found the criminal?" James asked.

"No. The constables have searched the grounds and have kept an eye out for travelers through the Hertfordshire inns, but they have found no one."

It would help to have a description of the man, but neither James nor Bobby had gotten a good look at him. All James had seen for certain during their scuffle for the pistol was the man's fair hair, and half the men in St. Albans had the same color hair.

James's head began to pound, cutting off all thought of the criminal. "The blasted fever comes at night, doesn't it?"

Coates stopped fluffing James's pillows and looked his master in the eye. "It arrives earlier than nightfall. It comes on after noon and lasts all through the night."

James tried to move his legs. He felt stiff, but the throbbing in his side was much worse than the discomfort in his limbs.

"I'll ask Mrs. O'Brien to prepare barley water," Coates said. "My mum always said barley water strengthens the body."

As James looked up at Coates, the servant's face blurred before his eyes. James blinked and when he opened his eyes he swore Coates looked just like the Honorable Barnard Bathwell of the Old Bailey. He had the same beady eyes, bulbous nose, and squat figure as the judge. Even the white hair was the same, although Judge Bathwell wore a wig and Coates's hair looked naturally white.

"Coates, by any chance are you related to Judge Bathwell?"

"No, Your Grace. Why would you ask?"

"You look just like him. He was the presiding judge for my last criminal client, Pumpkin O'Dool, you see, and Bathwell's appearance is quite fresh in my mind."

"Isn't Judge Bathwell under five feet tall, Your Grace?"

James smiled. "That he is, Coates." His manservant did recognize the similarities.

But Coates straightened to his full height, and James suspected he thought the comparison unfavorable after all.

"I'm an inch shy of six feet, Your Grace."

"But the similarities! You even share the same mole on your left cheek the size of a shilling. Look in the glass, Coates."

Coates didn't turn to look in the cheval glass. Rather his brows slanted in a frown, and he reached out to touch James's forehead, then stepped back abruptly. "I shall go see if Dr. Muddleton has arrived."

"Not that bumbling bloodsucker!" James shouted. "He's an idiot. I'll not allow those leeches near me again. I feel horrid afterwards, listless and drained."

"But, Your Grace—"

James waved his hand, cutting his manservant off. "Very well. Go then. I'm feeling tired again, blast it."

James shut his eyes and barely had time to rest before the door swung open and slammed against the wall. In marched Dr. Muddleton, followed by Bella and Coates.

"Ah, Bella. It's been days since I've seen you," James said.

Coates answered, "She was here an hour ago, Your Grace."

James smiled at Bella. She looked beautiful as always, with wisps of auburn hair framing her oval face. Yet there were shadows under her emerald eyes, and she looked tired— almost as tired as he felt. He wanted her to sit beside him and read, and he had a vague recollection of her doing just that. He reached out a hand, but the annoying surgeon took it as a sign for him to examine him instead.

"Your Grace," Muddleton said, pressing his meaty palm to his forehead, "the fever has returned." Muddleton rolled up his sleeves. "I must bleed him at once."

"No!" James bellowed. "No more leeches!"

Muddleton's lips thinned, and a swift shadow of annoyance swept across his face. "Very well then, Your Grace."

Muddleton turned to Coates and Bella. "He needs to drink water."

"What of the wound?" Bella asked. "The swelling and redness remain."

"No matter. Soon I shall remove the stitches," the surgeon said.

James could hear the worry in Bella's voice and see the tiny frown lines between her brows. He tried to smile, to put her at ease, but he was so damned tired all he could do was close his eyes.

"Bella! Bella are you there?"

She woke with a jerk and was at the side of the bed in a heartbeat. "Yes, I'm here." She removed the cloth on his forehead. Once cool, it was as hot as James's flesh.

"I was worried you had gone," James said.

"You needn't worry about that." She raised his head and placed a glass to his lips. "You must drink more water."

He shook his head and pushed the glass away. Water splashed on her sleeve and across the sheets. She bit her lip in dismay at her utter helplessness.

"Please, you must drink." But either he didn't hear her or he had no interest.

It had been ten days since she had found him fevered, and she was in a hell of her own making. Muddleton had been correct about one fact—the fever abated in the early morning hours and returned with each passing afternoon with the vengeance of a spurned lover.

Bella refused to leave his side when the fever struck. She spent hours changing the cool compresses on his forehead and lifting the water glass to his lips. Only when the endless nights had finally grayed into dawn and the fever broke would she leave to allow Coates to take over and care for his master. She would then eat, see to her personal needs, and nap if she was able.

In the back of Bella's mind, she knew she should take time to search for the ledger when she was not tending to the duke, but in her exhaustion she cared naught. If James died from the wound Rupert inflicted, she would never forgive herself. Rupert could bribe whomever he wished to blame her for her husband's death, and she'd welcome the chance to spend the rest of her life in jail.

Unbeknownst to Rupert, he wouldn't be completely wrong regarding Roger's demise.

She'd never felt guilt over Roger's death, but James's . . .

She cleansed his face and neck, all the while praying for a better night than the last. His handsome face was ruddy; his blue eyes held the glassy gleam of illness. He looked haggard and exhausted. Dr. Muddleton arrived daily and his prognosis grew more and more dismal with each passing day.

Harriet kept Bella informed of any household news. Bobby had fully recovered and was back in the stables. The "criminal" still had not been found, and Harriet had whispered in her ear that Rupert had not been heard from or spotted since the attacks.

James opened his eyes. "Read to me, Bella."

She picked up the Bible. "I shall continue where I left off in John."

"No. read what you've written."

"Pardon?"

"Your next article for the *Times*. Read it to me."

She was stunned. He was having an incredibly lucid moment.

"You must have written something all these nights," he said.

She had, but it was not a political piece. She had recalled reading about a young surgeon who had treated the fallen soldiers during Waterloo. He had since moved to London to practice medicine. His new methods of treatment were controversial, but the positive results could not be denied.

In desperation, she had written to the surgeon the day after Muddleton had first bled James. She pulled out a sheet of foolscap in the back of the Bible and unfolded a draft of the letter she had sent off to the surgeon.

Dear Dr. Grimsby,

I am writing to request your services for the Duke of Blackwood. He suffers from an infection from an injury when a pistol discharged. You will be generously compensated for your services and all travel expenses provided for. Kindly arrive as soon as possible as time is of the essence.

James grinned. "I take it you don't trust Dr. Muddleton?"

"He is a country surgeon who has little experience with injuries such as yours. Dr. Grimsby treated soldiers in the war."

"You think me worthy of saving then?"

"Of course! All life is worthy of saving."

"You do realize if I perish then there will be no one to contest the ownership of Wyndmoor. The place will be yours."

"You think that little of me?" The truth was as the days passed she cared less and less about the manor. What she had previously believed was the most important thing in her life, now seemed inconsequential and meaningless.

"I fear my memory is poor. Remind me to thank you when I'm no longer fevered," James said.

"For summoning the surgeon?" she asked.

"No. For caring for me in my time of need."

Chapter 18

On the fifteenth day of Blackwood's fever, Dr. Grimsby arrived by stagecoach at a posting inn. He was met by a driver and a footman and escorted to Wyndmoor Manor in the duke's carriage.

Bella and Coates greeted Grimsby expectantly at the door. A score of years younger than Dr. Muddleton, Grimsby had a long bony face with a nose that resembled a wedge of cheese.

"Where is the duke?" Grimsby asked.

Coates opened the door wide. "Upstairs, if you please." Bella and Coates were close on Grimsby's heels as he rushed up the stairs and swept into the duke's bedchamber.

The surgeon's gray eyes were like silver lightning as he took one look at his fevered patient. James lay motionless as he slept, his eyelids almost waxen in the beam of sunlight from the parted drapes. His pallid color resembled fireplace ash, save for the bright spots on his cheekbones and forehead.

"He's in a bad way. It's good you summoned me," Grimsby said. He lifted James's arm and spotted the short cuts of Muddleton's blade and the swollen telltale signs of the leeches. A frown creased Grimsby's high brow. "He's been bled?"

"Dr. Muddleton said it was the only way to fight the fever," Coates explained.

"Then he's a bloody fool!" Grimsby snapped. "The fever is from the infected wound, not any imbalance in his blood. Bloodletting has served only to weaken him."

Bella met Coates's concerned look, and an unmistakable meaning passed between them. Had they in their ignorance allowed Dr. Muddleton to further harm the duke?

Grimsby seemed to read their minds. "No sense blaming yourselves for an incompetent country surgeon."

Grimsby withdrew a rectangular case from his medical bag. He opened the mahogany lid to reveal a dozen surgical instruments. Razor-sharp knives with ivory handles, needles, forceps, trephines, and a saw that could only be used to amputate limbs.

A wave of nausea enveloped Bella.

"Summon your strongest footman," Grimsby ordered.

"Whatever for?" Coates asked.

"I must reopen and clean the wound, and the duke needs to be restrained," Grimsby said.

Sweet Lord! Bella thought. *How will he survive the pain?* James slept on, completely unaware of what the surgeon intended for him.

At Coates's stunned look, Grimsby prompted, "Go on, man. Get the footman and a basin of hot water and clean cloths while you're at it."

Minutes later, Coates arrived with a burly footman and the hot water. Bella assumed the water was to wash James, but Grimsby did the most peculiar thing; he used it to scrub his hands and a select number of instruments.

"I treated a soldier at Waterloo who survived after I washed away the grime of travel," Grimsby said as he lathered his hands. "Medicine is not a perfect science, you see. When one thing works, even if you don't understand the specific reasons, you do it again until you do. Some call it superstition. I call it good medicine."

The surgeon picked up his knife. "It's time to hold him

down. You at his shoulders," he directed the footman, "and you at his legs," he told Coates. Grimsby's eyes snapped to Bella. "I could use a good nurse to hand me my instruments. Do you have the stomach for it?"

Bella's heart pounded against her rib cage. She didn't think she had it in her, but if Grimsby needed her, then James needed her. She had seen to James's needs thus far; how could she turn away now?

She swallowed her terror and took a deep breath, meeting the surgeon's steely gaze. She nodded curtly, then watched in horror as Grimsby lowered the knife.

James was floating. The fever that he had feared and battled for days had worn him out until he could not recall why he had fought so hard. His heavy lids had finally slipped closed. Sleep was a sweet haven, a place where he could hear Bella's voice as she talked, calming and soothing. At first he had recognized the Bible chapters she had read from John and Luke, and then the stories had jumbled in his mind like complex legal statutes until he could only hear her voice. Later still he comprehended nothing at all, but he had *sensed* her presence. He had come to depend on her and her cool touch on his brow. He longed to touch her in return and kiss her beautiful lips, but that would require the effort of waking. Instead he allowed her comfort to ease his pain, and he had slept on.

Until the screaming woke him. His eyes flew open. Someone was skewering him alive, slicing into his side and innards. The screaming, he realized, was his own.

"Jesus," he gasped. "Sweet Jesus."

There were men hovering over him. A large beast holding down his shoulders, another his legs, while an emaciated-looking butcher was cutting into his side. James bucked, tried to throw them off, but the blade twisted and his vision blurred.

Intense agony seared his brain—unlike anything he had ever experienced—and threatened to make him black out.

"Almost done," the butcher said. "I've never seen so much pus. It's a wonder the infection didn't do him in days ago."

James was stopped from answering by another wave of pain.

The man uncapped a black jar, and for an instant James thought the bastard meant to pull out the dreaded leeches. But it was worse; he rubbed a substance on his wound that burned like the fires of hell. "Bastard!" James bellowed.

"Easy, Your Grace. The worst is over now."

James was dimly aware of the surgeon stitching him closed. Then he was no longer being held down. He tried to move, but the racking pain was still present, and his limbs wouldn't cooperate. Beads of sweat ran down his brow into his eyes.

The surgeon handed the jar to Coates. "This is a healing salve made of pitch and moneywort. You must apply it to the wound twice a day no matter how much he hollers. Understand?"

"Yes! Yes!"

"At Waterloo many a soldier was not as fortunate as His Grace to have survived two weeks of improper care. He's a strong one, he is. But there's no guarantee he'll survive the infection and the bloodletting. The next few days will tell."

Three days after Dr. Grimsby's arrival, Bella's prayers were answered and James's fever subsided. He would survive, thank the Lord, and for the first time Bella could breathe easy. Another week later, James's color and appetite had returned, along with his arrogance, pride, and surly disposition after having remained in bed for so long.

Bella opened the door to his bedchamber to find James struggling to kick the covers from his legs. Coates was frantically trying to dissuade his master from rising.

"I want out of this damned bed!" James boomed.

"But Dr. Grimsby's orders, Your Grace!"

"Tell him to sod off. I feel better, good enough to rise."

Bella shut the door behind her and Coates looked up, his gaze desperate and pleading at once. "Mrs. Sinclair! Perhaps you can talk some sense into the duke."

Bella nodded at Coates. They had grown fond of each other over the course of James's illness. Dr. Grimsby continued to check on his patient daily, but it was Bella and Coates who had shared the main burden of caring for James, and most importantly, the goal of wanting to see him healed.

Their motives, however, were of an entirely different nature. Coates was a dedicated manservant, while she felt guilty and responsible for the duke's suffering. But if she was truthful to herself, she knew there was more behind her altruistic behavior. She cared for James, genuinely cared.

"Hiding behind a woman's skirts, are you, Coates?" James said gruffly.

"Give me the jar and I will apply the salve and bandage him," Bella offered.

The relief was so evident in Coates's expression that Bella bit the inside of her cheek to keep from laughing.

"You're an angel in disguise, Mrs. Sinclair," Coates said as he rushed to hand her the salve on his way out of the room.

A chuckle came from the bed. "I suppose Coates knows you will have no problem keeping me in bed," James said, the unmistakable gleam back in his eyes.

Bella's grip on the jar tightened a fraction. "I see you truly are feeling better. Allow me to spare your manservant and see to your wound myself."

"The wound is closed and healed."

Bella placed her hands on her hips. "Perhaps, but at the moment I fear Dr. Grimsby more than you."

He grinned, and Bella's heart lurched at the devastating effect.

"Never let it be said I denied a lady," James said.

She set the jar down beside the bed and pulled up a chair. His charm had returned with his health, and she feared she was even more affected by it. He wrapped his hands behind his head and eased back down on the pillows.

James wore a loose white shirt and breeches, and Bella was thankful that Coates had had the foresight to dress his master before her arrival. Now that the danger of the fever had passed and James was lucid, she realized it was improper for her to tend him much longer in the privacy of his bedchamber. A fevered and deathly ill duke was one thing; a healthy virile duke was quite another.

Yet she suffered an odd twinge of disappointment at the thought of no longer seeing to his needs.

She raised his shirt and her pulse quickened. He had lost weight during his illness and his body was whipcord lean. She had never felt this instinctive awareness of him when he had lain unconscious. He had healed, and along with his renewed health her senses had leapt to life.

"Bella."

At the sound of her name, a tingling started in her limbs. "Yes?"

She thought she detected a flicker in his intense eyes, but he turned his gaze to the jar resting on the bed side table. "You best get on with it," he said hoarsely.

"Of course." She felt her cheeks warm, and she returned her attention to her task and carefully unwrapped the bandage. The wound no longer bore the scarlet streaks of infection, rather a raised rope-like scar where the stitches had been removed.

"See? It's healed," he said.

"Yes, it is remarkable. Dr. Grimsby was right to reopen the wound."

"I have a memory of you reading a letter requesting Grimsby's services. But when I woke to him hovering above me with a knife slicing into my side, I thought you had summoned a St. Giles butcher."

"It turned out that Dr. Muddleton was the butcher," she said.

His expression turned fierce. "You're right. For as long as I live, I shall never forget those horrendous leeches."

Bella picked up the jar and dipped a clean cloth into the salve.

James lay back and watched as she dabbed at his wound. Her hands were infinitely gentle. Tendrils of silky hair escaped her bun, framing her heart-shaped face and drifting her lavender scent in its wake. She worked quickly, her expression one of intense concentration.

The wound stung, and he sucked in a breath.

"I'm sorry if it hurts," she whispered.

"Anything is better than the fever."

Her eyes lifted to his, the clear jade hypnotic. For the hundredth time he wondered why she had remained by his side. His fevered memories were a jumbled mixture of dreams, but throughout them all he was certain of one thing—Bella's presence. She owed him nothing, least of all her loyalty, yet she had stayed.

He wanted her. His desire had nothing to do with any prior plan to seduce her and bend her to his will. This need was fierce and all consuming, encompassing every fiber of his being. His near escape from death had served to heighten his awareness of life, his awareness of *her*.

"Let me change the bandage," she said.

The task required her to lean closer. She bit her bottom lip as she worked, tying a fresh bandage firmly around his torso. His blood heated; his muscles tightened as raw lust rushed through him. He pictured her hands on him in erotic ways. Her hair trailing down his abdomen, her soft, white hands caressing his rock-hard manhood.

Her gaze snapped to his. "Am I hurting you?"

Yes, I'm throbbing with need for you.

His voice was gruff. "No, it needs to be done." He breathed in deeply, willed his body to relax, but succeeded only in inhaling her sweet lavender scent more fully into his nostrils. He had to clear his thoughts. Now was not the time for his cock to rule his head. There were other more pressing matters that needed to be resolved.

"Coates tells me they never found the attacker," he said.

"The horse thief?" she asked a little too eagerly.

"Was it someone you know, Bella?"

She sat back in the chair. "No. You asked me this before and my answer is unchanged."

"You accused me of having you followed. You were quite adamant about it as I recall."

"I told you I was mistaken."

He didn't believe her, not for a second, but he didn't press her. He had asked Investigator Papazian to look into the matter. He had not heard back from the wily Armenian, but then again, if the investigator had called upon him while he lay fevered, he would never have known. James made a mental note to summon him as soon as possible.

"Will you help me rise?"

"Don't be foolish."

"I shall attempt it on my own then."

"Very well, but I don't want you standing for long. You can sit in the armchair."

"Stubborn and bossy woman."

A rush of pink stained her cheeks. "Perhaps I am, but it appears you need a firm hand."

Wrapping her arms around his shoulders, she helped him sit. Her breath was warm and moist against his neck, and the soft curve of her breasts brushed against him. His heart thudded, and sweat beaded on his brow. He swung his legs over the side of the bed, then stood with her aid. His legs were wobbly, but his knees didn't buckle; rather it was his head that swam.

"Do you want to lie back down?"

"The chair, please."

She led him to the armchair and he sat. "Damnation, this is a nuisance. If Brent, Anthony, and Jack could see me now."

"You asked me not to write them, remember?"

"Yes, I remember. I had no wish for them to watch me lingering on my death bed."

She paled, and he felt uncomfortable that he had distressed her with a few careless words. Death was not a topic to make light of when it had been a grim reality days ago.

The problem was his pride. He had too much of it, and he couldn't bear to exhibit weakness. He had succumbed to the emotion in his youth when he had cried during the lonely holidays at boarding school. The students, excited and eager to return home, would wait for their families' arrivals. Too often James had remained behind, the vacant and eerily silent halls of the school a depressing and dreary existence.

But those years had long passed, and James refused to succumb to weakness now, especially in front of this strong, courageous woman who had survived the betrayal of a spouse who had abused her rather than cherished her. James had never forgotten the betrayal of his family as a child, and as a result he was fiercely loyal to those who stood by him as a man. His colleagues knew and understood this.

Bella had yet to discover it.

Whatever her reasons for caring for him, he would repay the kindness and do right by her. Gifting her Wyndmoor Manor was not sufficient. He wasn't the marrying kind, but she was. Even though her first marriage had been a tragedy, he had the power and influence to ensure her second was not. He was a duke who could see to it that she married a wealthy man. An old, filthy-rich man whose estate was not entailed and who would leave her a bloody fortune upon his demise.

If only he didn't desire her for himself. If only the thought of her with another did not make his thoughts race dangerously.

She pulled up a wooden chair and sat next to him. He liked her beside him. It felt right, comfortable. Reaching out, he clasped her hand.

"I owe you a debt for your tender care."

"You do not owe me anything for your care."

Something swam in her eyes. Regret? Pain? He didn't want her feeling either emotion. He wanted to see her smile, and so he said in a teasing tone, "I'll pay you with affection. A kiss to start."

Her plump lips parted in surprise as she read the desire in his face. "I shouldn't be here. It isn't proper. Coates should be the only one to tend you now that you're recovered."

"Do you want that?"

"No," she said softly, and again more firmly, "No."

For several heartbeats, the air between them was charged with awareness. Then he pulled her forward in her chair and kissed her. He hadn't meant for it to be anything but a brief kiss. He was still drained, but the moment their lips met, all thoughts of a quick encounter fled.

Weakness be damned. His blood heated, and his breeches grew uncomfortably tight.

Her lips parted on a sigh, and his tongue swept the sweet hollows of her mouth. She again tasted of strawberries and warm woman. She moaned and clutched his shoulders. She leaned closer, her full breasts grazing his chest.

He sucked in a breath. The thought struck him that he wanted her more than any other woman he had known. He didn't understand this need, this compulsion, only that she evoked untapped emotions within him. He deepened the kiss, savoring her sweet essence. Leisurely explored with a wild swirl of his tongue.

With a low moan, she pulled back. "Your injury," she whispered. "I don't want to hurt you."

He looked down into her face. Despite the dim light from the closed drapes, he was mesmerized by the jade pools of her eyes, clouded with passion. Her lips were parted, full and glistening, enticing him to possess and claim. As alluring and seductive as a siren.

Then her tongue glided over her lower lip, wetting it, and the lust that had simmered in his blood burst into an inferno. In one swift motion, he swept her onto his lap and sealed his lips to hers. This was no leisurely kiss, but one fueled by passion, need, and an emotion he didn't fully comprehend. An emotion only she had the power to wield.

He cradled her face in his hands as he smothered her lips with demanding mastery. To his surprise, she returned his kiss with reckless abandon. He soon grew restless, wanting more. His hands skimmed down her arms to caress the length of her back and the soft lines of her waist and hips. His touch was urgent as he grazed the side of her breast, then cupped a full mound. She moaned, her body instinctively moving toward him. His thumb grazed the nipple, taut beneath the fabric of her gown; then his fingers dipped inside the bodice to fill his hand with warm, womanly flesh.

She gasped and kissed him back, eagerly and urgently. When she squirmed in his lap and her bum cheeks rubbed against his arousal, his engorged cock throbbed in response.

His heart hammered; his need intensified. He had to have her. It was no longer a question of if. His fingers reached for the hem of her skirt. . . .

The door opened suddenly, and Bella jerked back just as Coates entered the room carrying a tray of food.

Coates froze when he spotted them, his eyes wide, his mouth gaping. "Pardon!" he sputtered, and turned to leave.

Bella jumped to her feet, two bright spots of pink dusting her cheeks. "No! Please set down the tray. I was on my way." With a swoosh of her skirts, she fled the room.

James ignored Coates's incredulous expression. His gaze remained on the open doorway. Something shifted inside him, an almost indiscernible emotion that reminded him of the

slight tipping of the scales of justice that had been artfully
displayed on his mantel in his Lincoln's Inn chambers.

James had witnessed it before from one of his clients. A
cold-blooded murderer who had escaped a near-death experience that had changed him. Vendettas were forgotten, longtime debts repaid, religion discovered. Life was too short, the
client had told him, to spend it battling his opponents.

James had never fully understood this client until now.

He had come to Hertfordshire to claim a piece of land and
a country home. But his motives had changed, along with his
mission. If Bella was in trouble, he swore to help her. And if
she wasn't, then he would ensure that she never had another
worry in her life.

Chapter 19

Over the course of the following days, James's health quickly improved. Dr. Grimsby returned to London, and James began a routine of vigorous physical exercise, which included hiking, swimming in the lake, and riding Maximus.

Bella's care had come to an end. There was no longer a reason to be close to the duke, and so she had resumed her efforts searching for the missing ledger.

She met Harriet in the spare room, where the trunks they had brought with them from Plymouth had been stowed. Painstakingly they had rummaged through each one. Bella had saved her mother's trunk for last, but now every item had been removed—her parent's miniature portrait, her mother's pearl combs, her books, notes, and writings, and a packet of documents. She had carefully examined the interior of the trunk and the curved top and flat bottom of the inside of the lid. No ledger had been hidden inside.

"We have searched every last one," Bella said, wiping her brow. "It's not here."

"Maybe the ledger is still in the Plymouth house," Harriet suggested.

Bella shook her head. "Rupert purchased the house and

searched it. He was convinced Roger had hid the ledger amongst my possessions."

Harriet shut the lid of the trunk she had just searched. "I wouldn't put it past him, but it is not here."

"What am I to do?"

"Nothing. Rupert has not been heard from since the incident in the stables. Rupert is bold, but he isn't stupid. I doubt he *intended* to shoot Blackwood. Both Bobby and the duke must have caught him unawares. Rupert knew if the duke died, he would be hunted for the murder for the rest of his days. He fled, I tell you."

Bella sighed. "I pray you're right, and he never returns."

"And Blackwood?" Harriet asked, arching a brow. "I take it you no longer consider him your enemy?"

Enemy? She could never think of James as her enemy. His impending death had changed her feelings toward him. That and the curious sweeping pull at her innards whenever she set eyes upon him.

"Do you still intend to seek the London solicitor's advice about Wyndmoor Manor?" Harriet said.

Bella knew she should. James would eventually leave for London and his ducal responsibilities, and the property dispute would be left unresolved. They had not been able to discuss the topic when he was sick, and ever since he had recovered and Coates had walked in on them in a scandalous position, she had been careful to avoid James and her riotous emotions. She still desperately wanted Wyndmoor Manor, yet the thought of fighting James in a court of law no longer felt right.

At Bella's silence, Harriet smiled. "You're battling yourself, aren't you?"

"What do you mean?"

"Bella, luv. You have nursed the man through his sickness. I know you better than anyone and your efforts weren't entirely out of guilt for Rupert's actions. Were they?"

"I'm uncertain—" she said hesitantly.

"Coates said Blackwood sent you a note requesting you to dine with him this evening."

Bella stiffened. "I had planned on declining."

"Why?"

"He's fully recovered! It would be unwise for me to spend more time with him."

Harriet's brow creased, her expression earnest. "Listen to me carefully, Bella. The heart makes its own rules. If only one could control it with logic, it would never be broken. But love and logic tend to stray from each other."

"I do not love him!" Bella said, but her voice sounded hollow to her own ears. *I cannot love him! He's a bloody duke, and I'm a country widow. Dozens of heiresses will throw themselves at his feet upon his return.* "Soon he will return to London, to his former friends, and to his new life as a duke."

"So? Nothing is stopping you for being with him now."

Bella had thought about it, God only knew she had thought of it many times. She could no longer deny the thrill of excitement at the prospect of being with James, of his warm flesh touching hers. She didn't fear intimacy with him like she had Roger. Nothing about the two men was similar, least of all in a physical nature.

James was devilishly handsome, and there were countless times she had to tear her gaze away from his profile. She had been attracted to him before he had been shot, and her feelings for him had only intensified since.

And when James had kissed her . . . had touched her . . . sweet heaven, she had melted in his arms. Her instinctive response to him was so powerful, she had been impelled by her own passion. If Coates had not chosen that moment to enter the room, she would have *begged* James to ease the shiver of wanting running through her body.

"Accept his invitation," Harriet urged. "Go and get the answers you need."

* * *

Bella wore the amethyst gown she had purchased while shopping with Evelyn in St. Albans. At the last minute, she tossed aside a pair of old serviceable stockings for the new black silk stockings and frilly garters. As she pulled the delicate material up her long legs, the sheer silk felt forbidden and delicious against her skin.

Then, opening her mother's trunk, she chose two pearl combs to adorn her hair. Parting her hair in the Grecian style, she used the pearl combs to sweep the tendrils from her face while the rest of her hair cascaded over her bare shoulders and down her back.

It had been years since she had worn her mother's combs. But tonight was special. She would go to James not as a fatigued and disheveled nursemaid concerned for his care, but as a woman accepting a handsome man's invitation to dine.

She descended the stairs, intending to go to the dining room, when Coates met her at the bottom of the staircase.

"His Grace awaits you in the billiard room."

Bella eyed him with puzzlement. "The billiard room?"

"Dinner will be served there."

She frowned as she made her way down the hall. How strange. What was James thinking?

She had forgotten about the billiard room. James had purchased the snooker table and had it delivered when she had been out of the house with Evelyn. At the time, she had sworn he did it to spite her. He had taken over one of the smaller parlor rooms and had the table assembled and a cue rack installed on the wall within the short time she had been gone. He had been quite aware that a country widow had no need of a billiard room whereas a bachelor could spend countless hours ensconced in the room with his friends.

So why would James prefer to dine there?

A sudden uneasiness plagued her, and a warning voice whispered in her head. Now that his recovery was complete, did he plan on turning her out? Was the billiard room a symbol for his victory?

She opened the door to find James leaning forward over the cloth-covered table, holding a cue and preparing to take a shot. With a quick thrust of his cue and a resounding crack, ivory balls scattered across the table.

She shut the door behind her. He lowered the cue, his gaze sweeping her face and figure.

"Thank you for coming, Bella. You look beautiful."

Her pulse quickened at the admiration in his eyes. "You look well, Your Grace."

"James," he corrected.

He turned away from the table to face her, and her breath caught.

He must have recently bathed for his dark hair was damp and curled around his collar. The candlelight heightened the rich mahogany of his thick hair and his bronzed, perfectly chiseled features. He was impeccably dressed in buff trousers, a striped waistcoat, and a navy jacket that accentuated his broad shoulders and narrow waist. The reflection of the flame in his eyes turned the deep cobalt into glittering sapphires. She hadn't seen him wear a cravat since before he was injured, and she was struck with how startlingly handsome he looked.

He appeared very much the powerful duke—all supreme and immaculate grandeur and unmistakable nobility. Yet he stirred dangerous and scintillating memories within her—the power and strength of his arms, the searing heat of his kiss, the first touch of his tongue against hers, the distinctive scent of his shaving soap, at once masculine and alluring.

"I thought we were to dine, not play snooker," she said.

"We are, but this room is much more intimate than the large formal dining room. Don't you agree?"

Yes, too intimate, she thought. It was difficult enough for her to resist him in a formal setting with the threat of the servants interrupting them at any time. But here she would be trapped in a small, private room that *invited* intimacy when she was struggling to keep it at bay.

James motioned to a table and chairs in the corner. The table was draped in a snowy-white tablecloth and fine china for two was set upon it. Until now it had escaped her notice, and she realized she had been consumed with watching him.

He walked to the table and held out a chair. "May I?"

His fingers brushed the tops of her bare shoulders as she sat, and a shiver of awareness ran down her spine.

There was a low knock on the door and a footman entered wheeling a cart with silver salvers bearing the Blackwood crest. Lifting the covers, the delicious aromas of turtle soup, roast lamb with a delicate mint sauce, and fresh vegetables made her mouth water. James uncorked a bottle of red wine and filled their crystal goblets.

The footman departed and Bella picked up her spoon. The food was exceptionally prepared, but she could have been eating cold porridge for all she knew. James's eyes feasted upon her as she ate, as if she were as delicious as the main course. She drained her glass and licked her lips nervously. His gaze dropped to her mouth, and he attentively poured her more wine.

"I received a letter from the dowager duchess this morning," he said.

There was uneasiness in her stomach, and she lowered her glass. "Your grandmother?"

"I never called her by that name."

"She provided for your education."

"Yes, but nothing more."

Bella's memories were clear of her own paternal grandmother. Warm embraces, showering kisses, and the aromatic smell of fresh baked bread. She was once again struck by the emotional coldness in which James had been raised.

His father's neglect. His grandmother's disdain. His half brother's belittling.

"She demands I return to London and take over my responsibilities," James said. "It seems my half brother, Gregory, has returned."

"Have you not yet spoken to him about . . . about your circumstances?" she asked.

"No, not since I've inherited the title. I can only imagine how the dowager duchess broke the news to him."

"Did you write her of your illness?"

His tone was harsh. "She deserves no explanations from me."

"Perhaps, but she's right in this instance. As the duke, you must return," Bella found herself saying. How odd that she would have been thrilled to have him gone not long ago and now the knowledge filled her with despair.

Taking a deep breath, she asked the question that had been hovering in her mind like a black cloud. "What will happen here? I mean no disrespect, but we have not resolved our dispute."

"Oh, but we have." He stood and took her hand. "Come. I want to show you something." Guiding her to the snooker table, he picked up a rectangular box that had been resting on its edge and handed it to her. "For you, my dear."

She hadn't noticed the box before, and she frowned in confusion. She opened the lid to find a stunning diamond and ruby necklace wrapped around a rolled piece of parchment. Her heart thundered in her chest at the priceless jewels. She slid the necklace from the parchment and unrolled it. It was his copy of the deed to Wyndmoor Manor.

"They are both yours," he said. "Thank-you gifts for your kindness in my time of need."

Speechless, she stared up at him. "You're giving me these?"

"I thought to buy you emeralds to match your eyes, but the

moment I spotted the rubies in the jeweler's window, I knew they were perfect. They are full of fire and spirit just as you are. As for Wyndmoor Manor, I know it is your heart's desire."

No, you are my heart's desire. At the gift of his deed, the remaining vestiges of the emotional barriers she had erected against him crashed around her like an ocean wave. Her heart took a perilous leap.

"Allow me," he said.

He took the necklace from her numb fingers and moved behind her. His fingers tenderly traced the line of her cheekbone and jaw before entwining in her hair and pushing the mass to one side. Setting the necklace around her neck, he hooked the clasp. His solid chest brushed against her back, and his warm breath caressed her nape—intoxicating and enticing. The priceless jewels rested between her breasts.

She turned slowly until his face was mere inches from hers. She wanted desperately to kiss him, wanted to touch him.

"How can I ever thank you?" she whispered.

"For the jewels or the deed?"

A smile touched her lips. "I'm particularly partial to rubies. How did you know?"

"Ah, but I'm guessing it is the deed that captures you."

"I thought the place reminded you of the old duke. Why did you give it to me?"

His eyes darkened, and his voice lowered. "Bella, I'm to leave tomorrow."

Chapter 20

Bella stilled. James reached out to caress her face, his touch gentle as a summer breeze. It was the gentleness that was her undoing. Her heart suddenly ached with an emptiness and yearning she'd buried for years. Hidden even from herself.

How strange to feel this way now when all she had craved was solitude after Roger's death.

Harriet's words haunted her: *The heart makes its own rules. If only one could control it with logic, it would never be broken. But love and logic tend to stray from each other.*

Love and logic could go to the devil. He was leaving. Without Wyndmoor Manor he had no reason to ever visit Hertfordshire, and with the deed to the property in her possession, she had no need to ever visit London. She would likely never see him again. The frightening truth was she was twenty-four years old, and a widow who would soon become a spinster. She had one chance to be with James, one chance to experience what she never had her entire life and what she most likely may never have again—true desire for a man.

She raised her hand to cover his, holding his warm palm against her cheek, anchoring him to her for the briefest instant. Then she stood on tiptoe and brushed her lips against his.

"Bella?" he asked, his voice gruff.

"Yes, James," she breathed.

She had what she wanted then, and he swept her into his arms. He must have sensed her emptiness, her urgent yearning, for his lips were hot as he plundered her mouth. Their tongues met and rich desire curled around her spine.

Still she felt him hold back. A stab of desperation . . . and lust drove her. She wanted to unleash his darkest desire, his fiery passion. She wanted to experience his strength and heat and yes—God help her—his notorious lovemaking skills. She wanted to experience all of him before time and duty tore him away.

She pressed against him and her hands slid beneath his jacket. The superfine material of his waistcoat felt luxurious beneath her palms. She grasped a fistful of the fine fabric as she kissed him in silent demand.

More, James. Show me more. Show me everything.

His mouth moved from her lips to nuzzle her ear. She held him tightly as his hot breath teased her lobe. He licked the delicate shell before sucking the lobe in his mouth. Liquid heat spread through her veins like molten fire.

She was vaguely aware of the snooker table brushing her low back. Her hands moved to the collar of his jacket and with a shrug of his broad shoulders, it fell to the floor. But there was his waistcoat. She wanted it off. Her fingers curled around his shirtsleeves, his muscles tightening beneath her hands.

"Do you want this, sweetheart?" he asked huskily.

Looking into the mesmerizing blue depths of his eyes, her answer was sure. "I want *you.*"

Her fingers went to the top button of his shirt. With a low groan he tore off his cravat and with impatient hands, he helped her unbutton his shirt.

She stared in awe, stunned by the changes in him. Gone was the lean patient she had treated, instead, here was a healthy, well-muscled man who had been dedicated to a vigorous routine of physical exercise. The scar was there, an angry ten-inch reminder of what he had suffered after her past came calling.

He caught her gaze. "Does my scar repulse you?"

"Oh, no." She traced the puckered skin down his side and lowered her head to kiss him there. "You're beautiful," she whispered against him.

He made a choking sound, then raised her face to his. "You're incredible."

He kissed her, and she felt his fingers at the fastenings at the back of her gown. He undid each button all the while kissing her lips, her neck, the swell of her breasts above her bodice. When the last button came loose, she pushed his hands aside and slipped the gown from her shoulders. The amethyst silk slithered down her body to pool at her dainty slippers. She stepped away from the gown and undid the top bow of her chemise. His gaze glittered as she pushed the chemise down her body, and she stood unabashedly naked before him.

His avid gaze traveled from her breasts to her long legs in the black silk hose and garters. His voice was husky as he looked at her. "I've imagined you naked a thousand times, but you are even lovelier than in my dreams."

Bella's eyes lowered to the bulge in his trousers. She wasn't a virgin; Roger had seen to that during the first months of her marriage. But it had been years since Roger had come to her bed, and the memories were abrupt, painful, and distasteful.

Without a doubt, she knew being with James would be entirely different. His kisses proclaimed pleasure and her body cried out for his touch . . . for him.

He lifted her up onto the edge of the table and, with an impatient sweep of his arm, ivory balls scattered across the table, some falling to the floor and bouncing across the Oriental carpet. Brushing his lips across hers, he murmured, "I chose to dine here to teach you how to play."

She eased back, her eyes devouring him, welcoming him. "Then teach me everything."

There was a wild flash in his eyes, like a predator about to pounce upon its long-stalked prey. A frisson of excitement pierced the base of her spine. The time for words was over. She'd wanted him for so long, she realized.

He stripped impatiently, tossing aside his boots and breeches. Her eyes roved his body. Years ago she'd seen a statue of Ares, the Greek god of war. She'd been fifteen at the time and thought the sculptor had created an impossibly unattainable version of the male form. She'd been wrong. James was broad shouldered and perfectly proportioned. His stomach had ridges of corrugate muscle that trailed down to his hips. Down to his large, rigid manhood.

Oh, my, she thought. She had imagined what he would look like, but he was different, so different, from her experience. Roger had been a pudgy, hairy man who cared only for his pleasure. But James . . . nothing about him looked soft.

At her intense look, he groaned low in his throat and captured her lips in a soul-searching kiss. His hard, muscled thighs pressed between her legs, brushed against her core, and desire like rich wine flowed in her veins and low into her woman's center. His hands caressed her breasts as he dipped his head to take a taut nipple into his mouth. Her body cried out from the wet friction of his tongue, his expert touch, as he leisurely lavished attention first on one breast, then the other.

He raised his head to capture her mouth with drugging kisses as his hands ran up her legs past her garters and caressed the soft flesh between her thighs. She moaned in delight, trembling with the flood of new sensations, and when his hand brushed the curls between her legs and his finger slid inside her, testing her wetness, she uttered a choked cry.

"How do you feel, sweetheart?" he asked.

"Hot. Hot and wicked," she panted.

He groaned. "Wicked is good."

He entered her slowly, giving her body time to adjust to him, but she was past the point of wanting him slowly, she wanted all of him . . . needed to feel his size and weight. She arched up, gasping, her nails raking his back and buttocks. Blessedly, he understood. Lifting her hips, he fully embedded himself in one smooth thrust. She cried out at the fullness of him and clung to his damp shoulders.

He stilled above her. "God, Bella. You're so tight," he groaned. "Are you all right?"

"Yes," she breathed. "Yes, yes . . . *yes.*"

He began to move, and Bella was quick to meet his thrusts. She was gloriously aware of the muscular cage of James's arms on either side of her and of the soft felt of the table beneath her. Staring up into his face, she knew she wasn't the only one lost. James looked just as intense, just as impassioned. He kissed her lips, her neck, her breasts as his thrusts increased in tempo.

Her body tightened like a bow and met his rhythm until her inner muscles contracted, and her pleasure peaked in an exquisite climax. Her pleasure triggered his. His head dropped forward, his body went rigid, and he released a growl that reverberated through her heart and soul.

James carried Bella across the room and laid her in front of the fireplace. He stretched out alongside her on the soft carpet. Spooning her body with his, her lush buttocks pressed against his groin, he placed a kiss on her shoulder. She sighed and rested her head on his bicep, her eyelids fluttering closed.

An unfamiliar feeling of tenderness swelled in his chest. He swallowed and tried not to think of what had just transpired between them, but to no avail. Nothing had prepared him for the real-life experience of making love to Bella. Not his erotic fantasies, not their heated kisses, not even the passionate thrilling encounter behind the stables the day of the fair.

She was splendidly uninhibited in her passion. Watching as she climaxed, her glorious dark red hair spread out on the

table, her long legs clasped tightly around his hips, had
heightened his own pleasure to a fevered pitch.

For the first time in his life, he had experienced a strong
connection to another person. An invisible web that bound
them. It petrified him to feel this intimacy—he who had
learned early on to remain aloof or suffer the pain of rejection.
She had managed to pierce his armor, to thaw the long-ago
frozen glacier that he identified as his heart.

Somehow she had gotten under his skin, and he had
become obsessed with Bella Sinclair. A part of him—the
helpless part—accepted this obsession as inevitable, just as
the rising and setting of the sun, and suspected where it was
heading. But the rest of his emotions were a jumbled mix of
foreign and fearful feelings.

He should rise and help her dress, carry her back to her
room and walk away. Use his power and influence to make
her dreams come true—whatever they may be. Instead he ran
his hand up the smooth curve of her hip and traced the side of
her breast. She stretched sinuously and turned her head to
look at him.

"Are you going to fall asleep?" he asked.

She smiled up at him. "I don't suppose Harriet would approve."

He laughed, and trailed his fingers across her breast. Her
nipples instantly hardened into rosy peaks and she turned
more fully in his arms. His arousal responded. He wondered
if he'd ever have his fill of her.

Her eyes widened at the feel of his erection against her
thigh. "What would Coates say if he found us like this?"

"I'm no longer ill. Coates knows better than to interrupt."

Her brow furrowed, and he inwardly cursed himself at his
hasty response.

"You've made love to other women that frequently then?"
she asked.

Made love? No, he never called the act by that name. He'd

been with many women, but he'd only made love to one . . .
to her. How to phrase it without sounding cold? "I won't lie
about my past, Bella. Celibacy has never been my strength.
I've never desired an emotional commitment."

She pressed against him, until their hearts beat as one.
"You were right when you had said there was no passion in
my marriage. Roger was much older and . . . and he only
came to my bed in the first months of our marriage. He was
always drunk, and it was painful . . . not pleasant. He had tried
thereafter . . . but he was unable. He said it was me."

Anger simmered in his veins. He had come to his own conclusions regarding her lack of experience, but not that her
husband had been an abusive alcoholic who had blamed his
impotence on her.

Sick bastard. The thought struck James that as a young
bride Bella had known a sharp betrayal. A betrayal similar to
his own. They had both been let down by those whose intrinsic duty required that they protect and care for them. James
pictured her, a scared seventeen-year-old bride at the mercy
of a sexually deviant older man.

What else was lurking in her past? Had Roger Sinclair
physically abused her regularly? No matter how horrific, such
was not uncommon.

His voice was a velvet murmur. "You are not lacking in any
way. You are a beautiful, desirable woman." It was true. He
wanted her again, wanted to be buried deep inside her, make
her cry out with pleasure.

She ran her palm down his chest, her eyes wide orbs of jade
as she studied his body. "*You* are beautiful. And your skill is
quite extraordinary. For the first time, I can understand why
Byron and his fellow poets are so popular."

"Then allow me the pleasure of welcoming you to touch
me at will."

She was hesitant at first, watching his face for any signs
that she did something wrong. Her fingers traced the corru-

gated muscles of his abdomen, then, lower, to wrap about his hardness. The pleasure was so intense, he nearly jumped out of his skin.

He rolled onto his back, taking her with him until she straddled him. When her softness rubbed against his cock, she gasped.

"Let yourself go, Bella," he urged.

He shifted his hips, rubbing more fully against her, until she was gloriously wet with wanting. She grew wild then, nipping his shoulders, kissing his chest, licking his nipples. Her hair trailed over him, sending exquisite sensations in its wake. He gritted his teeth, forced himself to remain still, allowed her to experience him at will.

At the end it was she who lowered herself onto his throbbing shaft. Inch by delicious inch she took him inside. She clutched his shoulders, and his hands clamped about her hips. He let her set the rhythm, slowly at first, then more urgently. Her hair was a silken curtain about her shoulders, her eyes closed, her breasts bouncing as she rode him.

Sweat beaded on his brow as he watched her, watched her take her pleasure and pleasure him in return. She was all slick need and fiery hotness. He lay back and watched as she peaked, taking him even deeper as her inner muscles tightened, urging him on to his own explosive climax. He breathed in deep soul-drenching drafts as she stole his will. There was nothing to stop it. He closed his eyes and surrendered.

Chapter 21

Bella stretched before the fireplace and studied James's face. "Did you know we were to be intimate here?"

James grinned and kissed the tip of her nose. "No. I thought to dine here and to show you how to play snooker. I'm leaving the table behind after all. But I'll admit this was a much more enjoyable use of the room."

He stood and helped her to her feet. He pulled on his shirt and trousers, then played the lady's maid and assisted her with the tiny row of buttons on the back of her gown.

He finished with the last button, and she turned in his arms. "Thank you for an unforgettable evening," she whispered.

"It is I who should be thanking you. Should you need anything, I can easily be found at Lincoln's Inn or at the old duke's home on Park Street. London is not far from Hertfordshire."

A hot ache grew in her throat, and she could only nod.

At her silence, his expression grew serious. Cupping her chin in his hand, he raised her eyes to his. "Bella, after the attack in the stables, I feel compelled to ask you one last time. Are you certain no one is following you?"

She swallowed. "Yes, I'm certain."

His dropped his hand. "Very well. My offer remains sincere. Promise you will come to me should you find yourself in trouble." Once more, his face displayed an uncanny awareness as though he could read her mind and discover her most hidden secrets.

Heart fluttering wildly, she wondered if he suspected the truth, then reminded herself that he was a barrister, trained to question every scenario.

"I promise to seek you out should anything befall me that I cannot manage on my own." The truth. With Rupert gone and in hiding, she had the rights to Wyndmoor Manor and could handle her future. Even if it meant harboring this loneliness for the rest of her life.

"May I escort you to your bedchamber?"

"Only to the door. I do believe Harriet would faint if she found us together."

He winked. "Do not underestimate her."

James took her elbow and they walked side by side through the halls and up the staircase. He halted at her door, brushed a quick kiss across her lips, then bid her good night.

Bella sat at the dressing table in her sitting room and stared in the mirror. Her face was flushed, her hair disheveled, her lips red and swollen from James's kisses. Lifting a hand, she touched her lips with her fingertips. Her eyes fluttered closed as she pictured their lovemaking.

James had made her feel desirable and worthy of his every kiss, his every glorious touch. If she lived to be one hundred years old, she would never forget tonight. Her heart ached under her breast, and she could no longer deny the truth. She had fallen in love with the Duke of Blackwood.

If only they had met before she was married, before he had inherited the title, before they had both desired Wyndmoor Manor.

She sighed. There was no sense wondering if. She was

thankful she had experienced him as a man and thankful she had title to the property. She was an independent woman at last. She was free to write and live her life on her own terms at last.

She opened the rectangular box and stared at James's deed. Going to her mother's trunk in the corner of the room, she placed the deed inside along with her own copy complete with Sir Reeves's scrawled signature.

The ruby necklace lay cool against her throat, and she impulsively decided to sleep with the jewels tonight as a reminder of what she and James had shared. Harriet would arrive soon and prepare her bath. Bella knew better than to attempt to hide tonight's events from the old woman. She could not help but notice the rubies, but even more telling, Harriet would see the glow in Bella's face.

She left the sitting room and entered the adjoining bedchamber. One of the maids must have already been there for the coverlet was drawn back.

Bella took a step forward, then froze.

A shiver of fear raced down her spine.

There was a dagger thrust into her pillow, pinning a note in place.

She pulled the dagger from the pillow, causing a burst of feathers to float above the coverlet. Her hand trembled as she read the note.

Bella,
    Meet me at midnight tomorrow in the back gardens with the ledger. Do not fail me. The duke lives. My next shot, whether for him or another, will be true.

Rupert had not even bothered to sign the note. Bella looked frantically about. The windows were shut and locked. There were no signs of forced entry. So how had Rupert entered?

Was it plausible that Rupert had walked in through the front door?

She felt as if every drop of blood had drained from her head. She had allowed herself to believe that Rupert wouldn't risk his neck by returning.

She had been terribly wrong. His desire for the ledger outweighed any risks. But the trouble was she had not found the ledger.

What was she to do?

Could she prepare a fake ledger? She swiftly dismissed the notion. She'd never recall all the transactions. She could beg Rupert's understanding, tell him the ledger was not in her possession, but she knew he would never believe her.

She bit her lip until it throbbed like her pulse. She had foolishly believed that her future was secure. James had gifted her with his deed, which would allow her to remain at Wyndmoor and write to her heart's content. She had the memory of James's lovemaking to warm her on the cold nights ahead, and a contract for the *Times* to keep her mind busy.

But such respite was not to be. Rupert's message was clear. He had shot and come close to killing the duke. Whether Rupert had panicked and fired unintentionally was not relevant. The fact that he'd returned proclaimed how desperate he was to retrieve the ledger. Next time he would kill. Who his victim would be, she could only guess.

None of it mattered. Only one option remained.

The door opened wide, and Harriet stood in the entrance.

Bella turned slowly, the dagger still clutched in her hand.

Harriet froze, mouth open. Then her eyes flew from the dagger to the blood-red rubies at Bella's throat. "What happened?"

"Help me pack. We're leaving for London."

* * *

James sat at the escritoire in his bedchamber and scrawled a letter to the dowager duchess. The content of the letter was brusque, the tone coolly impersonal—one of a barrister addressing a court. The gist of the letter: He would leave Wyndmoor Manor immediately, return to London in two days' time, and permanently move into the mansion on Park Street. Advise the servants of the new duke's arrival.

Not for the first time that evening, he acknowledged that his feelings for Bella had become complicated and the thought of returning to London held little appeal. Yet duty called, and he knew that he must return and conclude his business dealings at Lincoln's Inn, deal with his grandmother's demands, and confront Gregory. At least one item was certain—Bella would remain at Wyndmoor Manor. Gifting her with the deed ensured that. Her desire for the property had been utmost in her mind, and he need not worry she'd disappear and he wouldn't be able to find her.

He could wait until the time was right, until he heard back from his investigator regarding Bella, until all his business matters were settled and his inheritance properly claimed, before returning here and settling things between them. One night of lovemaking, no matter how extraordinary, had not satisfied this craving. . . .

Setting aside the pen, he was folding the piece of foolscap when the door opened. He turned, expecting Coates.

Bella.

His gut clenched at the sight of her. She was still in the amethyst gown with his rubies draped about her neck. Gone were her pearl combs, and her glorious hair framed her exquisite features and green, catlike eyes.

His attraction was immediate and total. Desire and possessiveness raged in his blood. Had she come to spend their remaining night together?

He stood. She shut the door and stepped forward.

But something was not right.

Through the searing lust he was slow to register the anxious look on her face, as if she was holding a mountain of raw emotion in check. Tension radiated from her, and she clutched her hands behind her back.

His initial excitement at her arrival in his bedchamber became concern. "Is something amiss?"

Coming forward, she extended her hand to place a document on his escritoire.

His deed to Wyndmoor Manor.

"I've changed my mind," she said. "I believe you should have the place. Does your offer still stand to pay me for the property?"

Something inside him shifted. Desire waned. Instinct and intuition reared.

"Why the change of heart?"

Her voice was flat. "I've reconsidered. It doesn't feel right. The place reminds you of your father, the old duke. You should be the rightful owner. I've decided that I'd rather go to London."

His eyes narrowed dangerously. "London? Whatever happened to your writing aspirations? You had led me to believe that being an independent landowner allowed you to finally live your life the way you chose."

"I can write in London. I'll be closer to my editor at the *Times*. . . . May even be able to meet him."

"But that would be fruitless, would it not? The editor believes you are a man."

She paled a shade. He fought the desire to shake her until she confessed the truth. It was no longer a question of *if* she was in trouble, but *what* the trouble was. What had happened in an hour's time?

"Will you honor your offer?" she asked again.

He walked toward her with measured steps, near enough that he could reach out and touch her should he wish to do so. He raised a hand to finger a curl at her cheek. She sucked in a breath, her green eyes pools of appeal. He detected her shiver of desire, but another emotion overpowered it—fear. It oozed from her—like one of his criminal defendants prior to testifying on the stand before an angry jury.

He quickly considered the turn of events. If she wasn't at Wyndmoor Manor, then she would be closer to him in London. He'd have to alter his plans. . . .

A thin chill hung at the edge of his words. "I'll honor my offer on one condition. You accompany me to London tomorrow."

"I accept."

Her answer was too quickly given. She was running from something . . . or *someone*.

He wouldn't ask again. He had attempted to extract the truth from her before, but to no avail. He would now resort to the legal strategies with which he was more familiar.

"Thank you," she said. "It seems I'm in your debt once again."

"Go, Bella. Go now and pack."

As soon as she departed, James went in search of Bobby. Well past midnight, he found the stable lad in his bed in the servant's quarters. James shook his shoulder.

"The horses?" Bobby woke with a start.

James shook his head. "The horses are fine, Bobby. I've come on a different matter. Bella and Harriet will accompany us to London tomorrow. The women will ride in my carriage as I prefer to ride Maximus. When we get to London the women plan to part ways with me. I'm expected at the mansion on Park Street. Bella's whereabouts, however, are unknown. I want you to stay with her. I want to know where they end up. Understand?"

"Will she protest?"

"It's no matter. Follow her, if need be."

Bobby grinned. "It won't be a problem, Your Grace. I grew up in the London streets and know my way around like the back of my hand. She'll never spot me."

Chapter 22

London was nothing like Bella remembered. Although she had been born here, she and her father had moved to the country when she was seven. Her memories were hazy—her small bedchamber in their modest brick home, the hawker's cries of "Fresh hot buns!" outside her window rivaling the church bell Sunday mornings, playing with the rambunctious neighborhood children, and the smell of flowerboxes in the spring.

They had left Wyndmoor Manor early the previous morning, had stopped at an inn for the night, and had pressed onward at the first touch of dawn. James, it seemed, was in a great rush to return to London. Bella had voiced no complaint. The hectic pace suited her, for each mile they put behind them hastened her distance from Rupert. London offered her a chance to hide and disappear amongst the hustle and bustle of the city. It also meant parting from James, but that would have happened whether or not she had stayed in Hertfordshire. He had a life here, and combined with his new title, his return was inevitable.

The city air was thick with the scent of coal smoke and impending rain. Sitting in the duke's luxurious carriage, she looked out at the cobbled streets as they wove around ramshackle hackneys, two-wheeled gigs driven by young gentlemen, and heavy horses pulling brewers' drays prodded by coarse trades-men. They passed a coffeehouse and the aroma of freshly ground beans made her mouth water. In the distance, the city's blackened chimneys grappled with church spires to crowd the hazy sky.

Harriet sat on the padded bench across from Bella, her gaze glued to the window, her fascination with the city evident in her expression. James rode Maximus beside the carriage. The women had protested, saying they would take a coach at the nearest posting inn, but James had refused, reassuring them he preferred to ride his horse.

The carriage stopped before an imposing structure built of stone, white brick, and marble. Letters etched in the stone proclaimed the building to be the Bank of England. To the east was the London Stock Exchange.

James dismounted Maximus and spoke through the carriage window. "I'll be but a minute."

Bella nodded and watched as James entered the bank. As soon as he was out of sight, Harriet opened the door and stepped down. "I'd best find us transportation. There are plenty of hack-neys on this street." Harriet shut the door, leaving Bella alone.

Minutes passed, and the temperature in the carriage rose. Bella's nerves were tense. She needed to be on her way before what little strength she had evaporated.

At last, James emerged from the bank with a packet tucked under his arm. He opened the carriage door and handed her the packet. "Payment in full for Wyndmoor."

"Thank you."

"I shall escort you to wherever you choose."

She tried to keep her heart cold and still. "No. We will be fine from here on. You need to attend the dowager duchess."

"Then allow my driver and Bobby to accompany you."

"That's not necessary. We have more than sufficient funds to rent a hackney cab and find a house."

She expected him to argue, but he offered her his arm instead.

She accepted his aid and stepped from the carriage. A bright shaft of sunlight broke through the clouds and struck his dark hair and perfect features. He was so startling handsome that her heart jumped. She wanted to kiss his lips for the last time. It didn't matter that they stood in a busy London street with passersby. The noise of the city thrummed in the background.

His expression shuttered, and he inclined his head toward the street. "Your cab is ready," James said.

The parting is easy for him, Bella thought, *and I feel as if I am leaving a part of my soul behind.*

She turned and saw that Harriet had flagged down a hackney cab and the driver was loading their baggage on top. They had left items behind and had taken only what was necessary and manageable.

James opened the door of the hackney. As she moved to enter, he touched her cheek and raised her hand to brush his lips across the back of her fingers. Pain squeezed her heart.

Lifting his head, dark blue eyes probed to her very soul. "Never forget my offer. Send for me should you need to."

Bella directed the driver straight to her childhood neighborhood—close to Portman Square and its magnificent mansions, but not so close as to be unaffordable by the working class. Time had changed the neighborhood, however, and the once well-swept cobbled streets were in disrepair, parts of them slick with horse dung and rotting refuse. Smocked tradesmen scurried about on their way to work, and children dressed in plain clothes rushed to the cotton factories.

The driver knew of a boarding house looking for a tenant and took them there. Bella stepped from the cab and looked up at a three-story red brick house with black shutters.

"You mean to stay here?" Harriet asked.

"It's perfect. Rupert will never think to search here."

The landlady was a thick-boned woman with an enormous

bosom and lips set in a perpetual sneer. "Third floor is empty. Rent is due the first of the month. No exceptions."

Bella paid the woman. It would do.

"What's yer name?" the landlady asked.

Bella gave the first alias that came to mind—James's suggested pseudonym for her writing career. "Mrs. Round-bottom," she blurted out.

The woman hesitated for a brief moment, her thin lips twitching, before tucking the rent money in her bodice and handing Bella a key.

Bella let out a held-in breath. Reason warned they couldn't stay in one place for long. If Rupert had inherited half of his twin's resourcefulness, there was a good chance he could find them.

But at least James would be safe.

The mansion on Park Street was a massive pile of stone and marble. James had set foot inside before, of course, but only on rare occasions as a young boy when he had been summoned by the dowager duchess.

The old duke's butler, Stodges, opened the door before James had a chance to knock. Straight-backed and serious, he had the look of a gunnery sergeant. The scowl James remembered as a youth, however, was a lukewarm smile today.

"Welcome, Your Grace," Stodges said. "The dowager is in the silver drawing room."

James nodded and followed Stodges across the marble vestibule. Priceless masterpieces from Rembrandt, Benjamin Marshall, Sawrey Gilpin, and Gerard Ter Borch hung on the walls. They turned down a hallway and James spotted a portrait of the old duke painted by renowned portrait painter Martin Archer Shee. The accuracy of the painting was remarkable and James stared at the dark, curling hair graying at the temples, aquiline nose, and mercurial blue eyes so similar to his own. The duke wasn't smiling; rather his mouth was thin with a cynical twist, giving him the stubborn, yet arrogant look James remembered.

The irony of James's current situation struck him. Just months ago he would have mocked anyone who even suggested he was the rightful heir. For his entire life, the mansion had been a taunting symbol of everything James had never been entitled to. He had been raised as the family outcast, only to suddenly learn that he rightfully *owned* it all.

Stodges opened the door of the silver drawing room, and James strode inside. Richly decorated with striped blue and silver silk drapes and a thick Oriental carpet, it was one of three drawing rooms in the house. The dowager duchess sat at a Roman-inspired pedestal card table with lion paw feet playing solitaire. As soon as she saw James, she set down her cards.

Stodges quietly departed and shut the door behind him.

Steel-blue eyes met James's own. "So you've finally arrived. I thought you were wallowing away in a drunken stupor in that insignificant country estate."

"What a splendid welcome. Did you not receive my note?"

She pushed back her chair and stood. "It's been weeks. I expected you to come home sooner."

Home. This place was no more a home than the boarding school in which he had resided his entire childhood. The fact that his grandmother did not recognize this spoke volumes of her own character.

Her mouth thinned with displeasure, and she shot him a cool stare. "We have much to discuss. You have a responsibility to this house and the title."

James made a show of glancing about the exquisite drawing room. "The mansion surely has suffered no ill effects during my absence. I'm confident you have kept all the servants in line."

"Do not belittle me. You are now a *duke.*"

"Yes, about that. Are you certain of my legitimacy?"

She appeared momentarily flustered. "I told you that your father confessed to me on his deathbed. I had a solicitor look into the marriage license and it was properly recorded."

"Ah, I see," he said softly, mockingly. "But numerous questions have been plaguing me these past weeks. Why tell anyone? It is no secret you have never approved of my existence. Why repeat what the old duke said? Why not take it to your grave? Gregory is still the old duke's son, and the title would have passed straight to him with no one the wiser. After all, he was raised and groomed to be the duke."

The dowager's hand fluttered to her chest. "Are you suggesting I lie? My heart will surely break."

"Please save your dramatics for Drury Lane. We both know your heart is as soft as a paving stone. You never act unless there is a beneficial purpose for you and your coveted status in the *ton*."

James had wondered about the dowager's true motives ever since she had stormed the Old Bailey Courthouse and delivered the news of his father's death.

"Come now," James prodded. "No one else is present, and you are free to speak the truth. It has to do with Gregory, doesn't it?"

Her eyes narrowed to slits, and she pointed a finger at his chest. "Now you listen to me. Since the time of the first Duke of Blackwood, the title has passed straight from father to son, and I have a responsibility to ensure its integrity. You are the true duke."

James didn't doubt her. "And what of Gregory?"

"He's not fit to bear the title," she snapped. "He's turned into a drunken wastrel and gambler. Worse, he's been snared by the evils of opium."

Opium!

When had Gregory begun to indulge in the highly addictive and destructive drug? James had suspected her reasons had to do with his half brother's irresponsible behavior, but had little guessed the extent of his troubles.

The dowager stepped closer and raised her chin. "I realize you believe I neglected you as a child, but I have watched you grow into a man. Your education—which *I* paid for—and your training at Lincoln's Inn have turned you into a shrewd and manipulative barrister. You would do the title justice, save one character flaw."

He couldn't help himself. His words were loaded with ridicule. "Please enlighten me as to which character flaw you refer, and I shall endeavor to exploit it at my leisure."

"Don't be daft. I'm aware of your rakish reputation, and I am not ignorant of the base needs of men. I also know of your aversion to marriage, which I suspect is due to your own parents' short, unfortunate union. I wouldn't dare ask you to curb your animalistic nature; however, you *must* marry and produce an heir. Thereafter, I trust you would exercise more discretion with your liaisons."

He had prided himself on distancing himself from his family years ago, yet the speed at which his temper rose was startling. *Control, James. You must not let her get under your skin.*

He took a breath, calming himself. She had said nothing that was not well understood. Most married men of the *beau monde,* and certainly the titled ones who married to increase their wealth, enhance their status, or both, took mistresses. After the precious male heir was born, many wives found lovers.

So why allow the dowager's words to anger him?

It was the notion that after a lifetime of being ignored, he was now expected to jump and do her bidding when she snapped her fingers.

There was a knock on the door and Stodges stood in the doorway. "Lord Gregory, Your Grace."

Gregory pushed past Stodges to march into the drawing room. Brown hair and eyes, he was dressed in trousers and a shapeless green coat that appeared three sizes too big. His pronounced cheekbones and sunken eye sockets reminded James of a cadaver.

Other than at the old duke's funeral, where James had only glimpsed Gregory, James hadn't seen his half brother in eight months, and he was struck by the change in Gregory's appearance. He appeared to have lost at least four stone in weight.

James recognized the telltale signs—the sudden weight loss, the sallow complexion, the dry cracked lips, the bloodshot eyes. He'd had clients who had gone down the same slippery slope into ruin. Indulgence in alcohol, gambling hells, sex, food, or opium came to mind. One excess could bring about the haggard appearance, but any combination would quickly take its toll on a man's health and mind.

Gregory stalked forward. "So the 'rightful' son returns."

"Hello, Gregory," James said. "We have much to discuss."

"We've rarely spoken our entire lives, and I see no need to start now. I've moved out of the mansion to a townhouse on St. James's Street."

"Good to know," James said.

Gregory scowled. "I intend to petition the courts to look into the legitimacy of your mother's alleged marriage to the old duke. I cannot imagine he would have been so smitten or sufficiently intoxicated to marry a parlor maid and trollop."

"I'd deem that a waste of time," James drawled. "I am an experienced barrister after all."

"Precisely," Gregory sneered. "Hardly proper material for a duke of the realm."

The dowager raised her hand. "Stop this nonsense, Gregory. The marriage license is legitimate. I had a trusted solicitor see to the matter, and he will testify to that fact in any court of law."

"You needn't worry," James addressed Gregory. "I am prepared to offer you an income."

"I don't want a shilling from you," Gregory said.

"Don't be a fool. What of Lady Caroline?" James asked.

"What of her?"

"Last I heard, you were to marry the Earl of Atwood's daughter. I understand finances are a foreign concept to you, but have you given any thought to how you will survive?" James said.

"Are you proposing a monthly stipend?" Gregory said.

"Yes, but not without proper consideration."

"Are you suggesting I *work?*"

"A novel notion to you, I see. Our father owned many properties. Although they are run by competent stewards, I could use a man to manage one of the properties. You would be an overseer, and I would pay you a generous amount for your services," James said.

Gregory looked to the dowager. "Are you going to sit back and allow him to mistreat me?"

"His idea has merit," the dowager responded.

Gregory pointed a finger at James. "This isn't over yet, *brother.*" He stormed from the room.

The dowager's eyes gleamed with satisfaction. "I was right. You have taken control with an iron hand. This Season is full of heiresses clamoring for a husband. Pick one."

James's temper finally snapped, and his voice hardened. "You had best heed my words, Your Grace. I'm not as easily controlled as Gregory."

Chapter 23

Seven o'clock the following morning, Coates entered James's bedchamber. As was his usual work habit at Lincoln's Inn, James preferred to rise early and was already awake and in his dressing gown.

"You look haggard. Did you spend your first night in this big mansion indulging in the old duke's fine whiskey?" Coates asked.

James eyes Coates warily. "What's irking you this morning?"

Coates dropped a handful of shaving materials onto the washstand. "Nothing. But if I am to dress and shave you, then I prefer to know what mood you are in."

"If you must know, I did not indulge in anything. I merely found it difficult to sleep in strange surroundings."

"Ha! As if you've ever suffered from such a problem in all the ladies' bedchambers of your past."

"That's just it. I've never *slept* in any of them."

Coates frowned. "The answer to your sleeplessness is simple. You should not have allowed *her* to leave."

His manservant meant Bella, of course. Coates had been prickly since he had learned James had paid Bella for Wyndmoor Manor and they had parted ways in London. It was no surprise that Coates had become Bella Sinclair's champion.

The man had sung her praises ever since James's fever abated and he had been sufficiently coherent to comprehend. She had helped nurse him, Coates had said. She had found and convinced Dr. Grimsby to travel to Hertfordshire, Coates had repeatedly reminded him. She had *saved* his life.

Everything James knew.

"I do believe I shall shave myself today," James said dryly.

"Fine." Coates marched out.

James went to the washstand. He had spoken the truth to Coates. There had been no whiskey last night, only the troubling quandary that had made him toss and turn in the magnificent master chamber for hours. Rather than enjoy the thick, feathered mattress, he had pondered the haunting look in Bella's eyes when she had asked if he would honor his offer to pay her for Wyndmoor Manor. She'd worn a similar expression when he handed her the envelope stuffed with banknotes outside the Bank of England.

Her corrupt, abusive husband was dead. So what else could she fear?

Picking up the shaving brush, James lathered his face. What Coates didn't know was that James had no intention of allowing Bella to slip through his fingers. He wanted desperately to help her, wanted to see her safely ensconced at Wyndmoor Manor—where they could resume where they'd left off and explore their fiery passion.

He lifted the razor, his hand halting in midair when the butler opened the door.

"You have a caller, Your Grace. It's—"

"Send him up at once." James expected Investigator Papazian with a full report this morning. Finally he would get the answers to the ceaseless, inward questions that plagued him.

But Stodges didn't move. "You have a *female* caller, Your Grace. Lady Caroline, daughter of the Earl of Atwood."

James set down his razor. "Gregory is not present."

Stodges cleared his throat. "She's requesting an audience with you, Your Grace."

"I see," James said, even though he had no idea why his half brother's betrothed would call upon him. "See her to the drawing room while I dress."

"Which one, Your Grace?"

James grit his teeth. "You choose," he snapped. The butler's rigid formality was at distinct odds with Coates's forthright attitude. Both were extremely irritating this morning. He had expected a meeting with his hired investigator, dammit, not a social call from an earl's daughter.

James finished shaving and dressed. He made his way through the maze of hallways, and found Lady Caroline in what Stodges referred to as the yellow drawing room. She sat on a pale gold settee and jumped to her feet when he entered the room.

She curtsied deeply. "I apologize for the early call, Your Grace, and I'm thankful you agreed to see me."

Tall and slender with honey-colored hair and light blue eyes, she was an attractive woman. The type of female he would have been interested in before . . .

Before what?

Before inheriting the title and rushing to Wyndmoor Manor? Or more precisely, before Bella Sinclair?

Irritated with his thoughts, he forced Bella from his mind. "How may I be of assistance, Lady Caroline?"

"We've never been formally introduced, Your Grace, but circumstances have been quite . . . unusual."

Unusual indeed. He knew Lady Caroline's father on familiar terms as the Earl of Atwood had sought out James's legal services to anonymously handle a sizeable gambling debt to a notorious London moneylender three years ago. Atwood's daughter—along with the rest of society—was ignorant of the earl's addiction. The privilege associated with a barrister-client relationship ensured Atwood's secret would be kept.

James smiled smoothly, betraying nothing of his annoyance at her untimely visit. "I do believe congratulations are in order. You are to marry my brother."

She stepped forward and the scent of her perfume—a cloying floral bouquet—enveloped the space between them. The sickly sweet smell permeated his nostrils, and he couldn't help but wonder why he found it so strong since many of the ladies of the *ton* preferred a similar perfume, and he had never found it offensive in the past.

"My engagement is a delicate matter, Your Grace."

"How so?"

Lady Caroline sighed, and James's gaze was drawn to her full breasts rising and falling against the artfully designed low neckline of her gown.

"It was never official."

"That is not Gregory's understanding," James said.

"He's mistaken. The reading of the banns has not begun. It was merely a loose arrangement between my father and yours."

"I see. And with the old duke gone you mean the arrangement is null and void."

"It's no longer simple. My father had agreed with the understanding that I marry a duke and become a duchess. Gregory is no longer the duke," she pointed out.

James knew her intent, but he asked anyway, "What's to become of it then?"

She came closer and placed her hand on his sleeve, her long, slender fingers curling around the fabric. Gazing up at him, she breathed, "*You* are now the duke. The agreement should be between us."

He recognized the eager gleam in her powder-blue eyes. Countless women had gazed up at him with similar expressions. For a brief instant, he was tempted to see just how far she was willing to go. To lose himself in a willing body and mindless sex.

But there was a sourness in the pit of his stomach that had little to do with the fact that she was Gregory's betrothed. Rather, he struggled with unfamiliar morals of a different sort. For the first time in his life, he felt like he would be betraying another's trust by indulging in a meaningless liaison.

He removed her hand from his sleeve. "I doubt my brother would agree with your interpretation."

She pouted, her eyes raking boldly over him. "May I confess a secret? I was glad when I heard of your legitimacy. I've seen you before at Lady Cameron's ball, and I found myself instantly drawn. I would make you a great duchess."

No doubt, he thought. She was everything he had enjoyed in a lover in the past. Beautiful, voluptuous, willing . . .

Yet she was clearly disloyal and conniving, both traits he'd ignored easily enough in a woman—whereas now they were as vivid as if emblazoned on her forehead.

A sudden image of Bella rose within his mind and along with it a fierce longing. He ached for the sight of her glorious auburn hair and fiery green eyes. He yearned to hear her delightful laughter, and he missed her tantalizing lavender scent—light and cool as a summer breeze across Wyndmoor's lawns.

She had drawn him from the beginning, like the first taste of fine wine. She was honest and loyal and beautiful and giving. At thirty-three years old, he had experienced his fair share of females, but never had he desired a woman as much as he wanted Bella Sinclair. And he had stood by and watched her ride away.

Coates was right. He should have insisted she stay, not allowed her out of his sight. Made her confess the truth to whatever she was running from.

At his silence, Lady Caroline said, "The dowager would understand. All you need to do is speak with her."

James's attention was drawn back to the woman before him. As he looked into her artfully seductive eyes, he felt inexplicably empty. "Gregory will be disappointed," he said. "He's lost the title and the woman he loves."

"He never loved me. It was nothing but a beneficial arrangement between our fathers."

"Even so. I'd expect my duchess to show more loyalty."

Lady Caroline opened her mouth as though she would speak, then closed it.

Just then there was a knock and Stodges opened the drawing room door. "Your appointment has arrived, Your Grace."

James took one look at the calling card the butler offered. "See him to the library. I'll join him shortly." He turned to Lady Caroline. "If you'll excuse me, I have a pressing business matter to attend to."

She curtsied. "You will think of my visit?"

"I shall not easily forget it, my lady."

"Bella! Look here! Blackwood's stable lad is outside your window," Harriet said.

Bella joined Harriet at the window and parted the frayed curtains to look at the street below. "You mean Bobby? Where?"

"There," Harriet pointed, "next to the gin shop across the street."

Bella spotted him then. Bobby stood in the shadow of the baker's boy, who was hawking fresh rolls from a tray hanging from a band around his neck.

"What's he doing here?" Bella asked.

"He's following the duke's orders. Careful now, you don't want the lad to see you. Then he'll know he's been spotted."

Bella dropped the curtain and whirled away from the window. "You sound pleased."

"I've had my suspicions about the duke's behavior," Harriet said. "He cares enough to have you followed."

"This is not good, Harriet. We need to move. If Blackwood

can find us, then Rupert will be able to as well. You haven't forgotten Rupert's threats, have you?"

Harriet's face fell. "No, luv. I haven't."

"We must leave immediately. We can slip out the back."

Harriet sighed. "I'll start packing."

Bella waited until Harriet departed before quickly glancing out the window. The baker's boy had wandered down the street. For a brief instant she could no longer see Bobby and she wondered if Harriet had been wrong, but a shadow between the gin shop and the adjacent building caught her eye. Bobby had slithered deep into the alley, but he remained.

She moved away from the window, pressing her back against the wall and staring bleakly into the dreary rented room. She shut her eyes, and a darkly handsome face rose in her mind.

Deep down, a part of her was relieved to know James cared enough to order Bobby to follow her. James's countenance had been a picture of relaxed acceptance outside the bank, too complacent as she had ridden away in the hackney cab with her belongings. His behavior had pained her, and she had believed that their lovemaking—which had been an earth-shattering experience for her—had meant as little to him as any one of his casual affairs.

But she'd wanted a clean break, hadn't she? She had known their night together in the billiard room was to be their last. She had been determined to grasp happiness, no matter how fleeting.

Her past had returned with a vengeance, determined to hunt and stalk her. Rupert wanted the ledger, no matter the cost to human life. And how could she live with herself if those she loved were killed?

And she did love James. He had burst into her life, and she had been swept away by his passionate challenge and his devastatingly handsome face. They had started off as enemies, but he wasn't the demanding, blue-blooded duke she had believed.

Yet it was his brush with death that had forced her to acknowledge her burgeoning feelings. James made her feel like a breathless girl of seventeen again—innocent, untainted—and everything took on a clean brightness when he was near. She had admired his intelligence, his driving ambition to succeed, and his thoughtfulness. He was a man who had fought for everything he had achieved, yet he maintained a natural charm and possessed an unwavering confidence. She had soon been lost in the flash of humor in his blue eyes, his generous nature, and his genuine interest in her writing.

She was torn.

Leave me be, James.

Find me and love me.

No! She was strong, she told herself. She had never allowed Roger Sinclair to break her. She had fought him tirelessly for seven years. Despite the fear in her heart he had inspired, she had learned to conceal her emotions from her husband rather than allow him to exploit them to his advantage. She had lied with a straight face, had hidden her deepest vulnerabilities.

And now, to protect the man she loved, she would reach deep within herself and find the strength to elude him and conceal her whereabouts.

Chapter 24

By the time James entered the library, his nerves were wound as tightly as springs. He found Investigator Papazian standing at the bay window, staring at the street below.

"Tell me you've discovered who's following Bella Sinclair," James said.

Papazian came away from the window. "I have. I've spent the month in Plymouth digging into her past. It seems Mrs. Sinclair's husband has a twin brother by the name of Rupert Sinclair of Somersetshire. Soon after his twin's death, Rupert returned to Plymouth and started asking the townsfolk where Mrs. Sinclair had gone to."

"Why?"

"Rupert told the people he was concerned for his sister-in-law's well-being since she was 'maudlin and hardly of sound mind.' Looking into his true motives, however, I discovered he purchased her marital home in Plymouth and has systematically dismantled it board by board."

"He's searching for something," James said matter-of-factly.

Papazian nodded. "I drew the same conclusion so I researched the man's finances. Turns out his accounts grew considerably during the height of Roger Sinclair's treasonous exports to the French, just prior to June of 1815 and the beginning of Waterloo."

"The brothers must have been business partners," James said.

"I suspected as much. I was able to find one of the workers that Rupert hired to tear down the Plymouth house. He said Rupert was looking for documents."

"I've had clients who kept two sets of business ledgers," James said. "One for the tax collector and the other for themselves."

"Since Roger Sinclair's death was unexpected, it would explain his twin's erratic behavior. After Rupert couldn't find the documents in the Plymouth house, he tried to track down Mrs. Sinclair. He must believe she knows where they were hidden."

"I'll be damned," James's voice grated harshly. "She's running from him. It explains everything. I never truly believed it was a horse thief that had attacked Bobby and shot me."

"You were shot?" Papazian asked incredulously.

"By Rupert, if I'm right."

"Mrs. Sinclair's husband was a bloodthirsty cur, and I believe it runs in the family. You'd best beware, Your Grace."

A coldness centered in James's chest. The fear in his heart was not for himself, but for Bella.

"Bella's hiding in London," James said.

"From what I've learned, the blackguard is quick-witted. Rupert Sinclair could track her down," Papazian warned.

James shook his head. "I'll learn where she is before then."

Just then the library door flew open and in scurried Bobby with Stodges on his heels in hot pursuit. Bobby's face was flushed, his red hair thrust up in disarray. Stodges panted heavily, his normally starched cravat wilted after his mad dash after the twelve-year-old boy.

"Pardon, Your Grace. He ran right past—"

"It's all right, Stodges," James said, dismissing the butler with a wave of his hand.

Bobby stumbled forward, his wide gaze riveted on James. "I've lost 'er," Bobby blurted, slipping back to his native cockney.

There was no need to ask who Bobby spoke of. "When?" James asked.

"They 'ad to 'ave slipped out the back door. I was watchin' the front."

"You were spotted, son," Papazian said.

"She's running from Rupert," James said. "He must have reached Bella the night before we departed Wyndmoor. It explains why she wanted payment for the place."

"Rupert Sinclair will soon learn of her departure from Hertfordshire," Papazian pointed out.

"He must already know. The remaining staff was aware we left for London. He'll head directly here, if he hasn't already arrived."

The pieces of the puzzle that was Bella Sinclair were beginning to fall into place. The night they had made love in the billiard room and he had given her the deed to Wyndmoor Manor, the joy had been stamped on her beautiful face. An hour later she had changed her mind.

Rupert must have confronted her. But how had the wretch entered the house? Rupert was villainous, and he must have followed in his twin's footsteps by threatening to harm her or Harriet in order to bend Bella to his will.

Bella had seen no choice but to flee.

She did not trust me to help her.

The disturbing thought barely crossed his mind before another followed. Bella had suffered too long under her husband's rein to be made a victim once again.

James's voice hardened. "I must find her before Rupert does. Time is of the essence."

"I suspect that they may not have gone far," Papazian said. "They will avoid the wealthy areas of the city, and it's in their best interest to stay away from the slums. It narrows our search."

"I can still help," Bobby said. "They may 'ave given me the slip, but they still 'ave to shop, and I know the neighborhoods and markets. I can keep an eye out for 'em."

James was shrewd enough to understand Bobby spoke the truth. The boy was a former pickpocket who'd grown up in thieves' kitchen, scurrying through the city streets and alleys.

"Both of you search," James said. "I'm going to Lincoln's Inn. My fellow barristers have contacts, former criminal clients, who will be able to aid us."

Wasting no more time, James headed for the vestibule, bellowing for his coat along the way. He was vaguely aware of the investigator keeping up with him until the man reached out and grasped his arm.

Papazian's face was earnest, his voice troubled. "There's more, Your Grace. When I was in Plymouth I spoke with her husband's former servants; one claims Mrs. Sinclair may have murdered her husband. It's not just the books Rupert Sinclair may be after, but vengeance for his twin's death."

The buildings that comprised Lincoln's Inn lined Chancery Lane. Even before the carriage rolled to a complete stop, James jumped down from the conveyance and headed straight for the Inn's main entrance, the Grand Tudor Gatehouse. He rushed through the sixteenth-century brick Gatehouse with its massive oak doors and entered the Inn's Hall.

It was a large oblong room with worn wooden benches and scarred tables in direct contrast to the elegant stained-glass windows. James knew he had as good a chance of finding his colleagues in the Hall at this time of day as he did in chambers. They met here early each morning, drinking coffee and discussing business before making their way to their shared chambers in the Old Buildings.

The hall was currently crowded with students and seasoned master barristers, known as Benchers—as they ate breakfast. The noise level rose as James walked farther into the room, and he heard barristers debating the latest legal statutes and courtroom procedures. James himself recalled sitting with his pupilmaster and discussing the complexities of criminal procedure and torts.

Sunlight streamed in through the stained-glass windows—artfully displaying coats of arms of the Inn's most prominent members—including Sir Thomas More as well as several of England's prime ministers. James scanned the room, his gaze focusing on the table closest to Sir More's window, where his friends customarily gathered.

Empty.

Several barristers waved in greeting, but they weren't his colleagues. James could only hope his friends weren't in trial at the Old Bailey or, in the case of Brent, away from chambers meeting with a client.

He left the Hall, walked back through Gatehouse Court, and this time headed for the Old Buildings, which housed the professional accommodations of the barristers. He rushed down a long hall lined with doors and brass nameplates engraved with the names of barristers until he came to his own chambers. Opening the door, he stepped inside.

The common room was precisely as he remembered. Rows of file cabinets lined the walls and a small table with stacks of paper waiting to be filed rested in the corner. Behind a weathered desk sat their middle-aged clerk, McHugh, copying a legal document two inches thick.

McHugh's jaw dropped when he spotted James and jumped to his feet.

"Mr. Devlin! Pardon, I mean . . . Your Grace. I wasn't expecting you."

"It's quite all right, McHugh. I was delayed in Hertfordshire and just returned. Who's in chambers this morning?"

"Everyone."

"Good. I need to speak with them. It is of the utmost importance."

McHugh straightened. "I'll summon them at once."

James went to his private office, and as soon as he opened the door, the comforting smell of books greeted him.

He had wondered if his office had changed during his absence, but he was relieved to find that very little looked different. The tall shelves of law books and statutes remained. A shorter shelf, where the books James had taken with him to Hertfordshire had been, was bare.

The surface of his mahogany desk, however, was a different matter. James had always amassed piles of papers. His desk had never been straightened at the end of the day, to McHugh's dismay. James thrived on the clutter, and he always knew beneath which stone paperweight a specific pleading, brief, or letter was located.

His desk was no longer covered with dense stacks of paper. His friends had sorted through his cases and had taken on James's clients. He understood the necessity, of course. His clients needed representation, and as the Duke of Blackwood, he could not continue to work as a barrister.

James walked behind his desk and sat, the soft springs of his leather chair squeaking as he leaned back. He realized how much he was going to miss it. He enjoyed the hectic pace, the demands of jury trials and ornery judges. He enjoyed the research, the heated discussions with other barristers. He *liked* helping his clients and offering them the best representation possible.

But fate had chosen otherwise, giving him different responsibilities. He would take his place in the House of Lords. Perhaps make a difference there. Yet he had never enjoyed politics or the twisted relationships associated with politicians.

His thoughts were interrupted as the door burst open and Brent, Anthony, and Jack entered.

"Where have you been?" Anthony asked.

"I was shot and near death with fever. Bella nursed me back to health."

"You're jesting?" Brent and Jack asked in unison.

James stood to face his friends. "Bella's in danger and I need your help. Her husband's twin, a man by the name of Rupert Sinclair, is searching for her and intends her harm. Last I heard she was in the mixed section of the city, close to Portman Square."

"What does he want with her?" Anthony asked.

"Roger Sinclair was a treasonous Plymouth exporter of guns and ammunition to the French during the Napoleonic wars. Rupert was his business partner. Incriminating ledgers are missing, and Rupert believes Bella may have them. There's also suspicion that Bella was responsible for her husband's demise, and Rupert wants revenge for his twin."

Anthony whistled between his teeth. "That's a lot of motive."

"Rupert Sinclair is violent. Not only did he fire upon me, but he attacked my stable boy," James said.

"I have two former clients who know the underbelly of London like none other," Jack said. "I'll contact them at once."

Jack was the top criminal barrister at the Old Bailey. Many of his clients came from the rookeries, and they all owed Jack a debt for escaping the gallows.

"I take it Papazian is on the case?" Anthony asked.

At James's curt nod, Anthony offered, "I work with other investigators as well. I'll speak with them."

"We'll both be in touch." Jack and Anthony left.

Brent went to a sideboard in the corner and poured two brandies, handing one to James. "Drink. You look like hell."

James accepted the glass and swallowed. James understood that Brent, who spent his days in chambers drafting boring letters patent, was not the type of barrister who had contacts such as Jack or Anthony.

James eyed Brent above the rim of his glass. "Don't worry,

Brent. I don't expect you to know the criminal types that Jack has on a string."

Brent frowned. "Stop talking utter rot. We've always been good friends. Tell me, do you love her?"

James lowered his glass. "What the hell does that have to do with anything?"

They had been close, and James's sexual exploits had never bothered Brent until recently. Brent was celibate; James was not. They had understood each other and had not allowed their differences to derail their friendship. But a few weeks before James had inherited the title, he had noticed a slight change in Brent's behavior, and their relationship had been strained.

"It may have everything to do with it," Brent said. "You are acting like a man in love. Have you thought about it?"

The truth was James had thought of it. Yes, he cared deeply for Bella and wanted her safe. Yes, he felt obligated to her for saving his life. Yes, he desired her above all others. It wasn't just a burning lust, one which would be satisfied after a romp or two.

And that was the catch. Wasn't it? The emotions she evoked within him made him feel out of control and he didn't like it, was battling it . . . and was failing miserably.

For the first time in his life, he pictured a home, a family. His obligations and duty as the new duke had nothing to do with these urgings.

But how could he love her? He was incapable of committing. He had often accepted the love of other women with a careless nonchalance. He had remained untouched because he had learned long ago that love was a dangerous weapon in the hands of others.

He had carried over his dislike of commitment not only in his personal life, but his professional existence as well. He was the only barrister in chambers who refused to specialize in any one type of legal practice. Unlike Jack Harding, who was the criminal jury master; Anthony Stevens, who handled domestic matters; and Brent Stone, who obtained letters patents, James chose to represent clients in both the criminal and civil arena at the Old Bailey.

Variety. Freedom.

It suited him.

His past mistresses had understood—if not at first, it soon became clear. But Bella Sinclair was not mistress material. She had made her preference clear when she had slapped him the day of the fair. He knew the truth of her character when she had cared for him as he lay weak and near death. No mistress would stay beside a man's sickbed, but would be off finding her next benefactor. Bella was a rare beauty and a true lady.

Nothing like the Lady Carolines of the *beau monde*.

Brent interrupted his thoughts. "Don't let your past destroy your opportunity for future happiness."

James set down the glass. "What the hell is it to you? When have you been in love?"

"I wasn't always this way."

"What are you saying?"

"Jack knows."

"Knows what?"

"I was married once. She died, and to this day I blame myself."

James was stunned. All he could think to say was, "Why does Jack know and not me?"

"I had to talk sense into him regarding Evelyn. He was being stubborn like you."

"Did it work?"

"They're married, aren't they?"

Chapter 25

As soon as James departed, Brent Stone went to his office down the hall. He quickly closed the door, slid the bolt in place, and went to the fireplace behind his desk. Pressing the base of a candlestick resting upon the end of the mantel, a stone loosened in the brickwork. He carefully removed the stone to reveal a hidden safe.

It had been six years since Brent had summoned his contact in the Home Office. Six years without an assignment, free of espionage, lies, secrets, and assassinations. He had thought he was done with the spy business, but fate, it seemed, had alternate plans for him.

Only this time *he* would contact *them*.

Brent made quick work of the safe. Inside was a four-inch stack of bills, a double-barreled pistol, a bottle of ink, and a miniature portrait of a fair-haired woman.

He reached for the portrait first. The artist had captured the woman's white-blond hair, the rosy hue of her cheeks, the sea-green eyes. She had been sweet innocence, completely without guile or the slightest tinge of malice. She had been clean and beautiful in soul as well as in appearance. Everything his ordinary world had lacked. Forcing his thoughts aside, he returned the picture to the top of the bills and removed the pistol and bottle of ink.

He shut the safe and carefully put the stone back in place and straightened the candlestick. When the safe had been installed all those years ago, he had laughed at the irony. The Crown's best safecracker in possession of his own safe. His superiors had used his talent for years to reclaim highly sensitive documents, priceless stolen artwork, and counterfeit plates used to print banknotes. There had also been the highly dangerous missions to steal military secrets from foreign diplomats and governments.

Brent's mathematical mind had excelled in safe cracking and the spy business, and he had been at the top of his game.

That is, until he had met and fallen in love with Grace Newbury.

But Grace had died . . . no, she had been murdered. A mission gone terribly awry.

Brent had immersed himself in his initial cover as a Lincoln's Inn barrister, obtaining letters patent where his engineering studies at Oxford aided his comprehension of mechanical inventions. His scarred soul and broken heart were suited to the isolation required for studying drawings and drafting patent claims.

His friends mistook his dedication to his legal practice and his celibacy for lack of interest in women when the truth was it was a form of penance for his sordid past and guilty conscience.

His superior, Hadrian, had repeatedly tried to persuade Brent to take on new missions, but Brent had refused.

Until now.

This time Brent would persuade Hadrian to act.

Brent's close friend needed him. James was in love with Bella Sinclair. The fact that James denied his own feelings was of no consequence. Brent could discern the truth, just as he had known that another legal colleague and friend, Jack Harding, had fallen in love with Evelyn Darlington some five years ago.

Now Bella's life was in danger, possibly James's too, and Brent couldn't stand by and allow James to suffer the same fate as he had, losing the woman he loved to a treasonous madman.

Brent had known many men like Roger and Rupert Sinclair. Traitors, gluttons, killers . . . men who would stop at nothing to advance their positions and their coffers no matter the damage to their country or the death of their countrymen. Brent had enjoyed taunting them, stealing from them, capturing them, and yes, killing a few of them.

Then he had met Grace.

He deserved his own life, Grace had said. He need not forever be a slave for the Crown and repeatedly risk his life, Grace had urged. They had secretly married and Brent had been ready to turn his back on espionage and spend the rest of his life with the woman he loved.

A flash of loneliness stabbed his heart. The years had only served to replace his initial grief with an inner torment that gnawed at his insides.

Brent sat at his desk and rested the pistol in the corner. Opening the jar, he dipped a pen in the ink. He wrote a single line on a piece of foolscap, then watched as the writing faded and finally disappeared in less than thirty seconds. He folded the note and sealed it in an envelope.

For a heart-stopping moment, Brent pictured Hadrian's eyebrow twitch when he opened the envelope.

Brent would surely pay a price for his request. His retirement would come to an abrupt end. His crazed double life would commence all over again.

He would break his promise to Grace.

Grace, my beloved. I pray you understand. I must help my friend.

Brent hesitated, the envelope in hand. Then he rose and unlocked his office door.

"McHugh," he called down the hall.

The harried clerk appeared moments later. "Yes, Mr. Stone?"

Brent handed McHugh the envelope. "Kindly have this delivered immediately. It's a legal opinion on the viability of Lord Quinn's patent." The lie came smoothly from Brent's lips—they always did. "I must leave for the rest of the day."

McHugh nodded. "Yes, sir."

Brent reached for his coat. He had one more stop before his true work could begin.

Chapter 26

It had not been difficult to slip out undetected from the boarding house once Bella had discovered they were being watched. Worry weighed upon her when she realized they would lose their first month's rent, but her concern had soon been replaced with the urgency to find new lodgings.

There were few lodging houses in London that suited Bella's precise needs. She desired to stay away from the fine townhomes and mansions for two reasons: to conserve their funds and to remove them from the attention associated with society; yet at the same time, she wanted to avoid the rampant crime that permeated the London sinkholes.

They found a second floor for rent near Covent Garden, and Bella shared a room with Harriet.

"No sign of the stable lad or anyone else?" Bella asked.

"No, luv," Harriet reassured her.

Ten days. They had been in this dreary house for a full ten days and each passing hour felt as slow as melting snow during a frigid January evening.

When Harriet left to prepare breakfast, Bella leaned against the door and sighed. The sparsely furnished bed-chamber was even worse than their prior lodgings near Portman Square.

She made her way to the corner and sat before the only table in the place—a drop leaf Pembroke table with a scarred top, wobbly leg, and a side flap with a broken hinge. She picked up a pen, dipped it in an inkwell, and tried to write.

The editor at the *Times* expected the second installment of her political piece, but for the first time in her life, she had lost her desire to write. Her mind was a blank slate, without inspiration or ideas.

James's image focused in her memory instead. Her lips tingled in remembrance of his kiss, and she suffered the dull ache of desire at the mere thought of him. She was trapped— trapped by the memory of his mesmerizing eyes, his touch, and her own rioting emotions when he was near.

She pictured him in London, rising to the challenges of his responsibilities as a duke of the realm. Was he in the House of Lords taking up his new position? Or was he in Lincoln's Inn discussing legal cases and clients with Brent, Anthony, and Jack?

She couldn't help but wonder if James was upset she had slipped his watchdog. Or was it simply a matter of gentlemanly concern that he knew she was settled? It was unreasonable to expect Bobby to follow her forever, and James himself had not knocked on her door to check on her well-being.

He had told her to seek him out should she need him. She needed him and desperately but for other reasons. Wicked, selfish reasons. She wanted to caress his perfectly chiseled face, touch her lips to his, feel the hardness of his chest against hers as he embraced her, as he made glorious love to her.

She pulled her drifting thoughts together. She refused to put his life at risk. Memories of James ill and fevered, with the blood-swollen bodies of the leeches on his arm, were forever imprinted on her mind. Harriet, who had been with her since childhood, was her responsibility and would stay by her side.

But James was a duke. . . .

Bella may have spent her life in the country, but she wasn't ignorant of society's demands. He needed to marry a woman of good bloodlines, one who could give him an heir. Neither was she blue-blooded, nor was she even sure she could conceive a child. During the first months of her marriage, Roger had bedded her and she had never conceived. She had been relieved at the time as she had never wanted Roger's child. But James deserved an heiress who could give him a son, not a widow with a crazed brother-in-law who had shot him.

After an hour of penning rubbish, frustration roiled within her, and she threw down her pen. It was useless. She couldn't write in her agitated state. She needed to escape the despair of the rented room with its broken furniture and stale air.

They were in need of food and other household supplies. In their haste to leave Wyndmoor Manor, they had left behind necessities. Seizing this opportunity to turn her mind in another direction, Bella reached for her bonnet, tied the strings tightly beneath her chin, and called for Harriet.

It was late morning by the time Bella and Harriet made their way to the main square of Covent Garden. The market and the surrounding streets were bustling with activity. Throngs of people meandered from stall to stall, haggling with overzealous merchants selling fruit, vegetables and dairy products. Hawkers roamed through the market peddling everything from fresh-cut flowers to pies, gingerbread, and sausages—all from trays hung about their necks.

Accustomed to the fresh air and quiet of the country, the shouts of the crowd, the stench of horse dung and human perspiration overwhelmed Bella, and she pulled her cloak more tightly about her.

Harriet must have sensed her anxiety for she reached out to squeeze her hand. "It's better this way," Harriet said in her ear. "No one will spot us here. In a few hours' time, this street will be no place for a lady."

Bella understood her meaning. When night descended, the market would fold up and the prostitutes would emerge in search of paying customers.

"Let's hurry, then," Bella urged.

They made several purchases—vegetables, butter, cheese, eggs, and a sturdy pot—and Bella discovered she could be quite proficient at haggling over prices. She was painfully aware that their money could quickly run out.

Only one item remained. "There," Bella said, pointing to a middle-aged hawker peddling fruit and crying out, "Fresh ripe oranges here!"

Rows of bright oranges and red apples made her mouth water. Bella headed straight for the fruit stand when a loud shout from a nearby merchant drew her attention.

"Stop! Thief!" The merchant lurched forward and grasped the collar of a passerby.

Bella strained to see, but the crowd, seeing a spectacle unfold before them, closed the space. People shoved and pushed, and Bella was jostled and separated from Harriet. Alarmed, Bella elbowed through the crush to where she'd last seen Harriet just as a constable barged past, barking, "Out of the way!"

The crowd parted like the Red Sea to let the official through, then closed the space in less than a heartbeat.

"'E should cut the thief's hand off, if ye ask me," a large man said on Bella's right.

"'E's just a boy," a woman in front of Bella turned to argue.

"So?" the man sneered, his top lip curling back to reveal swollen gums. "Boy or not, 'e's got no fear of God or the law."

Once again, the crowd parted as the constable made his way past, pulling along the "thief" behind him. He wore a patched corduroy jacket and a battered hat that shielded his eyes. As he came close, the large man bumped into him, and the hat fluttered to the ground to reveal disheveled red hair.

Bella froze as pulse-pounding recognition rushed through her. "Bobby!"

The lad's head snapped up to reveal his stark white face, his freckles bright blotches across his nose. "I didn't do it!"

"I believe you! Tell me what to do."

"Find the duke," Bobby pleaded. Then he stumbled, as the constable tugged forcefully on his wrist and dragged him forward. Seconds later the crowd closed in, swallowing up his small frame.

There was no question in Bella's mind that Bobby had been searching for her, just like he'd been before. Why else would he be in a Covent Garden marketplace? No doubt Bobby felt responsible for losing her the first time and sought to make it up to his employer, the duke, whom he idolized.

She felt no animosity, however, only fear for the lad, for she was certain he would be convicted of a crime he did not commit if she failed to act.

She must find James and quickly. He would know what to do. She owed Bobby, she told herself, since he had also been a victim of Rupert's malicious behavior.

Once the commotion in the market calmed, Bella found Harriet and escorted her home. Bella then returned to the street and hired a hackney cab. She went first to the ducal residence on Park Street only to be told by a sour-faced butler that His Grace was not in residence. Bella debated whether the butler had spoken the truth; then she recalled that James's friends spent their days at Lincoln's Inn. Surely they would be able to locate James.

When Bella informed the hackney driver of her new destination, he grinned knowingly and said, "Legal problem, miss?"

"Yes, and quickly if you don't mind," she answered.

The cab wove its way through the city streets before finally coming to a stop. She alighted and stared in wonder at a massive complex of sprawling buildings. "Which one is Lincoln's Inn?"

"All of them, miss."

At her blank look, the driver said, "Head for the Gatehouse."

She paid the man and headed for the impressive stone structure. As she came up to the Gatehouse, she gazed at the three coats of arms above the massive oak doors, the first showing a lion rampant. Her father had owned a book outlining the achievements of Sir Thomas More, one of the most prominent members of Lincoln's Inn. Bella had repeatedly read it to her father cover to cover as it had been one of his favorites, and she recalled a sketch of the coats of arms. Never had she believed she would visit the Inn and see it firsthand.

She understood the lion rampant to be the symbol of Lincoln's Inn as well as the arms of Henry de Lacy, Earl of Lincoln. The remaining two coats of arms belonged to Henry VIII, king at the time the Gatehouse was built, and Sir Thomas Lovell, member of both Lincoln's Inn and the House of Commons, as well as the Chancellor of the Exchequer who helped fund the Gatehouse.

She passed through the oak doors and stood in a charming Tudor-style courtyard with turrets and a small garden with flowering bushes.

She knew Lincoln's Inn boasted a library that contained some of the rarest books in the country. Under different circumstances, she would have loved to explore everything the place offered. She envisioned James in the library, surrounded by books and fellow barristers, and her heart ached for the sight of him.

"May I help you?"

Bella whirled to face a short, portly man dressed in a black barrister's gown and white wig.

"Pardon. I'm looking for the chambers of Brent Stone, Anthony Stevens, and Jack Harding."

"Ah." The man's face lit. "Make a left and head for the Old Buildings. You'll find their chambers easily enough."

She followed his directions and soon came to a long hall

lined with the nameplates of barristers. She passed two clerks whose arms were full of voluminous documents. The pair spoke in bursts of conversation, clearly intent on their duties and destination. They barely paid her attention as they rushed by. She continued onward until midway down the hall when she spotted the proper nameplate. She opened a door and stepped inside.

Chapter 27

Bella entered a common room lined with rows of file cabinets. A slender, dark-haired clerk sat behind a desk.

"Good afternoon," she said. "My name is Bella Sinclair. I'm looking for—"

The clerk's eyes widened behind thick, wire-rimmed spectacles, and he jumped to his feet. "Yes, of course! Mr. Devlin . . . I mean His Grace will want to see you. Please wait here."

He rushed down the hall and knocked on a closed door. Seconds later the door swung fully open.

"Bella!"

James's voice.

He strode forward, and she was struck by the fierce look on his handsome face. His meticulously cut navy coat emphasized his powerful shoulders and made his blue eyes appear the color of a stormy sky.

She was engulfed in a pair of wonderfully strong arms. His distinct masculine scent, his warmth, the brush of his breath against her cheek . . . all the emotions she had unsuccessfully tried to keep at bay rushed through her with a fierce longing. Her will melted like hot wax.

"Thank God!" he murmured. "Where have you been?"

She pulled back to look in his eyes. "I'm not here for a social call. Dire circumstances have arisen."

Sapphire eyes sharpened. James held her away from him as his gaze traveled her from head to toe. "Dire circumstances? Are you well?"

"Yes. Yes. It's not me, but Bobby. He was arrested for theft at a Covent Garden marketplace this afternoon."

His expression eased. "He'll be with the constable. I'll see to him soon enough. Right now I want to speak with you."

She shook her head. "I must head back. Now that I know you will see to Bobby, I must leave."

James's grip on her wrist tightened. "Oh, no you don't. You're not leaving my sight anytime soon."

A sliver of alarm raced down her spine. "Don't be ridiculous. Harriet is waiting—"

"Come with me." He pulled her behind him and across the hall into the room he had emerged from when she had arrived. He kicked the door shut behind them with a booted foot and slid the bolt into place, locking them inside.

She wrenched her wrist free. "Your Grace!"

"Don't worry, Bella. The chambers are vacant, and McHugh is leaving to file pleadings at the Old Bailey."

She whirled around and breathed deeply, hoping to calm her traitorous emotions and the tingling in the pit of her stomach. She glanced at her surroundings, suddenly curious to see where James had spent so much of his time.

Her eyes took in the tall bookshelves heaped with legal volumes. A large rosewood pedestal desk with drawers was stacked with papers and colorful stone paperweights. Behind the desk was a stone fireplace, and resting beside the mantel clock were the brass scales of justice. A sideboard sat beneath a tall window on which crystal decanters and scrolled silver candlesticks were arranged. On the opposite wall was a well-padded sofa beside a mahogany-top writing table with brass handles that could be wheeled close for convenience.

She could picture him in his office, his booted feet propped on the edge of the great desk, his brow furrowed in concentration as he read and studied case law.

She turned to find him watching her. "Do you miss it?" she asked softly.

He understood her meaning. "Very much. I doubt I will make a good duke."

The words tumbled out easily. "You'll make a wonderful duke."

He stepped close and fingered a curl at her nape. "You can stop pretending. I know everything about Rupert Sinclair."

She sucked in a breath, not entirely certain if her response was from the brush of his bold fingers or his words. "However did you learn—"

"I know."

Anxiety spurted through her, and she forced herself to breathe. "I see. So you hired a man to look into my past then?" she said.

His full lips curved in a smile. "There's no sense in my denying it. You remember Tom Jones, don't you?"

"Your school friend? Heavens! You can be cunning."

She wondered just how much James knew. "What did your hired man tell you?"

His eyes sharpened. "You want to know what I've discovered? I know your husband and his twin brother were engaged in treasonous exports to the French. I know Rupert Sinclair is searching for the incriminating evidence, and he believes you have it."

To her dismay, her voice broke slightly. "I do not have the ledger he wants. He's convinced Roger had hidden it in my belongings without my knowledge. Harriet and I have searched, but to no avail."

"I believe you cannot find the ledger."

"So you understand why I must leave," she said. "Please do

not try to follow me. I know Bobby was looking for us when he was arrested."

"If a twelve-year-old boy can find you, so can Rupert. You will be safe with me."

"No!"

"Bella, listen. I've been frantic with worry. You must trust that I can protect you."

"Who will protect you?"

She realized her mistake the moment the words left her lips.

His eyes flashed a gentle but firm warning. "I know it was Rupert in the stables."

"Then you must understand," she pleaded. "He's desperate and dangerous. He had no qualms about injuring an inno-cent boy and shooting a duke."

"If you had been honest with me from the beginning, I could have prevented it."

She felt the blood drain from her face, and she bit the inside of her cheek to keep quiet.

"Damn it, Bella. Now that I know who is after you, I can stop him. You must come with me until Sinclair is found and locked up," James insisted.

"Where?"

"To my home on Park Street."

She stared at him in astonishment. "You want an unmarried woman to live with you in the ducal mansion? Are you crazed?"

"Why? You had no problems residing with me at Wynd-moor Manor."

"But . . . but that was the country and the manor was mine! *You* insisted on living with *me!* This is London where the gos-sipmongers feast on the nobility. The scandal sheets will surely print—"

"I cannot believe you are concerned about a bit of gossip when you are running from a dangerous man."

"It's not only my reputation at stake, but yours," she pointed out.

He laughed at that. "I don't give a fig about the gossips or the scandal sheets. But I do care for your safety. If propriety truly disturbs you, I'll handpick the staff. No one need know of your presence."

At her hesitation, he said, "Stop carrying your burdens alone and let me take care of *you*."

Her heart took a dangerous leap at his words. She was tired, so damned tired, of fighting for her survival and battling the perpetual fear. First it was fear of her husband and now his diabolical twin. She desperately wanted to accept James's offer, to lean her weary head upon his shoulder and let him deal with Rupert. Confess *all* her secrets.

Bella wavered, and James pulled her into his arms.

"Let me, Bella," he said softly. "Allow me the pleasure of caring for you just as you did for me in my time of need."

If she weren't determined to keep her wits and remain in control of her emotions, she would have wept at his words.

"I see you need convincing, and I'm more than willing to assume the task." With slow deliberate movements, he unlaced her bonnet and it fluttered to the floor. He kissed her forehead, the tip of her nose, her cheek, then briefly brushed her lips. "Ah, Bella. I've been near mad in my search for you."

She sucked in a breath. He'd been that anxious to find her? She knew he'd sent Bobby to trail her after her arrival in London. She was stopped from wondering what else he had done by the stroke of his tongue against the base of her throat. Her pulse quickened, and she felt oddly light-headed.

His hands grazed the sides of her breasts, and then lowered to circle her waist. He drew back, and a frown marred his brow. "You've always been slender as a reed, but you are even more so now. Haven't you eaten since we've parted?"

Her body hummed deliciously from the pressure of his lips, and his intrusive statement regarding her weight seemed ludicrous. "I have had little appetite," she said, her voice surly.

"It's from the worry. No more worries, Bella."

"I'm afraid I don't know how to stop."

"I'll teach you. You must start by focusing on other things, more pleasurable things. Allow me to demonstrate." Lowering his head, he kissed her and cradled her face in his hands.

The touch of his lips was gentle at first, a soft brushing of his mouth, and she moved closer into his embrace, seeking more. She parted her lips on a sigh of pleasure, and his tongue slid into her mouth. Her lashes fluttered closed, and her fingers slid into his thick hair and pulled him closer. She loved the feel of him, the texture of his skin and the taste of his lips.

As he tore his mouth from hers, his blue eyes burned with unmistakable desire. "See? Your worries have already begun to ease. Come with me and let me take care of you."

How wonderful it would be to have someone of influence and power on her side. To not be alone. Harriet was old and didn't take well to moving from place to place. Bella's own finances couldn't maintain such a transient lifestyle. She loved James and no amount of logic or common sense could dissuade her feelings. She had tried to stay away, but fate had once again thrown this man into her path. Only this time, she wanted him, *longed* for him, and the fact that he knew the truth about the demon who was hunting her and he had still sought to find her made Bella's heart sing with delight.

"Yes," she said. "I will come with you."

He reclaimed her mouth, his kiss fierce with longing, and her thoughts scattered like dry leaves in a sudden gust of wind. Her back was pressed to the wall, her breasts crushed against his chest, and her head held between his large hands.

She knew the strength of those hands, knew the pleasure they could give. His desire was evident in the bold stroke of his tongue, in the strength of his embrace, and in the hardness that pressed against her belly. Bella's pulse beat erratically in response—and in what she now recognized as anticipation.

He desires me and this time I know what pleasure he can give.

His fingers loosened her hair, and the auburn mass cascaded down her shoulders and back. There was a low groan in his throat as he sank his fingers into the silken strands, angled her head, and held her captive for his plundering kiss.

She whimpered and reached up to push his jacket off his shoulders. She needed to touch him, to feel his heat and warmth and the comfort it could provide. He obliged her, shrugging out of his jacket. His fingers went to the fastenings of her gown and soon she was unbuttoned to the waist. Pushing down the delicate muslin of her chemise, he cupped her breasts in his hands and lowered his head to lick a taut nipple. She arched into his caress, wanting to scream from the intense pleasure. Never had her breasts been as sensitive as when he touched them, caressed them.

She couldn't imagine intimacy with any other man. James had singlehandedly banished her fear and her sordid memories of Roger. He had taught her that a man's touch need not be a brutal assault, but filled with a tenderness that sent delightful shivers of wanting down her spine.

Her need intensified, hot and heavy between her legs. He tugged his cravat free and the white silk floated to the floor. With trembling hands she unbuttoned his shirt. She kissed his neck, his shoulders, and her hands roamed the muscular planes of his chest. He was even more stunningly virile than she remembered.

He reached for the hem of her skirt and his fingers slid up her leg, past her garter to push her drawers aside. Then he touched her. Sliding into her silken folds, his thumb caressed her sensitive nub.

Bella's legs weakened. If his arms hadn't been supporting her, she would have slid down the wall. She arched her back as he devoured her breasts with his mouth and aroused her to frenzy with his fingers. She held on to his shoulders, her nails leaving crescent-shaped marks in his flesh. She wanted to lick and taste every inch of his heated skin.

"Ah, Bella. Have you missed me?"

Her mind was languid as passion inched through her veins. "Yes," she sobbed. "Oh, yes."

Her gown and undergarments slid to the floor. She experienced a moment's uncertainty that she was left in nothing but her stockings and garters in broad daylight while he remained clothed. Then all thought left her when he kissed her as if he was starving for the taste and feel of her.

Boldly, she reached down to cup him, feeling the ridge of his erection through his trousers. A primitive rumble came from deep in his chest.

"James," she moaned. "I need you. . . ."

He ripped off his shirt, and she freed his manhood. Hot, hard, it moved in her hands. He raised her leg, giving him fuller access to her as his finger slid deep into her wet, hot sheath. Her hips moved toward him of their own accord.

In one fluid motion he lifted her in his arms. He cupped her bottom, and her legs straddled his hips. She looked down and realized his intent as he slowly lowered her onto his hard erection until he was embedded inside her. She gasped and clutched his shoulders as he carried her to the sofa. "I'm going to fall—"

He silenced her with a kiss. "Trust me, Bella. I won't let you go."

Trust him. With each step he took, he slid deeper inside her, fusing their bodies together. The delicious pressure was enough to melt her bones.

He pushed the writing table aside, laid her on the sofa, and covered her body with his. He braced himself with one forearm on the sofa, entwining the fingers of his other hand in her hair. Staring into her eyes, he withdrew, then slowly thrust again. Passion radiated from the soft core of her body, and she bit her lip to keep from screaming her pleasure.

At her soft mewling sounds of delight, he increased the tempo of his strokes, setting her aflame as he plunged into her again and again. Through half-lidded eyes, she looked up at the fierce ecstasy etched on his face and knew she loved him.

"Sweet, Bella," he gasped. "How I've missed you."

His tender words and the stroke of his body aroused her to a fevered pitch. He covered her mouth, smothering her screams, as she reached a cataclysmic peak and exploded in the cradle of his arms. Once, twice more he thrust within her, then stiffened with his own release. She closed her eyes as a deep feeling of peace entered her being and cradled his head to her breast.

Chapter 28

James lay on his side beside Bella, his heartbeat gradually slowing. He trailed his hand down her arm to rest it on her hip. When McHugh had knocked on his door and announced Bella was present, he had jumped out of his seat. And when he had spotted her standing in his chambers, his relief had been overwhelming. She was safe, thank the Lord, and he would never repeat his past mistake by allowing her to leave again.

He wanted to linger with her in his arms, pressed against his heated length, but he felt a pressing need to take her straightaway to Park Street. He kissed her nape, and sat.

"Let me help you." Reaching for his handkerchief he made to cleanse her thighs of the evidence of their lovemaking.

"Let me." She blushed, and he thought she had never looked so beautiful.

He dressed quickly, then helped her with her gown. With a firm hand on her elbow, he escorted her out of Lincoln's Inn and to his carriage. As he was about to speak to his driver, Bella touched his sleeve.

"You're concerned for Bobby, aren't you?" Bella asked.

He was, but his utmost concern was for her safety.

"Yes, he is on my mind. But I plan to go to the Bow Street Magistrate's Office and settle matters later," he said.

"Go see him now, please."

James shook his head. "I want you safely ensconced at Park Street first."

"Then take me with you. Surely I'll be safe in the magistrate's building."

He couldn't argue with her logic. There wasn't a safer building in all of London. He had been fraught with worry when Bella had disappeared in the city, and he was very much aware that she had needed coercing to stay by his side. He didn't want her to reconsider her decision and slip away from his home while he left to aid Bobby.

"All right," he conceded.

Turning back to the driver, James instructed the man to take them to Bow Street.

Bella settled across from him in the well-padded carriage and smoothed her skirts. "I believe Bobby's innocent. Will he be ill treated?"

"I'm not worried about abusive treatment from the constables. Rather if Bobby is forced to spend the night in Newgate, there's no telling what consequences he could suffer."

Her eyes widened. "Surely they wouldn't imprison him with the other felons? He's just a boy."

"The prisons are full of boys. Officials do not discriminate based on age or the type of crime. He could sleep beside a cold-blooded murderer for all they would care."

"How horrible!"

At her fearful expression, James regretted his words. His intention had not been to disturb her, and after all she had experienced at the hands of Rupert Sinclair, he wanted to offer comfort, not additional worries.

Reaching out, he lifted her hand and brushed his lips across her knuckles. "Please do not worry about Bobby's legal dilemmas. I will take care of him," James assured her. "I'll also send a coach for Harriet and your belongings as soon as we depart Bow Street."

They traveled in silence for the rest of the journey. As the driver maneuvered the elegant carriage through the city streets, Bella sat stiffly. Twice her lips parted as if to speak, but she turned away instead to gaze out the window. Her fingers clenched her skirts, and she nervously licked her full bottom lip.

His attraction for her was immediate and profound. It didn't matter that he'd just made love to her in his chambers. That she had been glorious in her passion, urging him to take her as she'd clung to him, all liquid heat and soft feminine curves. That his own release had been intense, earth shattering. He wanted her again. . . .

Yet even now she appeared as skittish as a doe, as if she would throw open the carriage door and dart away. He knew she was reconsidering his proposition to stay with him at Park Street.

She'd felt obligated to protect *him,* for Christ's sake, even at the expense of her safety. No one had ever cared for him in that way, not his father or his grandmother—those who should have. His gut response to Bella's retreat, her desire to flee him, had left a vicious vulnerability in its wake. It made him uncomfortable, insecure . . . *fearful* of his inability to hold onto her. Disturbing emotions that affected him in a way he'd not thought possible.

At a time he needed to focus with shrewdness and clarity, to hunt down the predator that threatened her, he was distracted at the prospect of her running away, of *her* leaving *him*.

The answer to his dilemma crept into his consciousness. There was only one way to bind her to him, to make her truly his. . . .

This time she would be the one who needed convincing. He thought of the possibilities. He understood who he was—a seasoned barrister trained to analyze a challenge. He could only approach the deed as a well-thought-out legal strategy.

The carriage took a final turn and stopped at the corner.

James jumped down and lowered the step for Bella. "It's near the end of the day. I hope to catch the head magistrate before he departs."

He placed her hand on his arm and proceeded down the street. He came to a stop, and Bella gazed up at the brick and stone building.

"There's no sign," she pointed out. "If I was coming on my own, I'd have no idea it housed the magistrate's office."

James winked. "Barristers don't need a sign. We're all familiar with Bow Street."

He held the door for her, and Bella stepped inside. A massive guard stood in the corner of the marble vestibule. His tanned and weathered face broke into a grin when he spotted James.

"Last I heard you inherited a title. What would bring a duke here?" the guard asked.

James smiled in return. "Legal business, of course, Ralph. Is the magistrate in?"

"You're in luck. He's in his office. One of your colleagues is already with him."

James halted. "Who?"

"The patent fellow in your chambers. Mr. Stone, I believe," the man said.

What the devil is Brent doing here? James thought.

His bewilderment must have shown for Bella said, "Perhaps Mr. Stone is helping Bobby?"

James didn't answer and walked down the hall, Bella by his side. They turned the corner and continued down a corridor, passing offices with no identifying nameplates. The heels of Bella's shoes echoed off the marble floor and bare walls as she kept pace beside him until James stopped at the last door.

Just as he raised his hand to knock, the door opened and Brent Stone emerged. Both men halted.

"James! What are you doing here?" Brent asked.

"I'm here to aid Bobby. He's been arrested for theft."

"Your stable boy?"

"Yes. Why are you here?" James asked.

"I'm on good terms with Magistrate Hadrian Sheridan; I thought to speak with him about the nefarious Rupert Sinclair." Brent's gaze shifted to Bella. "I was concerned for Mrs. Sinclair's safety, you see."

James eyed his friend. He couldn't help but wonder if Brent's interest was due to James's comment in chambers that he'd never expected a patent barrister to be of assistance in a criminal matter.

Had James insulted Brent? Or was there more to the man's presence at Bow Street?

"I'd like to speak with Sheridan myself," James said.

Brent nodded. "Wait here."

Brent stepped back inside Sheridan's office. Muffled words were exchanged, and then Brent reappeared. Holding the door open with one hand, Brent motioned for James and Bella to enter.

Hadrian Sheridan was a large man with shoulders that appeared a mile wide, a fleshy face, and strands of dishwater-brown hair combed over a shiny scalp. He sat behind a walnut desk, smoking a pipe.

James and Brent waited for Bella to sit before occupying wooden chairs in front of Sheridan's desk.

"I ran into the duke and Mrs. Sinclair outside your office," Brent told the magistrate. "I explained my visit to unearth any helpful information regarding the whereabouts of Rupert Sinclair."

Sheridan lowered his pipe. "Seems Sinclair's been a busy man. Illegal exports of arms during England's pivotal battles against Napoleon. Treasonous activity for certain." The magistrate's voice was gravelly, as if he had chewed on a mouthful of stones.

"What can we do to help?" James said.

Sheridan looked to Bella. "I understand your deceased

husband was Rupert Sinclair's twin. Were they identical in appearance?"

"They bore a strong resemblance to one another," Bella said.

"If you can provide a portrait or sketch of your husband, I can show it to my runners. They can keep an eye out for Rupert," Sheridan said.

Bella paled a shade. "I'm sorry. I do not have a portrait or any likeness of my husband's image."

"Then I have a man on staff that is excellent with sketches. Can you give a solid description of Rupert?"

"Of course. I'll do my best to recall every detail that may be of assistance," Bella said.

"I'll be certain my foot patrols see the sketch," Sheridan said.

The magistrate turned to James. "Mr. Stone tells me you are also here on legal business. Why would a new member of the upper crust bother himself with barrister responsibilities?"

"My stable lad was wrongfully arrested this afternoon at a marketplace in Covent Garden."

"Ah, I see. If you vouch for him as a duke, I'll have the boy released later today," Sheridan said.

"Thank you. I'll send a man to fetch the lad."

"I'll do it," Brent said. "You have enough concerns with Rupert Sinclair roaming the streets."

Sheridan walked them to the door and called for an assistant. Seconds later a uniformed man appeared and introduced himself as the sketch artist and escorted Bella down the hall.

Sheridan gave Brent a sideways glance before returning his attention to James. "London is a large city, but rest assured, Your Grace, the government has eyes everywhere."

James shook Sheridan's hand before the magistrate returned to his office and shut the door.

James was left alone with Brent.

"What was that about?" James asked Brent.

Brent shrugged. "I thought to act in some way. Treason has never sat well with me."

James was not fooled by Brent's nonchalance. There was something disturbing about his longtime friend that James couldn't quite identify. Brent had always been secretive about his past. Others may have found it disconcerting, but James had never been bothered by it. But this was different. Brent was different.

Willing to help Bella, yes; yet a strange undercurrent, a leashed dangerousness, simmered in Brent's piercing blue eyes.

Brent turned and—just as quickly as it had appeared—the flash was gone, and in its place returned the respectable and reserved barrister.

"I never meant to insinuate you weren't as cunning as Jack or Anthony," James told Brent.

"I know." Reaching out, Brent clasped James's shoulder. "But I want to do whatever I can to help."

It was dark outside by the time Bella finished with the sketch artist. James studied the drawing, memorizing each line of Rupert Sinclair's face—the square wall of his forehead, the stubborn jut of his chin, the slightly crooked nose.

James had wondered if Bella's husband had looked exactly like his twin. Throughout his legal career, James had encountered more than one set of twins—either clients or witnesses for the prosecution. Several pairs, he recalled, had been identical in appearance, and others, had displayed little resemblance to each other. But Bella had said Roger and Rupert Sinclair had looked alike.

As for her not having a portrait of her husband, James wasn't surprised. If any had existed, she'd probably left them behind or destroyed them.

Bella pushed back her chair from the writing desk she had spent the last hour huddled over with the sketch artist. She stood and rubbed her lower back, the strain of exhaustion written on her face. She rubbed her eyes, and James suspected they burned from concentrating on the artist's work as Rupert Sinclair's image had slowly come into focus.

James dropped the sketch on the table. "You're exhausted."

Bella opened her mouth to protest, but was stopped short when her stomach growled. Her face burned brightly.

He cocked an eyebrow. "How long has it been since you've eaten?"

"Not too long," she said defensively. "I had dry toast and tea this morning."

"There's a pleasant inn off the beaten path called the Harvest Post. I'm friendly with the proprietor, and the place serves good food and wine."

When she looked like she was going to continue to argue, he said, "Don't try to deny you're hungry. I'm famished as well. And the inn is a short ride away."

"Now that we're in town, it's inappropriate for us to intimately dine together without a chaperone."

"Don't be concerned. The Harvest Post is on the outskirts of London on an isolated road. It's hardly the type of establishment to be visited by the *haute ton*."

She let out a sigh of resignation. "All right." She turned to fetch her coat, which hung over the back of her chair. "I suppose if the place is as out of the way as you suggest, there is no risk that we will be seen."

They stepped outside to where his driver waited at the corner, and James helped her into the carriage.

The journey to the inn did not take long. Soon the city street lamps faded and the wheels of the carriage slowed and swayed on the dilapidated cobblestones of the rural road. The well-lit inn shone like a welcoming beacon in dimness.

The proprietor of the Harvest Post greeted James warmly. Farnsworth had been embroiled in trouble with his business partner, and James had settled the dispute between the partners, freeing Farnsworth to run the inn on his own.

Exchanging pleasantries and laughing with James, Farnsworth himself escorted them to the inn's sole private room. A waiter appeared with a bottle of red wine, and James ordered the inn's specialty, a hearty rabbit stew, for both himself and Bella.

After tasting the first forkful of stew, Bella's eyes closed in delight. "Mmmm. This is delicious," she murmured.

His mind burned with the erotic memory of the first time they made love—of Bella sprawled naked across the snooker table, strands of her luxurious dark auburn hair in vivid contrast to the green felt, her eyes half closed and her lips parted in pleasure.

James watched, enthralled, as she drained her wineglass, then licked a lingering drop from her full lip with the tip of her tongue.

He busied himself with refilling her glass, then cleared his throat, forcing himself to focus on the important issue at hand rather than the desirable woman across from him.

"Tell me," he said. "When did Rupert Sinclair first contact you?"

"Weeks ago in Wyndmoor's stables. He confronted me there before . . . before he attacked Bobby and shot you. I haven't seen him since the stables. Except . . ." She twisted her napkin in her lap. "Except, he had left a note on my pillow the night we dined together at Wyndmoor. He wanted to meet for me to hand over the ledger. My bedroom window was shut and locked. I've no idea how he gained entry."

"That was the night you asked me to pay you for the deed to Wyndmoor?"

She nodded. "Yes. I never found the ledger and I had no choice but to flee." Her eyes widened, and she whispered, "He threatened to harm you a second time."

Again she sought to protect him. His heart hammered, and

his breath burned in his throat. He truly would enjoy killing Rupert Sinclair.

"I'm even more convinced my plan is sound," he argued. "You must live with me until Sinclair is arrested and you are no longer in danger."

"I'm still uncertain. What of your grandmother, the dowager duchess?" Bella asked.

"Do not concern yourself with her. The Park Street mansion is enormous. One could wander for days without seeing anyone but a servant. You can have your own wing if you prefer."

When she made to protest further, he said, "I'm sending for Harriet, remember? She can act as your chaperone."

"Surely the dowager will see through such a ruse."

"I don't care what she believes. I want you safe."

For a long moment, she looked back at him. "No one has ever concerned themselves with my safety before."

"Then allow me to be the first. You cannot run from Rupert indefinitely. The man must be brought to justice for his crimes."

"Which ones?" she asked. "His past treasonous actions or for shooting you?"

"Both. My only regret is that your spouse expired before he could be held accountable for his abominable treatment of his beautiful wife."

She stilled, her hand resting on the stem of her glass. The candlelight brushed her elegant features—her heart-shaped face, her catlike green eyes, her wildly tempting lips. She was breathtaking and maddening at once. An arousing combination. The air thrummed with awareness between them.

Awareness and unmistakable anxiety.

Her voice was a tremulous whisper. "Whatever do you mean by Roger's 'abominable treatment'?"

James leaned across the table, his eyes locking with hers. "Make no mistake, Bella. My investigator was thorough. He spoke with the Plymouth townsfolk. Your husband was the worst type of man, and spread lies of your frail mental state. We both know you are anything but frail and are of strong, sound mind. But it was his abuse of his beautiful wife that was truly vile. He was a sick man, and his death was a far too easy escape for his crimes."

A flicker of relief flashed across her features before her eyes lowered to her glass.

James wasn't fooled and knew the reason. She feared his investigator had stumbled across the additional rumors—that she was responsible for Roger Sinclair's death. James didn't care if she had pushed the drunken fiend down the stairs or not. God knew, he would have done it for her had her villainous husband lived. But he kept his knowledge hidden. She need not face everything, not now, when he desired her cooperation.

"Roger had an obsessive and addictive nature," she said, meeting his gaze. "He was consumed with amassing a fortune, by whatever means necessary. When trade with France ceased, the demand for French goods heightened, and he realized the money to be made. He started small with French brandy, lace, and perfume, but his greed soon took over and he began exporting munitions. He was addicted to brandy as well, and when it came to me . . ." She swallowed, then went on to say, "He was fiercely jealous. First of my writing, which he immediately prohibited, then of any attention I received from the women and men in Plymouth. I lived in fear of his volatile temper and his abuse, and through his threats against the one person I cared for he ensured I never ran away."

"I've observed his type in my legal practice. Demented souls who cannot be rehabilitated. Many are addicts of alcohol or opium, others respectable tradesmen with dark secrets and violent tendencies. Rupert Sinclair shares your husband's traits. We can work together and see this through to the end. But you must agree to live under my roof," he said.

She inclined her head. "If that's what you truly wish, then I'll go with you."

Profound relief swept through him. He raised his glass, and said, "A toast then, to our agreement."

She drank, and he was quick to refill her glass.

There was a low knock on the door. The waiter entered to remove their plates, and James ordered more wine. Dessert was served, strawberries with Devonshire cream. Bella visibly relaxed and seemed to enjoy his company, just as he enjoyed hers.

Which was entirely foreign. Women had always served a single purpose in his life thus far—mutual pleasure. He wasn't immune to Bella's charms in that regard. Even now his gaze was repeatedly drawn to her luscious mouth as she licked the cream from each strawberry. The dessert was a concoction to arouse and inflame him. Yet it was her keen intelligence and courage that drew him and prompted this fierce possessiveness.

Eventually the conversation slowed. She yawned, then stretched.

James pushed back his chair. "I don't want you falling asleep in your chair, Bella. We should head home."

He helped her to her feet. She swayed slightly and smiled up at him with heavy lids.

He chuckled. "You've had too much wine."

"Don't be a ninny, James. I'm certainly not drunk, just relaxed."

He rolled his eyes. "A ninny? No one has ever accused me of such a crime."

She giggled, then threw his words back at him. "Then allow me to be the first."

Chapter 29

Bella leaned on James in the carriage. Since arriving in London, the stress had worn on her, but now she had a defender. A powerful duke on her side, a man who had stolen her heart. She could share her burdens and cease looking over her shoulder in fear of Rupert's retaliation for her not finding the ledger he so desperately sought.

The carriage wheels rolled over a rough patch of country road, and James pulled her more firmly against his side. The hardness and warmth of him was comforting and arousing at once.

There were complications, of course. This time, she had *agreed* to live under his roof. But in her wine-induced state, she pushed her worries aside.

Bella looked up at him, her cheek brushing his coat. "How can I ever repay your kindness?" she asked.

His hawklike gaze looked fierce in the carriage lamplight. "A kiss is sufficient."

Yes, she thought and raised her chin.

"But we should not, Bella."

She frowned. "Why not?"

"You're inebriated."

"I am not," she huffed. "I'm merely a bit tipsy. You said diversion would work to ease worry, remember? I'm only following your suggestions." She raised her lips to within an inch of his.

His gaze dropped to her mouth. "Serves me right," he ground out. "A woman who can argue like a barrister." He pulled her close, and his head lowered. . . .

Just then a loud crack sounded outside, and the carriage jerked to a sudden stop.

"Stand and deliver!" a voice boomed outside.

James sat upright. "Christ! It's highwaymen."

"Highwaymen!"

James reached beneath the bench seat for a knife—a wicked-looking four-inch blade that he slipped into his boot.

Fear spurted through Bella. She had heard of highwaymen, pirates of the rural roads who preyed on vulnerable carriages at night. Never had she thought she would fall victim to one.

Her gaze flew to the window. It was dark, save for the torches held by the robbers. There were two . . . no, three . . . men, one mounted on a horse. Their driver was on his knees, a look of terror on his pale face as a highwayman held a knife to his throat.

"Do they know you are a duke?" she whispered.

"For certain. No doubt they've targeted the ducal crest on the side of the carriage," James said.

Seconds later, the door was jerked open. A large, bald man holding a club the size of which she'd never seen stared at James. "Get out of the carriage. And empty yer pockets."

Heavens! It was the size of a tree branch, yet the man held the club with ease in a meaty fist, as if it weighed no more than a small branch.

"You're making a grave mistake," James said in a hard voice.

"Me? I don't think so, me lord." The man jerked his head toward Bella. "The chit stays inside. Ye get out. Now."

"Stay here, Bella," James commanded before hopping down and closing the door.

Icy fear knotted inside Bella, and she strained to see out the window. The ruffian holding a knife to their driver began to search his pockets. The third highwayman stood apart from the rest, clearly the leader. He wore a hooded cloak and was of average height. A terrifying thought struck her.

Could it be Rupert Sinclair?

James threw a purse at the feet of the bald man. "Take it and go."

Bella watched as the leader raised his hand and made a quick slicing motion across his throat. A signal to kill James?

No! her instincts screamed out.

Without further thought she flew from the carriage and flung herself at the bald man's arm. She was no match for him, and he struck her across the face and threw her like a rag doll. Her head split in pain as she fell to the ground.

James had a fiery, angry look that was completely unfamiliar to her. With lightning quick reflexes, he reached into his boot and came up with the blade in his hand. His eyes were hard and merciless as he slashed the arm of the bald highwayman and then hurled the knife at the ruffian who held the driver. With an eerie swoosh, the blade struck the man in his gut.

"Let's get out of 'ere!" the leader shouted.

From where she lay, she saw one of the ruffians turn and flee and heard the sound of horses' hooves pounding over the dirt road.

"Bella! Look at me!"

She turned to find James beside her on the ground. Her head hurt; every movement ached like the devil.

"They were going to kill you," she mumbled.

He gently gathered her into his arms and stood. "No, sweetheart. I was ready for them. You risked your life. Why?"

"I couldn't let him hurt you."

James cradled Bella in his arms inside the carriage. He had told his driver to rush to the Park Street mansion.

"I'll be fine," Bella insisted. "The brute struck my cheek. I've suffered worse in the past."

Lord! What hell had she lived through? Roger Sinclair was lucky indeed that he was already six feet underground.

As for tonight, when the highwayman had struck Bella and thrown her to the ground, his heart had slammed into his ribs. Bloodlust had consumed him, and he had attacked with murderous intent.

She had risked her life when she had left the safety of the carriage. James stared down at her upturned face in wonder. She may have been emboldened by the wine, but he knew it was her courage that had made her leap from the carriage and throw herself at the hulking criminal. She could have been killed, taken from him before he could truly make her his.

His voice was harsher than he intended. "You shouldn't have left the carriage."

"He was going to kill you. I had to act."

"No. I was watching and knew their intent. You could have been gravely injured."

"But—"

"Promise me that you'll never do that again. That you'll never disobey a direct command and risk your life again," he said.

She bit her bottom lip, a nervous habit he now recognized. He curbed the impulse to shake her until she agreed.

"I was never good at taking orders, but I'll try."

James laughed; he couldn't help himself. How could he stay angry at her when he wanted to kiss her?

Tightening his arms about her, he kissed the top of her head. "Then that will have to do for now. Rest, Bella. I'm taking you home."

Lady Blackwood, the dowager duchess, was in the midst of one of her intimate parties. Forty guests—all influential members of the *beau monde*—stood around a long table in the silver drawing room, where a mesmerist, Master Ormond, was in the process of hypnotizing Lady Booth, who had volunteered for the task.

Her ladyship was well aware that her intimate soirees were the talk of the *ton* and that many would sell their souls to garner an invitation. She prided herself on serving the finest champagne, exquisite food prepared by her own highly sought-after French chef, and offering the most unique entertainment via the mesmerist. When Lady Booth barked like a dog, the guests collectively laughed, then clapped.

But the dowager knew the excitement behind tonight's soiree had nothing to do with any of these offerings. The thrumming excitement and tangible curiosity of the gossips was not due to the talented mesmerist but the shocking discovery of the new Duke of Blackwood. The guests lingered, requesting more and more outrageous tricks from Master Ormond, all in the hopes of catching a glimpse of James.

Lady Caroline was in the thick of the crowd. The dowager knew Lady Caroline's game as she herself would have played the same way had she learned her betrothed was no longer first in line for the title, but a penniless younger son. Lord knew Gregory had his faults—the drinking, gaming, and the opium dens—but Caroline had never given Gregory's addictions a second thought.

Until now.

If Lady Caroline wanted to become a duchess, she had no other choice than to set her sights on James. Caroline had tried. The dowager knew, of course. Her personal servants were as efficient as the Regent's top spies when it came to eavesdropping. The dowager couldn't blame Lady Caroline for trying, but still . . .

Gregory was her grandson. She may not have wanted him to inherit the dukedom, but she felt a tinge of sympathy that he would lose both the lady and the title.

For Caroline would never have Gregory now.

But neither would she succeed in snaring James.

The dowager knew this deep in her bones. James Devlin was his own man. He had ruthlessly carved out a career as a successful barrister when many illegitimate sons would have spent their lives begging for every shilling from their wealthy relations.

But not James Devlin. He had lived life on his own terms, accountable to no one.

His life had changed overnight with his father's deathbed confession. He'd have to marry and produce an heir. Despite his irritation when they had last spoken on the subject, James was shrewdly intelligent and fully aware of his duty. As a boy he had sought his father's approval—even his acceptance— like a puppy begging for his first bone.

Life was ironic indeed. Now that James had his father's title and wealth, he exhibited not gratitude at his fortune, but disdain.

She should have anticipated his cynicism. James had been a barrister and a rogue his entire adult life. His exploits with women were as well known as his success in the courtroom. As far as she was aware, he had never fathered a child and had never desired to have a family. Now duty required it.

When James had failed to return from Hertfordshire, the dowager had inquired and had learned a lovely, young widow by the name of Bella Sinclair was in residence. Knowing James, the dowager had understood why he had tarried.

The truth was the dowager desperately wanted grandchildren and the sooner the better. At eighty-two years old, her time was running out. The chest pains that had plagued her over the past year had increased in intensity and frequency. Yet she refused to succumb before ensuring the future of the dukedom before she died. If Lady Caroline was not to his liking, then James must choose another and quickly.

The dowager was considering which ladies from titled and wealthy families she would want to bear her grandchildren and strengthen the dukedom, when the drawing room door was kicked open with startling force and James stalked in with a young woman in his arms.

The guests spun from the mesmerist, mouths gaping open at the sight of the tall, sinfully dark and imposing man who glared down at them with an ominous expression.

The dowager came forward, and James's blue gaze snapped to her. "Who are all these people?" he asked rudely.

The woman in his arms started to struggle. "James, let me down. I'm fine now."

His arms only tightened around the lady. She appeared dazed and cradled her cheek with her hand, but she was strikingly beautiful with rich auburn hair and green eyes.

"Pardon," she said. "I'm Bella Sinclair. We were alone in James's carriage when we were waylaid by highwaymen on the way here, and if he hadn't acted swiftly, we'd both have been gravely harmed."

The guests stared agog; a group of young ladies in the corner giggled behind their fans. Master Ormond stomped his foot. "Enough! My demonstration is ruined!"

James's fierce countenance silenced the temperamental mesmerist.

The guests followed in fascination as the new Duke of Blackwood spun on his heel out of the drawing room, calling for Stodges to summon a physician. Then James carried the woman across the marble vestibule and marched up the grand staircase.

Lady Caroline's eyes narrowed as she placed her hand on the dowager's sleeve. "His first social appearance as duke and he brings a harlot into the house," she spat.

The dowager felt her chest tighten. "Watch your tongue, Caroline," she admonished. "The lady is not a harlot." *She just may be this house's salvation, and the answer to my prayers.*

Chapter 30

Bella woke when a cool hand brushed her brow. She opened her eyes to foreign surroundings and a strange-looking man standing by the bedside looking down at her.

"I'm Dr. Sterling. You were struck cruelly across your face, Miss, but I suspect the pain you're no doubt experiencing is more from indulging in too much wine than the blow."

Bella raised her hand and felt a bandage on her right cheek. She rose on her elbows, then sat up with the doctor's aid. Her stomach flip-flopped, and her head felt as if an elephant had sat upon it.

Sterling poured a glass of water and offered it to Bella. She took it and obediently drank.

"The dowager wants to see you after I complete my examination."

Bella coughed and handed the glass back. "The Dowager Duchess of Blackwood?" she croaked.

"Yes."

Bella's gaze darted across the elegant room. It was done in shades of light peach from the matching coverlet and canopy of the four-poster to the drapes, to the spray of peach flowers in the Oriental carpet. The furnishings were made of exquisite rosewood, and there were delicate lace runners atop the nightstand and the bureau—

Her eyes flew back to the bureau and the silver-handled brush and comb resting upon it. *Her* brush and comb.

She looked closer and spotted her mother's trunk with its curved, decorative top besides two others. When on earth had her belongings been delivered? She had been with James. . . .

Memories of last night rushed back with a vengeance. She had been famished and there had been the rabbit stew at the Harvest Post. Then there had been the delicious warmth and strength of James's arms in the carriage, only to be interrupted by the frightening highwaymen, and afterwards . . . dear Lord, she had humiliated herself before the dowager and all of her guests.

She looked at the physician. "Is His Grace well?"

Sterling nodded. "His Grace was uninjured in the attack. He has been quite persistent and has spent most of the night pacing outside your door. I insisted he leave so that you could rest."

"I see," she said.

"Allow me to finish my examination." Sterling came so close she could see her reflection in his pupils. He looked into each of her eyes, had her follow his finger from side to side, nodded once, then stood straight.

"Normal," he said. "You shall suffer no ill effects. You may rise and dress, but do not venture from the house." He snapped his medical bag closed. "If you need me, I can come by tomorrow afternoon to check on you."

He opened the door to leave just as a maid entered carrying a breakfast tray. She was followed by a short, elderly woman with steel-gray hair, who swept into the room with the bearing of a queen. Her blue gaze settled on Bella sitting in the great bed.

Blue eyes strikingly similar to James's.

Bella instantly comprehended.

The Dowager Duchess of Blackwood.

"Your Grace." She struggled to rise, the tangle of bed-clothes and her throbbing temples making the task exceedingly difficult.

The dowager raised her hand. "Stay. I'd rather you not exert yourself."

Bella's arms sagged from the effort, and she nodded in compliance. "I must beg your pardon for last night."

The dowager's chin rose a notch, and it was immediately clear that she was a formidable woman who was unaccustomed to having her authority challenged. Bella recalled James's story—that this woman had harbored no affection for the motherless bastard of the old duke.

"Last night was unexpected," her ladyship said. "The most important members of society were present. They always attend my parties, you see. I know of you, Mrs. Sinclair. You were married in Plymouth. Your husband was a wealthy merchant and landed gentry. Was he not?"

At Bella's stiff nod, she continued. "After his death you went to Hertfordshire, where you ran into James at Wyndmoor Manor, correct?"

Bella nodded mutely. It appeared the dowager knew the bare facts.

"It's important I know everything. Is there anything else?"

Nothing I would ever admit to. "No, Your Grace."

"Good. James has seen fit to move you into this house along with your former nursemaid. As if a servant could stand as a proper chaperone." The dowager tsked. "That won't do. That won't do at all."

"Please forgive my intrusion. I shall leave immediately," Bella said.

"Leave! You shall do no such thing, young lady," the dowager snapped. "I realize you have spent your life in the country, but you must understand the gravity of the situation. I had considered other candidates, mind you, but James is quite headstrong. I may be old, but I'm not blind. I saw the way he acted toward you last evening. Heavens, all of society saw. If I want to see his duty done before I depart this earth, then I'll not complain how he chooses to do it. Understand?"

Bella had no idea what the old woman was rambling about, only that her headache had slid to the base of her skull, where it throbbed with a vengeance, and so she found herself nodding for the third time.

The dowager marched to the window and threw open the drapes. Bella's hand immediately came up, shielding her eyes from the bright light.

"It's already midmorning. Time to dress. Jenny shall see to your needs."

The maid that had been silently standing in the corner holding the breakfast tray jumped to attention.

"But Harriet sees to my needs," Bella protested.

"Jenny shall serve you this morning," the dowager retorted in clipped tone that forbade any argument.

After a moment's hesitation, Bella asked, "Is His Grace home?"

"He departed quite early to meet with the constables regarding the criminals that had waylaid you; although I believe there's little chance they will be found. The back roads have been swarming with such vermin."

"Is he expected home soon?" Bella asked.

"Do not worry, my dear. With you here, I'm certain he'll return shortly. I expect he'll want to set the details, of course."

Bella wanted to ask what details the woman referred to, but with her head pounding and her stomach churning, she needed a moment's peace to compose herself.

Bella held her tongue, and the dowager marched out of the room.

* * *

With the maid's help, Bella dressed, nibbled on buttered toast with a light layer of jam, and washed it down with three cups of weak tea. Her stomach settled and her headache subsided. The maid bobbed a curtsy and a footman arrived to escort Bella through the labyrinth of halls to meet the duke.

As Bella ventured down the staircase she couldn't help but notice that the mansion was truly stunning—the grandest she had ever set foot in. The marble vestibule was gargantuan in size with gleaming black-and-white Italian marble. Resting upon a center pedestal table sat an Oriental urn with dozens of fresh, cream-colored roses.

The library, she learned, was in the back of the house, and she followed the footman past no less than three drawing rooms, each decorated in their own color schemes and styles of Greek, Roman, and Chinisoire décor. The dining room was furnished with Chippendale chairs in the Rococo style, a table which could comfortably hold fifty guests, and a magnificent chandelier with crystal prisms like a shower of diamonds. They continued onward, past a music conservatory, complete with a polished pianoforte, harp, and two violins resting upon chairs before music stands.

At last they reached the library, and the footman opened the door for her to enter.

James was standing before a tall mahogany bookshelf, studying the colorful spines of the volumes. He turned at her entrance, his hawklike gaze traveling her figure, then resting on the bandage on her cheek. He frowned and stepped forward.

"How do you feel today, Bella?" he asked.

"Better now."

He motioned to a settee, and then sat beside her. His stare was bold as he assessed her frankly. "The physician said you are not to exert yourself."

She smoothed her skirts, immediately conscious of her appearance. The maid had shaken out her gowns and hung them in the wardrobe. She was wearing a demure navy gown with long sleeves and pearl buttons down the front. Her hair was brushed and pulled back into a knot. Save for the bandage, she looked as acceptable as an applicant for a governess position in a fine household—completely different from the disheveled and intoxicated woman of last night.

Unnerved by his scrutiny, she looked to the bookshelves that had captured his attention moments ago. "It's a fine collection. Is it yours?"

A smile curled the corners of his lips. "No. I've had little time to move my collection from my Lincoln's Inn chambers here. These," he said, pointing to the books, "belonged to the old duke. He had a voracious hunger for knowledge and was quite intelligent."

"Like father, like son," she blurted out.

He stiffened, and she feared she had struck a nerve.

"It is of no consequence now, is it?" he said.

She had the maddening urge to reach out and touch him, tell him that his father's abominable treatment had been wrong, that he had been worthy of love as a boy and that she loved him as a man.

She cleared her throat, and said instead, "Your grandmother came to see me this morning. She said you were meeting with the authorities regarding the highwaymen. She believes it's unlikely they'll capture the criminals."

"Do you believe that?" he asked.

She considered his question. "You wounded two. I saw one go down with my own eyes. Can the authorities not find him?"

"His accomplices must have taken him with them. When I returned last night—"

"You returned?" she asked incredulously.

"I had to see to you first. After you were settled and the physician called, I went back with Coates. The wounded highwayman was gone."

She bit her bottom lip. "Oh, my. The dowager said highwaymen have been plaguing the back roads."

"The constable told me the same thing. I, on the other hand, do not hold with his opinion."

"What do you mean?" she asked.

"I do not believe they were local criminals."

She sucked in a breath. "You think Rupert Sinclair was involved?"

"What did *you* see last night, Bella?"

She hesitated, her thoughts filtering back. "It was dark outside. One of the highwaymen remained apart from the others, and he struck me as the leader. He was cloaked, and I couldn't identify him as Rupert. But he gave a slicing motion with his hand across his throat, and I knew he had signaled his accomplice to kill you."

She frowned, allowing her subconscious thoughts to surface. "Thinking back, it makes no sense. Why kill the victim if you had already robbed him? They knew you were a duke by the crest on the carriage. Murdering an aristocrat would have sealed their doom, for the authorities would scour the area until an arrest was made."

His mouth was tight and grim. "That's right. I believe Rupert hired them to commit murder."

Her hand fluttered to her breast. "Are you trying to frighten me?"

The intensity of his gaze unnerved her. "I'm drawing logical conclusions. Now do you see why I want you under my roof? I was furious when that criminal struck you and threw you to the ground. I was also scared to death that you had been hurt. I've never had such a beautiful guardian."

She was taken aback by his passionate admission.

At her silence, he prodded. "Bella, what do you recall of last night after the attack?"

Other than making a complete fool of myself? she thought.

"We walked in on your grandmother's party."

He chuckled. "That is quite an understatement. Not only

did we walk in on the festivities and interrupt her pompous mesmerist, but we simultaneously became the main entertainment. You introduced yourself by name to the dowager and all of her guests and admitted to having an illicit affair."

Alarm rippled along her spine. "I did not!"

"You used my Christian name and admitted to being alone with me without a chaperone in the middle of the night."

"But surely you can explain—"

He leaned forward, a silken thread of warning in his voice. "Explain that we fought over a country property and lived together during the battle? Or explain that your crazed brother-in-law had shot me and is hunting you for a ledger that will prove the treasonous activities of your deceased husband?"

Her headache was returning, and her voice sounded shrill to her own ears. "This is not my fault! I did not ask for your protection or for you to bring me to Park Street. I sought to leave Lincoln's Inn alone. I had my own lodgings. I would have been fine."

"Fine?" he asked impatiently. "You wouldn't have lasted another week without Rupert finding you."

He was right, she knew it deep in her gut, yet a rebellious streak remained. "Then what should we do?"

"We can solve the problem with my grandmother and aid your situation by marrying at once."

"Marry! You cannot be serious."

"Oh, but I am."

He didn't appear upset at the notion of marriage as she would have predicted; rather a flicker of emotion—satisfaction, perhaps?—passed over his face, before he hid it with a smile.

"I thought you never wanted to marry, never wanted a family. That you thoroughly enjoyed your bachelorhood."

"When I had first met you at Wyndmoor, I had no idea of your past. Things have changed between us, and what you had earlier said is true. I insisted you leave Lincoln's Inn with me and come live under my roof. I will share the blame for last night's circumstances."

"You do not need to marry me. Many an heiress will be eager to—"

"The titled ladies of society do not interest me; they never have," he said.

"And your grandmother? What does she think of this?"

"For the first time, she is in agreement with me. She insists I act honorably."

"Of course! She wants grandchildren. An heir to the dukedom. And duty requires you produce the next generation."

"Yes, that does seem to be high on her list," James said dryly. "She has it in her head that she will be your chaperone and *properly* introduce you to society."

The dowager's conversation now made sense to Bella. She had woken in a fog, both from the blow to the head and the free-flowing wine of the prior evening. Bella hadn't understood the dowager's meaning, but in light of James's proposal everything had become clear.

There was desperation in Bella's voice. "Her reasoning is illogical. She knows I am a widow who has never borne children. I could be barren."

"I don't believe that to be true. You had said that you were not with your spouse in the biblical sense often. As for the dowager, I told her your husband was impotent. She understands it's not an uncommon ailment in older men with much younger wives."

Bella felt her face redden. She had been the one to tell James that Roger had been unable to bed her after the first months of their marriage, but never had she anticipated that the dowager would learn such intimate details.

"But I don't want to remarry. I swore never to—"

Bella halted when James leaned forward and cupped her chin tenderly in his warm hand.

"Stop," he said. "You are too young to be jaded. Your first

marriage was a farce, a despicable arrangement to a mentally deranged old man. You are beautiful and young and desirable. By refusing my offer you are exposing yourself to the villainous exploits of Rupert Sinclair. You cannot fight this battle on your own, and as your husband I will be in a much better position to protect you. Last night's debacle should have made that perfectly clear. Otherwise you will have to keep running from place to place looking over your shoulder. Is that what you wish?"

"No, but—"

His fingers lowered; his thumb rubbing the wildly beating pulse at the base of her throat. "Plus we are up to our necks in scandal. You cannot leave me at the gossips' mercy—or, heaven help me, the dowager's—can you?" He gave her a grin calculated to melt a lady's heart.

Her heart pounded, and she felt light-headed. How on earth could a man be threatening and charming at once?

"I'm an untitled widow; my father was a merchant. I'm hardly duchess material."

He laughed, a deep, rich sound. "I'm a barrister, raised as an illegitimate son, hardly ducal material."

Once again, she had the distinct impression he had thought of this before, had considered proposing and had seized the opportunity of last night to launch a well-formulated argument as to why they should marry.

His hand slid down her arm and grasped her fingers. "Perhaps my proposal wasn't what you expected. Let me remedy it." He rose from the settee and walked to a pedestal desk in the corner. Picking up a square box, he strode to her side and knelt on one knee. "Bella Sinclair, will you do me the honor of becoming my duchess?"

He opened the box to reveal a stunning oval ruby surrounded by brilliant diamonds nestled in folds of black velvet. She stared in shock.

"It belonged to the last duchess and has been in the family

for five generations. My mother never wore it, but I believe my wife should."

"Oh, James," she breathed. "It's beautiful."

He slipped the ring on her finger. "Bella, the years I spent with other women were in hindsight a waste. I had yet to meet my match. I wandered aimlessly, bored and never satisfied. And then you held a fireplace poker over my head, and my life has never been the same since. We are intellectually and physically compatible. It is more than most couples ever dream of obtaining."

She swallowed at his admission. It wasn't a romantic declaration of undying love, but his motives were honorable. He sought to make things right, to protect her on two fronts. First from her brother-in-law, even though James was now aware that it was Rupert who had shot him. And second from her tattered reputation after she had carried on in front of his grandmother and her guests. He may not love her, but he cared for her, and she had fallen helplessly in love with him.

A knock on the door interrupted them, and the butler entered.

"Not now, Stodges," James said tersely.

Stodges paled a shade, but held his ground. "Her ladyship wishes to speak with you."

A split second later, the dowager swept inside. Shrewd blue eyes took in the large ruby on Bella's left hand.

"Splendid," she said. "I see congratulations are called for."

"I do believe Bella was consenting to marry me," James said.

Bella smiled weakly. "Yes, I suppose I have."

The dowager clapped her hands in delight. "Stodges," she called, "my best champagne."

For the next hour, Bella smiled and sipped expensive champagne as the staff and the dowager wished her future happiness and a herd of children to carry on the House of Blackwood. James took it all in stride, leaning against the sideboard, a grin playing at the corners of his mouth. He really had accepted the turn of events with ease. She pushed her suspicion aside. There was no way he could have planned the embarrassing scene last night.

He hadn't anticipated the highwaymen or her scandalous speech at the dowager's party. But had he wanted to marry?

The dowager interrupted her musings.

"I realize your year of mourning has not passed, but I see no sense in waiting. James is a duke after all, and I have an influential position in society. The rigid rules have been bent before, I assure you, and since I will act as your chaperone, you will be accepted. I shall throw a ball in James's honor as the new duke and formally announce your engagement. You shall require a new wardrobe, of course, but that shall not pose a problem. You are quite lovely, my dear."

A ball. A new wardrobe. It was all happening so quickly. What of Rupert? The ledger was still missing, and Rupert was still an ominous threat.

Bella looked to James. He didn't seem the least perturbed. Rather, he appeared surrounded by an air of calm—rakishly good-looking and confident. In short, he seemed very pleased with himself.

Chapter 31

Bella spent the remaining afternoon with the dowager learning the names, titles, and material wealth of the lords and ladies to whom she would be properly introduced—or, in certain instances, reintroduced after last night. A future duchess, the dowager instructed, had a rigid code of propriety that must be followed.

After the dowager deemed their first lesson finished, Bella was dismissed to change for dinner. She opened the door to find Harriet in the sitting room.

"Harriet!" Bella threw herself in her old nursemaid's arms.

Harriet's face beamed. "Congratulations! A duchess! The news has traveled like wildfire with the servants below stairs. I'm thrilled."

"But it's all happened so suddenly."

"Not really, Bella. Blackwood has wanted you for some time. The man is head over heels in love with you."

"No. He feels indebted and responsible for me," Bella argued. "He hasn't mentioned love."

Harriet surveyed her kindly. "A dominant male like Blackwood will not easily speak eloquent words of love. You must judge him by his actions."

Bella sighed and sat on a settee beneath a window overlooking the street. "His grandmother is planning a grand ball in James's honor and intends to announce our engagement, but Rupert still roams the city. We were waylaid by highwaymen, and James suspects Rupert hired the criminals."

"I heard about the highwaymen," Harriet said in a dull and troubled voice.

"Then you must understand my fear. If Rupert hears of the ball, surely he will try to sneak in and confront me for the missing ledger!"

Harriet sat beside Bella and stroked a loose curl from her face. "Don't fret, luv. Blackwood must have a plan. You no longer have to carry your burdens alone."

Harriet spoke the truth. As James's wife, Bella would be safeguarded. As a duchess, she would have her own power. Then why was there a creeping uneasiness at the bottom of her heart?

Dinner turned out to be a grand affair. Bella had hoped to have a word in private with James, but as she descended the staircase, the front door opened and James's friends filled the vestibule. Bella was delighted to see Lady Evelyn standing beside Jack Harding.

"We've come to celebrate and wish you happiness," Evelyn said.

James's fellow barristers came forth one by one and kissed her cheek. Brent Stone offered her a warm, charming smile, his handsome countenance relaxed. He then turned to slap James heartily on the back and gave him a look that said, *I told you so.*

Anthony Stevens was another matter entirely. He was polite, but distant, tilting his brow, looking at her uncertainly. His dark eyes showed the dullness of disbelief, and he seemed confused by it all.

No doubt, Bella mused. Anthony's legal career was spent

trying to find ways to free men from their marital vows, and now another of his close friends was *volunteering* to be leg-shackled.

James placed Bella's hand on his sleeve and headed for the dining room. There was a warm possessiveness in his touch when he guided her to her chair. His fingers brushed her collarbone and the tops of her shoulders and lingered. When his gaze fell to the creamy expanse of her neck, she blushed and struggled to contain the dizzying current racing through her.

Liveried footmen entered, carrying trays of lamb, fowl, and ham. The sideboard was laden with a dozen vegetable dishes, each served from gold-rimmed chafing dishes bearing the Blackwood crest. The wine was selected to complement the flavor of the dishes, and numerous footmen assured that the guests' glasses were never empty.

The dowager was notably absent, and Bella learned she had a prior engagement. James seemed more than happy at his grandmother's absence and seized the opportunity to discuss last night's attack.

Bella understood that James shared his friends' confidence, and she was not surprised that they all seemed to know the details of Rupert's treason and his quest for the ledger. As Jack Harding's wife, Evelyn would know as well.

"Rupert Sinclair has resorted to hiring criminals," James said. "I've no doubt the highwaymen that attacked us last night were recruited by him."

"It's not difficult to hire local riffraff, and the man has the means to pay them," Jack Harding said.

Bella spoke up. "Which brings me to my point. Is it wise for the dowager to hold a ball announcing our engagement? Rupert will attempt to gain entrance and could cause grave harm."

"Exactly," James said.

"You plan a trap, then?" Anthony asked.

"I do. We can leak news that the ledger has been found and

is in my possession. Make it impossible for Rupert Sinclair *not* to make an appearance," James said.

Brent grinned in approval. "It's a bold move. He'll come for you, for certain."

"I'm planning on it," James said. "But I don't want him anywhere near Bella."

Bella stared wordlessly across at James, her thoughts a crazy mixture of hope and fear. She no longer doubted James's ability to defend her or himself. When James had been shot in the stables, he had been distracted by aiding an unconscious and bleeding Bobby; he hadn't anticipated Rupert's presence. But last night James had been ruthless with the highwaymen. Blue eyes blazing, he had dispatched his knife, his actions swift and unhesitant.

No, she knew James could handle Rupert. Rather, what had her heart pounding was his willingness to put himself at risk for her. Harriet's words ran through her mind.

A dominant male like Blackwood will not easily speak eloquent words of love. You must judge him by his actions.

What little Bella knew of men, she knew one thing to be true—a man wouldn't risk his life for just any woman.

James turned to Bella, seemingly oblivious to her rioting emotions. "Thanks to the physical description you gave the artist at Bow Street, we all know what Rupert looks like, and we will be alert to his presence. The element of surprise is on our side."

"Jack and I will stay with Bella at the ball," Evelyn said. "Brent and Anthony can stay with James."

"We'll all be armed, and I'll retain extra men to act as footmen and keep a lookout," James said.

All voiced their approval of the plan.

Despite her initial apprehension at hearing James's plan with such unanimous agreement, Bella experienced a profound relief like she had never known. She'd been alone for so long, but now she had James and his friends on her side. She was accepted here, not looked down upon as weak-minded or maudlin—the way Roger had painted her to the Plymouth townsfolk—but a woman worth helping, worth *saving*.

Ever since her marriage, Roger had isolated her from her friends and from her father until she had withdrawn into herself out of fear.

But now she was free to be herself, free to share her concerns and problems with people willing to help her and powerful enough to make a difference. Freedom, she now understood, didn't necessarily mean single as a widow, but could mean being James's wife and accepted into his circle of friends. Marriage with him would be a partnership, not a legal prison. It would offer her protection and security, and, yes, *love*.

After the guests departed, the dowager returned from her function. Not wishing for another lesson on her future duties as a duchess, Bella retired to her room. Any private conversation with James, it seemed, would have to wait.

She was dressed in her nightgown, curled up on a leather arm chair and reading a draft of one of her writings when the low knock sounded.

Setting her notebook aside, she rose and cracked the door to find James leaning against the doorjamb. His hot gaze took in her prim nightgown and loose hair.

"Were you asleep?" he asked.

"No. I was reading."

He slipped inside and locked the door.

For an instant, she wondered if she should insist he leave. His grandmother was somewhere in this mansion, even if she slept an entire wing away. Then he gathered her in his arms and kissed her with such tenderness she was lost.

"Ah, Bella," he whispered against her ear. "All day and night you were beside me and I could not touch you. My frustration knew no bounds."

"James," she breathed. "We need to talk about this plan of yours."

He kissed her forehead. "Later. Much, much later."

He took her hand and led her into her bedroom.

She followed. "You've turned me into a wanton."

"Yes. *My* wanton."

His passionate kiss dissipated her thoughts, left her trembling with need. She was helpless to stop herself then. All of her loneliness and worry melded together in one upsurge of devouring yearning.

His fingers were rough with the tiny buttons of her nightgown, and with a frustrated growl, he ripped the fabric until it slid down her body to pool at her bare feet. She helped undress him until they were skin to skin.

His hands cupped her breasts, teasing, kneading. His lips seared a path down her throat to her breasts; then he devoured her flesh.

She felt wanton indeed. Wanton and desired . . . and cherished.

They fell to the bed in a tangle of limbs and deep sighs. He shifted her to the edge of the mattress, her legs dangling. He kissed and licked his way down her soft belly and blew his breath on her silken curls. Then he set his mouth to her hot core.

She gasped, her eyes flew open and her fingers tangled in his dark hair. She tried to twist away, but he gave her no reprieve, his hands tightening on her waist. His tongue laved her, bold and wicked, caressing her most intimate flesh with infinite tenderness.

"James! I don't know if—"

"*Shh.* Let me pleasure you this way."

The tip of his tongue flicked over her aching bud, and she moaned. His seductive expertise, his ruthless gentleness, the merciless stroke of his fingers in her slick, feminine folds banished her inhibitions and she lay drowned in a floodtide of desire. Passion inched through her veins, and molten heat flooded her loins. She'd never felt pleasure so acute, and her body felt as if it were half ice and half flame.

She tugged on his hair. "James," she pleaded. "I need . . . I need you inside me."

He rose above her and smoothly eased into her with one powerful thrust. She arched up to meet him, frantic to take him deeply, completely. He sensed her need, sensed her desperation and took her with powerful strokes. The heat between them flared into an inferno, joining him to her forever. She clutched his powerful shoulders and shut her eyes, savoring each moment, each blissful feeling as blood pounded through her heart, chest, and head.

"I love you," she gasped. "I love you, James."

James lay with Bella in his arms. Her body was warm and pliant, sated in the aftermath of their passion.

She loved him. His heart swelled, and he knew a relief so great it made him tremble. He wanted to spend the entire night holding her. He didn't give a damn what his grandmother thought. But it was the notion of causing Bella any embarrassment that counseled discretion. He would have to tear himself away from her and make his way back to his own bedchamber.

She nestled against his shoulder. "Are you concerned?" she asked softly.

"No."

"Hmmm."

He rose on his elbow and looked down at her. "Do you trust me, Bella?"

"Yes," she said without hesitation. "But Rupert won't stop until he has the ledger."

He brushed his lips across hers. "Then I shall have to stop him."

She gazed up at him and chewed on her bottom lip. "James,

there's something else I must tell you. Something that may change your mind about marrying me."

"Nothing you can tell me will change my mind."

She took a deep breath, then said, "The day Roger died we fought horribly. He confronted me at the top of the landing and when he raised his hand to strike me, I raised my own in defense and he . . . he tripped and fell. I fear I may have . . . killed him."

James sighed. "You didn't kill him, and I wouldn't blame you if you did."

"How do you know?"

"I told you once my investigator was very thorough. Roger Sinclair's own servant said he was raging drunk and in a foul temper that day. If you raised your hand to protect yourself, then it was self-defense."

"I feared the worst. That you would think I was a . . . murderer," she said.

"Listen, sweetheart. Even if you pushed him down the entire length of the hall and threw Roger Sinclair down the stairs to his death, I would not blame you. He was an abusive husband and deserved his fate."

Her voice was weak and unsteady. "Rupert blames me. He said he could easily bribe one of the servants to testify that I pushed him."

James's eyes narrowed at Rupert's malicious threat. "He'd never succeed. It's one thing to threaten a vulnerable widow, but quite another to threaten my soon-to-be bride, a future duchess." He placed a finger under her chin until she met his gaze. "Don't you know, Bella? I'd never let anyone harm you."

She pulled his head down and kissed him hungrily.

He groaned. "That is not the way to get me to leave this bed tonight." He stood and slipped on his trousers.

She lifted her head from the pillow. "Where are you going?"

He held up her ripped nightgown. "This is torn beyond repair. Let me fetch you another."

Taking the bedside candle with him, he entered the sitting room and went straight to a trunk in the corner. It was a small trunk with a lid with a curved top inlaid with ivory and mother-of-pearl. It was a good guess as to where a maid would store a lady's nightdresses. He lifted the trunk's latch and looked inside to find a miniature portrait of a couple he assumed were her parents, Bella's books and writings, other papers bound with brown string, and a pair of jeweled combs that he recalled her wearing. Not a stitch of clothing was stored inside.

As he was closing the trunk his hand halted in midair. It wasn't the contents that grabbed his interest, rather a pinch that felt like a pinprick on the tip of his forefinger as he tried to close the lid. Raising the lid once more, he studied the interior with renewed interest.

Both the interior and underside of the lid were lined with luxurious, crimson velvet. He'd seen one of these before. A client had been accused of stealing his aunt's trunk, not for the expected contents inside, but because of a false lid that held a secret compartment storing banknotes.

James felt along the velvet lining of the underside of the lid. At first there was nothing, but when he tore a small section of the velvet, he felt a faint ridge along one side. Pressing on the ridge produced a slight click, and the bottom of the lid opened to reveal an inner compartment. Heart pounding, he reached inside and removed a bound sheath of papers.

The ledger.

"I found it!"

A muffled voice sounded from the other room. Seconds later, Bella appeared in the doorway, the sheet wrapped around her slender frame. Dark red tresses covered her bare shoulders and the tops of her breasts.

He grinned and held up the ledger.

"Oh, my!" She rushed forward. Her gaze flew from the ledger in James's hand to the open trunk. "All these years I had no idea my mother's trunk had a secret compartment. And Roger had hid the ledger right beneath my nose."

"We have it now, Bella." James scanned the pages and whistled through his teeth. "Solid evidence of treason. I shall turn it in to the authorities. Rupert Sinclair is doomed."

She flew to his side and embraced him. "Oh, James," she breathed. "I do love you."

Chapter 32

Waking alone, Bella stretched in the large bed, her limbs sore after last night's delicious bout of lovemaking. She rolled to the side and inhaled James's scent on the feathered pillow. She knew he had departed her bedchamber late last night to preserve an appearance of propriety. But she missed him and longed for the mornings after they were married when she could wake in his arms.

She still couldn't believe he had found the ledger and that it had been hidden in her mother's trunk all along. How could she not have known of the secret compartment?

Looking back, she wasn't surprised Roger had discovered the compartment. He'd had five locked drawers in his desk, and two safes in his library that she had been aware of, and she suspected there were others. A man as devious as Roger had need of many hiding places.

Bella rose and dressed quickly. Hoping to catch a glimpse of James before he departed for the day, she rushed into the breakfast parlor, where the smell of cooked bacon wafted to her. The room was empty but a sideboard was laden with chafing dishes heaping with eggs, toast, biscuits, and yes . . . bacon.

Instantly, bile rose in her throat and she feared she would be sick on the expensive Brussels carpet. She turned and fled back up the stairs, racing down the long hallway to her room. She made it to the chamber pot just as nausea overtook her. She wretched, her stomach contracting painfully. A sheen of sweat rose on her brow, and she felt faint.

Bella pulled the bell cord and sat on the edge of the bed. A maid arrived, and Bella instructed her to fetch Harriet.

Minutes later Harriet entered the room, her eyes flying from Bella's pale face to the chamber pot.

"When was your last monthly flow?" Harriet asked.

The question alarmed Bella, and her mind raced back. She had not had her courses since . . . since before she had been intimate with James at Wyndmoor Manor, well over a month ago. She had always been as regular as clockwork.

"You could be pregnant," Harriet said.

Bella shook her head numbly. "I could be ill."

"Have you been tired of late? Your breasts sensitive?"

She was and they were.

"I never conceived with Roger. I'm most likely barren," Bella argued.

Harriet clucked her tongue. "Roger was much older. And he had not successfully bedded you after the first months of your marriage."

Bella rested her head in her hands; the harder she tried to ignore the signs the more they persisted.

"Sweet Lord," Bella gasped. "What am I to do?"

"Nothing, luv. You're to be married. Tell Blackwood."

"Tell me what?"

Bella and Harriet started at the sound of the deep, masculine voice in the doorway. In her haste to aid Bella, Harriet had left the door open. James now stood in the entrance of the room, his brows drawn downward.

"Your Grace." Harriet bobbed a curtsy, then snatched the chamber pot and fled the room.

James came and sat beside her on the bed, rubbing her back and whispering soothing words. Dismayed, Bella shut her eyes. She didn't want him to witness her ill, didn't want to tell him this way.

Yet slowly she felt the tension ease from her shoulders. James poured her a glass of water from the pitcher beside the bed and wiped her brow with a clean cloth.

"Are you unwell, Bella?" he asked.

"I'm with child," she whispered.

He captured her eyes with his. "Are you certain?"

"I believe so. I went downstairs to the breakfast parlor only the find the smell of bacon suddenly repulsive. I've always loved bacon."

James smiled as if her explanation made perfect sense. "When Evelyn was with child she could never stand the smell of certain foods. In the beginning of her pregnancy, Jack was desperate to get her to eat."

"Are you displeased?"

He cradled her in his arms. "I'm pleased, Bella. *Very pleased,* to be precise. Even more that we are to marry." His voice took on a serious tone. "No child of mine will be raised with the stigma of illegitimacy."

"The dowager shall have her heir after all," she whispered against his shoulder.

"If I have my say, it will be a girl."

She raised her head. "Truly? A girl?"

He grinned. "Yes, a little girl with rich auburn hair the same glorious shade as her mother's. A little girl I can cherish and spoil and bounce on my knee as I read to her every night."

Her heart lurched. She was reminded of Wyndmoor's tenant children. All had adored him. Without a doubt, she knew James would be a wonderful and loving father to his own child.

She was relieved he wanted the child, but at the same time she was flooded with uncertainty. The undeniable truth was that he had mentioned duty and devotion to the child, but not love for her.

The following week was spent in a flurry of activity. The invitations for the ball were sent out, and Bella had begun her fittings with the modiste for a new wardrobe suitable for a future duchess.

As for James, she rarely saw him. His days were spent transferring his remaining cases to his friends at Lincoln's Inn or in his library office poring over the books alongside the stewards of all the ducal properties he had inherited.

His training as a barrister was evidenced in his handling of his new responsibilities. He was a shrewd businessman who refused to allow others to handle his newly acquired estates without his involvement. As for the nights, he sensed her concern and desire for propriety. She was nervous sharing a bed beneath the same roof as his grandmother. James had respected Bella's wishes and had not knocked on her door in the middle of the night.

She missed him. Lord, did she miss him.

Two days before the ball, the dowager accompanied Bella to the modiste for the final fitting of the gown Bella would wear to the event. Harriet came along, for the sole purpose, the dowager said, of learning how to properly dress her mistress.

The women entered the Bond Street dress shop. As soon as the owner saw who had walked into her salon, she rushed forth. A middle-aged French woman with a large bosom, Madam Marie had dark hair slicked back in a knot at her nape. She clapped her hands and a young assistant appeared holding an exquisite gown of silver satin.

"Ah, you are pleased with the gown, no?"

Bella's breath caught as she touched the fine fabric. When she had first learned the cost of the gown, she had been shocked. She could feed a small household for a full month for such an enormous amount. The dowager was quick to point out that James had insisted she was to purchase whatever she desired.

"If you'll follow me into the fitting room." Madam Marie escorted Bella through the salon to the fitting room and pulled back a blue curtain. The dressmaker pulled the curtain closed and helped Bella into the gown.

Bella walked to the two mirrored panels mounted on the wall that allowed the shop's customers to view both the front and back of their clothing. She turned in a circle, noting the seamstresses' work. The gown fit like a glove, from the tight bodice to the nip at the waist, to the slender flare of her hips. She couldn't stop herself from thinking of James's reaction when he first spotted her at the ball.

"It's stunning, no?" Madam Marie said.

Bella twirled the flowing skirts about her legs. The silver satin felt light as air. She'd never owned anything so luxurious, so costly.

"It's beautiful," she breathed.

"You will make a lovely bride for your duke."

Bella's heartbeat skyrocketed. She may not have initially planned to marry, but her future seemed as bright as the chandeliers hanging from the ceiling. She was marrying a man she loved, a man as different from Roger as night from day. She had finally escaped her bad memories—memories that had been built over the seven horrific years of her marriage.

She need not fear her wedding night or the years thereafter, waiting for his touch to turn into a brutal assault. Rather, thoughts of the coming nights with James were exhilarating, exciting.

The dressmaker removed a pin from a pincushion at her waist. "The hem needs work. Head up, shoulders back for me."

Bella complied. Madam Marie was in the process of pinning the hem when the curtain was swept open. The dowager stood in the doorway, her gaze raking over Bella's figure in the silver gown.

"It will do just fine for the ball," the dowager said. Her eyes snapped to the dressmaker. "I require a moment alone with the lady."

Madam Marie's lips tightened around a mouthful of pins. She stood, grabbed her pincushion, and rushed out. She was clearly accustomed to taking orders from her aristocratic customers.

The dowager stepped inside and pushed the curtain back in place.

The elder woman's hawklike gaze made Bella nervous. "Is something wrong?" Bella asked.

"James was successful in obtaining a special license from the bishop. It helped that I was always very generous with my donations to the church in the past, you see. You can be married immediately after the ball," her ladyship said.

Not for the first time, Bella wondered why the dowager had been so quick to accept her. Bella knew the woman wanted a grandchild, but at the same time, Bella was not a titled heiress. The only money she had in her possession was what James had paid her for Wyndmoor Manor.

Just as Bella was pondering these thoughts, the dowager sagged against the door frame. Her posture was awkward, her upper body bent slightly at the waist. Her face went pale, her lips parted, and her breathing came in quick, little gasps.

Bella rushed forward. "Your Grace?"

The dowager held up a shaky hand. "It's nothing. . . . It will pass."

Bella took the woman's arm in a firm grasp and guided her to a chair in the corner. "How long have you suffered from these chest pains?"

"It's nothing."

"I beg to differ. It's your heart."

The dowager lifted her head. "How . . . how do you know?"

"My father suffered from a weak heart."

The woman's voice was fragile and shaking. "I thought . . . your father died in a carriage accident."

"He did, but he often experienced a painful tightness in his chest."

"My son, the old duke, died of a weak heart. I . . . I must have passed it to him."

Bella stood. "Let me call for help."

"No!" The dowager grasped Bella's wrist like a claw. Her cobalt eyes blazed in her face with desperate determination. "No one must know."

Uncertainty flooded Bella. She wanted to summon aid, but the dowager was adamantly against it. She knelt by the woman's side and held her hand.

"It will pass soon," the dowager said in a weak voice.

Thirty seconds, then a full minute, passed as the pair remained in the fitting room. Bella glanced at the closed curtain, torn by indecision. She had made up her mind to call out when the dowager's pain subsided, and the woman could speak easily once again.

Thank the Lord! Bella thought. She experienced a flooding relief, a numb comfort that death had been avoided. It was the same when her father had suffered through an "episode." What could be worse than complete helplessness?

The dowager released her grasp on Bella's wrist. "You must think my treatment of James as a boy was abominable."

Bella hesitated, torn by conflicting emotions. "He was your grandson, no matter his birth mother."

The dowager's face crumpled. Gone was the haughtiness, the superior aristocratic air, and in its place was an old, frail woman.

"I have my regrets," the dowager said. "You must understand when my son, James's father, came home from Oxford on holiday he was a hellion. Fathering a child with a parlor maid was one thing, but then he claimed he loved her and disappeared with the chit. I was furious. I'd not have my son, the heir to the dukedom, make a laughing stock of the family. He eventually came crawling home, saying the maid was dead and an infant son born. I provided for the child, and my son settled into his role as a proper duke. I never knew they had married."

"But James was innocent."

"Yes, I made a mistake. Gregory was spoiled and indulged. I've turned a blind eye to his habits, but truth be told, I'm relieved James is legitimate. He'll do the title justice. I fear my time is running out to make amends and see his heir," the dowager said.

A tumble of confused thoughts and feelings assailed Bella. Should she confess her secret? Consummating their union before marriage was not something any woman would want to tell her grandmother-in-law.

But the dowager was dying.

Bella took pity on the woman. "You may see your heir sooner than you believe," she said.

Her face lit. "You're with child? I knew the moment James carried you into my party that my prayers had been answered."

James arrived home from Lincoln's Inn to learn that Bella and his grandmother were out of the house. Stodges informed James that the women were shopping, choosing slippers, fans, and jewels for tonight's ball.

James was looking forward to presenting Bella to all of society on his arm. He had kept his distance from her over the course of the past week because he found that he could not be in the same room with her and not touch her. He had wanted to show respect for her wishes, but damned if it hadn't cost him. Just a glimpse of her at the top of the staircase, in the gardens, over dinner, was enough to set his heart pounding.

The wedding could not come soon enough.

I've turned into a lovesick fool, he mused. He wanted her as his wife and the thought of her having his child did not terrify him. Rather, he was thrilled.

A child he could love the way he was never loved. And if he had a son there would be no boarding schools, no seasonal visits. James would spend time each day with his child, share meals with him, and teach him how to ride and hunt, how to read and write, and how to never doubt he was loved.

There was a knock on the door. Stodges wasn't near so James opened the door himself. Gregory stood on the front steps.

"Good afternoon, Gregory. The dowager is not home," James said.

"I've come to speak with you," Gregory said.

James opened the door, and Gregory stepped inside. James studied his half brother with a critical eye. Gregory appeared to have cleaned up his appearance for today's visit. His moss-colored jacket and matching waistcoat had been tailored to his shoulders. But the tailoring revealed how cadaverously thin Gregory had become. He looked like a man in need of his next meal.

It's the damned opium that eats away at his flesh. The decreased appetite for food increases the need for the drug.

James motioned for Gregory to follow him to the library and offered him a whiskey.

Gregory accepted the glass and sat in an armchair across from him. "I realize congratulations are in order."

"You must be speaking about my upcoming nuptials."

"No. I'm speaking of your unborn heir."

James set down his glass and leaned forward.

"Oh, don't try to deny it," Gregory said. "I was here yesterday to discuss another matter with you when I witnessed the dowager ordering one of her loyal footmen to fetch a cradle from the attic. The old bat was going on and on about the heir to the house of Blackwood. The cradle, she said, belonged to our father. I easily surmised the truth after that. You need not worry, brother. I can keep a secret."

James was surprised to hear the dowager knew of the babe. Bella must have told her. But why?

"I find it hard to believe you've come here today to wish me happiness," James said.

Gregory ignored his mocking tone. "No wonder you acquired a special license. You had best marry quickly to ensure the child is legitimate. You wouldn't want it to be looked down upon as you were."

James's eyes narrowed. "Tell me what you want."

"I'd like to speak of the allowance you had mentioned. I spoke in haste. I realize our father had deemed to leave his heir everything. He has not left me with a shilling."

"As I mentioned before, if managing a ducal estate is not to your liking, I have many business interests. Some are even listed on the London Stock Exchange. I would be willing to pay you to assist managing them." James knew it would be an act of charity, rather than business sense, but despite it all, Gregory was his half brother.

Gregory laughed bitterly. "It's no wonder you don't understand. You were a barrister, for Christ's sake. You were never meant to have the title. I, on the other hand, am a gentleman. We don't work."

James's voice hardened. "Don't be a fool. Circumstances have changed. I hold the title now, and I'm not inclined to hand it over. Accept what I'm offering. I can be generous, Gregory."

"What do you know of generosity? You have taken my title, my wealth, and my betrothed."

"I never touched Lady Caroline."

"She's cried off our betrothal."

"Perhaps you should look to yourself," James said.

Gregory scoffed. "What are you implying?"

"I can help you with the opium. I have aided former clients.

There are physicians that specialize in treating those that are addicted."

Gregory's face became red and blotchy with anger. "You think I'd agree to have you lock me up?"

"Don't let the opium ruin your life."

"The opium hasn't ruined anything. *You* have."

James scraped back his chair. "If the purpose of your visit was to attempt to use the knowledge of my unborn child against me, then you have failed. Go now, Gregory, before I change my mind about my financial offer."

Chapter 33

Bella stood beside James in the ballroom, greeting a long line of well-wishers. The dowager had announced their engagement moments ago, and the ballroom swelled with extravagantly dressed guests all eager to congratulate the new Duke of Blackwood and his betrothed. Bella spent the next hour smiling and curtsying, completely surprised at the number of people James knew—judges and barristers as well as influential members of society and the government. Then there were the dowager's acquaintances, who carried themselves with the haughtiness that Bella associated with the titled and wealthy individuals of the *ton*.

A viscount with a curled mustache that resembled a walrus bowed low before Bella and peered down her bodice. Bella rolled her eyes and stole a glance at James standing beside her. Among the garish colors worn by the male popinjays, James looked strikingly handsome in simple black-and-white evening attire. He stood tall and broad-shouldered, his hawk-like features arresting and elegant, conveying a compelling sensuality that captivated her.

As the evening progressed, it was clear the ball was a huge success. There were no whispers of her unladylike interruption at the dowager's private soiree. Lady Jersey herself, one of the powerful patronesses of Almack's Assembly Rooms, kissed Bella's cheeks in congratulations and invited her to a Wednesday evening at that establishment's hallowed halls on King Street.

At last the line of well-wishers dwindled, and Bella spotted Evelyn and Jack taking a turn on the dance floor. Brent and Anthony stood by the refreshment table near the open French doors leading to the terrace. She understood their intent. Without an invitation permitting Rupert entrance through the front door, he would have to sneak in through the gardens. She assumed James's hired men were among the numerous footmen stationed at the doors and seeing to the guests' needs in the ballroom.

They had all seen the sketch she had provided to the Bow Street Runners. They knew whom to look out for.

In between dances, glasses clinked and laughter floated throughout the ballroom. Yet Bella remained tense, her eyes darting every few minutes to the open French doors.

James reappeared by her side. His gaze appraised her form-hugging silver gown from head to toe. "Have I told you that you look beautiful tonight?"

His heated glance made her senses reel and brought a hot blush to her cheeks. "Four times to be exact, Your Grace. But I must admit to finding your flattery quite thrilling."

He grinned devilishly. "Then I promise not to disappoint you in that regard." He held out his hand. "Shall we dance, my dear?"

He led her to the dance floor just as the orchestra struck up a waltz. As he whirled her across the floor in his arms, she was painfully aware of the attention they received and forced a smile on her face. Only her quickened breathing revealed her nervousness.

"Bella, love. What are you thinking?" he asked.

"It's past midnight, and Rupert has not made an appearance. Could we have been wrong?"

His hand tightened on her waist. "It's unlikely. I leaked word that the ledger has been found, and Jack told a former client who is well-connected in the underworld that an incriminating ledger will soon be turned over to the authorities. Rupert cannot afford but to try and seize it. I suspect he is waiting for the perfect opportunity."

"Then we must give it to him."

The dance ended and he escorted her off the floor. "What are you suggesting?" he said.

She leaned close and whispered her plans in his ear.

He jerked back, his eyes darkening. "No, Bella. I'll not permit you to put yourself at risk. The night of the highwaymen has already aged me ten years."

"I wouldn't be at risk. I'd have you and your friends watching out for me. It's a solid plan."

"Still—"

"This is our last chance," she urged. "I wouldn't want Rupert to make an appearance at our wedding." She stepped close, her silver skirts brushing his legs. "Please don't be stubborn about this, James."

He let out a rough laugh. "I see I will never stand a chance against your persuasive techniques."

With her hand resting upon his sleeve, she was aware of the coiled tension in his body. She gazed up at his profile, and was struck by his determination.

He guided her to where Anthony and Brent stood, and James motioned for his friends to join him in a corner. Quick words were exchanged and plans made.

Brent looked surprised, but nodded. Anthony's lips curled in a calculated smile.

"If we do this," James instructed Bella, "then you must follow my precise directions. Do not leave the main path of the gardens."

"I promise," Bella said.

Though together they strolled through the crowd, smiling

as they passed couples on the dance floor as if they hadn't a care in the world, Bella's composure felt as fragile as an eggshell.

As they stepped outside onto the terrace, the cool night air felt wonderful on her overheated skin. Couples there nodded in greeting, and two men smoked cigars in the corner. Lit lanterns bobbed in the slight breeze, and the full moon hung overhead, a luminescent ball. The scent of roses from the garden filled the air with a heady perfume. It would have been perfectly romantic if not for her troublesome brother-in-law.

James leaned against the balustrade and made a show of laughing at one of the guest's jokes. Bella knew he was trying to attract attention should Rupert be lingering in the gardens below.

James lowered his head, his breath brushing her ear. "Let's go. Anthony and Brent should be in place by now."

He whisked her down the terrace steps into the sculpted gardens below. Lanterns on the main stone path illuminated their way past white stone benches and graceful statues of Greek gods and goddesses situated along the path.

As they followed the walkway farther into the gardens, the bright light of the ballroom faded and the noise of the crowd became a far-off din. James guided Bella to one of the benches, and they sat down together.

Around them, the chirping of the insects blended with other night sounds. Some sixth sense told her Rupert was here, and the hair on her nape stood on end. James must have sensed it too for he tightened his hold on her hand.

With a rustle of shrubbery a dark figure emerged from the bushes. Bella started, then gasped as Rupert stepped onto the stone path and into the moonlight. He held a pistol in his right hand.

"Move and I'll shoot her in the head," Rupert said tersely.

James stood slowly, an ominous expression on his face. "Rupert Sinclair, I presume."

Rupert sneered, turning the pistol on James. "That's right. And you must be the Duke of Blackwood. We were never formally introduced in Wyndmoor Manor's stables."

James's smile did not reach his eyes. "I assume you've come for the ledger. The contents are quite interesting, I assure you."

Rupert waved the pistol in the direction of the mansion. "Go inside and get it. Bella stays with me."

James held out a hand, his expression suddenly contrite. "All right. I'll go. Just don't hurt her." He turned to leave, and Rupert lowered his pistol an inch. Just then James pivoted swiftly on his heel and lunged for Rupert. They hit the ground hard, the pistol flying out of Rupert's hand. Both men scrambled for it.

"Stop!" Another male voice.

Bella whirled around to see Brent Stone rush from the bushes and kick the pistol out of reach. He held his own pistol to the back of Rupert's head as Anthony Stevens came forth and snatched the discarded weapon from the ground. A tall man wearing a footman's uniform stood beside Anthony.

Sweet Lord! Bella sagged in relief.

James's gaze never left Rupert Sinclair's face as he dragged the man to his feet. "Anthony and Miller, escort Bella back to the ball."

Bella didn't argue when Anthony and the footman moved to her side.

James was going to interrogate Rupert, and she wanted to put as much distance as possible between herself and the man who looked so much like her dead spouse.

James forced Rupert deep into the gardens, far from the ballroom terrace and the lit torches. "Pass the maze and head for the stream," James told Brent.

An intricately designed maze wove through the center of the gardens. An acre past the maze, a stream ran through the remaining property and bordered a back road. The isolated stream was far from the ballroom, and would suit James's needs precisely tonight. Guests with dainty ballroom slippers and finery would never venture out this far.

They came to the end of the maze, and James heard a trill of feminine laughter coming from deep within the shrubbery.

James pushed the muzzle of the pistol into Rupert's neck. "Not a sound," he growled.

Rupert stiffened, but remained silent.

They continued onward, past the maze, until the sound of running water echoed off the stone embankment of the stream.

James shoved Rupert forward, and he tripped and fell in the mud at the stream's embankment.

"All I want is the ledger, and then I'll go back to Somerset-shire," Rupert said.

James's voice hardened ruthlessly. "You'll never get it. You're going to Newgate."

Rupert stood and wiped his muddy hands on his pants. His mouth lifted in a menacing, sarcastic smile. "So you've been taken by her? Bella was my brother's whore. Did you know he enjoyed beating her and kept her on a tight leash?"

James growled in rage. For the first time in his life, he felt he could kill another human being in cold blood. He kicked the blackguard in the gut, and Rupert doubled over. James pulled Rupert's head back by his hair and punched him square in the nose. Blood splattered across James's clothing. He raised his fist again, fully intending to beat Rupert to a bloody pulp, when Brent grasped James's arm.

"Let me question him," Brent said.

"No!"

Brent's grip tightened. "Stop, James. Let me do it."

Though the hostility and fury James felt for Rupert Sinclair cried out for revenge—thirsted for it—Brent was right. James would kill Rupert before he obtained the answers he needed. Brent, on the other hand, was level-headed and not in a murderous mood. James clenched and unclenched his fist and released a held-in breath before finally lowering his arm.

Brent stepped in front of Rupert. "Who else was involved in your exports to the French?" Brent asked.

Rupert remained silent.

"What other documents are there?"

Again silence.

"You truly are desperate to have hired the highwaymen."

Rupert looked up at Brent. "Go to hell."

Something flickered far back in Brent Stone's eyes—an ominous glint like that of a predator certain of his prey's doom.

Brent grasped Rupert's hand. With a slight twist, there was a crack and Rupert dropped like a stone, howling in agony. Brent stood above him, a frightening look of utter detachment on his handsome face.

God's teeth! James thought. Who would have thought Brent had it in him?

Brent looked and sounded as if he were on a stroll in Hyde Park, completely oblivious to the pain he was inflicting.

"Did you hire highwaymen to attack the duke and Bella?" Brent asked.

"No!" Rupert screamed.

Brent twisted his grip a fraction more, and Rupert was reduced to wailing and begging. "No! I swear it on my twin's grave!"

Several seconds passed before Brent released Rupert's hand. "He's telling the truth," Brent said, matter-of-factly.

Fear gripped James's gut, tight as a vise. "The highwaymen were paid to kill. Then who hired them?"

"Who has the most to gain if you're dead?" Brent asked.

Gregory.

His half brother's name resounded in James's head.

"Gregory's highwaymen failed to kill me. He knows that Bella's carrying the heir and we're to wed the day after tomorrow by special license. He'd have to kill her, too."

"Go to her," Brent urged. "I already summoned the constable, and he's waiting on the back road. I'll deal with Rupert."

Chapter 34

After Anthony escorted Bella to the ball, he headed back to the gardens. The footman who had accompanied them returned to his post by the terrace. Bella lingered at the refreshment table, sipping a glass of bubbling champagne, her outward façade of calm masking her inner turmoil.

At this moment, James was questioning Rupert Sinclair. Just the sight of Rupert in the gardens had sent a spurt of panic through her. For a heart-stopping moment, Bella had seen her dead husband standing before her. Rupert looked frighteningly similar to his twin, and her mind froze with the same terror, the same dread as when Roger had hovered in the threshold of her bedchamber and leered down at her. It had taken every ounce of willpower not to run from the gardens, screaming like the madwoman Roger had once proclaimed her to be.

Then James had spoken in a calm, deep voice, and she recalled he was by her side.

"Ah, here is the soon-to-be duchess." Bella jumped and turned at the feminine voice behind her.

A tall, slender woman with blond hair and blue eyes approached. The satin bodice of her turquoise gown accentuated her breasts, and diamonds glittered at her throat and ears. She was accompanied by a man of average height with brown hair and eyes.

"Lady Caroline, are you enjoying the evening?" Bella said.

Bella recalled meeting Lady Caroline, the daughter of the Earl of Atwood. Their encounter had been brief as the line of well-wishers at the ball had been significant, but Bella had not missed the sidelong glances the lady had cast in James's direction.

"The dowager's events are always a success." Lady Caroline's painted lips curved in a smile. She motioned at the man beside her. "I would like to introduce Lord Gregory Devlin."

The man stepped close and bowed. "I apologize for my late arrival, Mrs. Sinclair."

Bella curtsied, masking her surprise. "It's a pleasure to meet you, Lord Devlin."

So this was James's half brother, the privileged sibling who had been raised in the ducal mansion while James grew up in a boarding school.

He was exceptionally dressed with a plum velvet jacket, matching embroidered waistcoat, and black breeches, but the well-tailored, padded jacket could not disguise his gauntness. His sunken cheekbones, pointed chin, and pallor that resembled old parchment gave him an ill appearance. He assessed her with unveiled interest.

"I see what has captivated my brother," Gregory said with a smile. "I'm fortunate to have found you alone for a moment this evening. You see, I commissioned an artist to paint a landscape for my brother as a surprise engagement present. I'd love for you to view it and give your opinion."

"What a thoughtful gift," Bella said. "There's no need for my approval. I'm certain James will be most pleased."

"Regardless, I'd like your opinion. I had it delivered to the library. It will take but a moment of your time. Will you have a look?" he asked.

Bella had no desire to view a painting. She glimpsed at the open French doors, hoping to see James enter the ballroom.

At Bella's hesitation, Lady Caroline said, "I've had the pleasure of seeing the work. It's a lovely landscape. However, as Blackwood's betrothed, you would be in a much better position to give an opinion."

Bella struggled to suppress her frustration. It took all of her restraint not to rush to the terrace and scan the gardens below. But Lord Devlin was watching her with such an earnest expression, like a student eager for his teacher's approval. How could she say no? He was James's brother, after all.

She made herself smile. "Of course. It would be my pleasure."

Lord Devlin's face brightened. He escorted Bella and Lady Caroline out of the ballroom and into the hall.

They reached the library door, and Caroline halted and waved at a passerby. "Please excuse me. I see Lady Henley, and I have yet to speak with her tonight." With a swish of her voluminous skirts, Lady Caroline turned and walked away, leaving Bella alone with Gregory.

He touched Bella's sleeve and smiled. "I have a confession to make. The painting is a peace offering. I must admit that James and I have not always seen eye to eye, but I'd like to make amends."

"I'd like that as well, my lord," Bella said.

"Since you are to be my sister-in-law, please call me Gregory," he said.

He opened the library door, and she stepped inside. The smell of lemon polish and old books reached her. Bella blinked as her eyes adjusted from the brightly lit ballroom and hallway to the dimness in the library.

She heard the door close and then Gregory's footsteps as he came close.

"Where is the painting?" she asked.

The library faced the opposite side of the mansion as the

ballroom, and only faint rays of moonlight illuminated the space through the windows.

"In the corner beside the lamp."

She followed him to the back of the room. All she could see was the outline of tall bookshelves and a desk situated before a window.

She bumped her hip on an end table, and a sense of uneasiness swept through her. Reaching his side, she looked to where he was pointing on the wall. "There's nothing here. Are you certain it was delivered to the library?"

"I'm not certain of anything, Bella."

"Whatever do you mean?"

Her unease exploded into alarm when she turned and found him holding a knife.

"Gregory! What are you—"

Before she could finish her sentence, he pulled her against him and pressed the knife to her throat.

"I apologize for my ungentlemanly behavior, but you have left me no choice."

"I don't know what you're talking about," she gasped. Panic welled inside her, tying her gut in knots.

"Believe me, I never meant for this to go so far. But you interfered with my plans for James."

She grasped onto the thought. "Yes, James! He can help you. Just let me go find him!"

Gregory laughed bitterly. "There's no need. He's going to find you. Only it will be too late for you and his unborn child."

She stiffened in shock. He knew about the child. How? James would never tell. Other than Harriet, the dowager was the only other person who knew.

A terrifying realization struck her.

"It was you with the highwaymen! You hired those criminals to kill James!"

Gregory cackled. "They failed, didn't they? You weren't

supposed to be in that carriage. But now that James intends to marry you swiftly because of the brat in your belly, I had to change my plans. You're ruining everything."

He meant to kill her and the babe. Fear pulsed hard and fast in her blood, paralyzing her.

Think! her inner voice cried out. How could she fight him? Even with a ballroom full of people on the other side of the house, he could slit her throat before she could let out a scream.

"Please, just let me go and I'll never speak a word," Bella said.

"You must think me an idiot."

"No, I don't. It's not too late to stop this."

"We must go now. Come." He pushed her forward, keeping the knife pressed to her throat.

She dragged her feet, and tripped on the carpet. "Wait!" she cried out. "You can't mean this!"

"Quiet!" he hissed in her ear and covered her mouth with his other hand.

He couldn't intend to take her out the front door. The mansion was packed with guests, and footmen were stationed outside escorting people to and from their carriages. She hadn't noticed the library's French doors, which led into the gardens on the side of the house. They wouldn't be seen.

She struggled and pulled at the hand that covered her mouth. The blade pressed into her throat. She winced as it pierced her flesh, and she felt a rivulet of blood trickle down her throat.

He opened the French doors and pushed her through. Her heart sank when she saw the waiting carriage on the side road.

Gregory's grip on the knife tightened as they approached the carriage. The driver stepped down, and a hard fist of fear knotted her stomach. He was an enormous man, over six feet six inches in height with a scar that ran down the entire right side of his face. Where his eye should have been was an unsightly, puckered scar.

Gregory shoved her into the carriage and took the seat across from her. The door slammed shut, and the carriage swayed as the driver hopped into his seat. Seconds later, they were off at an alarmingly fast pace.

"You won't get away with this," Bella said. "Surely someone will notice that we departed together."

"Only you will be missing, my dear. I will return shortly to the ball. Your body, on the other hand, will be found floating in the Thames days later. Society will assume you drowned yourself rather than marry a barrister turned aristocrat."

"That's ridiculous!"

"Is it? I overheard James speaking with his hired investigator. Your deceased husband had accused you of being mad. Once it's known, everyone will understand your rash behavior. Your child will never become the next heir to the title."

Raising her chin, she glared at him. "James has inherited the title; you never will."

Gregory's cold brown eyes flashed with contempt. "It was an unfortunate inconvenience that the highwaymen I retained did not succeed with their assignment. But be assured, accidents happen all the time, my dear. Something can be arranged to dispose of an unwanted half brother. The dukedom will then revert to me."

They had all been wrong. It wasn't Rupert, after all. Would James realize it was his own brother who desired to have him killed? More importantly, would he discover the truth in time?

"Is Lady Caroline your accomplice?" she asked.

"No. Alas, the lady believes I am to bribe you to disappear. She does not know you are pregnant. She wants you gone, but she is not a murderer. I'm not blind and know she is scheming to seduce James in order to become a duchess. She has no idea that I will eliminate both you and James. If she wants to be a duchess, she will have to marry me."

Bella's voice was shrill. "James is your *brother*. How can you do this?"

Gregory pointed to himself. "*I* am supposed to be the duke. *I* was born and bred for the position, not that conniving barrister. He had the audacity to suggest I work for him. Work! As if I'd ever entertain the notion. He's nothing but a bloody bastard!"

She bit her lip to keep from screaming that James had never been a bastard, but had been the rightful heir all along. Then the coach came to an abrupt stop, and Bella grasped the seat to keep from being thrown into Gregory's lap.

The door opened and the driver loomed in the doorway.

"Out!" Gregory shoved her from behind.

Stumbling from the carriage, she looked up in horror at Gregory's massive accomplice. The man's one good eye turned on her, and his mouth curved in a malicious smile.

Evil, she thought. Cold hard eyes just like Roger's before he had struck her in a drunken fit. She shivered.

Taking in her surroundings, Bella's dismay heightened. They had pulled off the main road, and a dense copse of trees loomed ahead. The spot was completely isolated from travelers; even were she to scream at the top of her lungs, no one would hear. Gregory pushed her into the wooded area, and she tripped twice over fallen branches.

When he jerked her to her feet, she shot him a withering glare. "James will learn the truth. He'll kill you."

Ignoring the comment, Gregory grabbed her arm instead and dragged her through the trees. His accomplice went ahead, slashing at low-hanging branches with a knife. She saw it then: a glimmer of moonlight reflecting off the surface of a lake in the distance.

"Stop!" she cried out, panicked. "The dowager knows I'm not insane. What if you're discovered?"

Gregory sneered at her. "The witch is old and is only concerned with the future generation of the House of Blackwood. With James dead, she'll need me to produce the next heir."

Gregory addressed his scarred accomplice. "Don't mark her. Make the drowning look like a suicide, then dump the body in the Thames."

Sheer black fright swept through her, and she knew her survival was in her own hands. She needed to buy time until James could find her. She struggled wildly, kicking at Gregory's legs and scratching at his hand. Gregory grunted twice and slowed, but then he tightened his grip and continued to drag her toward the lake. His hand was an iron manacle on her wrist. In a last desperate attempt, she bared her teeth and bit the back of his hand until she tasted blood.

With an ear-piercing scream, Gregory released her wrist. She stumbled back, then gained her footing and sprinted deep into the woods.

She heard their shouts behind her. "Stop!" Gregory's shrill voice. Followed by: "Go after her!"

Pulse pounding and frantic, she gathered her voluminous skirts in a fist and ran as fast as her legs would carry her. Low tree branches and brambles scratched her face and arms and tore her gown. Stones cut the bottom of her slippers and bit into the tender soles of her feet. The dense trees blocked the moonlight, and she could see only two arm lengths in front of her. She could hear the pounding footsteps of Gregory's accomplice gaining ground.

He was going to catch her. She needed a place to hide. But where? She turned sharply to the right and spotted a large, fallen oak. She scrambled over its massive trunk, then crouched low against it. Sweat trickled between her breasts in the tight bodice.

Booted feet snapped a nearby branch on the forest floor, and a man's heavy breathing came close.

"There's no sense 'iding. If ye come out, I'll make it quick fer ye."

His ominous words had the force of a lightning jolt to her already pounding heart. She needed a weapon. Her hands felt about the forest floor, resting on a rock the size of her fist. She grasped it in her right hand.

The man stepped onto the fallen tree, discovering her hiding place.

She looked up at him with wide, panicked eyes. "The duke is coming. He'll track you down!"

The corners of his mouth twisted in a malevolent smile, and he reached down for her.

Bella feinted to the side, and threw the rock, aiming for his forehead. It struck his good eye instead.

The man howled through clenched jaws and fell to his knees.

Bella jumped to her feet and sprinted back toward the clearing, toward the moonlight. Her lungs felt as if they would burst in the tight bodice, and her arms and legs ached from her mad dash. She cleared the woods, risking a glance behind her, when she ran straight into Gregory and fell down heavily.

He loomed above her, his face red and blotchy with anger. "Bitch! There's no escape from your fate."

Just as he grasped her wrist and wrenched her to her feet, the sound of pounding hooves could be heard on the dirt road. Gregory's head jerked around.

The shouts of men followed, and Bella spotted the riders. There were three in all, one in the lead riding a black stallion. Judging by its size, it had to be Maximus.

"James!" Bella cried out.

Gregory pulled Bella against him and pressed the knife against her throat.

"Killing me will gain you nothing," she hissed. "He is the duke. He has always been the duke."

"Shut up!"

The riders came close, and James pulled back on the reins. Anthony and Jack followed on their own mounts. James took in the scene. His gaze met hers, a frantic need shining within the sapphire depths of his eyes, but when he turned to Gregory they held a murderous fury. He held a pistol in his hand.

"I never knew you had a death wish, Gregory," James bit out as he jumped down from his horse.

"Death wish! It's not me that's going to see their maker this night."

"The opium has addled your brains." James aimed his pistol at Gregory. "You're outnumbered. Throw down the knife and step away from my woman."

Anthony and Jack aimed their own pistols at Gregory's accomplice as he ran into the clearing, blood running down his face.

Gregory backed up a step, taking Bella with him. "No! You shouldn't get everything!"

James's expression hardened. "It's over, Gregory. There's no way out. Let her go."

"So you can have me arrested?"

"No, so you can get the help you need."

Gregory continued urging Bella backward. With the knife pressed to her throat, there was only one way to go. She dropped her chin then whipped her head back with all her might, smashing into his face. Gregory stumbled, dropping the knife away from her throat. She followed with an elbow jab into his stomach. Gregory fell backward, taking her down with him. A heartbeat later, she heard the deafening crack of a pistol firing and felt the whiz of a bullet by her ear.

Chapter 35

The acrid scent of gun smoke burned his nostrils as James dropped his pistol and rushed to Bella's side. "Bella!"

Bella struggled to sit. "Thank God you came!"

He gathered her in his arms. "Are you hurt, darling?"

"No. I'm all right, but Gregory—"

Gregory writhed on the ground, clutching his arm and howling.

"I don't care about him," James said. He held Bella tightly to his chest, his breathing ragged. When he rode into the clearing and saw Gregory's knife pressed against Bella's throat, he'd never been more terrified in his life. Thank God he had reached her in time.

After discovering Rupert wasn't responsible for the highwaymen's attack, James had sprinted into the ballroom. Hearing from Lady Evelyn that she had last seen Bella leave with Gregory, James's heart had dropped to his stomach. He had fetched Maximus and raced to follow the coach. James dared not think of what would have happened had he not learned of Gregory's deception in time.

Jack now had his pistol pointed at Gregory's accomplice while Anthony tied the man's hands behind his back. They would take care of the criminal.

James brushed a gentle kiss across her lips.

Gregory cried out behind James. "You shot me!"

James lifted his head and narrowed his eyes at Gregory. The bullet had struck his arm, just below the elbow. James's intent had been to disarm him of the knife, not kill him. "You're lucky I'm a good shot, Gregory. I could have aimed for your skull."

"You bastard!"

James rose, ready to finish the job with his fists. Bella's touch on his chest halted him. "No, James! He's injured."

"He's going to the gallows."

"This can be handled quietly. A public scandal would devastate your grandmother," Bella said.

"She can handle herself."

"She's dying."

That stopped him. "It's her heart," she whispered. "I witnessed it myself."

"Just like my father, the old duke?"

Bella nodded. "The family name is important to her. Let her keep its integrity."

Gregory started wailing. "There's so much blood."

"He needs a doctor," Bella said. "I don't want my future husband and the father of my child to be tried for murder."

Anthony and Jack jumped to attention. "You're to be a father?" they asked in unison.

"We'll talk later," James said.

The pair bound Gregory's arm and lifted him onto Jack's horse. "The ball will be over by now; it should be safe to return to Park Street," Anthony said. "I'll ride ahead and call for a doctor."

James lifted Bella onto Maximus and mounted behind her. They reached the house where the dowager came charging outside demanding to know where the guests of honor had run off to. She stopped short when she caught sight of Gregory cradling his bloody arm close to his chest.

Entering the house, James ushered all to the drawing room, where they told the dowager everything. After listening intently, she marched up to Gregory and slapped him full across the face.

"To murder your brother and his betrothed! How could you!"

"I couldn't let them marry! The baby would be the next duke. The title is rightfully mine!"

"No," she snapped. "It never was. And I'm thankful for that fact."

"What do you want to do with him?" Jack asked.

James looked at the dowager. "It's no secret Gregory's a slave to the opium. There are facilities to help addicts. They are not pleasant, but the results can be positive and they're confidential."

"I'd rather rot in prison!" Gregory shouted.

"Don't tempt me," James said.

Anthony arrived with the doctor, and the dowager directed her footmen to carry Gregory upstairs and barricade him in one of the bedchambers.

"I think it best to avoid a scandal, Your Grace," Bella said.

The dowager paused, her lips pursed. "Yes. Once Gregory is able to travel, he can be admitted into a facility under a doctor's care. As for you two," she said, glancing at James and Bella, "I shall tell everyone that you ran off to marry at the end of the ball. It will be the romantic gossip of the decade."

"I'll agree to that," James said. "I want to marry now. I'll not wait a minute longer to marry the woman I love."

The dowager clasped her hands together as she hurried to the door. "I shall have to wake the priest."

Finally alone, James found Bella staring up at him with wide, jade eyes.

"Did you mean what you said?" she whispered.

There was no reason to ask what she was talking about. He gently held her hands in his. "When I learned Gregory had taken you, I nearly lost my mind. And when I saw him holding a knife to your throat, my world came crashing down upon me, and the truth in my heart became clear. I love you. I've loved you for so long now, even before I woke up to find you by my bedside after I was shot. Looking back, I started to fall under your spell that very first night I stepped into Wyndmoor Manor and you came close to splitting my skull in two, then accused me of being a burglar. You were a fiery challenge who turned into a passionate, intelligent woman that I cannot live without."

"Oh, James," she breathed.

He kissed her forehead, both eyelids, and brushed his lips across hers. Her mouth was warm and sweet, and when he pulled back she breathed lightly between parted lips.

He cupped her cheek in his hand. "Forgive me for not speaking the words sooner, darling. I foolishly feared to love, to open my heart and risk rejection."

Love meant bearing his soul, risking emotional pain, and he'd spent his entire adult life barricading himself from that danger. Since his family's rejection, he had learned not to trust or to need, and he had looked back upon his lonely childhood years in the boarding school as a form of weakness. After becoming a successful barrister, he had sworn never to be weak again. As a result, he had buried his feelings for Bella. He had justified his actions of wanting to keep her close in order to protect her when he had been too frightened to admit the truth to himself. It was time to take a leap of faith.

"I love you with all my heart, Bella. Nothing else matters— not my career or the dukedom and all the fortune that comes along with it—if you are not by my side. I want to marry you, have children with you, and grow old with you. After all that's happened tonight, will you still have me?"

Crying out with joy, she threw herself in his arms. "I love you too, James. Yes, I'll have you today, tomorrow, *forever.*"

The dowager had been right. They did have to wake the priest. Father Stevenson entered the church, his collar askew, and tufts of white hair sticking up from his scalp in disarray. If he resented being dragged from his bed in the middle of the night to perform a marriage, one stern look from the dowager turned his frown into a welcoming smile. All traces of annoyance dissipated as he opened his worship book. Clearing his throat, he began the marriage ceremony.

Although the wedding was on short notice, it turned out to be a beautiful event. Lady Evelyn held Bella's flowers and Brent stood as James's best man. Harriet sat beside the dowager, and Jack and Anthony behind them.

After the vows were exchanged and the couple pronounced man and wife, James pulled Bella into his arms and kissed her. He was still kissing her when the priest departed, followed by Jack and Evelyn, arm in arm. Brent slapped Anthony on the back, and on their way out Brent said, "I told him so a long time ago."

James would have kept kissing Bella, but she turned her head and blushed prettily. He followed her gaze and realized the dowager had remained behind and was watching them with a most uncharacteristic expression on her face. James could have sworn he saw a tear in her eye.

"We're married now, Your Grace. It's sanctioned by the church," James said.

The dowager made a little huff and turned away, but before she departed, they heard her mutter, "True love. Who would have thought?"

Epilogue

Four years later

Bella's pen flew across the paper, and a thrill of excitement hummed in her veins as the story unfolded before her. It was always this way when her thoughts flowed freely, and she had a solid block of time to write. An imminent deadline always helped.

Her editor at the *Times* had liked her proposal for her next piece, and Bella had eagerly accepted their generous offer.

The door burst open.

"Mama! Mama!"

Bella looked up from her writing. Her four-year-old son, Alexander, and three-year-old daughter, Catherine, were standing in the doorway. James came up behind them.

"They want to kiss you before they go down for their nap."

Bella scraped back her chair and gathered her children in her arms. "Would you like Mummy to read you a story first?"

"Yes!" they cried out in unison.

"You know your mother is working," James said gently.

"I don't mind."

"You spoil them," he teased.

"I enjoy it." She hugged both children before glancing up at James. "The dowager wants to take them on a picnic tomorrow."

"Can we, Mummy?" Bella smoothed her daughter's red curls away from her face to reveal green eyes, the shade of which was identical to her own.

Alexander smiled. "She promised me chocolate!"

Bella's lips trembled with the need to smile. No doubt the dowager had promised Alex chocolate. At four years old, Alex had his father's dark hair, blue eyes, and lethal charm.

James rolled his eyes, and Bella let out a burst of laughter.

The dowager had lived to see her great-grandchildren after all. It was her stubborn will, James often said, but Bella knew he was shocked by her interest in the children. As for Gregory, he had been released from a facility and remained under a doctor's care. He had struggled to overcome his need for the opium, but she was hopeful. James no longer wished his half brother dead or imprisoned, but neither did he trust him around Bella or the children.

The nanny came and James handed the children over. As soon as they were alone, James pulled Bella into his arms and nibbled the side of her neck. "Will you spoil me later?"

"James! You are incorrigible!"

"Yes, and you too from your behavior last night."

"James!"

Bella fought the need to melt into him, then gave up entirely and did just that. "Oh, James."

He brought his mouth to hers. "I've been thinking. Now that the children are older, it's time for us to get away. Wyndmoor Manor is beautiful in the spring, remember?"

Oh, yes. How could she forget? It was spring when they had first met there.

"Are you asking my permission?"

He chuckled. "Last I recall, Wyndmoor Manor belongs to you, and I feel obliged to ask permission from the owner."

They had made a game of passing the deed back and forth

between them for each wedding anniversary for the past four years. It was an unconventional symbol of their love.

She smiled a secret smile. "I do believe the billiard room is still there. You never did teach me how to play."

He brought his mouth to her ear and whispered wickedly, "Your wish is my command, my duchess. I shall endeavor to teach you everything."

Author's Note

The idea of two owners purchasing the same property from an unscrupulous seller first came to me in a real-estate-transactions course in law school. Before I started writing this story, I researched early nineteenth-century English property law. If two buyers disputed ownership, the first to record the deed was generally the owner.

The idea of registering titles rather than deeds did not come about in England until the Royal Commission on Registration of Title in 1857, and was not officially in the statutes until the Land Registry Act of 1862.

In the United States today, we have title insurance that protects the buyer against financial loss due to any defects in title, claims, liens, or taxes. With the invention of computers, buyers and lenders can more easily ascertain this information with a stroke of the keyboard.

It was a pleasure to write this book, and I hope you enjoy the book as much as I have enjoyed writing it!

If you enjoyed IN THE BARRISTER'S BED,
please look for Tina Gabrielle's other
barrister historical romance:

IN THE BARRISTER'S CHAMBERS

Turn the page for a special excerpt.

A Zebra mass-market paperback and eBook on sale now!

Chapter 1

April 5, 1814
London, Old Bailey Courthouse
Honorable Tobias Townsend, presiding

"They ain't whores!"

"What would you call seven women who live under your roof then, if not a brothel?" Prosecutor Abrams asked, stalking forward.

"Me lady friends, they are," Slip Dawson explained.

"All seven of them?"

"Me mum always said I 'ad a way with the ladies," Slip whined.

"Did your mother tell you to freely share your women with all the men of the City of London?" Abrams asked sharply, giving the accused a stony glare.

An imposing barrister at the defense table jumped up. "I object, my lord. The prosecution has not brought forth *one* man 'from the City of London' to testify as to bedding any of Mr. Dawson's lady friends."

The judge sighed and rested his chin in hand, a look of complete boredom on his face. Four of the twelve-member jury rolled their eyes; others snickered.

Evelyn Darlington sat perched on the edge of a wooden bench in the center of the spectators' gallery. Her eyes never wavered from the defense barrister—the only man in the room she knew—Jack Harding. He was the reason she was here, witnessing this spectacle, along with all the other observers in the packed courtroom.

The late-afternoon sun streamed in through the windows, raising the temperature in the crowded room by twenty degrees. Too many unwashed bodies in too small a space should have repulsed her.

Instead, she sat in her seat completely enthralled.

Jack Harding was precisely as she remembered him, as only a few lines near his eyes gave away the years that had passed since she had last seen him. He was tall—over six feet three inches—with chiseled features that gave him a sharp and confident profile. His eyes were a deep green that reminded her of the ferns that thrived during the summer months. His lips were curved in a smile, but she knew they could be either cunning or charming, or both.

Beneath his barrister's wig, she knew his thick brown hair had an unruly wave that he had often impatiently brushed aside when he was concentrating on a legal treatise. He was dressed in a black barrister's gown that would make the complexions of most men appear sallow, but the dark color only served to enhance his bronzed skin.

But perhaps his most fascinating appeal was his attitude of complete relaxation as if he were unperturbed by the judge, jury, prosecutor, and even the audience sitting in the courtroom staring at him. He was infused with a confidence that made one hang on every word that fell from his lips. Without a doubt, Jack Harding probably had women, from all stations in society, swarming around him.

A snort beside her drew her attention. "'E's got 'em by the throat, 'e does."

Evelyn turned to look at the man seated to her left, a squat fellow with beady eyes and fleshy jowls. The overpowering stench of onions wafted from his skin. He smiled, revealing no teeth and swollen gums.

She shifted inches to the right only to brush up against a heavyset woman with a bloodstained apron, sleeves rolled up to her elbows, and work-roughened hands. A butcher's wife, no doubt.

"'Tis a matter of time till old Abrams gives up." The woman laughed and rubbed the calluses on her hands. "Ain't nobody can git past that Jack Harding."

Just like old times, Evelyn thought. *Jack Harding could charm the habit off a nun and cunningly argue the most complicated legal points while doing so.*

But that's why she was here, watching him . . . waiting for him. For the years, it seemed, had only polished his raw talent.

The rest of the trial went as expected. Prosecutor Abrams argued about Slip Dawson's entourage of female inhabitants. Jack countered each argument by pointing out the prosecution's distinct lack of evidence followed by a number of witnesses who testified as to Slip's "stellar" character and good standing in the community.

Exactly eleven and a half minutes after the start of the trial, the judge cleared his throat, cutting off Prosecutor Abrams in midsentence.

"As all of the relevant evidence has been presented," Judge Tobias said, "I ask for the jury to deliberate on the charges and come to a verdict."

The jury, not bothering to leave the courtroom, huddled in the corner.

In what must have been record speed, the foreman stood— his barrel-shaped chest puffed up with self-importance. "We the jury find Slip Dawson not guilty of keepin' a brothel."

The spectators burst into cheers, turning the courtroom into a scene of chaos. Hands reached out to give Slip Dawson a hearty slap on the back as he proceeded out of the room—a free man.

The pounding of Judge Tobias's gavel was a distant thumping, completely ignored by the people.

Evelyn stared as Slip passed, a cockeyed smile on his face, and she wondered how many of today's observers were patrons of his "lady friends."

Her gaze returned to Jack Harding.

Jack extended his hand to Abrams. The prosecutor looked like he had sucked on a lemon, sulking in defeat, but he shook hands with Jack nonetheless. Jack then bent to gather his papers and litigation bag from the desk.

She waited until he turned to make his way out of the courtroom, then stepped into the aisle.

"Mr. Harding," she called out.

He stopped abruptly, his gaze traveling over her face, then roaming over her figure before returning to her eyes. His lips curled into a smile.

"I believe you have the advantage of knowing my name. How can I be of assistance, Miss . . ."

"Lady Evelyn Darlington."

His brow furrowed in confusion before his eyes widened in surprise.

"Why, Lady Evelyn! I don't believe it. You were a girl the last time I saw you. It's been a long, long time."

"Ten years since you were a student studying under my father to become a barrister at the Inns of Court."

"Ah, yes, my pupilage. From what I remember, you always had a voracious appetite for the law. You often visited your father's chambers, listening to his lectures. I have vivid memories of you following me around, taunting me with your extensive legal knowledge."

Heat stole into her cheeks at his words. "From what *I* recall, you needed the additional tutelage."

He laughed, a rich, pleasant sound. "Touché, Lady Evelyn.

I probably did. Now please tell me, have you come today to watch the proceedings? Many do."

She shook her head, then looked up at him. "I've come to seek your services."

"My services? No one seeks out my 'services' unless they are in trouble. I cannot imagine you in trouble." A sudden frown knit his brow. "Last I heard, your father, Emmanuel Darlington, inherited his brother's title and is now the Earl of Lyndale. I understand he is currently lecturing at Oxford. Is he well?"

"It's not about my father, but a close acquaintance."

"Ah, I see. What crime has your friend committed?"

"None! He's been wrongfully accused."

"Pardon, Lady Evelyn," he said. "I meant no offense. What crime has he been accused of?"

She looked to both sides, her eyes darting nervously back and forth, then whispered, "Murder."

He cocked an eyebrow. "A serious offense, to be sure. Who is he?"

She took a deep breath and gathered her courage. "My soon-to-be betrothed."

He stiffened visibly, and a shadow crossed his features. "I'm very sorry, Lady Evelyn, but my docket is completely full. Murder trials take a significant amount of time to properly investigate and prepare, and I would be remiss to even consider representing your acquaintance."

A thread of panic ribboned through her. "But you must. If not as a service to an innocent man wrongfully accused, then as a favor to a girl you once knew."

"I can refer you to a number of proficient criminal barristers. I am not the only—"

"Then as a favor to my father, your former pupilmaster."

He hesitated, and she knew she had struck upon a nerve. Her father was a revered Master of the Bench—otherwise known as a Bencher—by many students, and she knew Jack was no exception. From what she recalled, Jack Harding owed Lord Lyndale even more than most.

He shifted the papers in his hands, then nodded. "I cannot promise anything, understand, but perhaps this conversation would be better suited elsewhere."

Relief coursed through her that he was even willing to further discuss the matter. "Yes. Certainly."

His hand cupped her elbow, and he led her out of the courtroom. As they weaved their way through the halls of the Old Bailey, she was conscious of his tall frame beside her, his firm fingers on her sleeve. She glanced up at the clear-cut lines of his profile and was once again struck by his air of authority. In this legal arena, he radiated a strength that drew her eye, impossible to look away.

He slowed his pace so that she could keep up, and a group of barristers waved as they passed. A voluptuous woman with a scandalously low bodice, a bright yellow flower tucked between her breasts, gave Jack a jaunty wave.

Evelyn couldn't help but ponder whether she was one of Slip Dawson's "lady friends."

"You are quite popular, Mr. Harding," Evelyn said.

"I am known as the people's lawyer."

"At the expense of the Crown's prosecution?"

His humor apparently returned, his eyes lit with laughter as he looked down at her. "You must not judge me too harshly, Lady Evelyn. From what I gather, my reputation is the very reason you sought me out today."

He was correct, of course. She had done her research. No other barrister, within the two jurisdictions covered by the Old Bailey—the City of London or the County of Middlesex—was a more successful criminal barrister than Jack Harding.

"You're right," she said. "I would be nothing short of lying if I said I hadn't followed your accomplishments over the years. I just never anticipated that I would so urgently require your services."

And she did *desperately* need his aid—a life depended upon it. For that reason alone, she refused to take no for an answer. She must convince Jack Harding to take the case, no matter the cost.

Chapter 2

Jack proceeded down a long hall, passing several more courtrooms, until he came to a stop before a door with a brass nameplate labeled CLIENT CONSULTATION. He reached for the handle, opened the door, and motioned for Evelyn to enter.

His gaze roamed once again over her form as she swept by. He had been stunned to learn that the beautiful woman standing in the middle of the spectators' gallery, waiting for him, was Lady Evelyn Darlington—the daughter of his pupilmaster when Jack was a mere student, striving to become a barrister. She had changed much in the ten years since he had last seen her poring over her father's papers. She had been a child then—close to twelve—now she was a woman full grown.

Her golden hair was piled in an elegant style atop her head. A few loose tendrils had escaped the pins and brushed the slender column of her throat. Her facial bones were delicately carved, and her lips temptingly plump. But it was the turquoise eyes, the shade of a tropical ocean—exotically slanted and tipped with thick lashes—that made his breath hitch.

She wasn't as tall as he preferred his women, but even in the demure blue gown she wore, any man could see she was generously curved.

She made a circuit of the room, taking in her surroundings—

a small desk in the corner, wooden chairs lining the perimeter of the room, and a bookshelf containing several well-used law books—with wide-eyed interest, and he was struck with a thought: Evelyn Darlington may have grown into a beautiful woman, but her scholarly aura seemed quite the same. She appeared quite serious, unaware of her beauty and how it affected men.

He closed the door, strode forward, and placed his bag and the papers he had been holding atop the desk.

Her eyes widened at the thick stack of litigation documents. "It's a wonder you can sort through such a voluminous amount of paper. Are they all pertaining to Mr. Dawson's case?"

He chuckled at the unmasked fascination in her voice. "Hardly. I was not lying when I said my docket was full. Truth be told, your friend will be better off with another barrister. There are several highly competent barristers we passed on the way here. I can escort you to any you choose today and request that they take the utmost care with the case."

"No," she rushed. "None other will do. You have not lost of late."

His gaze sharpened at her admission. "I'm flattered that you think so highly of me and that you have followed my career, but at the same time, I never anticipated that you would seek to hire me. Does Lord Lyndale know that you're here?"

Thick lashes lowered. "No. I haven't told my father of my intentions to retain you."

"He doesn't approve of your choice of betrothed, does he?"

She hesitated for a heartbeat before answering. "It isn't relevant."

"Ah, he doesn't." Her hesitation spoke volumes, just as when a witness paused those few critical seconds before formulating an answer on the witness stand. It usually meant a lie was forthcoming, or in Evelyn's case, an omission of importance.

He motioned for her to sit in one of the chairs in front of the desk. He ignored the chair behind the desk and occupied the one across from her.

Leaning forward, he said, "Tell me everything."

She took a deep breath, her breasts straining against the fabric of her bodice. "Mr. Randolph Sheldon, my soon-to-be betrothed, is under suspicion of murdering an actress in the Drury Lane Theatre."

"An actress? Was she his lover?"

Her cheeks flamed red. "No! She was a distant cousin."

"Why is he suspected?"

"He was seen fleeing from her bedroom window."

"Let me guess. Her body was found in her bedchamber?"

She shifted in her chair and twisted her hands on her lap. "Yes. She was to give him something."

He ignored her obvious discomfort and continued his questioning. "How was she killed?"

"She was . . . stabbed, wearing only her night rail."

"Who discovered her?"

"The neighbor heard screams, and she called the constable. Witnesses claim they saw Randolph jump from the window."

"That is enough evidence to cause concern," Jack said. "The prosecution will surely seek to indict him."

Evelyn's chin rose a notch. "But he's innocent! I've known Randolph for years. Our families were neighbors at our country estates in Hertfordshire. We took many summer strolls together."

"I still think it best that Mr. Sheldon be represented by another lawyer. I don't see how my representation would aid your father."

"Don't you see? If we are to be officially engaged and the reading of the banns begun, it would affect Father's career at Oxford, for his daughter to be engaged to an accused murderer!"

Jack leaned back in his chair. All his gut instincts warned

him not to get involved with Lady Evelyn Darlington, but she was right. The resulting scandal *would* adversely affect her father's career.

And he did owe Lord Lyndale. If it was not for the eccentric Master of the Bench, Jack would not be practicing law, would not be enjoying his success, wouldn't have more money than he knew how to spend, and certainly wouldn't be basking in the fickle affections of the *ton*. In fact, it would be safe to say, Jack would be nothing at all; he would most assuredly be wenching, gambling, and drinking to excess.

But what disturbed Jack more than Evelyn Darlington's being besotted by a man who most likely killed another woman in cold blood was the fact that Lord Lyndale clearly was unaware of his daughter's intentions to seek out his legal services.

That and the undeniable truth that he was drawn to Evelyn himself.

Looking into Evelyn's mesmerizing blue eyes, Jack struggled to hold on to his firm resolve.

The lady is nothing but trouble, he mused. She had been a minx as a girl—an I-know-it-all-better-than-you-ever-will tormenter—and as a grown woman she was wildly beautiful. His attraction was its own warning. He never mixed business with pleasure. It always led to disastrous results in the courtroom.

His mind whirled with excuses. He would speak with her father, explain the circumstances to him, and he had no doubt in his mind that Lord Lyndale would understand that he did not have the time to take on a murder client. He would be doing his former pupilmaster a service by informing him of his daughter's clandestine activities.

Reaching out, she grasped his hand, her eyes imploring. "If it is a matter of money," she said, "please be assured that you will be paid."

Jack froze, every muscle in his body tensing. His blood

always ran hot after a trial, and her touch—however innocent—tempted him to reach out and take the victor's spoils. A kiss, at the least. He wondered what her reaction would be if she knew the effect she had on him.

"It has nothing to do with money," he said tersely. "If I'm to consider taking on your friend's—Mr. Randolph Sheldon's—case, then I insist on speaking with your father first."

"My father? Why?"

"I owe him a great deal. I won't go behind his back and take on a case involving his own daughter, even if you are not the accused."

She sat upright as if her laces suddenly had been pulled tight. "Fine. If you insist."

"I insist."

She stood and turned to leave. "As I'm sure you're aware, my father is a busy man—"

He reached for his pocket watch with a flourish, then looked at her. "I'm available now. I had expected Slip Dawson's trial to take longer and had cleared the remainder of my day. From what I recall, your father never liked to work through the evening meal and should be returning home soon."

Jack stood and opened the door for her. He gave her his most charming smile as they returned to the main hall of the Old Bailey. He would meet with Lord Lyndale, enlighten him as to his daughter's intentions, explain why he could not take on the case, help his daughter find a suitable lawyer to defend her anticipated betrothed, thus fulfilling any ethical obligations. He expected to be in his chambers at Lincoln's Inn of Court within two hours' time.

It was dark outside by the time they arrived at Lord Lyndale's town house in Piccadilly. They had traveled by separate conveyances, Evelyn choosing to take a hackney cab while Jack traveled in his phaeton. As soon as Jack was alone, he removed his barrister's wig and gown, laid them beside him on the padded bench, and ran his fingers through his hair. She had been worried about her reputation, traveling unchaperoned with a bachelor, and Jack was more than happy to accommodate her concerns. He didn't want to learn more than was necessary about her troubles.

Why bother? He didn't plan on taking them on.

They now stood on the front steps while Evelyn rapped on the door.

"Shouldn't your father's butler have opened the door by now?" he asked after a full minute had passed.

"Hodges is well into his eighties. His hearing isn't what it used to be," she explained.

Just like Lord Lyndale, he thought. *He would take troubled students under his wing and keep on an elderly butler when most other members of society would have let the old servant out to pasture years ago.*

Evelyn fished into her reticule, searching for her key. The task was made harder by the dusk, with only the dim glow of the street lamp to aid her. Finally she withdrew the key and was inserting it into the lock, when the door pushed easily open.

"That's odd," she said. "Hodges must have forgotten to lock the door."

They stepped inside the vestibule. It was dim here as well, and the lingering scent of a pipe filled the space. The distinctive smell of the tobacco triggered a memory of Emmanuel Darlington at the podium in the classroom, pipe in hand.

"Father?" Evelyn called out.

Jack took a step forward and bumped into a long-case clock in the corner. He heard Evelyn shuffle forward, then the sound of flint strike iron as she sought to light a lamp.

Hands outstretched so as to avoid walking into anything more, he made to reach her side, then tripped over something on the floor. He barely registered what sounded like a low moan, when Evelyn screamed and something shattered across the floor.

Jack twisted around, just in time to see a figure dart forward. Jack launched himself at the shape, grasping a fistful of coat, when a heavy object came crashing down upon his temple.